DAMNOS

FALL OF DAMNOS · SPEAR OF MACRAGGE

SPREADING OUT, THE necrons had enveloped them. Bolters tracked and fired to compensate, relying on advanced targeting sensors – the mist was so bad that the enemy were literally appearing as if from nowhere, and in numbers.

'Brother, my flank has been compromised.' It was Atavian through the comm-feed in Iulus's helmet.

'Close up battle-formation, there are more necrons than we first believed.'

An affirmation rune flashed on Iulus's retinal display. The tac-icons representing the Devastator squad started to move closer to the Immortals. Iulus noticed there were several red markers that remained static.

Squad Fennion and the two Devastators – they were the rearguard. Glory belonged to others.

'Take and hold the ground.' Those had been his orders during the mission briefing. Thirty Ultramarines to keep a simple esplanade from the enemy. It had seemed like overkill; now, Iulus Fennion wasn't so sure.

Visit blacklibrary.com *for the full range of Space Marine Battles
novels, novellas, audio dramas and Quick Reads, as well as many
other Black Library exclusives*

DAMNOS

FALL OF DAMNOS · SPEAR OF MACRAGGE

NICK KYME

BLACK LIBRARY

For Will and Beth.

A BLACK LIBRARY PUBLICATION

Fall of Damnos first published in 2011.
Spear of Macragge first published in 2012.
This edition published in Great Britain in 2016 by
Black Library,
Games Workshop Ltd.,
Willow Road,
Nottingham, NG7 2WS, UK.

10 9 8 7 6 5 4 3 2 1

Produced by Games Workshop in Nottingham.

Damnos © Copyright Games Workshop Limited 2016. Damnos,
Space Marine Battles, GW, Games Workshop, Black Library, The
Horus Heresy, The Horus Heresy Eye logo, Space Marine, 40K,
Warhammer, Warhammer 40,000, the 'Aquila' Double-headed
Eagle logo, and all associated logos, illustrations, images, names,
creatures, races, vehicles, locations, weapons, characters, and the
distinctive likenesses thereof, are either ® or TM, and/or © Games
Workshop Limited, variably registered around the world.
All Rights Reserved.

A CIP record for this book is available from the British Library.

UK ISBN 13: 978 1 78496 179 4
US ISBN 13: 978 1 78496 180 0

No part of this publication may be reproduced, stored in a retrieval
system, or transmitted in any form or by any means, electronic,
mechanical, photocopying, recording or otherwise, without the
prior permission of the publishers.

This is a work of fiction. All the characters and events portrayed
in this book are fictional, and any resemblance to real people or
incidents is purely coincidental.

See Black Library on the internet at

blacklibrary.com

Find out more about Games Workshop
and the world of Warhammer 40,000 at

games-workshop.com

Printed and bound by CPI Group (UK) Ltd, Croydon, CR0 4YY

It is the 41st millennium. For more than a hundred centuries the Emperor has sat immobile on the Golden Throne of Earth. He is the master of mankind by the will of the gods, and master of a million worlds by the might of his inexhaustible armies. He is a rotting carcass writhing invisibly with power from the Dark Age of Technology. He is the Carrion Lord of the Imperium for whom a thousand souls are sacrificed every day, so that he may never truly die.

Yet even in his deathless state, the Emperor continues his eternal vigilance. Mighty battlefleets cross the daemon-infested miasma of the warp, the only route between distant stars, their way lit by the Astronomican, the psychic manifestation of the Emperor's will. Vast armies give battle in His name on uncounted worlds. Greatest amongst his soldiers are the Adeptus Astartes, the Space Marines, bio-engineered super-warriors. Their comrades in arms are legion: the Astra Militarium and countless planetary defence forces, the ever-vigilant Inquisition and the tech-priests of the Adeptus Mechanicus to name only a few. But for all their multitudes, they are barely enough to hold off the ever-present threat from aliens, heretics, mutants — and worse.

To be a man in such times is to be one amongst untold billions. It is to live in the cruellest and most bloody regime imaginable. These are the tales of those times. Forget the power of technology and science, for so much has been forgotten, never to be re-learned. Forget the promise of progress and understanding, for in the grim dark future there is only war. There is no peace amongst the stars, only an eternity of carnage and slaughter, and the laughter of thirsting gods.

CONTENTS

FALL OF
DAMNOS

PROLOGUE
274973.M41

THE PRIMARY GENERATORS were dead. No litanies to the Machine-God, no entreaties to the Omnissiah were about to revive them. The last tremor had been the largest – the Mandos Prime fusion stations were down.

It was the job of Gorgardis and his crew to repair them.

'Critical failure across all facilities,' the exofabricator muttered. His breath fogged the air with the cold from the permafrost.

'My lord,' a voice crackled through the vox-implant in Gorgardis's ear. The heavy ice and some kind of latent, as of yet unspecified, radiation marred his reply with static.

'Present,' said the exofabricator, distracted with his scanner read-outs. The seismographic returns were incredible, more than merely tectonic plate shifts. Perhaps the planet was destabilising.

The voice's next words made Gorgardis stop what he was doing.

'We've found something.'

He licked his lips, tasting the blandness of ice crystals, and put away the scanner. Artak's position in the facility came up on the retinal display of his optic implant. It was flashing, and a small binaric code indicated the other exo-fabricator was a further eighty-six point two metres down.

Gorgardis paused to think, the logic engines supplementing his organic brain functions making swift correlations. 'I'll be right down,' he said, and made for the nearest rail-lifter.

MUCH OF THE hard ice around the structure had melted, but it was buried so deep and seemingly without end that it was impossible to tell just how big the thing was.

There were icons upon the smooth outer wall. It looked like metal but very dark, shimmering, almost vital. Despite a wealth of experience in runic symbolism and semiotics, Gorgardis didn't recognise any of the iconography.

'Unknown provenance,' he muttered, tracing his hand over the symbols but being careful not to touch them. He turned to Artak, who was waiting anxiously behind him. Gorgardis waved him on. 'Bring up the servitors – drills and hammers, heavy-bore.'

MAGOS KARNAK OBSERVED the pristine surface of the half-buried ruins with cold detachment.

'Incredible…' he breathed. It had been many years since he'd experienced awe, let alone expressed it through his organic vocal cords. Karnak was mostly machine, but he still retained the gamut of human feeling. Presently, it was being stimulated to a greater extent than he'd thought possible since his apotheosis from the flesh.

Mechadendrite scanners performed a full spectral, auditory and metallurgic analysis of the structure, feeding the results to the tech-priest's machine-cortex for later study. An initial review made little sense.

'And you went to every length to open it?' he asked.

Gorgardis gestured to the half-dozen wasted servitors slumped in a pile nearby. 'We exhausted our every resource,' he said.

Upon witnessing the slab-sided ruins, he'd summoned the tech-priest of the facility at once. Karnak had been swift to respond, bringing in his adepts: a horde of enginseers, transmechanics and genetors. The tech-priests were baffled.

Gorgardis went on, 'Returns from our sonar-staves reveal that this is but one structure amongst a series of many. Most are buried deep beneath the ice bed.'

'And this?' Karnak referred to a floating grav-bench on which several items of alien origin were arrayed.

Gorgardis singled out a six-legged creature with silver chitin across its back and mandibles not so dissimilar from mechadendrite tools.

'My best estimate is a repair drone of some sort. It's dead.'

'Or dormant,' Karnak countered, his gaze absorbing and cataloguing the other mechanical finds on the bench. Some were perhaps weapons; others were harder to classify. Partial degradation from exposure to ice moisture made the task difficult but not impossible. 'I'm taking all of them,' he decided, before showing Gorgardis his back and driving away on the tracked impellers he had in lieu of his legs.

'M– my lord?'

'All finds are to go to Goethe Majoris where they can be better studied.'

Gorgardis made the sign of the Cog and went about his orders.

'Seal this site,' Karnak added by way of afterthought. 'Its secrets will be revealed to us in due course, Omnissiah be praised.'

ACT ONE: EMERGENCE

CHAPTER ONE
779973.M41

THE VOX-TRANSMITTER WAS wretched with interference, so Falka hit it again.

'Keep doing that and you'll break it,' said a deep and sonorous voice behind him.

When Falka turned, his smile was broad and bright enough to light up the whole mine. 'Jynn!'

He seized the woman in a bear hug, lifting her off the ground. Even in her environment suit, she felt the steel of his girder-like arms.

'Easy, easy!' she warned, mock-choking.

Falka put her down, ignoring the questioning glances from the rest of the shift. Riggers, drill-engines and borer-drones advanced towards the darkness of the vast ice-shaft like an army. They were accompanied by menial servitors and heavy-set chrono-diggers. Like Falka and Jynn, the human contingent of the labour force wore bulky environment suits to stave off the cold and make the twelve-hour cycles possible.

'Where's your rig?' asked the big man. He'd stripped back the thermal protection on his arms, revealing faded gang-tats and wiry grey hair. 'I didn't see it.'

Jynn pointed to a docking station, one of many in the massive ice cavern. Like most of the mining vehicles it was squat, decked out with plates and protective glacis and only partially enclosed. A crew of three menials and a pair of chrono-diggers stood around it awaiting her return.

'She's all mine,' she said proudly, adjusting the thermal-cutters, flare-rods and chain-pick fastened to her tool belt from when Falka's bear hug had dislodged them.

A klaxon sounded and an array of strobe lamps filled the cavern with an intermittent amber glow. They started walking.

'You look good,' said Falka a moment later.

Jynn gave a wry smile. The ice concourse underfoot crunched as they moved. It was hard-packed by industrial presses to create a serviceable roadway for the mine entrance. Most of the light was artificial, though some natural light filtered down from the bore hole above them at the entrance's threshold.

'What I mean,' Falka struggled to say, 'is it's good to see you back at the ice-face. I thought after Korve, you might–'

'Honestly, Fal, I'm fine,' she said, brushing a strand of errant hair behind her ears and pulling down her goggles.

Falka did the same – close to the vent a fine spray of ice chips saturated the air. Environment suits managed the worst. Get one in the eye and you'd know about it, though.

'Just with the 'quake and all that…'

She stopped and glared at him. The other workers flowed around them to their riggers and crews. The first few cohorts had already begun descent.

'Seriously, Falka – just drop it. Korve's dead and that's it.'
The big man looked distraught. 'Sorry.'

She lightly gripped his shoulder. 'It's all right. I under–'

'Rig-hand Evvers,' a shrill, imperious voice interrupted.

Jynn had her back to the speaker and groaned inwardly
before she turned. 'Administrator Rancourt,' she replied
politely.

A hawkish man, trussed up in thermal gear and flocked
by a retinue of scribes and aides, approached them. Despite
the cowl drawn up around his small head and the padded
mittens he wore, the administrator still shivered.

'I had not expected to see you on shift,' he said, fashioning a poor smile. It was meant to convey warmth but only
exuded his awkwardness.

'Nor I, you…' she muttered.

'I beg your pardon. I'm finding it hard to hear under all
of this.' He gestured to his cowl and thermal coat.

'I said it's rare to see you, administrator… at the ice-face,
I mean.'

Rancourt moved in close to Jynn.

'I've told you before,' he said. 'You may call me Zeph.'

Falka broke his stoic silence to grunt.

Rancourt's gaze moved to the giant. 'And Rig-hand
Kolpeck. Don't you have a shift to go to?'

'We both do, administ… ah, *Zeph.*' She tugged lightly on
Falka's arm, urging him to join her.

The big man looked like he'd rather stay and squeeze
Rancourt's neck, but he followed anyway.

'Of course, of course,' the administrator blathered, shooting a dark glance at Falka. 'I have much work to attend to.
In the Emperor's name,' he added, pretending to look at a
data-slate proffered by one of his toadies.

'May His glory watch over us all,' Jynn replied.

Heading in the direction of the vent, the air suddenly felt as if it were actually getting warmer.

'He still stalking you, then?'

'Leave it, Fal. I can handle it. He's harmless enough.'

Falka grunted again. He was prone to doing that. 'Eyes and ears,' he said, peeling off towards his rigger and crew.

'You too,' said Jynn, diverting to her vehicle. She'd put one boot on the boarding stirrup when the concourse trembled. She slipped, snatching a holding rail to steady herself. A second tremor shook some debris from the roof. More violent than the first, it sent men and servitors sprawling.

'What the feg was–' she muttered over the vox-bead.

A high-pitched keening cut her off.

She fell, the intensity of the sonic burst forcing her to press her palms to her ears. 'Throne!' Jynn gasped, grimacing against the auditory pain.

The keening became a hum, throbbing at the back of the skull, but at least she could stand. Around the ice cavern, the walls were shaking. Sections of the ceiling rained down on the labourers in a cascade. The cries of one man ended abruptly when a slab of permafrost crushed him.

Jynn staggered. It was just like with Korve. Memories came flooding back, but she suppressed them, focused on surviving instead. 'Not yet, dear heart,' she whispered, finding some resolve. 'Not yet.'

Falka was on his feet too and rushing over to her.

'You hurt?' He had to shout to be heard above the ice-quake.

Jynn was about to answer when a massive cold cloud ripped through the vent in a bright white bloom. The rig-hands closest to the shaft were shredded by the host of shards within the cloud. Snow crystals fogging the air were tainted a visceral red.

A burst of hard, emerald light followed, refracted from the angular descent shaft beyond the vent. Shouting echoed from the icy dark, injured and desperate men trying to control some unseen catastrophe. The shouts became cries, and then screams. There was something else too... a sort of discharge, as of an energy beam or perhaps a heavy generator.

The winches slaved to the adamantite descent lines at the vent threshold started to retract. Someone was coming up.

'We have to get out,' said Jynn. Then, with greater urgency as the emerald light issuing from the vent intensified, 'All of us – right now!'

Falka nodded.

'No!' she cried, seizing the big man's arm as he made for the vent.

He looked back at her nonplussed. 'People are down there, our people. They might need help.'

Jynn was shaking her head. 'They're gone, Fal. This way, come on.'

'Wha... but...'

'They're *dead*! Now, come on!' She heaved and he followed, reluctant at first but then with more conviction. Something was scurrying up the shaft. It sounded like a horde of giant, mechanical ants.

The first of the rig-hands from below made it to the ice cavern. He was dead. Men screamed, terrified, when they saw the flesh of his partly flayed corpse. Surgical, precise, horrific – it was as if the layers had been stripped anatomically.

More followed, equally gruesome.

Jynn and Falka were running, shouting at anyone who would listen to join them, yanking environment suits or shoving them bodily. *Down tools and flee.* This was not a rescue; it was a full-scale evacuation.

She found Rancourt cowering behind a rigger, getting his aides to peer around its armoured flanks and provide him with updates. Several of his entourage were dead, one from fright when the keening blast had struck; another to the sudden avalanche from the ceiling.

'Get up!' She seized his collar and pulled. 'Get up! These people need guidance. The surface must be told what's happening down here.'

'What *is* happening?' he shrieked, unwilling to stand at first, casting fearful glances towards the vent where the emerald glow was now spilling into the ice cavern.

Jynn looked over her shoulder, still hanging on to Rancourt's suit. 'Falka!'

The big man gently moved her aside and threw the administrator over his shoulder.

'Unhand me! I am an officer of the Imperium. Release me at once!'

'Shut up.' Falka smacked Rancourt's head into the rigger just hard enough to leave him dazed.

Then they were running again. The remnants of the administrator's retinue followed without need for coercion.

The exit shaft and the rail-lifters were just a few metres ahead. The light from the surface was like a soothing balm as it touched Jynn's sweat-slick face. She glanced back.

Several more rig-hands from below had made it to the ice cavern. Though they were far away and her view was unsteady on account of her fleeing for her life, she made out… *creatures* attached to the miners. The rig-hands were thrashing and squirming. Eventually they fell and the swarm dispersed, silver beetle-like creatures the size of Falka's clenched fist, leaving a flensed corpse in their wake.

'God-Emperor have mercy,' she breathed.

Larger, bulkier shadows were reaching the end of the vent shaft. A coruscating emerald beam lanced from the darkness, throwing a spider-like creature into sharp relief. Like the beetles it was metallic, but almost the size of a rigger. The beam, fired from one of the creature's mandibles, struck a fleeing rig-hand and atomised him. The afterimage of the man's flayed skeleton was seared into Jynn's retinas just before it collapsed into ash and she looked away.

'Move, move!'

They raced into the nearest rail-lifter. About sixty rig-hands had joined them on the access plate, and Falka gunned the engine as soon as they were all aboard.

Jynn gazed to the distant surface as the heavy winches began to drone. She willed the oval of light from the ground-zero bore point closer.

Below them, the other rail-lifters started up – fifteen in total, all screaming, engines hot, towards the upper world.

One of the cables snapped, lashing wildly with the sudden slack. A beam from one of the spiders had severed it. Rig-hands screamed as they plunged to their deaths. Others, clinging on, could only watch in horror as the beetles already scaling the shaft wall sprang from their perches and landed amongst them.

Jynn saw a few of the miners let go and embrace death by falling rather than face being flayed alive.

The hard drone of a warning klaxon sounded from farther up the shaft. The oval of light was becoming a rectangular strip, narrowing by the second.

Rancourt, having recently regained consciousness, put away his command-stave. Falka saw him do it and rounded on him.

'What are you doing? The others will never make it.'

The administrator's pupils were dilated, his eyes wide and haunted. 'Those th-things…' he stammered. 'They can't be allowed to get out.'

'Bastard!' Falka punched him, a solid blow to the chin that put Rancourt back on his arse, and then ripped the command-stave from the administrator's trappings. 'Show me how to stop it,' he said, bearing down on him, threatening more violence.

'Leave him.' Jynn wrenched the big man's shoulder. She had a strong grip and made him turn.

'You're defending this worm?'

'He's right, Fal.' The sides of the shaft blurred past and the displaced air snapped at Jynn's hair.

Falka shook his head. Those men and women were his friends. 'No!' He was about to beat down on Rancourt again when Jynn smacked him hard in the chest with the flat of her hand. It didn't hurt the big man but it got his attention.

'He's right,' she said again, continuing in a small voice when she looked below – her mind tried to blot out the carnage and horror. 'We can't let them get out.'

Falka's grimace became a snarl as he pounded at the holding spar with impotent rage. 'Hold on,' he growled, moving towards the engine. 'We're about to breach the surface.'

The rail-lifter cleared the slowly closing shaft doors and after a few more metres broke into the pale Damnosian sun. Another miner called Fuge kicked open the exit ramp and the sixty or so survivors pounded it across to the arctic tundra of the upper world.

Though the sun was shining, an icy wind brought a chill and kicked up slurries of snow and frost eddies. The barren wastes of Damnos had never looked so bleak.

There was no need for conversation. What could any of them say, anyway? So the sixty survivors made for the distant comms-bunker, marching in file, heads bowed against the wind and ice. Behind them the shutting of the shaft door was like a death knell for the hundreds still trapped within.

850973.M41

THERE WAS STILL no word from Damnos Prime, and the Valkyrie gunships Lieutenant Sonne had deployed from Secundus to investigate were also quiet. It didn't take a soldier's instincts to realise that something was wrong.

'We're experiencing a full communications blackout in the northern regions all the way to the Tyrrean Ocean, colonel,' he gave his report to Quintus Tarn. The commander of the Damnosian Ark Guard peered over steepled fingers into the shadows of his operations chamber. His mood was pensive. Leaning on the desk with his elbows, he hadn't stirred the entire time Adanar Sonne had been in his presence.

Behind the colonel a planetary map showed the location of each and every manufactorum, drilling-station, mining complex, refinery, labour-clave and outpost on Damnos. Unlit lume-globes represented the stations that Kellenport, the planetary capital, had lost touch with. Precious few of the globes were lit.

The wave of darkness emanating from the north reminded

Adanar of a slowly creeping shroud. 'We picked up a group of refugee mine workers from one of the outposts near Damnos Prime,' he offered.

Tarn looked up at Adanar for the first time since he'd entered the room.

'How many?'

'Thirteen, sir.'

'Are they saying anything?'

'I don't know yet, colonel. They were picked up by a patrol. Apparently, they'd been trekking across the tundra for several weeks. Administrator Rancourt is amongst the survivors,' Adanar added.

'Inform the lord governor and bring them all to me as soon as they arrive at Kellenport.'

'Yes, sir. Is there anything else?'

'Do you have a wife and child, Lieutenant Sonne?' asked Tarn. The colonel was staring right into his eyes.

'Er, yes… Yes, I do.'

Though Tarn smiled, his eyes were despairing black gulfs.

As if seeing them for the first time, Adanar noticed the stubs of tabac in a silver tray to the commander's left; on the right was a vox-unit. Its message received light was flashing silently.

'Is something wrong, sir?'

'Listen,' Tarn answered simply.

He broke the steeple of his fingers and replayed the vox-message blinking insistently on the unit. The opening segment was fraught with static, natural interference on account of the distance and the weather conditions. Slowly, a voice resolved through the auditory crackle.

'…*found something, sir…*'

Adanar recognised the hard timbre of Major Tarken. He didn't know the man personally but his reputation preceded him as one of the most lauded combat veterans amongst the Ark Guard.

Colonel Tarn tapped a rune on the vox-unit and a grainy hololith issued from a projector-node. It took a few seconds to synch to the audio. Major Tarken appeared in jagged resolution.

'Image-servitors accompanied the platoon,' the colonel explained unnecessarily.

Major Tarken was speaking to the picter. *'The manufactorums at Damnos Prime were silent, but there is definitely something here.'*

The view swung downwards at the major's request, revealing several skeletal remains.

'Could be labour serfs or rig-hands...'

Adanar caught Tarn's hooded gaze. 'Was this a live feed?'

'Up until about twenty minutes ago.'

The picter swung up again. Panning left and right, it showed Tarken's men advancing in echelon formation. The sound kept cutting out, succumbing to crackling interference or the occasional hiss of static, but it seemed quiet. Mist from the cold exuded off the walls in a fine veil. Tarken's kit and that of his men was wet with the moisture and crusted from it flash-freezing.

'...moving into the main drilling area now...' Tarken was whispering and brought up his lasgun. Somebody shouted from up ahead, a scout off-picter.

'Where was this?' asked Adanar, utterly enrapt on the hololith.

'Dagoth Station, three hundred kilometres north of Secundus at Halaheim.'

A flash on the pict was too bright to be static. Someone had started firing.

'*Contacts! Contacts!*' Tarken was running and the whir of the servitor's tracked impellers could be heard as it shifted gear to keep pace with the major. Though largely stable, the additional momentum made the image blur and haze. The whine of lasguns was getting louder over the audio, too.

Adanar leaned in closer. Tarken had reached his frontline and was taking up a position behind some riggers evidently in for repair. Around thirty men adopted similar postures and hunkered down. Farther ahead, men were shouting. The scouts were discharging weapons and Tarken was trying to raise their sergeant on the vox.

Something garbled came over the vox-return, twice filtered for Adanar's ears and totally indiscernible.

The picter was still shaking, although the servitor had stopped behind the major.

'Can we steady it?'

Tarn didn't answer. He was fixated on the hololith.

Something was appearing through the mist. An emerald glow coloured the fog suddenly, as if tainting it. Shots from the scouts ended with its arrival.

'*Holy Throne…*' Tarken was levelling his lasgun over the makeshift barricade. A beam snapped out of the dark, ugly and green, and one of the riggers was shorn in two. '*Holy fegging Throne! All weapons, bring them down!*'

The chamber lit up with over thirty las-bursts. Tarken's troopers went to full automatic, draining their power packs with an abandon and urgency Adanar had never seen before in professional soldiers.

The things coming out of the fog, they were… *nightmares.* It was the only word Adanar could think of to describe them. Huge, broad-shouldered skeletoids with strange, glowing carbines attached to their arms. Energy coursed up and down the wide tubular barrels and was expelled in bright lances of dirty emerald.

They moved like automatons, neither speaking nor slowing as a barrage of las-bolts hammered them.

'Increase fire!'

The picter zoomed in, blurring the image at first but then focusing in on one of the metal skeletons. Its eyes blazed with a terrible fire, suggesting a crude sentience that chilled the lieutenant's blood even removed, as he was, from the firefight and the moment.

Adanar saw the creature jerk spasmodically as it was struck by countless las-shots. It must have taken over ten well-placed bolts to down it. Chunks of metal flew off its carapace body, fused rib-plate and punctured presumably vital systems before it fell.

The picter lingered. Horrified, Adanar watched the broken components slowly reknit as las-fire raged around the creature's prone form. Wires snaked across the ground finding other wires and, like sewn flesh, drew the shattered pieces together. Metal became as mercury, dissolving into liquid before being drawn to the torso as if magnetised. Impossibly, the skeleton rose intact and fired its terrible beam weaponry again.

'...all back... Fall back!'

Tarken stood up to order the retreat. The vox-man next to him was spun by a glancing hit from one of the beams. Half of his face and right shoulder were missing, simply stripped down to glistening bone.

It was more rout than retreat.

Major Tarken took a hit to the chest. His carapace armour dissolved on contact, so too his uniform and under-mesh, his skin and flesh and bone. A hole opened up in his back, what remained of blood and innards cauterised before Tarken crumpled in a dead heap.

The image-servitor was the last to fall. Unarmed, Adanar assumed it presented the lowest level of threat to the creatures.

Just before the report ended, a looming skeletal face filled the screen. Balefires smouldered in its eye sockets and spoke of unfathomable hatred.

A squeal of binaric or something like it keened through the speaker. Adanar winced and recoiled. When he'd opened his eyes a split second later, the screen was dead, frozen on the skeleton's face.

The lieutenant was sweating, his heart racing in his chest. He licked his lips. They were dry and his voice croaked at first. 'What are those…?' He coughed, clearing his throat and tried again. 'What are they, colonel?'

A figure emerging out of the darkness behind Tarn had Adanar reaching for his laspistol. He only relaxed when he recognised Magos Karnak.

The tech-priest's timbre was as cold and unforgiving as Adanar imagined the skeletons to be. 'Ancient and terrible, and they are here, lieutenant.'

'What the hell is that supposed to mean?'

Tarn interjected, switching off the hololith and stopping the dead-air audio feed. 'It means they have come for us, for this world.'

Adanar bit back his anger – he was only reacting to his irrational fear. 'With respect, sir, that explains shit-all. What's going on?'

'The lord governor has been informed,' said Tarn, 'and is being secured in a Proteus-class command bunker with his generals as we speak. He intends to conduct operations from there.'

'Very wise, sir, but what precisely are we dealing with here?'

'The *Nobilis* has been contacted and is adopting geo-stationary orbit above the capital.'

Tarn was talking as if he'd lost it. Adanar wanted to shake him. 'Sir!'

'They are coming to Kellenport, Sonne. I sent over fifty thousand men to Damnos Prime and Secundus, and all the stations inbetween. All of them, our fleet at anchor in the Tyrrean – dead, all of them.'

Adanar nearly choked. *'What?'*

Karnak advanced into Adanar's eyeline, the whirr of his tracks drawing a scowl from the lieutenant.

'That scrambled piece of binaric was a data-burst,' the magos explained. 'There was a message encoded within it. Based on a proto-Gothic linguistic system, it was easy to discern the meaning. My xeno-linguistic savants took approximately thirteen point two-six minutes to decipher it.'

'Are you looking for praise, magos?'

'No, I am merely suggesting that the simple encoding was deliberate. They *wanted* us to hear it.'

'Hear what?' asked Adanar.

Colonel Tarn activated a different message spool on the vox-unit. After a few seconds of charged silence an unearthly voice issued from the speakers. It resonated with age and archaic menace, as if drawn from the grave or the depths of a planet-eating black hole.

We are the necrontyr. We are legion. We claim dominion of this world… Surrender and die.

'Throne of Earth,' Adanar could only rasp. He found his composure again after a few more seconds. 'Surely, it means surrender *or* die?'

Karnak uttered a sombre reply. 'No, Lieutenant Sonne, the translation is accurate.'

'In the Emperor's name, what are these things?'

'Death, lieutenant – they are death. Adanar,' said the colonel, getting to his feet at last. 'Take your family and get out of Kellenport. Go south. Do it quickly, before it's too late.'

020974.M41
Aboard the Nobilis

THE BRIDGE WAS frantic with activity.

Captain Unser barked orders at his command crew from a gilded throne inlaid with operation-gems and picter-slates. 'Get me firing solutions on those war cells, now!'

Naval ratings scattered as Unser's flag-lieutenant cracked the whip of his tongue in relaying the captain's commands. Far below the sub-command dais, servitors slaved to control-pits worked tirelessly to manoeuvre the ship, responding to the dictates of their helmsman; others processed and relayed back firing information, making minor weapons adjustments that would be fed down to the gun-decks.

'Melta torpedoes at forty-four per cent, my lord,' said the flag-lieutenant, Ikaran.

Unser's eyes flashed in the sepulchral gloom of the bridge. The long scar he'd earned whilst posted in support of the Plovian VI Imperial Guard looked like a vertical grin on the left side of his face. 'Give 'em another dose, sir.'

Ikaran relayed the orders and the message bled down through the ship to the gun-decks.

Unser smiled, his mouth pulling at the injuries that chronicled a life that had only ever known war.

He loved this. He absolutely… *Loved. It.*

The *Nobilis* was invincible. A capital ship, the largest in the line, Dominator-class – it was an expression of Unser's undeniable will and righteous anger. Dread enemies had come to Damnos, unearthed from the very bowels of the world. Though he had not seen them up close, Unser was determined to send them back to whence they came, turning them into the corpses they already resembled.

'Torpedoes away, lord,' said Ikaran.

'Bring it up.'

The bridge picters delineating the forward arc of the command dais came online. They showed a view of realspace and the half hemisphere of southern Damnos. Bright, blazing contrails invaded the vista as the torpedo payload sped earthwards.

Unser leant forward, revelling in the power. 'And in three… two… one–'

A series of bright blooms lit the world's surface from the massive impacts. The *Nobilis* was at the cusp of the mesosphere and close enough to see the effect of the incendiaries on the ground.

Ikaran had his hand to his ear, a comms-officer on board the ship reporting back to him.

'Hits on eighty per cent of targets, lord.'

Unser allowed himself to sit back. He gripped the arms of his command throne like a triumphant king. 'Another barrage, if you please.'

THE AIR WAS hot and sweaty on the gun-decks. Thousands of crew and hauler-servitors scurried in packs as the order came down from the bridge.

Overseer Caenen applied the lash to increase their efforts.

'Sweat and blood, dogs,' he drawled, bawling above the heavy drone of the engines and loading machinery. His hellish gaze followed the ammo hoppers, hoisted by teams of swarthy, soot-stained men, and glowered. 'The cap'n wants another, we give him another!' The lash cracked out again and the crews of torpedo tubes five through ten picked up the pace. All down the port-ventral aisle of the *Nobilis's* gun-deck, the scene was the same. Overseers urged their crews with threats and cajoling, just like any good Navy men.

In less than three minutes the next barrage of torpedoes was prepared, the tubes locked, their deadly cargo primed for launch.

A wave of green 'ready' runes flickered down the hot darkness of the gun-deck. Vox communication went to the gunners who angled the tubes mechanically from their firing nests according to solutions provided by the bridge. All was in harmony, the perfect machine with the men of its crew its blood and sinew.

Caenen leapt down from his pulpit, stepping on a servitor's bent back so he didn't have to use the stairs. He grunted when his boots met the deck in a heavy *thunk*, berating a man for getting in his way and punching out another as he moved to a viewport.

The tiny aperture afforded a limited view of realspace, but enough to witness a torpedo barrage. Tearing open the iron hatch, Caenen wiped the grime and warp-frost from the many-layered plascrete protecting them all from the void and simply looked.

To the overseer, a bombardment was a thing of beauty. Even the many slummer-whores he had bedded, in spite of his scars and his lack of hygiene, paled. She, the *Nobilis*, was his true mistress… and the bitch had quite a slap in her.

When the launch tubes failed to vent, Caenen frowned. He wiped at his heavy breath where it had fogged the viewport, but he hadn't missed it. The tubes were still full. He was about to start shouting and bawling again, ready to apply his boot to the fegger who'd screwed him, when a dense, ultra-concentrated beam speared from the surface.

'What the shi–'

WE ARE INVULNERABLE.

The thought was a comfortable one and Captain Unser was enjoying this feeling of pre-eminence when the weapons failure rune on his command-slate spoiled it.

'Mister Ikaran, report!'

The flag-lieutenant had his hand to his ear again, getting information from the comms-officer. 'A jam, lord. We'll have to repack and acquire new firing–'

The massive energy spike raging across all of the pict-screens on the bridge arrested Ikaran's recommendations.

'Lord, our shields will be–'

'Impossible,' breathed Unser, sitting up so he might defy his imminent death more staunchly. 'They don't have… Up here… we're invinc–'

A bright flare of emerald light filled the bridge, blinding the crew and scorching their flesh despite the plascrete shielding on the viewports. The *Nobilis's* shields capitulated in seconds, one after the other, and the once mighty vessel's armour was sheared away like parchment by the necron beam. It impaled the bridge and lanced the heart of the ship. Plasma drives erupted in conflagration, sending roiling firestorms across all decks. Munitions and artillery cooked off in the blast, killing thousands. The main breach caused by the beam's hungry trajectory resulted in several more sub-breaches – crewmen, equipment, entire bulk-heads and sub-decks were vented into the void, flash-frozen.

IN THE GUN-DECKS, Overseer Caenen didn't even have enough time to curse before the torpedo wall was ripped away and the entire gunnery crew, all two thousand, three hundred and fifty souls, burned to death before being expelled into the cold night of space.

LORD GOVERNOR ARXIS had not always been in the business of politicking. Unfortunately, it was a necessary evil when running a world of the Imperium. Such a task required a strong hand and a firm belief in the Emperor. Deviation from the creed could not be tolerated; the people lived to serve His greater glory and the glory of mankind.

Arxis had once been Imperial Guard, a general no less, and now he sat amongst his generals, the trappings of politics forgotten and the familiar mantle of soldier resting firmly upon his shoulders.

It was comforting.

The news he'd just received about the *Nobilis* was not.

'Throne, the entire ship? In one attack?'

Field-Marshal Lanspur nodded sombrely. 'Captain Unser bought us some ground, possibly even some time with the barrages the *Nobilis* was able to make, but the ship is dead, my lord – all twelve thousand, three hundred and eighty-one souls.'

'Merciful Emperor…' Arxis was staring into space, finding it hard to comprehend what the necrons had done. He looked up at his commanders. The sixteen men arrayed around the metal table in the Proteus bunker looked back with carefully neutral expressions.

'The astropathic message?'

'Has been sent,' replied the governor's choirmaster, a robed adept called Fava who was in charge of all interstellar communication to and from Damnos. 'We got it out just before the blackout.'

Though most short-wave vox transmissions were still in effect, anything longer range, certainly off-world communication, was utterly dead. The necrons had some kind of jamming shroud fouling it.

'Then we should pray to the Golden Throne that it reaches allies quickly. For now, we marshal what defences we can.' Arxis was about to address his Master of Ordnance, a short, pugnacious man who was loyal like a bloodhound, when a dull scraping sound stopped the words in his throat and altered them. 'Did you hear that?'

The scraping was getting louder, resonating against the metal inner walls of the bunker.

Several of the governor's military staff nodded.

Sytner, his chief bodyguard, drew a pistol. 'Sire, we have to move you. Now.' He said it forcefully but without panic. Sytner had been a storm trooper, serving in the same regiment as Arxis back in the day. The lord governor trusted the stocky man, recognised the urgency in his tan face, and nodded.

Beneath them, the ground trembled. Sytner stepped in, pushing the lord governor behind him and tipping the table back with one hand. Like the pillars of termites that formed in Damnos's arid zone, a column of metal-flecked earth spiralled upwards from the ground. The bunker floor was several-centimetre-thick ferrocrete, but the tunnellers bored through it anyway.

A beetle-like creature, silver-backed and dirty with earth,

poked out at the apex of the pillar. Sytner shot it with his laspistol, pitching it onto its back, legs twitching.

'By the ice-hells, what...' Gaben-dun leaned in for a closer look. The pillar erupted in front of him and in seconds the Master of Ordnance was swarmed with the beetle-creatures. He fell writhing, the weight of the diminutive necrons bringing the big man down, and screamed.

'Throne of Earth,' gasped the choirmaster, seeing moist bone poking up from the chitinous mass assailing Gaben-dun. 'They're *eating* his flesh!'

'Out! Out!' shouted Sytner.

Lanspur and four of the other commanders had also drawn sidearms and put themselves between the carnivorous beetles and the lord governor.

'Open fire!' snapped Sytner and the crack of las filled the chamber along with the stink of fyceline.

Silver beetle-creatures split in half and spun off the corpse. A few las-bolts even pierced poor Gaben-dun, though the Master of Ordnance was little more than a sack of slowly dissolving meat by now.

When they were done with their first kill, the swarm converged on the rest.

Sytner and his fellows were soon shooting at the ceiling and the walls as the beetles scuttled towards them without impediment. A larger tremor shook the chamber and the room just as they were retreating into the bunker's annexe.

A vox-unit switched to open frequency crackled to life, adding to the confusion. Frantic reports came over the speakers from the outside: of the walls being compromised; of the enemy inside the defences, seemingly appearing out of thin air; of high-pitched beam weapons and the screaming of their victims.

Arxis clenched his fists impotently as the floor caved in completely, taking Lanspur with it, and a much larger insectoid lumbered into view.

Men were being flayed alive outside…

One creature, its carapace glistening silver and suggestive of an arachnid construct, became three. Sytner's las-bolt caromed ineffectually off the hide of the first. Its mandible claw snapped out and severed the man in two. To his credit, Sytner didn't scream.

The choirmaster did, just as his face and torso were melted off by the second spider's beam-spike. It started as a death-shriek then ended in a wet gurgle of sloughed flesh and matter.

The rest of the command staff didn't last much longer. Scarabs claimed them – the lord governor could think of no better way to describe the beetle swarms – or the arachnids butchered them.

Arxis was alone, surrounded by foes, trapped by the illusory protection of his own Proteus bunker.

He had time to kneel before he died: a prayer to the Emperor on his lips and the barrel of a laspistol to his temple.

When he squeezed the trigger, the weapon groaned and failed. Exhausted during those first frantic moments, the power pack was out.

Arxis closed his eyes before the claws took him.

CHAPTER TWO

IT WAS GOOD fortune that placed the Ultramarines within the vicinity of Damnos. Although it would later be questioned what exactly was *good* about it. The desperate astropathic message delivered with Lord Governor Arxis's seal of verification was deciphered quickly by the sightless adepts aboard the *Valin's Revenge*.

Its captain, the dauntless Sicarius, had no compunction about ordering the vessel and his vaunted Second Company to the beleaguered world with the utmost haste.

The strike cruiser translated in-system amidst a debris field. Tracking augurs identified the stricken shell of the *Nobilis*, a vast Navy capital ship. The *Valin's Revenge* was undoubtedly smaller and lacking the same level of firepower, but it was also more manoeuvrable and boasted one of the most lethal payloads known to the galaxy.

Helmsman Lodis, long-serving of the Chapter, drew the vessel in close. In the void, the engine surges, the slight amendments to heading and bearing, might have seemed glacially slow but they were not. Whickering gauss-beams from the necron arc-obliterators on the ground, many kilometres long, tried time and again to skewer the strike cruiser. Each time Brother Lodis manoeuvred the *Valin's Revenge* out of harm's way or used the debris to ward them. Shields flickered with the glancing impacts, several minor hits were confirmed by the damage crews but still the ship drew closer, coming in line with Sicarius's perfect assault vector.

Hunks of the *Nobilis*, floating listlessly through the void, presented a serious threat to the strike cruiser's integrity. Volleys from the vessel's laser batteries sheared the larger sections in half. The lesser pieces of debris merely rebounded off the *Valin's Revenge's* armour.

It was a feat of bravura that finally allowed the exact attack point to be reached. Ventral drop pod bays vented in seconds, like tiny arrowheads launched from an unseen bow. They sped towards Damnos in formation, bearing Angels of Death and slim hope to the populace.

Finally capitulating under the necron gauss barrage, the shields broke down and the *Valin's Revenge* sustained a critical blow. Its payload delivered, Helmsman Lodis was content to retreat into the void, beyond the range of the guns, and lick his wounds.

For now, at least, Sicarius and his brothers were on their own.

DEEP PERCUSSIONS SHUDDERED through the walls of the drop pod.

The gauss-streams were getting closer. Warning runes flickered across the control console, urgent and red. Despite the thickness of the ceramite arrowhead in which the

Space Marines were cocooned, the internal temperature was rising, not just with the heat of re-entry but from the proximity of the necron's anti-aircraft cannonade.

Sicarius was unmoved.

'Hold to your purpose, Lions,' he addressed his command squad. Except for Veteran-Sergeant Daceus, the rest of the nine-man retinue was masked by their cobalt-blue battle helms. 'We roar!'

The engine drone forced his shout into a bellow. The captain's retainers voiced a reverberant war cry as one. It was a sound to stir Sicarius's Talassari blood.

None would ever eclipse the Second, they were preeminent amongst the Ultramarines. Even Agemman's First were looking over their heavy-armoured shoulders.

His wide eyes flashed like stars as he roared again. 'Victoris Ultra!'

The reply was in mid-repeat when the gauss-beam clipped them, shearing away a portion of drop pod. Part of Brother Argonan went with it, most of his right shoulder and a chunk of torso. The blood vacating his body in the high-velocity pressure release of the pod vented like red streamers through the breach.

'Apothecary,' said Sicarius, donning his helmet and nodding to the only one of the squad armoured in white.

Brother Venatio leaned over to the stricken Argonan, unclasping one of his grav restraints to do so. Situated alongside him, Veteran-Sergeant Daceus instinctively seized the Apothecary's cuirass to steady him.

Punching a hole through Brother Argonan's gorget and chestplate with his reductor drill, Venatio quickly removed the sacred progenoids within and secured them in an ampoule-chamber mag-locked to his belt.

'Remember him,' Sicarius told his warriors. The wind had built to a shriek inside the compromised drop pod. Outside, visible only through the ragged trench in the hull, the world blurred like smeared paint. 'Avenge him,' the captain concluded.

His gaze flicked to a series of read-outs on the control console. Their trajectory was still sound. The metres to planetfall clicked past on electronic tumblers at a fearsome rate.

'Twenty-eight seconds and counting, High Suzerain,' Veteran-Sergeant Daceus announced, using one of Sicarius's many honorifics.

The physical testament to his many deeds was plain for all to see in the medals and laurels that bedecked his armour. Sicarius was a warrior born but he was also not one to shy from ostentation.

'Bolters and blades ready, sergeant,' he growled, gripping the hilt of the sword of Talassar. Tempest Blade was its name. Even Sicarius's weapons had laudations.

'Hot hands and ready swords!' barked Daceus to the rest.

Snap-slides from bolters being primed filled the noisy drop pod interior. Flames were tearing off the point where the gauss-beam had glanced them and ended Argonan's life. None aboard gave them notice. All eyes were on the embarkation hatch.

LIKE THE THUNDER-SMITE of a storm god, the drop pod touched down and sent impact cracks webbing across the surface of Damnos. It was one wound amongst many the planet had suffered.

A pneumatic pressure hiss preceded the exit ramp

slamming down. Seconds later Sicarius was bounding through it, cape flaring, Guilliman's name on his lips.

He speared a necron warrior, half-cooked by the drop pod's incendiary flare. Another nearby had rapidly self-repaired and was advancing with automaton-like implacability. Sicarius pummelled its torso with a blast from his plasma pistol. Breaking into a run, he got close enough to behead it. The green balefires in its eyes guttered and died.

Behind him, the hard *chank-rattle* of bolters sounded as Daceus and the others opened up. Energy beams, viperous and emerald green, streaked through the smoke before Sicarius's retinal scanners could resolve a better view. A gauss-beam scudded over his pauldron, stripping it back to naked ceramite with the barest touch.

The necrons' balefire eyes appeared in the gloom like dead stars. The few they'd destroyed around the drop pod were just part of the vanguard.

More were coming.

THE THANATOS FOOTHILLS loomed in the distance like bad omens. The drop pods had got them as close as they could.

The ground running up to the snow-crested mounds was over three kilometres of debris-choked mire. Fanged by ice shards and dotted with arctic sinkholes, it was treacherous.

Scipio Vorolanus ate up the metres eagerly, his 'Thunderbolts' keeping pace alongside him and in spread formation. He checked the dispersal on his retinal display. A series of ident-runes showed good separation and fire-arc discipline.

'Move!' he said into the comm-feed, spurring his warriors as one.

Through the smoke-fog and the dust palls from the sundered refinery complex, shapes were moving ahead of them. They strode, slow and purposeful. Whickering emerald gauss-beams preceded them.

A grunt of pain, an armoured silhouette crumpling to Scipio's extreme right signalled a hit. Brother Largo's rune went to amber as the tac-display in Scipio's helmet registered a serious injury.

Just a few more metres…

A long line of silver-grey, flecked with pieces of ceramic, opposed them. The necron fire was a relentless barrage now. Another Ultramarine battle-brother fell to its fury.

+*Halt!*+

Scipio was stunned into obedience by the figure running just ahead of him. The word resolved in his mind rather than his comm-feed, a psychic impulse that could only be defied by one with sufficient will.

Varro Tigurius dropped into a crouch, gauss-beams flashing against a kine-shield the Chief Librarian had raised around him.

'Get to cover. Hunker down!' Scipio ordered, slamming behind a shattered wall in the gutted remains of the half-destroyed refinery.

The place was a grim mortuary, littered with the bodies of Damnosian labourers and indentured Imperial Guard troopers. There'd been a battle here, a hard-fought one that had ended badly for the human natives.

Scipio barely gave them a second glance. It had not always been so. Black Reach and the many hard years that followed had changed him.

Fifty metres of spar-studded, wire-drenched courtyard stood between the Ultramarines and the necron firing line.

Tigurius had brought the Space Marines to a sudden stop behind a ragged barricade before the final charge.

Peering through the gauss-laced haze, Scipio engaged the comm-feed. 'Specialists to point, on Vorolanus.'

Brothers Cator and Brakkius moved up, crouch-running, a few seconds later. Scipio clapped Cator on his shoulder guard. 'Plasma and meltagun at either end, brothers.' Both nodded as one, taking position at the edges of the wall.

Chips of rockcrete and semi-flayed plasteel slivers forced Scipio to duck.

'What are we waiting for, brother-sergeant?' asked Naceon.

Scipio had his eyes on the courtyard – there was more than merely war-churned earth beneath its shattered flag-stones – and didn't look back.

'For thunder and lightning.'

Telion had taught him when to wait and when to strike; the Master Scout's expert tutelage and influence, presently engaged in other war zones, would be missed on Damnos. Scipio gestured towards Tigurius, a couple of metres ahead of them. 'Watch and be ready.'

A coruscation of electricity suddenly wreathed the Librarian's ornate battle armour and he pressed one gauntleted palm to the ground. Instantly, the azure energy banding him leapt into the earth and ripples of psychic force went searching through the no-man's-land.

Like gruesome marionettes jerking to horrific un-life, the necron 'flayed ones' sprang from their ambuscade. They'd been buried just beneath the surface of the earth, poised to attack the Ultramarines as they charged. A minefield of sorts, but one littered with an animate and deadly enemy rather than merely explosives.

Two of the ghoulish creatures juddered and expired from

Tigurius's lightning arcs, the flayed human skin draped across them like cloaks and cowls burning off in a noisome flesh-smoke. Several more came on, having lost the element of surprise, but slashing with razored finger-talons anyway.

Scipio roared, 'Space Marines – unleash death!' The flare of his bolt pistol framed the hard edges of his crimson battle-helm in jagged monochrome.

A plasma bolt took one of the flayed ones in the chest, annihilating mechanical organs and processors. The necron collapsed in a heap, quivered and then phased from existence as if it had never even been there.

Another sloughed away under the beam of Cator's meltagun. Despite the rapid self-repair engines of the necron's advanced mechorganics, the damage was critical and it too was teleported away.

Naceon had leapt the barricade, full-auto adding thrust to his battle cry. 'Ultramar and the Thunderbolts!'

Impact sparks riddled the onrushing necron, jarring but not stopping it. Naceon saw the danger, bringing his bolter's combat-bayonet low to block, but was too late. Finding the weak points of Naceon's armour joints, the flayed one punched several fatal wounds into the Ultramarine before slicing open his gorget.

Naceon's head rolled like a dud-grenade into the dirt.

'Guilliman and the Temple of Hera!' Scipio invoked a blessing as he cut into the metal clavicle of Naceon's killer. The chainsword bit deep and jammed.

An expressionless silver rictus, stained with blood, reared towards the sergeant. A bolt pistol burst took off the necron's left claw-hand before it could slash him. Scipio then butted it, snapping the creature's neck so its head lolled at an unnatural angle. He thumped his chainsword's activation stud again, muttering a quick litany to the machine-spirit within, and it churned to life. Dropping his pistol, Scipio drove the blade two-handed clean through the flayed one's body and out the other side. As he stepped back, ready to strike again, the two mechanical halves slid diagonally and fell in opposite directions.

Scipio had barely recovered when a second necron was advancing upon him. Without his bolt pistol, he adopted a rapid defensive stance.

The flayed one exploded before it could engage, sparks and machine-parts flying like frag.

A pair of hard eyes, glowing with power and set in an ice-carved face, regarded him.

+*Take up your arms*+

Scipio gave a curt nod of thanks to Tigurius, his soul ever so slightly chilled by the Librarian's gaze, and retrieved his bolt pistol.

There was little time. The flayed ones were vanquished, Brakkius and Cator were finishing the wounded at close range, but the line of gauss-flayers remained.

Scipio waved his squad forward after Tigurius. Catching the Librarian's battle-signal on his retinal display, he opened up the comm-feed again.

'Squad Strabo. Bring fire from heaven.'

Hidden behind the wreckage of a refinery tower, ten bulky figures arrowed into the air on plumes of fire. The roar of their ascent jets made the necrons look skywards. Half of the creatures switched their aim, but the gauss-stream was too late and not nearly enough.

Hit from the front by Tigurius and Squad Vorolanus, and from above by Assault Squad Strabo, the necron firing line disintegrated, leaving the Ultramarines the victors.

In the aftermath, Tigurius eyed the distant Thanatos foot-hills. The forbidding arc of necron pylons and the long noses of gauss siege cannon blighted the horizon line. Sustained particle whips and focused energy beams bombarded the city of Kellenport relentlessly.

'They will be well guarded,' counselled the Librarian, without acknowledging Scipio's presence but answering his question before he'd even asked it.

'We'll need a way to breach their defences,' Scipio replied. Behind him, his squad and that of Sergeant Strabo secured the battle-site.

'A dagger rather than a hammer,' said Tigurius. 'But not one wielded by the hand of a Space Marine,' he added cryptically, turning his attention onto the sergeant. 'Does something trouble you, Brother Vorolanus?'

Scipio shifted uncomfortably in his armour, wishing he hadn't removed his battle-helm.

'No, my lord,' he answered, truthfully. *Nothing, except your psyker's interrogation.*

Tigurius smiled and it was, at once, a deeply incongruous and unsettling gesture.

'Perhaps it should be,' he said, and left Scipio to plan the next stage of the assault.

Brother Orin was at the sergeant's shoulder before he could reply.

'We've secured the battle-site, my lord.'

Scipio re-donned his helmet. 'Retrieve Naceon's body and replenish ammo. We advance,' he replied, left to wonder at Tigurius's meaning.

THEY SAW IT as a star-fall from the heavens. All who manned the Kellenport walls, their tired bodies and weary souls crying out for succour, knew it for what it was. No mere meteor shower, although celestially that was how it first appeared.

No, it was salvation. Or so they all hoped.

Adanar Sonne surveyed the dispositions of his troops on the city battlements. They'd lost much of the outer ground beyond the core. Several of the defensive walls had fallen, those ringing the heart of the city. Ferrocrete, armaplas and adamantite had been made a mockery of by the necron flayer technology. The horrors it could inflict upon flesh and blood were even worse to behold.

The necrons had some kind of device, a phasic-generator the tech-priests had postulated. It had allowed the bulk of their awakened troops to teleport directly behind the Ark Guard's defensive positions. Fortified walls, bunkers, fields of razor-wire – they were no impediment to the mechanised advance of the necrontyr. Isolated pockets of resistance in these outer zones, 'the wasteland' as it had come to be known, fought still. Their lasgun reports diminished to the same ratio that the emerald flash of gauss-flayers increased. Soon they'd be silent and the metal host would come for the survivors cowering within the city's core.

Adanar could make out the remains of the lord governor's Proteus bunker in the snow-choked battlefield. How they had managed to extract him was unknown, but he was rumoured to be alive, albeit comatose and in critical condition. The body of Tarn, the former commander of the Ark Guard, lay amongst the corpse-tide. Their icy graves were barely settled when the necrons had begun marching over them. Tarn had been a brave man, and honourable. His rearguard action had allowed Adanar to lead the bulk of the troops behind the inner walls of Kellenport, all the way back to the western gate and the Courtyard of Thor. It was only delaying the inevitable but it gave them all a few more hours to contemplate their fate.

A sea of metal horrors extended all the way to the horizon line, their balefire eyes adding to the chill colonising the hearts of the men. In the distance, arcane pyramids, newly unearthed, hove into position. Every burst of infernal light from their cores seemed to bring fresh monsters into the fray. This legion of death would not be denied, but despite his fatalism Adanar would not yield without making a fight of it.

Behind him, the dense thud of *uber*-mortars and long-cannons could be heard. Their reports, though loud and earth-shaking, had started to pale in comparison to the necron barrage. Slowly, they were being drowned out.

We are all drowning… in our fear. Death, slow and terrible, has come to my world and there is no escaping it.

Adanar flinched reflexively as another of the artillery stations was sundered. A vast cloud of smoke belched across the Ark Guard platoons waiting in the Courtyard of Thor to fill the inevitable breaches in the wall.

Lasgun fire rained from the battlements, a steady shriek of energy that the necrons waded through as if it were nothing but an insect swarm. Shielded by bunkers, hunched below plascrete bulwarks or hastily erected barricades, the Ark Guard were holding out. For now, at least.

Rotational guns – las and autocannon, heavy stubber and bolter – slaved to a rail network, spat muzzle flashes into an alien darkness. Not only had the necrontyr brought a comms shroud to blanket the regions before them, they had summoned an unnatural shadow too. Running hot on its tracks, Adanar watched a team wheel an autocannon in position only for it to be vaporised by necron heavy fire before it could shoot. Ammo buckets attached to the platform went up in a fiery cascade, shredding the crew and several more Ark Guard nearby. Below, platoon sergeants saw the hole and ordered more men into the gap.

'Sir.'

Adanar was dimly aware of someone addressing him.

The voice became insistent. 'Commander Sonne.'

He glared at Besseque, his aide. The man was shorter by a head than Adanar and had his cold-coat buckled all the way to his chin. His goggles were perched on his hooded head and covered in rime-frost. Shivering, Besseque saluted before going on.

'Acting-Governor Rancourt has just been on the vox. He wants a battalion sent to the Capitolis Administratum. He says if the area outside the walls can be cleared then an extraction from the Crastia Shipyards will be possible.'

Adanar fought the urge to strike Besseque, but it wasn't the messenger's fault. He cursed the day that Rancourt returned from the ice wastes alive.

'Request denied,' he answered flatly.

The Capitolis Administratum was an isolated bastion out in the wasteland. From his vantage point on the wall Adanar could discern its troops fighting hard against necron aggressors. Somewhere inside, Zeph Rancourt had secreted himself, deep within the governmental chambers. Perhaps that was where they'd moved Arxis to, as well.

Mercifully, only the lesser necron constructs were harrying the bastion's high walls. Wave after wave of scarab creatures assailed the Ark Guard platoon and the capitolis storm troopers charged with its defence, but they were holding. The necron war cell diverting its attention in the bastion's direction suggested that situation was about to change.

'It's a suicide mission,' Adanar muttered, and brought his attention back to the broader killing-fields.

'What should I tell the acting governor, sir, he won't–'

'Tell him to feg off for all I care, Besseque! There are no more men, no spare battalions. It's ov–' Adanar caught himself before he went too far. He lowered his voice, just for the aide. 'It's over, Corporal Besseque. This world is our tomb.'

Slowly, Besseque nodded and backed away. The hollow anger in Adanar's eyes was reflected in the corporal's fearful pupils.

Adanar didn't watch him go. He returned to observe the assault. Hard to see, as a sudden snowfall shawled the more distant defensive walls, but a line of shattered tanks punctuated the outer marker of the city where they'd first tried to meet the necrons. The enemy had annihilated the armour columns with perfunctory ease and then used their swarm creatures to gut the machine innards of the Imperial tanks and convert them into more necron warrior constructs. How foolish the humans had been to think anything other than hiding behind the walls of the capital would extend their lives, albeit fractionally.

'How much of a fool,' whispered Adanar. He rubbed his finger over a locket-charm chained to his wrist. There were two picts nestled inside, memories of the wife and child now slumbering beneath the Damnos earth like so many others.

'I'm sorry,' he said, ghosting the air with his breath, the din of the battle all around him receding. He felt the scar on his face, the ache in his shoulder and back from when he'd tried to save them. When the hab had collapsed and… and…

Adanar shut his eyes.

Tarn, the poor dead fegger, had been wise to tell him to flee with his family. A pity Adanar had not heeded him.

'I'm sorry,' he echoed, talking to the phantoms in his mind. He wiped away a tear, crystallised on his cheek, and the battle rushed back. They were stretched. He needed more men. Once the phasic-generator was in range it wouldn't matter. Not long now. He'd be with them soon enough.

Some of the Ark Guard in the courtyard were pointing at the sky.

Adanar followed their gestures and saw… *comets*. Armoured comets, cobalt-blue and streaked in flame, emblazoned with an icon he had seen depicted in tapestries and triptychs, if never in real life.

Ultramarines.

The Space Marines had come.

WHEN ORDERED TO join the gate-guard, a soldier surrendered all semblance of control and accepted his fate was no longer in his own hands. Even firing a weapon was pointless. Engaging the enemy was impossible. The first moment a gate-guard would know of the enemy was when that enemy was bearing down on him, breaching the very portal he had sworn to protect.

Falka accepted the duty grimly. He never trembled like the other men did when the earth shook and the gate shuddered from artillery impacts. He gripped his lascarbine, felt the reassuring weight of the ice-pick tugging at his belt loop, and waited. He thought of Jynn, lost in the ice storm. It seemed like years, but in reality it was just months. She'd got them out of the mine and died an ignominious death for her bravery. Sometimes, the Emperor's sense of humour was a cruel one. Falka's last sight of her had been the ice bank collapsing, Jynn and a dozen or so others falling to the abysmal white of the frost-gale.

Now all he had was the gate. He had lived, she had not. It would count for something, Falka decided. He'd seen, first-hand, what had happened in the outer zones – 'the wasteland'. Ferrocrete and plasteel were no barriers to these creatures, these *necrons*. They filled the air with their threats, their promises of annihilation and domination, and there was nothing the Ark Guard could do. This was a menace that could materialise through walls or *inside* bunkers. There was no place on all of Damnos to hide. So, it was with a certain irony that Falka regarded the western gate.

When the phasic-generator, an arcane device spoken of in fearful whispers by the men, got close enough or attained enough power, they would be tooth to nail with the necrons. Flesh against metal, the humans did not stand a chance.

'You were the lucky one, Jynn,' muttered Falka, and the sadness plucked at his stomach, making him feel sick.

'Trooper Kolpeck.' It was the gate-sergeant, a hard-edged brute called Muhrne. 'Save your prayers until they're at the gate.'

'With respect, sir,' Falka replied, 'it won't matter a shard. They'll pass the western gate and be on us without warning.'

Muhrne nodded sagely. 'So, like I said: save your prayers.'

Falka laughed before his gaze was drawn to the sky and he saw the stars falling, setting the clouds aflame.

THE DROP PODS hammered into the earth with concussive fury. Adanar watched a wave slam into position around the Capitolis Administratum, burning scarabs off the walls with the displaced heat of their re-entry. Slab sides like the edges of an arrowhead crashed open with a hiss of venting pressure and a missile barrage disgorged from within. Tiny explosions, combining to form much larger ones, erupted throughout the necron ranks in close proximity to the bastion. Adanar had expected Space Marines; instead he got a fusillade that was punishing the enemy hard with automated precision. The defenders, pushed close to the brink of defeat, rallied at once. Redoubled las-fire spat from the walls adding to the carnage.

Adanar's vicarious exultation was short-lived as the phasic-generator came into range and so too did the necron warrior cohorts. Several war cells translated *through* the Kellenport walls and fell upon the vanguard Adanar had positioned in front of the Courtyard of Thor. A strange sensation emanated from the newly arrived enemy, something brought on by the effects of the generator's recent activation. The world spun vertiginously and Adanar was forced to cling to the battlement for support. He heard screams, echoing through the fog of sudden dislocation, and assumed several of the Ark Guard stationed on the wall had fallen.

'Sergeant,' he began, spitting out the word through gritted teeth.

Sergeant Nabor was on his knees, blubbering like an infant with his hands over his ears.

It had affected the entire garrison.

Adanar tried to move, thinking he was stepping back when in fact he went forward. He reached for his laspistol, hoping the sudden discharge might return his senses, but grabbed for the empty air on the left side of his belt, instead of the holster on his right.

'Throne of Earth,' he garbled, as an errant trickle of blood wept from his nostril and touched his lip. The copper tang was intense, almost acidic.

Below, through his tunnelling, kaleidoscopic vision, the vanguard was being slaughtered.

A voice, inhuman and metallic, resolved on the breeze.

Heed my words for I am the Herald and we are the footsteps of doom. Interlopers, do we name you. Defilers of our sacred earth. We have awoken to your primitive species and will not tolerate your presence. Ours is the way of logic, of cold hard reason; your irrationality, your human disease has no place in the necrontyr. Flesh is weak. Surrender to the machine incarnate. Surrender and die.

Adanar found his laspistol – it was as if it'd been placed in his trembling grasp – and pressed it to his forehead.

'Surrender to the machine incarnate,' he echoed macabrely. 'Surrender and die.' A thought, so small and insignificant he barely felt it, entered his brain and he paused for a few life-saving seconds. The trigger pull never came.

The comets from heaven crashed home, flooding the plaza beyond the walls with cobalt-blue angels, and the terrible sensation abated.

Weeping openly, Adanar put down his gun and praised the Emperor.

'Thank you, my loves,' he sobbed, rubbing at the locket-charm. 'Thank you.'

Mustering his resolve, ignoring the fact Sergeant Nabor had forcibly evacuated much of his brainpan across the battlement, Adanar issued the order to open the western gate and empty the Courtyard of Thor.

The tide had turned.

CHAPTER THREE

Aboard the Valin's Revenge *prior to drop pod assault*

SCIPIO KNELT ON the assembly deck, blessing his weapons before launch. Less than fifty metres away row upon row of drop pods waited, cinched in their launch tubes.

'As I anoint this holy bolter with these words of benediction, so too do I commit myself, body and mind, to the service of the Emperor. I swear by Guilliman's blade and for the glory of Ultramar that Thy will be done.' Holstering his bolt pistol, Scipio drew his chainsword from a sheath on his armour's power generator and pressed the still blade to his forehead. 'Make my hand into a ready sword; let my faith and certainty of purpose be my shield. For I am Adeptus Astartes, Ultramarine, pre-eminent of all Chapters. So swears Lord Guilliman.'

'So swears Lord Guilliman,' echoed a deep voice behind him.

Scipio smiled and turned, sheathing his weapon. 'Didn't think I'd see you again so soon, brother.'

Iulus Fennion had a face like a slab of carved granite and displayed about the same amount of emotion. He clasped Scipio's proffered hand and tiny cracks sprang out from the corners of his eyes in what could have been amusement.

'A dangerous mission into the Thanatos Hills,' Iulus replied, all business. His square jaw and flat nose shifted like a mountain crag as he spoke, and the stubble on his chin and head reminded Scipio of grit rather than hair.

'Is that concern I hear, brother?' Scipio asked, releasing his grip and patting his fellow sergeant on the shoulder.

Iulus shrugged, pretending to run a final check over his wargear. 'A statement of fact. As part of the main push to relieve Kellenport, I won't be there to watch your back.'

'I can think of no better to perform such a task, either,' Scipio replied with genuine bonhomie. 'Or perhaps it's you that's in need of protection.'

Iulus grunted something when the pair were interrupted by a third figure.

'Brother-sergeants.' Praxor's greeting was friendly enough, but a chill entered the air at his arrival nonetheless.

The three clasped vambraces in the manner of the old way once favoured by Macraggian battle-kings.

'A glorious campaign is in prospect,' said Praxor Manorian. 'Our Lord Sicarius will bring many laurels to the Second this day.'

'Cast off your politician's mantle, Praxor,' growled Iulus, finding the other sergeant's vainglory distasteful. 'It is war, plain and simple.'

'There is more than mere soldiery at play here. We need to be seen to be supporting our captain.'

Scipio snorted. He hadn't seen Praxor in many weeks – he originally believed he'd been secluded in the practice cages, but later discovered he was involved in senate dealings concerning Calgar's eventual successor. 'Support for what? Sicarius's elevation?'

Praxor looked nonplussed, his thin face taut like wire. Together with his silver hair, the sergeant had the haughty cast of a statue. He was certainly inflexible enough when it came to Ultramar politics. 'Yes, what else?'

Iulus shook his head. 'We three have debated this point at length, and I still maintain it is unfitting talk for warriors. Agemman is First, therefore he sits at Lord Calgar's right hand. I vaunt Sicarius as much and as readily as any in the Chapter, as any in the Second, but the law of ascendancy is what it is.' The grizzled veteran folded his arms as if that were an end to it.

'Just because you have a uniquely simple view of matters does not mean everyone else has, Iulus,' chided Praxor. 'Every victory, laurel and laudation we garner for the Second brings us closer to our rightful place, at the head of Calgar's table.'

Bored of the debate, one that had been waxing and waning for over a century, Scipio began inspecting the seals on his power armour. 'There is no struggle, save that devised by your imaginings, Praxor,' he said dismissively. 'You've been spending too much time in temples with the legates, senators and magistrates instead of on the battlefield. I liked you better when you were a slave to the battle-cages. At least that improved your blade-craft.'

Iulus laughed, a rare concession to humour for him, but Praxor returned a serious expression. 'It is no trivial matter, Scipio. Our Chapter's future and who shapes it is of the utmost importance to all of us.' He relaxed a little, realising he was being goaded. 'And besides, the struggle is plain to see.'

Scipio frowned, bidding Praxor to clarify.

'Or did you not see Helios in the mission briefing? Him and four others of the First – Agemman's watchmen.'

'You see conspiracy and spies where I see only fellow battle-brothers–'

'They are not alone,' interrupted Iulus, pointing further down the deck where three mighty Chapter wardens stomped into view.

The drop pods meant to convey the Dreadnoughts were slightly larger than the rest and designed to accommodate their bulk. Ultracius, Agnathio and venerable Agrippen – veterans all, formerly battle-brothers but now warriors-eternal entombed within sarcophagi of ceramite. Their mechanised shells were festooned with honour gilding and reliquaries, purity seals and oaths of moment. Each bore the sigil of the Ultramarines proudly and was armed with a brutal array of weapons.

'Agrippen is First, is he not?' said Iulus, rubbing at the rough texture of his chin as he considered what it must be like to fight for the Chapter as a Dreadnought.

'Aye,' uttered Praxor darkly. 'He is.'

'You'll turn us all into company separatists with this talk, brother,' Scipio warned. 'It's not fitting.'

Praxor turned on him, flint in his eyes and ice in his voice. 'Eventually you'll need to find your loyalties, Scipio. The Second fight and die as one.'

Scipio smacked away his brother's coaxing hand before it touched his shoulder. 'No, we the *Chapter* are as one. Politics be damned.'

'It is for the good of the Chapter that I speak!' Praxor was clearly becoming exasperated. As if remembering where he was, he lowered his voice. 'And by supporting our captain, we are achieving that aim. There will come a time when political schism is inevitable. You won't be able to hide behind your indifference then, Scipio. Your hand will be counted, as will every other sergeant and captain's.'

'Then I hope that day is long in the coming, brother. For it holds no interest for me.' It came out harder than Scipio had intended.

Praxor's expression went from animated to one of resignation. 'As you wish.' He saluted, somewhat crisply, and stalked away to find his squad. By now the assembly deck was thronged with battle-brothers from the Second. There were elements from other companies too: specialist forces the Ultramarines would need to face the necrons. Praxor only had issue with those warriors from the First, perceived as a threat by the paranoid brother-sergeant.

'He craves the captain's validation still, even after all this time,' said Iulus. 'Space Marines have long memories and pride, the same as any man.'

'I would see Praxor's pride lanced swiftly before it overtakes his reason.'

Iulus only nodded.

Scipio scowled at Praxor's back as he departed. 'He's a fool.'

'Perhaps.'

A raised eyebrow gave away Scipio's surprise. 'You agree with him?'

'I am a soldier, brother. I care not for the politics of advancement. Calgar will appoint the right successor, I trust in that. But I'm not blind, either. Agemman is looking over his shoulder, and Sicarius has his gaze fixed on what's ahead of the First Captain. Power struggles are inevitable in any organised structure – they don't need to be a bad thing, either.'

'You sound more like a Salamander, all tedious pragmatism and fatalistic acceptance.'

'Better to accept what you cannot change and learn to adapt than rail against the immutable and end up wasting time and effort.'

Scipio gave the facial equivalent of a shrug, indicating his interest in the matter was at an end. 'Battle calls, brother,' he said. Squad Vorolanus was gathering around their drop pod, awaiting their sergeant. 'May Guilliman guide your hand and the Emperor shield you.' His gauntlet slapping Iulus's pauldron made a dull ring before he turned away.

The hard-faced brother-sergeant seized Scipio's forearm, stopping him.

'Those heavy guns,' he said, releasing his grip. 'They won't be easy to knock out, even with Lord Tigurius at your side.'

'It is I who'll be at *his* side, Iulus.'

Scipio hadn't seen the Master of Librarians throughout the muster but somehow felt his presence. Varro Tigurius was formidable in the psychic arts – to take to the field with him was a great honour, but also a source of trepidation for the sergeant. What misgivings might he uncover in Scipio's turbulent mind?

Iulus brought him back. 'Even still, you'll be far from the rest of us.'

Confusion creased Scipio's brow. Did Iulus doubt him for some reason?

'The necron pylons *will* be destroyed, brother.' His eye-line strayed to the distant figure of Antaro Chronus as he inspected the Ultramarines armour. 'Rest assured of that.'

The master tank commander would not be deployed with the first wave, but Thunderhawk transporters stood ready on the launch bay for when the enemy beam weapons were silenced and passage opened for the Predators, Whirlwinds and Devastators in Chronus's arsenal.

'I don't doubt it. Antaro's cannons will be a welcome friend in a sea of foes when you do.'

'What is it, then? All this evasion.' Scipio's eyes narrowed. 'It's not like you.'

'I give you counsel, that is all,' Iulus said plainly. He paused, as if deciding how and if to proceed. Good advice given at a bad time by a friend was always harder to hear; it was even harder to give. 'You are becoming like him.'

Scipio's face stiffened. It had lost much of its youthful exuberance over the last century, only the close-cropped hair remained the same. 'More allusion. Are you sure that's not Praxor Manorian under all that grim and sturm?'

Iulus didn't return Scipio's smile.

'I am my own man, Iulus.'

'I don't doubt that.' The sergeant had his hands up in a plaintive gesture. 'But these creatures are not ork, nor are they eldar or even Traitors…'

'I know what they are, brother.'

Warning sirens were sounding, signalling the imminent drop pod assault.

Further counsel from Iulus Fennion would have to wait.

Sicarius, ever the last to walk the assembly deck, ever the first out onto the battlefield, had just arrived with his Lions. The captain and his command squad strode with an imperious air about them. As they closed on their drop pod, the slab sides of the inverted arrowhead grinding open to allow them access, Sicarius spoke. 'Glory to the Second,' he roared, a broad grin splitting his patrician jawline. He lifted the Tempest Blade and its edge glittered in the half-light. 'Let's give them a taste of Guilliman's wrath.'

The necron cannonade had begun outside the thick walls of the *Valin's Revenge*. The rapid manoeuvres by Helmsman Lodis and the close proximity of the blasts resonated through the hull and shook the assembly deck.

Sicarius laughed it off, even as he was enjoying the bellowed affirmations of his men.

'I am my own man,' Scipio repeated, watching Sicarius and the Lions of Macragge climb aboard their drop pod. It was something he and Iulus should also be doing.

'Just watch yourself, brother. Promise me that at least.'

Scipio nodded, not liking the hint of anxiety in Iulus's eyes. They clapped pauldrons, their brief disagreement forgotten, and made for the drop pods.

It would be a long time before they saw each other again.

WHEN THE LIONS were in their positions and the access hatch was closing, Sicarius's expression changed. Swathed in shadows, with only the internal lumes of the pod interior to light it, his face took on a much darker cast.

'These revenants are not like the greenskins,' he warned. 'The warriors outside this covenant are Second Company – there are none better – but they require steel and fire, not cold hard facts. Let the tactica briefings give them the knowledge they require to do their duty. You, my Lions, are *chosen*. You, as I do, will know what we face on the Damnos soil.' Sicarius looked to his second-in-command.

Veteran-Sergeant Daceus narrowed his eyes. He swept his gaze across the other eight Space Marines in the drop pod. A countdown timer had begun. Intermittent vox-chimes signalled the imminence of launch; the shuddering impacts felt against the hull conveyed its urgency.

'There have been few reported sightings, let alone

engagements with these creatures. We, the Second, have yet to lock blades with them but they are a foe unlike any other. Your tactica briefings are inloaded to your retinal displays – I suggest we all analyse that data during launch. Their technology, resilience and ability to self-repair are all in there.'

The vox-chimes were getting closer together as the countdown started to reach its final cycle.

'There is no drill, no amount of training or physical honing that can prepare you for this foe,' he went on. 'Preparing for the unknown, adapting to face the unforeseen scenario, it is what we Space Marines excel at. We are not the Guard, mere men, who would balk and pale in the face of this enemy. We are Ultramarines, but our mettle will be tested here – yours, the valiant Lions, most of all. To be chosen means something. It is more than honour, it is responsibility. Inspire your battle-brothers, for we will need inspiration and visible courage this day.'

Each of the warriors present met Daceus's hard eyes. Vandius, their Company Banner Bearer, wore a determined expression – his duty was to keep the standard of the Second aloft. Gaius Prabian, as Champion, was charged with keeping Sicarius alive and allowing him to lead the line – Daceus didn't envy him, but there was steel in his eyes and aggression. Of the others, all showing grim resolve and ready violence, only Venatio remained carefully neutral. The Apothecary knew his task would be hardest of all and it carried the most weight – in his hands was the future of the Chapter, the harvesting and safeguard of the gene-seed.

'Trust in the Codex, and in your captain,' Daceus concluded. 'Through that we will triumph.'

'You all know my mind,' said Sicarius. 'Know this, also: I

do not want this fight. I desire to gild our banner with victory, to elevate our station, to glorify our Lord Calgar and the Chapter. But our chances of victory here, on Damnos, are almost none. We will do what is needed, because it is asked of us and as Adeptus Astartes it is our solemn calling, but we are stepping onto a dead world.'

He thrust out a clenched fist.

The move was immediately mirrored by every warrior in the drop pod, until ten spokes of ceramite formed a wheel of brotherhood around the interior.

'Courage and honour.'

The words were returned to Sicarius, spoken with stern conviction.

The vox-chimes reached a long sustained whine. Launch engines were burning outside the drop pod. The bays opened in unison. There was a sense of weightlessness, then of gravity pulling them downwards through the atmosphere. Temperature gauges rose; so too did the sound of the necron guns.

The liberation of Damnos had begun.

CHAPTER FOUR

IULUS ISSUED A series of orders using Ultramarines battle-sign and his squad tightened around him in a defensive cordon centred on the drop pod. Sicarius and his Lions had landed ahead of them. Somehow, impossibly, even their transport was more eager than everyone else's to close with the enemy.

Necrons were thronging the plaza. Hot beams from their gauss-flayers turned the accumulated snow to slush that detonated wetly beneath Iulus's armoured tread.

'Dense separation, suppressing fire,' he bellowed, voice grating through his vox-grille. Iulus seldom wore a battle-helm, preferring for his squad to see his face and the fury therein, but on this occasion he was glad of it. The snow-fog occluded the view. Retinal sensors built into his helmet lenses overcame that easily, the reddish blur of the unique necron heat signature readily discernible in his field of vision.

Staccato bolter fire, clipped and precise, rewarded the

many training drills he'd put the 'Immortals' through during his tenure as their sergeant. Several of the automatons jerked and bucked against the bolt storm before collapsing into the snow-slush.

'Advance and execute,' he continued.

The Immortals moved on their sergeant's lead, charging up to the stricken necrons. Three battle-brothers hung back as the others went ahead of the enemy casualties. The loud *crack-bang* of single headshots and the sonorous report of a phasal shift filled the air.

Iulus had read the tactica briefings extensively. Nothing barring critical system damage would prevent a necron's ability to self-repair. He was taking no chances.

'Report,' he barked into the comm-feed.

'Eliminated, brother-sergeant.' Three identical replies came back before Iulus's squad were reunited. The dense *chud-chud* of a heavy bolter, unleashed by 'Guilliman's Hammer', Tirian's Devastators, sounded from the left. It was paired off with another weapon, the two cannons giving off intermittent barrages that overlapped at the beginning and end of their ammo cycles. The *foom* of missile tubes provided a low chorus to the percussive refrain of the bolters. Explosions, hazy through the mist, bloomed. Snow and frag spat in diagonal bursts. It was brutal, but in the distance necrons were rising from the carnage.

'Temple of Hera.' Iulus had moved ahead of the Devastators, but caught the flare of muzzle flashes and the fading contrail of expelled smoke in his peripheral vision as they advanced. There was little to no cover on the plaza, the necrons had levelled it with their cannonade, but that was why Space Marines wore power armour – ceramite battle plate was all the cover they needed.

From the right, Brother-Sergeant Atavian brought up a second squad of Devastators, the Titan Slayers. Their weapons brought swift death to the mechanoids. Even the necrons' enhanced repair ability couldn't save them from the searing beam of a lascannon or the metal-sloughing effects of a multi-melta. Iulus stayed close to Atavian, advancing in an oblique line. Engage, take ground, engage – enacted as if on the training ground.

The first few raiders had been the exploratory elements of a vanguard. The reddish heat signature blurs on Iulus's retinal display suddenly increased as the Ultramarines reached the shadow of the first of Kellenport's defensive walls. It was overrun and the sound of desperate Guardsmen fated for death resolved on the breeze like a requiem.

Spreading out, the necrons had enveloped them. Bolters tracked and fired to compensate, relying on advanced targeting sensors – the mist was so bad that the enemy were literally appearing as if from nowhere, and in numbers.

'Brother, my flank has been compromised.' It was Atavian through the comm-feed in Iulus's helmet.

'Close up battle-formation, there are more necrons than we first believed.'

An affirmation rune flashed on Iulus's retinal display. The tac-icons representing the Devastator squad started to move closer to the Immortals. Iulus noticed there were several red markers that remained static.

Squad Fennion and the two Devastators – they were the rearguard. Glory belonged to others.

'Take and hold the ground.' Those had been his orders during the mission briefing. Thirty Ultramarines to keep a simple esplanade from the enemy. It had seemed like overkill; now, Iulus Fennion wasn't so sure.

A swarm of beetle-like creatures droned out of the fog, mandibles champing.

The Immortals turned with battle-honed efficiency and cut them down. Brother Galvia cried out as one of the creatures clamped onto his forearm. Iulus stepped in and excised the mechanoid with his chainsword. A stamp of his armoured boot ceased the beetle's squirming after it was removed. A bolter salvo exploded another with mass-reactive fury before it could refashion itself and attack anew.

'They're hard to keep down,' breathed Galvia. 'I've never seen such–'

A gauss-beam skewering his shoulder and upper torso cut him off. Iulus reached for Galvia, who grunted and slumped to his knees. Blood-stained slush spattered his armour viscerally as he fell hard.

The wounding preceded a fusillade of gauss-fire as the necron vanguard force tried to pin them. Enfilading beams streaked across the trio of Space Marine squads diagonally while more of the drone beetles pressed an assault from the front. Iulus had one arm under Galvia to support him; with the other he wielded a whirring chainsword with menace. He swatted the first scarab-like creature, cracking its carapace but not disabling it; a second he carved with a heavy downward swing. A third latched to his vambrace but he was able to shake it off and crush it under his boot.

Another dug into his back, gnawing at the power generator. Emergency icons flashed up on his retinal display warning of an imminent energy drain. Iulus reached for the creature but staggered when a pair of scarabs fastened themselves to his pauldron. He cried out as one attached itself to his battle-helm. Below, Galvia screamed in agony and frustration.

'Aristaeus!' The comm-feed was wretched with interference. The creatures were slowly disabling it.

The low *whoosh* of pressure release and the acrid stench of promethium filled the air as Iulus and Galvia were consumed by fire. Aristaeus had kept the aperture of his flamer narrow. Both Ultramarines emerged from the conflagration blackened but otherwise unscathed. Smoking, burning scarabs writhed about on the scorched earth. Iulus crushed one underfoot before dispatching the others with a desultory burst from his bolt pistol.

He waved Aristaeus forward. 'Bring the heat.'

The Ultramarine had lost his battle-helm in the fight and wore a scarred grimace instead. His eyes became hateful slits as he unleashed the full fury of his flamer.

The swarm died in a nucleonic storm and Iulus was readying to advance when his retinal display was overloaded by a beam hit to his eye. He cried out, dropping his chainsword so he could rip his helmet off before it corroded through and the gauss-flayer started in on his face, but still held onto Galvia.

The battle-helm hit the ground with a dull *thud* and rolled, the right ocular lens partially dissolved, the ceramite around it bare and raw.

'Set me down,' Galvia mumbled. Even lying on his side, an unknown number of internal organs ruptured, he triggered his bolter. The swathe of shells found several marks and the scarabs exploded aerially like flak.

Iulus resisted the urge to touch his injured face. It hurt but pain-suppressing chemicals were already flooding his system to combat the pain and keep him fighting.

With the gauss-fire intensifying around them, forming an almost lattice-like web of emerald, any ordinary soldier would have retreated. Bolt pistol blazing as he stooped for his chainsword, Iulus's order demonstrated that Space Marines were no ordinary soldiers.

'Hold the line and return fire. In Guilliman's name!'

The Ultramarines were dauntless, but so too were the implacable necrons. One side would have to break. The low booming voice, rendered through a vox-caster, decided which side that would be.

'For the Chapter and the Lords of Ultramar!' The assault cannon of Brother Ultracius whirled into a blur of muzzle flare. Out in the cloying snow-fog, Iulus saw necron raider constructs torn apart. Instantly, the gauss enfilade lessened.

Ponderous but redoubtable, the Dreadnought had taken a little longer to reach the hold-point than the rest of the rearguard. It had been a long few minutes before his arrival but now the veteran warrior had arrived, Iulus knew the tide was with them.

'Defend the line; maintain it until the veterans of the Second can join you.' It had been a sound plan and one that suited the sergeant's intractable nature.

What was more, Ultracius was not alone.

'I am the warrior eternal of my Chapter. Long live Macragge and the Empire of Ultramar.' Where Ultracius was bombastic and glorifying, Brother Agnathio was unshakable and pragmatic. He moved with the slow but inexorable purpose of a glacier, his multi-melta scything the distant raider formations with impunity.

'Spread and engage,' bellowed Iulus, taking advantage as the necrons faltered, 'slow and exacting.'

He nodded to Agnathio, who had pounded up alongside him.

'Good to have you with us, venerable one.'

'I am the avatar of my Chapter's will. I serve eternally.' The Dreadnought's mind was not as lucid as it had once been. Agnathio knew not what year, what conflict he was embroiled in, only that he fought for the glory of the Ultramarines. A part of Iulus relished the simplicity of that existence as much as another part pitied it.

'For Ultramar.'

'Aye, for Ultramar!' The multi-melta sang its shrieking refrain again, spearing the necron constructs that were moving to engage them at closer quarters.

Tirian's gravelly voice came over the comm-feed. 'They're adopting more aggressive protocols.'

'They react,' said Iulus, 'as if directed. These shells are automatons with only hate and fell technology to animate them, but a will is at work here. Engage and destroy.'

Iulus felt his grip on the esplanade tightening. Despite the change in tactics, the necrons would not prevent him making a fist and holding the ground indefinitely. It was then, as the rearguard was fanning out and punishing the necron vanguard, that two things happened almost simultaneously to change the complexion of the battle.

First, the massive gates behind the Ultramarines opened and a human Guard force poured out, lasguns flashing. Second, a larger and much more densely packed necron cohort emerged from the fog ahead. They were bigger than the raider constructs and more heavily armed. Iulus was forced to reassess the internal boast he had made. His fist had become an open palm, clinging with fingertips. The tide had shifted again. Instinctively, the Ultramarines closed ranks. Even the Dreadnoughts paused in the face of this latest threat.

'Bring them down,' Iulus roared as the necron elites

unleashed a gauss-storm of terrifying potency. 'Give them nothing!'

Estimating thirty of the hulking necrons and factoring in the remnants of the raider constructs that were still operational, Iulus made a quick assessment of their odds. His conclusion was muttered defiantly. 'We need more men.'

THE SKY ABOVE Kellenport was wracked with incandescent thunder. The city was a distant silhouette, leavened only by the flash of explosions.

Scipio wanted to be there, alongside his brothers Iulus and Praxor, but that was not his lot in this war. Instead, he was crouched in a slowly melting mire of slush and hard earth, peering through a pair of magnoculars.

'How does it look, brother-sergeant?' asked Largo, flat against the escarpment on his armoured chest.

Power armour didn't really lend itself to stealth missions, it was too bulky and better suited to more direct engagements, but without any of the Tenth to reconnoitre the Thunderbolts were being used as de facto scouts.

'Busy,' Scipio grumbled. He handed Largo the magnoculars for a look. He was bearing his earlier injury well, the sergeant noted. Barely a flinch when Scipio had forced him to twist and reach for the scopes.

'Their picket lines look thick even without magnification,' added Ortus, sighting down the barrel of his bolter. Despite the fact the Ultramarines assault force was still several kilometres away, he could tell that the war cells protecting the pylons and gauss-obliterators were numerous. He had a good eye for that. Ortus spent most of his training allocation on the firing ranges. He could deploy his weapon like a sniper rifle, so accomplished was his aim.

'Find the leader and you have my permission to take the shot,' replied Scipio, before shuffling backwards down the ridge on his stomach. Part of their scouting task, as well as assessing the level of resistance, was to find the necron hierarch commanding the force. Imperial tacticians, those who were privy to the threat of the necrontyr, had postulated that rather than being unfeeling automatons the necrons actually adhered to a series of 'protocols' not that dissimilar from a servitor's. Their logic-engines were far more advanced, of course, but by removing the sentient will that guided it, a war cell would resort to secondary functions. Their tactics would become less adaptable and more predictable. Such a disadvantage made them easier to defeat and increased the likelihood of a full scale 'phasal retreat'. These were all theories, however. There wasn't enough battle-data yet recorded that allowed any firm conclusions to be drawn concerning potential necron weaknesses.

Tigurius obviously thought the reasoning was sound – Scipio agreed – and so charged his 'scouts' with finding the hierarch leading the cell defending the artillery. So far, they'd had little luck in doing so.

Largo was putting the magnoculars away when he asked, 'How will we breach it?'

'Not this way, that's for certain.' As he was returned to the present, Scipio brought to mind the densely thronged access routes through the hills to the necron artillery. As well as the ubiquitous raider constructs, there were larger elites and even semi-ephemeral ghosts patrolling the enemy picket lines. They'd formed concentric rings around the mass of heavy cannons in the centre. While the ghosts phased in and out of existence, the raiders and elites stood still and unspeaking like metallic sentinels. Scipio suspected they would wait like that until the galaxy burned and the universe itself ended, if commanded to do so. At least orks bickered, even the alien tyranid chittered and the Traitor hordes exalted and chanted: these soulless machines just stood in abject silence. Despite Scipio's Adeptus Astartes hypno-conditioning, it was unnerving.

'Perhaps a diversionary attack to draw out the bulk of their troops, allowing Strabo and Ixion to neutralise the guns.'

Scipio shook his head at Largo. 'There are too many and they won't move. That's a defensive force. Whatever protocol it's operating on will keep them from coming at us.'

He'd seen enough of the necrons, their mechanistic idioms, their logic-engine style tactics, to know that they couldn't be coaxed or goaded. Only a certain and direct imperative would force the mechanoids to alter their battle-routines. Somehow, the Ultramarines attacking the Thanatos Hills had to find it. If executing the necron leader was the key to that, there was still a lot of work to be done.

His eyes narrowed when he spied a rocky promontory overlooking the artillery. 'How does that look to you?'

Largo went back to the scopes, magnifying to enhance the view. He scowled. 'Impenetrable.'

'No route through the terrain?'

'We need gunships and speeders,' Largo replied.

'A pity they are locked down aboard the *Valin* then,' added Ortus.

With the necron cannonade still in operation, not only

was Kellenport subject to constant bombardment but Antaro Chronus could not deploy his tanks and any aerial support was denied to the Ultramarine spearhead.

'What are your orders, sergeant?' asked Largo after the silence started to become uncomfortable.

Scipio's expression was foul with frustration. 'Return to camp. Then we go deeper. There has to be a way through those pickets without taking them head-on.'

SCIPIO FOUND TIGURIUS alone, looking out onto an ice expanse. Snow flurries chased each other across the barren tundra like arctic devils, whipped into sudden frenzy by the wind.

There was a rime of frost coating the Librarian's cheeks, nose and forehead but he seemed not to notice. Though his eyes were open, he was locked in a psychic trance. It took Scipio a few seconds to realise before he fell into respectful silence and waited.

'The direct approach to the Thanatos Hills is denied to us,' Tigurius said without even turning around, 'and we have yet to locate the force leader.'

Scipio suddenly felt quite redundant in the face of the Librarian's prescience. 'Is it *that* easy to read my mind?'

Tigurius faced him, wiping at the crust of frost veneering his features. 'Your mood anyone could read.'

'Transparent too. I must attend to that upon our return to Ultramar.'

'I admire your optimism, Brother Vorolanus. You think our victory here is certain?'

Scipio tried not to balk before the Librarian's penetrating gaze. He didn't think Tigurius was interrogating him psychically but couldn't be sure. 'Far from it. These creatures are like nothing we've ever faced. I also believe our sternest challenges are to come.'

Tigurius nodded. 'Yes, I–' He collapsed before he could finish.

'Master!' Scipio sprang to the Librarian's aid. He was clutching his head and screaming in mental agony.

The air was filled with the scent of burning and Scipio noticed rivulets of arc-lightning spilling from Tigurius's eyes. His power armour was hot with psychic energy. Tendrils of smoke were coiling off every plate of ceramite. Seizing his force staff, the Librarian tried to anchor himself and channel some of the energy away.

Even through his gauntlets, Scipio was feeling the heat. His fingers smouldered but he clung on to Tigurius in spite of the pain.

'Master,' he hissed through clenched teeth. Below them the Ultramarines assault force was readying to move out, unaware of the unfolding crisis.

Just as Scipio thought he could hold on no longer, the baleful energy that had gripped Tigurius slowly started to dissipate. In a few seconds it was over and the Librarian could stand unaided.

'They know we are here,' he gasped, a wisp of smoke escaping from his mouth into the cold air. 'And what we intend to do.'

Scipio looked to the direction of the enemy cohorts, though they were far away. 'How will they respond?'

Tigurius looked him in the eye. It disturbed the sergeant to see the obvious disquiet there. 'Nothing. They will do nothing.'

Frowning, Scipio asked, 'What?'

'Because they believe our efforts are in vain, that there is no possible way for us to achieve victory.' Tigurius licked his lips and for a moment Scipio thought he might stumble again when he gripped his shoulder. 'I touched their minds. Fathomless, ancient, they think this world is their own. They want to reclaim it, to eradicate its population, to annihilate us. Damnos is doomed.'

'You... you *spoke* to them?'

'One of their number, part of the hierarchy, communicated with me. He called himself the Herald. But I saw something else, a fragment of the future.' Tigurius's respiration became elevated, and he clenched his fingers into claws as he fought for recall. 'It's like trying to grasp a wisp of cloud... The truth eludes me, brother. A dark pall is clouding my prescience. Another of their kind...' The Librarian wrinkled his brow, seeking an appellation. 'The Voidbringer. He is the one we are looking for.'

'And this glimpse of the future,' Scipio asked. 'How does it bode for us?'

Tigurius's voice rang with the forbidding timbre of prophecy. 'Ill, brother. It bodes ill for all of us.'

PRAXOR WAS EXULTANT. Fighting by his captain's side, he felt empowered. His squad, the 'Shieldbearers', had fought hard to stay within striking distance of the Lions. Praxor had never seen such purpose and fury from the Second's pre-eminent warriors and Sicarius's retinue. To be counted one amongst them, to become one of the High Suzerain's inner circle, was one of the brother-sergeant's most fervent desires.

'Guard against pride, brother,' Iulus had once counselled him. He sounded like Orad. But the Chaplain was long dead and Praxor's ambitions very much alive. It wasn't pride so much as idolisation and that fact – one the brother-sergeant was ignorant of – was precisely why the senators of Macragge, indeed the Masters of the Chapter, debated Sicarius's tenure so furiously. His apparent growing cult of personality was regarded as vulgar by some, as Invictus reborn and a return to the glorious golden age of the Ultramarines by others. Some in the Chapter, the oldest campaigners, felt the sons of Guilliman had been diluted by the breaking of the Legions. The many subsequent Founding Chapters all held allegiance to Ultramar but were autonomous otherwise.

Agemman, as captain of the First and with therefore the largest number of veterans in his company, was in the ironic position of recognising the importance of heroes like Sicarius but at the same time being wary of his popularity. He wanted the old days, just not ushered in by the Grand Duke of Talassar.

'Advance with all speed, stay with the captain!' Praxor was running and his squad ran with him. They moved in a 'V' formation, bolters blazing. Kill-shots were few, but the objective was to burst through the packed necron vanguard and strike deeper into the mechanoid ranks like a spear.

They had bypassed the first defensive wall already. Sicarius had studiously ignored the pleas for help and deliverance from the stricken Guardsmen still battling to hold it, his face undoubtedly a mask of hard indifference, focused on his mission. To do otherwise, to give in to compassion, would be the end for all of them. At least, that was what Praxor believed.

A necron construct sprang out of the fog, seemingly materialising from the very air. It glided in tandem with three others; no, it wasn't gliding, the moves were almost serpentine, like a snake reared to attack. It was supported by a long, segmented tail that ended in a broad barb like a scythe. Its torso was equivalent to the raider constructs Praxor had already dispatched on their charge through the breach in the first defensive wall, but its arms ended in razor talons. There was something incorporeal about it, as if it were only partially in the material realm or somewhere between solidity and necron phasal shift.

Acting on instinct and too close to fire, Brother Vortigan swung at it with his bolter's bayonet. The monomolecular blade should have carved into it, but slipped through the creature as if parting vapour. Like a whip, the tail lashed around and speared Vortigan in the neck. The talons found weak points in his armour between plastron and greave. The Ultramarine spewed a film of blood into his helmet that speckled the lenses before he fell.

Praxor cried out Vortigan's name and swung at the same time. His power sword crackled, as if reacting to the creature's nature, and he clove off a limb. Then he drove the point of the blade through the wraith's gear-like intestine and it shuddered and phased out.

The other three were in amongst the Shieldbearers, whose charge had now faltered to a stop. Krixous was down, his forearm severed, but still lived. A melta-blast from Tartaron maimed another wraith, sending it back to whatever abyss spawned it. The other two weaved in and around the slow-moving Space Marines, who swung and fired with little effect. Praxor was reminded of the gorgons of old Calth, cave-dwelling harridans that could turn men to stone with a glance. Such was the necrons' speed, it appeared as if the Shieldbearers were indeed petrified.

Praxor rallied them quickly, ordering them to corral the

creatures and bring them to Tartaron's meltagun. Another died with its living metal turned to mercury, the fourth the sergeant dispatched himself with a determined thrust of his power sword.

Agony lanced Praxor's shoulder and he realised there was a fifth wraith he had not accounted for. Its barbed tail sent Tartaron sprawling before he could fire, whilst the creature jerked and twisted around the clumsy bolter shells railing at it. The troopers were of no consequence. It wanted Praxor. Only the sergeant's blood would do. He'd dropped his bolt pistol. He heard it skitter across the ice before he lost it in the mist. With a grunt Praxor shrugged off the talons and managed to half turn before the tail barb cut his legs from under him. He fell hard onto his back, a flicker in his retinal display indicating the power to his armour had been briefly compromised. It returned with a whir of servos, and the piston-grinding swipe of his power sword was too slow for Praxor. A flick of the wraith's talons sheared his vambrace and forced his fingers to part. Like the bolt pistol before it, Praxor's blade spun away from his grasp and he was suddenly weaponless.

'Shoot it!' he growled, determined to show the mechanoid his unswerving hate before he died.

Bolter shells crashed around it, but were like exploding flares for all the damage they caused. The wraith phased through the bursts, advancing on the Ultramarines sergeant who was crawling away on his back.

'You'll have to work for it, scum.'

The necron seemed willing to oblige, darting forward on its tail with talons primed.

A shock of lightning bent its skull-head at an awkward angle. It tried to turn when the bolt hit again. Only it wasn't lightning, Praxor realised. It was a power mace. A crozius arcanum.

Trajan bludgeoned the wraith until its restorative programming kicked in and it phased out. Where the necron's face was skull-toothed metal, the Chaplain's was gimlet-eyed bone studded with platinum service bolts.

'Arise, brother,' he said with a deep, silken voice utterly unlike his predecessor's, 'for the Chapter finds you wanting.'

Praxor ignored the Chaplain's proffered hand. His power armour's systems were fully operational again. 'I can stand unaided.'

'A pity your pride didn't keep you on your feet,' Trajan snarled. He regarded the Shieldbearers. 'These creatures are fleshless abominations. They are an affront to the machine-spirit and cannot be allowed to live. Purge them all and let faith guide your holy bolters!'

Then he was gone, lost to the snow-fog as quickly as he'd arrived.

'I can see why Sicarius wanted him,' said Tartaron, his tone wry. It swiftly changed to contrition. 'I'm sorry, sergeant. My aim should have been better.'

Praxor clapped his pauldron. 'We live, don't we? Your aim was sound. Get Brother Krixous and follow on my lead. Captain Sicarius is not far ahead.'

'Are you still with us, Brother-Sergeant Manorian?' It was Daceus through the comm-feed. The veteran-sergeant was only metres in front of them with the Lions, and waving the others on.

Contrary to his initial beliefs, the point of the spearhead had been slowed to a man. Beyond the first wall, the battlefield was thronged with the necron vanguard. Praxor made out the black ceramite of Trajan nearby. The

Chaplain was everywhere, it seemed, singing litanies of hate against the alien and the abomination, as he swung his crozius. Squad Solinus, 'The Indomitable', formed an honour guard around him.

'He prefers his warriors to carry the Victorex Maxima,' said Tartaron with disdain.

Praxor's eyes hardened. 'They are the heroes of Telrendar, brother. Would that the Shieldbearers be so vaunted.'

'Apologies, brother-sergeant,' Tartaron replied, head bowed.

'Come on. We are missing the battle.' Praxor ordered them forward, but within he was burning with envy at the honours garnered by Solinus. At Damnos then, that was where they would earn their laurels and perhaps even Elianu Trajan would find the Shieldbearers worthy of his company.

IN THE WASTES, little more than rubble and accumulated ice, Agrippen had continued his irresistible advance. Spider-like constructs the size of attack bikes had impeded him, but the great warrior had battered them aside with his power fist, swathing the remains in glowing-hot promethium from the flamer attached to his wrist. A vast ball of plasma tainted the ice storm cerulean blue as the last of the spiders was engulfed and destroyed. After it was done he came to stand shoulder-to-shoulder with Sicarius, the old juxtaposed against the new.

'To the captain, for the glory of Ultramar!' The Dreadnought's augmented voice was lucid and powerful. Rare amongst the Chapter, he was one of few veterans of old that still remembered who he was and what time period he was fighting in. With Agrippen not being one of the Second,

Praxor had been surprised to learn the warrior-eternal was part of the force led by Sicarius. Perhaps the captain desired to show solidarity towards the First or maybe he wanted Agemman to hear of his prowess from one of his most loyal and forthright warriors. None could doubt the word of Agrippen – it was spoken with thunder and the weight of ages.

The breaks in combat were brief, but a patch of open ground had formed at the site of the spearhead's last victory. Sicarius occupied a half-ruined promontory overlooking the wastes. A shell of some manufactorum or perhaps a lectory – it didn't matter. The structure's blasted plateau, the burned-out remains of a second floor, was stable and expansive enough to allow the captain and all his officers the benefit of its vantage. It also offered a moment to take stock and reanalyse as the Ultramarines squads regathered for a fresh offensive.

'We should hold here, my lord,' advised Agrippen from the ground floor below. Broad and strong it might be, but even if the Dreadnought could have reached the second floor his mass would have crushed it. 'Our forces in the Kellenport plaza can reinforce us.'

Sicarius surveyed the distant battle lines, the drifting smoke and emerald flash of the necron guns. To his right, the Capitolis Administratum still stood. It was isolated but now ringed by a defensive cordon of Deathwind drop pods.

'How long will their payload last?'

'Another few minutes, captain,' Daceus replied. 'Guard forces are en route to liberate the acting governor and his staff.'

'Largely irrelevant, brother-sergeant,' said Sicarius. 'The leaders of Damnos are spent, just like their armies, but without those missiles cleansing our flank we'll become exposed and forced back.' He shook his head, looking down on Agrippen. 'Advice noted, brother, but we advance. Let the rearguard hold our lines.'

'My lord.'

'Yes.' Sicarius had removed his battle-helm to wipe the sweat from his brow. His eyes were as hard as sapphire and belatedly Praxor realised it was he who had spoken and that the captain's gaze was fixed on him.

'The mechanoids have cut off our way back.' He pointed east, to where the vanguard had flowed behind them like the living metal from which the necrons were infernally constructed. 'Our forces are split in two.'

'Then it is fortunate we do not turn back, isn't it, sergeant?'

'I–' Praxor was wrong-footed. Sicarius already knew, and didn't care. Vortigan was dead, Krixous at least was being tended by Brother Venatio – his stump in place of a hand was swathed in pinkish gauze and bandage. His Larraman cells had clotted the blood quickly but there was still some residual fluid. The casualties amongst the Second were rising, though. How many more would fall in this insane gauntlet they were running?

'Do you know what a gladius is, brother?'

'Of course, my lord, it's–'

Sicarius nodded. 'Yes, and I trust that you know. I trust that you can wield bolter and blade, that you can lead your men and inspire them to greatness.' He put his hands on Praxor's shoulders like a father to a son. He sheathed the Tempest Blade to do so. The weapon was still humming eagerly despite the ferocious tally it and its wielder had reaped. 'So too must you trust me.'

Praxor bowed his head. 'I meant no offence, Lord Sicarius.'

'Chapter Master Calgar is your lord, I am your captain. That is all the loyalty and deference you need afford me. Remember the gladius?' He nodded as Praxor did, their eyes meeting. Sicarius let the sergeant go and mimicked a thrust with his hand. '*We* are that gladius, driving at the heart of our enemy.'

'But the mechanoids have no heart, brother-captain,' chimed Daceus, to facilitate his leader's point.

'And so they must be fought another way. The necrons respond to one thing, and one thing alone,' Sicarius said. 'Punishment. If we hurt them enough, they will yield. To do that we must bring their masters out into the open. *They* are the heart. Spear that and the machine will fail. I want these creatures to notice me. I want them to recognise my wrath as a threat to their existence. Achieve that and Damnos has a chance.'

So moved, Praxor fell to one knee, his power sword held across his body. 'I am honoured to serve by your side, Grand Duke of Talassar.'

'Then you had better stand, for we shall press on, find the command node and bring glory to our Chapter.'

The Lions roared with their captain. So did Praxor, but as he was getting to his feet he noticed that Agrippen stayed silent. The time for reflection was over. A large necron war cell was resolving out of the mist and heading for them.

Sicarius grinned ferally. 'In Guilliman's name, and for Talassar. War calls us, brothers...'

As one they replied, 'We shall answer!'

FALKA WAS SECOND through the western gate after Sergeant Muhrne, running on pure adrenaline. Most of the Ark Guard behind him didn't want to die, nor did they want to fight. If anything, it was fear and mad fatalism that drove them into the wasteland. A part of Falka hoped it was the cobalt-blue angels that had suddenly arrived in their midst compelling the men, a smaller vestige of him dared to believe that some spark of bravery and pride still burned within Damnos.

'We shall not surrender!' he heard Sergeant Muhrne bellow. 'On, on, on!' he roared.

As they closed on the battlefront, Falka was glad he would meet his death head-on and not trapped behind a gate waiting to be crushed by fallen masonry or vaporised by a faceless necron artillery barrage. At least this way he could be proud when reunited with his ancestors, he could look Jynn in the eye and say, 'I died with honour, defending our world.' He hoped he would see her again soon, but was determined not to waste his life. It would be worth something to these mechanised bastards.

The Ark Guard were four hundred strong when they left the Courtyard of Thor, just under two battalions. Ominously, the western gate was closed behind them. The resonant din of it being sealed broke some of the men who turned and ran back, pounding against the metal impotently with their fists. The commissars on the battlements put them out of their misery with precise pistol shots and the wailing ceased. Not that the rest of the Ark Guard could have heard it. The shattered plaza drowned out the noise with the cacophony of war. Not just any conflict, though – this was Space Marine warfare, and it was brutal.

Falka marvelled and balked at the Angels of Death. They were as resolute and indefatigable as the necrons. When he and the rest of the Guardsmen had managed to get two hundred metres from the gate unscathed, he dared to hope that with the Space Marines' help they might yet save Damnos. Necron warriors, turning their baleful gaze upon the humans at some proximity warning within their machine brains, crushed that assumption quickly.

Muhrne was the first one Falka noticed. The pugnacious sergeant couldn't even scream as the gauss-beam flayed him. Metal and cloth became particles, skin and flesh turned to dust, organs liquefied until there was nothing left of Muhrne but a charred skeleton. Even that cracked apart when it hit the ground.

Falka ducked instinctively, though it was really just luck that spared him during that first headlong charge. Charred skeletons were exploding all around him as the necrons exposed the weakness of the human form so horrifically. He was shouting, incoherent and wordlessly, but it kept the fear down. He also realised he had yet to fire his gun, so intent was he on running the length of the plaza. Falka checked the load and hauled the trigger. His first shots went wide and too fast. He was still running and needed to conserve his ammunition. Keep going at that rate and he'd be out in a few seconds. The barrel flash, though ineffective so far, brought attention. He dived behind a rubble pile, thanking his saints as the gauss-beam careened away without killing him. Falka took a second to realign himself and was moving again. He had about twenty others with him. Judging by their shoulder patches, they were from several different squads. The gauss barrage had scattered them; the Ark Guard's discipline and coherency broken in seconds.

'What do we do?' one man asked.

It took Falka a few moments to realise he was talking to him. He wished Jynn was there, fighting by his side. She was a warrior; at least her natural instincts suggested it. She would have been an asset to the Ark Guard.

'A hit, even glancing, from those flayers and we're dead men,' said Falka. He tried not to let the fact that so many were hanging on his words disturb him. He slapped the hard flank of the ruin they were hiding in. It wasn't much, just the worn-down footprint of a defensive barrier. Each man was crouched low, keeping out of the gauss-beams streaking above them.

One man, Falka didn't know his name – he was a professional soldier, not a conscript from the mines like himself – rose a fraction to wipe his brow. An emerald flash filled the ruins and the nameless man slumped down without his head, the ragged neck stump cauterised. Two of the others had to be restrained from fleeing before Falka could continue.

He looked down at the decapitated corpse grimly. *That's the fate that awaits us all.*

'Stick to the cover, what little there is. And make for the Angels. The Space Marines will protect us.'

'We've been sent to our deaths,' one lad sobbed. His helmet didn't really fit him. Falka took off his and gave it to the boy. It wasn't a much better fit but it seemed to galvanise the lad.

'Aye, and we'll meet it on our feet, defending our people like heroes of Damnos.' He reached over and patted the boy on the shoulder. 'All right, son?'

The lad nodded. The lasgun looked awkward in his hands. Falka turned away, unwilling to see his fear any longer.

Crawling to the edge of the barrier, he waited until the whine of gauss-beams diminished and then risked a look over the top. Through the mist and carnage, he saw a squad of Space Marines giving battle. They'd abandoned the sanctuary of their landing vessel – it looked like an inverted spear-tip with its sides split open and laid flat on the ground. A black scar surrounded it, slowly obscured by falling snow.

Warriors from heaven, indeed.

Falka tried to turn that realisation into hope.

'Come on,' he shouted to the men. 'With me!'

CHAPTER FIVE

IT WAS COLD in the ice cave, but it came from more than just the temperature. There was a chill that emanated from inside, a hollowing of spirit and resolve that would kill her far quicker than a drift or even being crushed beneath an avalanche of compacted snow. It pressed against her body. She felt its weight against her torso and her left shoulder. Her legs she could no longer feel. Her bored-out heart was simply numb.

I am dead, she realised. *I am dead – my body simply doesn't know it yet.*

It was black inside, not white at all, underneath the snow. She knew it must be a cave that she'd broken through to, because of the quiet. No screaming, no weeping or mewling. The moaning had stopped too. It had started out as belligerent anger at their situation and a refusal to accept it. Then it became doleful. In the end it just *was*. She was ashamed to admit that she missed it.

I am dead and that's why I am cold.

Then she saw a light, a tiny pinhole that turned her black world into powdery grey. Noise followed, a sort of shuffling then a scuffing. Finally, she realised it was digging. *Something* was digging her out.

She panicked, but she couldn't move. Vaguely, she remembered snapping on the distress beacon and how stupid that decision had been, even born of desperation as it was, given what stalked the drifts.

I wish I was dead. The digging sound was getting closer, it became a wet scrape and a hard rasp of metal chipping into ice as the hole widened and her world lightened with every stroke.

Why can't I will my body to accept that I am dead?

Her fingers trembled, and she realised she could move them. They seized the pick half-frozen to her belt and leg.

If I am alive, then I will fight…

The edges of the hole collapsed as they were torn away by sharp metal blades and her dark world expanded exponentially.

Then you'll be the dead one.

She tried to shout, but her larynx was dry and frozen stiff, so all that came out was a choking rasp. In her mind, her fingers freed the pick and brought it down on the creature's head, buried it in its skull. But her arm didn't respond. All she could do was grip the haft, and that wasn't nearly enough. She couldn't even fight. She could only submit, and it was this that bothered her the most. When the blades were done, the shadows of them loomed over her, blotting out her newly-risen sun. Faced with the sheer terror of it she found her voice, and screamed.

Jynn awoke.

* * *

THE CHAMBER WAS bathed in a sickly emerald glow. The light came from channels and conduit lines describing esoteric runes, sigils from an elder age lost to history. It limned bulky sarcophagi and weather-grained tombs, rubbed to mirror sheen by the action of the elements. They had been underground for a long time. Sleeping. They didn't know what imperative had woken them, what pre-programmed scenario had activated the resurrection protocols of the tomb spyders, but they were conscious again – the long dream was over and vermin were abroad in their dominion.

The Undying sighed, though he had no breath to expel from his mechaorgans, nor did his fleshless torso heave. It was affectation, a piece of extant learned behaviour that persisted in the cold existence of the now. He had trouble remembering that, differentiating between what *is* and what *was*. They all did. All except the Architect.

'Your logic-engines are functioning without imparity.'

It was a statement of machine-fact, not a question. The Undying did not question, he did not need to. He was knowledge, aeons and aeons of it. He was pre-eminent but he was also still in a pseudo-torpor. The scarabs refashioned his beautiful mechaorganic body, re-attaching his limbs and re-energising his weapons, while the tomb spyders tended to his revivification casket.

The Architect made a slight bow. The sound of shifting servos and gears within his unseen workings testified to it. 'You are still weak, my lord. Your strength is returning, though.'

'The others are waking too.' The Undying's machine-voice was deep and resonant, but not on account of the resurrection chamber. His baleful eyes narrowed to fiery slits as they regarded each of the four portals that led to the upper echelons of the tomb in turn.

'We live,' said the Architect. 'Do you remember me, master?'

The Undying nodded slowly. 'So many lives,' he muttered.

'We have awoken to interlopers infesting our sacred realm.'

The Undying's reply was a bellicose rumble. 'Excise them.'

'I am waking the rest of the royal house. We shall be one again soon.'

'I desire to move, to command the legions. My sky-chariot–'

'Has long since turned to dust and memory,' the Architect interjected. He did not touch the Undying, for that was to invite his overlord's wrath, but his tone was conciliatory. They had all lost so very much to gain so very little.

Our flesh for metal, our veins and blood for circuits, our very being sacrificed for the machine.

Some felt it more than others, which was the real reason why the Architect was in attendance. The Undying would not fully awaken for several hours, but other, lesser lords would.

A flash of translocation lit the grand tomb chamber. When it abated, the Architect was in a different room. Using his chronomancy, he had descended several levels in a nanosecond. The catacombs were dank and sealed. It was fear. Fear of contamination that drove the necrons to such lengths. And for good reason.

A shriek of anguish broke the silence in the catacombs but none of the insects toiling slowly and methodically gave it heed. The Architect merely looked towards the sound, his long lamellar cloak fashioned of bronze sigil-ingots clanking as he moved.

Another revivification casket had opened behind him.

Now he faced it, he saw the awakened lord within. This one was ripe with putrefaction, the decaying flesh that swathed it long since turned to rot.

The Architect glared. His real name was Ankh the Herald of Dismay, a title self-appointed. He would need to cow this one. Rabid and disillusioned, he would need to direct him quickly and forcefully if he was to be of any use. Unlike the Undying and the other dynastic nobles, Ankh did not fear the flayer disease. He had many arcane items to protect him. Caution was still wise, though – he took a step back.

Ankh stretched to his full height, making the most of his cryptek's skull panoply and brandishing his rod of office like a threat. His appearance was that of a skeletal, metal-skinned sorcerer. There were devices about his person, amulets and speculums, star-compasses and fathomless orbs. A vial of liquid adamantium attached to his belt by an ornate chain contained his predecessor; the mirror of the speculum trapped another of his would-be usurpers a nanosecond out of synch with the rest of reality.

'Do you remember who you are?'

This one gibbered, hunched as if broken, as it looked on with fervent eyes. For a second, Ankh thought the tomb spyders had revived him too early and that the scarabs would need to deactivate him again. The doubt passed when the lord spoke.

'My robes,' he said, holding up the flaps of skin draped about his metal frame, 'they are wretched. Where is my tailor?' He paused, staring at his bone-that-was-not-bone limbs and blood-stained torso. 'Where is my flesh! My skin!' He wailed, then just stopped.

Ankh glared, patient. Revivification was not easy.

'Wait,' said the other. 'Wait…' A deep melancholy affected his voice, though it was still the timbre of the mechaorganic. 'Waaaaiiiit…' he rasped, almost like a sigh. 'Oh, how I miss the flesh.' He caressed the putrefied skin layering his body, pulled down the flesh-mask over his rictal countenance. Emerald orbs of hateful desire burned through the ragged human sockets.

'You are Sahtah, the Enfleshed,' Ankh told him.

'Am I a butcher, a skin-surgeon?' Sahtah asked, looking up and brandishing the razored talons that replaced his fingers. Inadvertently, he'd snipped several pieces of skin from his grisly mantle and they hit the floor of the chamber with a soft thud.

Ankh's eyes flared brighter. They were like fire-tempests of sudden excitement.

'Yes.'

The forbidding tones of the Undying echoed inside his skull from the mind-link to the grand tomb chamber. 'The fourth is due. The royal hierarchy is incomplete.' He was saying it by mechanised rote, still not fully lucid, but even in his millennia-spanning dementia, the overlord was right.

Ankh shifted back. He arrived and scrutinised another part of the chamber where the shadows were darkest.

'He comes…'

The darkness shifted, coalescing like the formation of a black hole into something of substance. It came with a susurrus of sound like air vacating the lungs of a corpse, only much longer and louder. Flaps of parchment, pieces of old cloak materialised on an unfelt breeze. A figure stepped from the penumbra, whole and imperious. It clanged the butt of its staff against the metal floor and with each percussive blow stepped forward until a lord of metal and night-shrouds was revealed.

Where the Architect's jaw was angular, almost pointed, this one's was square. His brow was heavy and he bore an icon stamped to his forehead. Ankh could not recall its meaning. Though less than the others, he too had lost much during transition.

'Why am I summoned?' the arrival demanded. 'The fleshed are reinforced with their armoured saviours, the genebred ones.'

'Flesh cannot prevail against metal,' droned the Undying in a moment of slow-returning lucidity. 'Hearts and minds of mortals cannot endure against the machine.'

'As you can see,' said Ankh, gesturing to their overlord, 'our master is waking. So too are the other cells. The royal house must form, Tahek.'

The shrouded lord snarled. 'Address me as Voidbringer, cryptek.'

'Tahek Voidbringer, you are summoned,' said Ankh with unnecessary ceremony. He fed a crackle of power through his staff but failed to goad the other lord. 'An enemy has arrived on our world. It fills our resurrection chambers with the plebeian and thins our scarab hive.'

'They are in my midst?' asked Voidbringer.

'Plotting to eliminate our pylons and gauss-obliterators. I theorise they plan to deploy further reinforcements from the vessel we struck in orbit.'

'I will slay them, then.'

Only the voice of the Undying stopped Voidbringer from turning and merging with the darkness. 'No.'

Ankh took over again, herald in every way. 'You will continue with your primary mission. Defend our artillery.' His eyes narrowed, partly in pleasure at the rage emanating from Tahek, partly in anticipation of what was to come. 'Sahtah the Enfleshed will hunt them down. He has need of a new skin.'

From a small black crystal attached to his body, Ankh projected an image of the lower catacombs where he'd been a few seconds ago.

Voidbringer glanced at Sahtah with disdain. 'I need no help.'

Sahtah was an outcast in necron society, a noble who had become little better than a beast. Proximity to other lords was strictly forbidden, the possibility of infection real and abhorrent. None amongst the royal house wanted to be cursed as a flayer.

Ankh drew Tahek's gaze. 'Focus on your task,' he said. 'Bring the night.'

The necron's eyes narrowed, a pair of tiny flames inside two pools of abject night. 'I obey,' he rasped, his voice disappearing into the shadows, as did the Voidbringer himself.

Ankh turned to Sahtah in the image-cast. 'Your servants await you,' he said. 'Follow them. They will lead you to the surface.'

Sahtah looked around at the disembodied voice in the chamber. His confusion was forgotten when he saw the other flayed ones approaching.

'So ripe,' the Enfleshed marvelled, regarding a pair of hunchbacked necrons skulking into the wan light of the catacombs. He reached out for their capes of skin but retracted his claws – the mirror of their own – not daring to touch, shamed by his own rotten rags. 'So fresh. A slave's attire should not eclipse that of his lord.'

The flayed ones bowed to him.

'So, renew your robes,' uttered Ankh, adding resonance to the voice that Sahtah was hearing, 'with the flesh of our enemies.'

Like a hound let slip from its master's leash, the Enfleshed leapt from his revivification casket and scurried after the slaves as they went to hunt.

The image phased out and Ankh put the crystal away.

'I long for proper sentience again,' groaned the Undying.

Now he and the Architect were alone.

Ankh considered the motions of the scarabs and tomb spyders, perceived the ethereal presence of his wraiths as they patrolled the deeps of the tomb. More and more cells were awakening. With the first hierarchy at full strength, the rest of the royal house and with them the entire legion would not be long in waking.

'Our numbers multiply. It will be soon, my lord.'

'I long...' the Undying moaned again, trailing off when his mind fell into oblivion again.

'We are legion,' said Ankh, partly to himself. With a gesture, he summoned a column-shaped node from the resurrection chamber floor. When his skeletal fingers closed on the icon inscribed at its apex a tiny coruscation of lightning fashioned a web-matrix between them and bathed Ankh in its light.

On the surface, several levels up, projection nodes churned into position; the activation runes delineating display dais lit up.

The Herald spoke and his graven image was broadcast to all who still lived on Damnos.

ADANAR FELT AS hollow as the clanging of the western gate when it was shut. He heard the flat reports of the commissars' pistols as they brought down the deserters. He closed his eyes when he thought of the four hundred who'd left the Courtyard of Thor. He doubted they'd last long against the necrontyr but someone had to go and get Rancourt – the administrator-turned-acting governor was the closest thing to Imperial authority left on Damnos. Not including the Space Marines, of course, but theirs was a different remit.

Adanar doubted he'd ever even meet them. What consequence was he to them? What were any of them? The Emperor's Angels were as cold and aloof as the necrons. The only difference was the Space Marines weren't trying to eradicate them.

The people needed a figurehead – Zeph Rancourt, loathsome as he was, had to fulfil that role and bring some sort of stability to Damnos. Kellenport was the last city on an unremarkable world, but it had to have unity if it were to survive.

Adanar recalled cheering at the sight of the azure arrowheads streaking through the heavens. People were praising the Emperor for their deliverance, for the saving of Damnos.

The Space Marines were formidable. They could do what no ordinary man could. They could turn certain defeat into victory, but these creatures… they were even a match for the Angels of Death. And all the while the emerald artillery barrage went on unabated.

'Send four battalions down to the Courtyard of Thor to replace our losses,' he said to the air. He'd forgotten Sergeant Nabor was dead, slumped in a pool of his own brain-ooze.

Adanar raised Corporal Besseque and gave the order down the vox. He also tasked him with getting another sergeant to help man the walls and relay instructions to the other officers.

'And get a message to Acting Lord Governor Rancourt. A force is on its way to bring him back to Kellenport.' Adanar had wanted to add, *and the safety of its walls*, but couldn't bring himself to lie that heinously. He was about to request a status report when a hololithic image materialised in the smoky haze over the battlefield. Adanar recognised the voice of the Herald of Dismay.

Your saviours are not angels sent to deliver you. There is no deliverance. We, the necrontyr, reclaim this world. Your saviours cannot stop us. We are not creatures of flesh and emotion, but of circuit and reason. We are the machine, and the machine will not be denied.

The hololith, rendered in grainy emerald, crackled and faded. It left a pall of despair in its wake. Adanar could almost sense the collective groan of the men under his command.

Hope, so cruelly given, was being snatched away. He could feel it.

'What have I to be thankful for?' he asked, remembering the premature celebrations while the artillery barrage raged all around him. He regarded the fire-blackened streets, the shattered plaza, the collapsed towers and ruptured domes of his city. 'What have any of us?'

SMOOTHING THE THINNING hair of his greasy scalp, Rancourt paced the floor of the medi-bay for what felt like the hundredth time. He had wanted position, power and all that came with it, but not in these circumstances. He was lord governor in everything but name, a de facto potentate, but of what? A rock, a fegging rock soon to be extinct or declared *excommunicate xenos* by the Imperium.

'Am I not a dutiful servant?' he asked the recumbent form on the medi-couch next to him. The room was bare and stank of sanitation fluid. It was tiled, and besides the couch, contained a single chair that Rancourt had yet to sit in. A chrono on the wall above him no longer functioned. Wouldn't matter if it did; he'd lost all sense of time. Ever since the mine, ever since…

He crushed the thoughts, not wishing to relive the days after that, the bitter struggle for survival in the ice wastes.

'Oh, Throne…' he murmured, pressing his hands hard against his forehead in an effort to push out the memories. 'If you'd have seen what we had to do. If you'd–' He stopped suddenly when his gaze met that of Lord Governor Arxis, laying on the medi-couch. 'You… you bastard! Leaving me with all of this. I don't want it, I tell you. I don't, but I can't give it back, can I? Can I?' He tossed the chair and it cracked several tiles when it landed, bending a leg.

Rancourt's fists were clenched and he was about to pound on Arxis when he stopped and caught his breath. His arms, so full of nervous anger just moments ago, fell to his sides. Instead of lashing out, he leaned in and spoke softly into the lord governor's ear.

'Help me,' he pleaded. 'Tell me what I'm supposed to do.'

A knock on the door made Rancourt start and he straightened, wiping away the tears on his face. 'What is it?' he snapped, turning to face Sergeant Kador who'd just entered.

'We've just received confirmation that we're moving you to the Kellenport wall, my lord.'

Rancourt shrank back as if stung. He stopped when he touched the medi-couch and could go no further. 'Is it safe?'

'Safer than the Capitolis at this time,' answered Kador

a little ruefully. 'The Space Marines are here, my lord, and they are reclaiming the outer defences, including this bastion.'

'Then I should stay, shouldn't I?' Rancourt was nodding. It looked like he was trying to convince himself. 'If the Adeptus Astartes are my protectors.'

'They won't be staying. Once we have the outer walls, Commander Sonne has vowed to garrison them again so our saviours can press the assault and liberate our world.' Sergeant Kador outstretched his hand. 'You need to accompany me, my lord.'

'Very well,' Rancourt replied, not entirely sure. 'What of Lord Governor Arxis? How do you plan to move him?'

Kador frowned. 'I don't understand.'

'It's very simple, sergeant,' Rancourt replied in exasperation. 'How do we get him from the capitolis to Kellenport?'

'We don't. He's dead.'

Rancourt was about to protest when he looked around. The room was bare. All the equipment, the life-preserving machines were gone… because they were no longer needed. The lord governor hadn't survived his injuries in the Proteus bunker.

'Of course… Yes, I will leave now. Lead on, sergeant.'

IULUS WIPED THE sweat off his brow with a heavy hand. Despite his advanced physiology, the wound he'd sustained in his shoulder was slowing him. Ahead of the squad, Agnathio led the line. His armoured bulk bore the worst of the intense gauss-barrage. A fusillade of beams staggered the Dreadnought and Iulus willed the venerable one to endure it.

Slamming a fresh clip into his bolt pistol, Iulus released

a tightly controlled burst. The hulking necron in his sights bucked, sparks cascaded off its armoured body, but it came on undaunted. Galvia and Urnos added their bolters to their sergeant's barrage, but to little effect.

Still firing, Iulus levelled his chainsword at the seemingly invulnerable necrons. 'Throw up a wall, brother.'

Aristaeus opened up his flamer, bathing the front line with a wave of super-heated promethium. Implacable, the mechanoids just ploughed through it, their bodies trailing with tendrils of fire and smoke.

'Oath of Hera,' breathed Galvia. 'They are unstoppable.'

Somewhere in the distance las-beams stabbed into the flames, but they were as insect stings to the monstrous automatons.

Iulus realised the Guard had engaged the enemy, but discounted the humans as an asset almost immediately. The Second were alone. He was determined they would triumph. It rested on the necron elites. Break them and the plaza was won.

Iulus grunted. 'Tough, but not inviolable. Close the gap and intensify.'

His Immortals advanced in Agnathio's shadow, crouched low and widely dispersed, but stalled as the warrior eternal faltered. His armour, his mighty sarcophagus that had endured for centuries over countless campaigns, was slowly being eroded.

'Venerable one. We need to move!'

Agnathio levelled his multi-melta and sent a blast into the necron elites. It cut one of the mechanoids in half and it phased out.

Iulus rallied his warriors. 'See! They are not indestructible.'

A second necron lost a limb but, incredibly, self-repaired,

its living metal reflowing and its wires re-stitching before Iulus's very eyes.

'Mercy of the primarch...'

Agnathio was not to be denied and strafed the line. The wounded mechanoid was only partway through its regeneration cycle when a salvo of mass-reactive shells from the Dreadnought's storm bolter tore it open. Balefires dying in its eyes, the necron phased out.

'I serve the Chapter eternally!' Agnathio was about to advance again when a plume of fire exploded from his motive servos. Haemorrhaging smoke and machine-fluid, one of his trunk-like legs seized.

A cry was ripped from his vox-emitter as a raw, burning line jagged up his sarcophagus. Visceral matter was leaking from the wound and Agnathio's agony resonated around the plaza.

Iulus felt a tremor of disquiet. He had never seen the Dreadnought hurt before. A small part of him hadn't thought it was possible that he would ever witness such a thing.

'Brother-sergeant.' Agnathio's speech was broken and fizzed with static, in part from the damage done to his vox-emitter and in part from the pain he was enduring. He even had to fight the din of the gauss-assault to be heard. 'You must take... the gate alone, brother. I can go no further.'

The gate? Then Iulus realised. Agnathio was back at Chundrabad, where he had fallen over five millennia ago when he was a mere battle-brother.

Iulus had no time to reply. A piece of armour plate was ripped from the Dreadnought's shoulder, flung shrapnel embedding in the sergeant's pauldron. Agnathio turned in the direction of his aggressors, unleashing a salvo from his storm bolter. It was to be his last as the weapon attached to his power fist burst apart in a cloud of exploding ammo. Like a pugilist that had taken too many beatings, Agnathio jerked and rocked as the blows rained down.

Iulus had seen enough. He pressed the comm-bead in his ear and spoke into his gorget vox-grille. He might have lost his battle-helm and with it the retinal display, but he could still command.

'Brother-Sergeants Tirian and Atavian, bring hell and fury!'

A barrage hammered from either flank. The sharp tracers and missile contrails blended together furiously as the Devastators concentrated fire on the hulking elites.

A storm of hot frag exploded in the necrons' midst but they came on implacably. Their numbers had thinned but they merely closed ranks and drove at the Ultramarines, laying down an emerald curtain of fire. Some of the casualties were rising, picking up their slowly reconstituting bodies and rejoining the rear echelons.

The Ultramarines had to get close, make certain of their kills. Iulus tightened the grip on his chainsword.

'Immortals! Hand-to-hand. Engage and destroy!' He ran headlong at the necrons, ignoring the gauss-beams glancing off his armour.

On his right shoulder, Urnos was struck in the chest and pitched off his feet. Iulus lost sight of him in the rush. 'Low and fast.'

Nearby, a terrible thunder shook the frost-caked earth as Ultracius joined them. A spew of assault cannon shells ripped a ragged hole in the elites, interrupting their fire pattern and allowing Iulus and his squad the precious seconds they needed to close the gap.

His first swing was like striking the bulkhead on a battleship. Sparks churned into the air but the blow left little more than a scar against the necron's torso. Up close the elites were even bigger, dwarfing even the Space Marines. Iulus ducked beneath a swing of its gauss-blaster. There was strength in the attack and even used as an unconventional bludgeon, the weapon was potent. A burst of fire raked the sergeant's left side but it only stripped away paint and surface armour. He rammed his bolt pistol into the creature's neck cavity and pulled the trigger.

Spitting shards of metal opened up a dozen shallow cuts on his face but the necron's head came away, leaving behind a sheared spinal column. Iulus kicked it over with an exultant roar before it phased out.

'Taste the fury of the Immortals!'

A savage blow to his solar plexus cut his victory short. He felt his armour plastron crack and struggled to breathe before his multi-lung kicked in to take up the slack of his collapsed organ.

One of the hulking necrons regarded him curiously. 'You are not immortal, flesh-thing. They are before you. They are your doom.'

Chainsword screaming, Iulus swung, but the mechanoid blocked with its arm and butted him.

Groggy, he shook it off.

Around him, he was acutely aware of his squad fighting hard with bolter and blade. Somewhere in the dense throng of the necron elite, Ultracius was avenging the crippling of his fellow Dreadnought. A heavy necron form was tossed into the air before landing back down into the melee and disappearing.

Ultracius was relentless. 'Guilliman watches over us. Do

not be found wanting in his hallowed sight!' The assault cannon shrieked and a half-dozen mechanoids were ruined, their shattered bodies flung into the closing mist.

Iulus took a blow against his wounded shoulder and felt the bone crack. His guard was split in two and fell away uselessly. He brought his chainsword around for another swing, this time ramming the blade where the necron's innards should be. The creature pulled the blade away, losing skeletal fingers to the chain-teeth, and brought its gauss-blaster up one-handed. With a feral shout, Iulus severed the weapon where it was conjoined to the necron's wrist and rammed the sword in again.

Iulus rejoiced as he drew out a modulated scream from the monster, but it came on undeterred.

'Desist. Your efforts are futile.' Bereft of its gauss-blaster, the hulking mechanoid smashed the Ultramarine's shoulder repeatedly with its wrist-stump. The other hand closed around Iulus's throat with three clacking digits. Its grip was incredible and the sergeant felt his trachea being crushed immediately. Without his battle-helm, the seal between it and his gorget was compromised and his throat was exposed. The necron had analysed this weakness and exploited it.

Mag-locking his bolt pistol – its clip was spent and he had no room to insert a fresh one – Iulus took a two-handed grip on his chainsword and drove it deeper. His sight was darkening as his air supply dwindled to a trickle.

He spat a last, defiant breath. 'Die, you soulless dog.'

Then the darkling world closed around him and Iulus felt his fingers slipping on the chainsword, losing their grip on the haft and his life.

* * *

FALKA WAS IN charge. He didn't know how, but he was. At least fifty men, most of the paltry survivors from the four battalions, were looking to him for orders. They'd left the flattened ruins behind them and had made it to a second line of broken-toothed defences. From here he'd formed the fifty into a firing line and got them to man the still-operational heavy guns behind the barricades and in the hollowed-out pillboxes. The bunkers and walls were prefabs, set up by Commander Sonne just before the *Nobilis* was destroyed and their hopes with it. They hadn't lasted long; the garrison behind them a few seconds longer. Now, what was left provided scant cover but it was better than nothing.

'Keep your head down and your lasgun charged,' Muhrne had said during basic training. Falka missed the tough old bastard already. His bones were ash by now. It didn't seem a just fate for such an honourable man.

'Feed the cannon,' he shouted at a heavy stubber team down the line, 'and watch for jams. Keep the barrel cool,' he bellowed at another working a tripod-mounted multi-laser. 'Don't let it overheat. It overheats, and you're dead.'

Throne, he even sounded like Muhrne. Maybe his spirit was alive and well, and fighting the battle through him. Falka hoped so.

He'd found a pair of magnoculars clutched in the cauterised limb of some dead officer. The rest of the soldier's body was gone, presumably atomised by the enemy gauss-flayers. The battling Ultramarines weren't far, but the scopes allowed Falka to get a good look without needing to be up close and personal. With the Emperor's Angels in their midst, the necrons had stopped shooting at the Ark Guard. Falka wanted to keep it that way... at least for a while.

Through the scope's infra-red – conventional vision was

largely useless for detailed observation in the snow-fog – he saw the Space Marines had committed to close assault against a wedge of necron warriors. Even the Angels looked diminutive compared to these hulks, but they had some kind of towering war machine to even the odds. Falka caught only glimpses of the gargantuan machine, swinging fists and shredding necrons with its fearsome cannon at close range.

The other Ultramarines were not faring so well, ill-suited to hand-to-hand combat against such heavily-armoured opponents. They fought valiantly, though, and Falka felt a swell of courage fill his breast. Lowering the scopes, he eyed the open ground between the barricades and the melee. Narrowing his vision, he reckoned on thirty metres. He let his lasgun sag on the strap around his shoulder – it was almost out, anyway – and hefted his ice-pick.

Damnosian permafrost was hard. It didn't break easily, especially in the deep caverns beneath the surface. Falka had once seen a man swing at the ice-face and miss. Instead of burying the pick-blade in the meat of his thigh, he'd sheared his leg off completely. It was so sharp it went straight through the bone.

Across the blasted esplanade, another group kept up a constant las-barrage. Falka nodded to his vox-man. 'Tell them to give it everything.' Then he growled at the others crouched around him, his makeshift command squad. 'I'm going over into *that*,' he said, meaning the frenzied melee. 'I won't ask any of you to come with me.'

Eighteen hard-faced men, some soldiers, some conscripts, drew blades and picks grimly.

Falka smiled. 'That's what I hoped you'd say.' He shouted to the gunners. 'Keep firing but try not to shoot us.'

Then he vaulted the barricade and ran towards death.

* * *

THEY WERE IN deeper than before, hunkered down in a tight defile with thick ice-shawled rocks hugging their shoulder plates. Scipio scowled as the frostbitten crags scraped his armour. He'd wanted to pare the powered suits down for better manoeuvrability, remove all but the body armour and leg greaves. Tigurius had forbidden it. The necrons were too dangerous, their technology too advanced, to go up against without full protection.

Behind Scipio a heavy *clank* echoed down the gorge as Largo slipped and cursed. The noise was carried away on the howling wind but his finger slipped into the trigger-guard of his bolt pistol anyway. The necron patrol below continued without pause. Whatever sensors or auspex-devices they possessed were being foiled by the weather and the altitude just like the Ultramarines scanning gear.

Scipio glanced over his shoulder. 'You eager for a fight, brother?'

Largo held up his hand, signalling contrition.

Ortus, who was a metre behind him maintaining the rearguard, smiled thinly. He scoured the way they'd come through his bolter sight. The falling snow was settling over their tracks nicely. After a few seconds of intense and still interrogation, he nodded to Scipio.

Crawling on their stomachs, heads low against the arctic wind riming their features with tiny spines of hoarfrost, they moved on.

After the initial recon had drawn a blank, Scipio had been forced upwards. Somewhere across the sheer-sided cliffs that bent around the necron artillery like a crooked spine was a rocky canal. He was intent on finding it. The Ultramarines needed a way to bypass the defensive cordon, something the necrons had overlooked. Being isolated from the main battle group in the mountains was risky. Pressing on beyond the outer marker Tigurius had provided could even be considered reckless, but the mission demanded Scipio locate a route through which to assault the pylons and gauss-obliterators.

Ducking into a natural alcove, he raised the other squad members on the comm-feed. '*Venetores*, report.'

With Naceon's death earlier, it left the Thunderbolts with nine. To tackle the mountain, Scipio had broken them up into combat squads of three. Unconventional as far as the Codex was concerned, but small groups would serve the Ultramarines' purpose better.

After Black Reach, Telion had told him that the Codex was not a book of strictures, nor was it meant to be an inflexible and comprehensive tactical manual.

'It is our primarch's wisdom,' he had said, 'distilled for all of us to utilise as we see fit. Some in the Chapter are old and hidebound, but as Adeptus Astartes we must adapt. The spur that does not bend before the sudden storm will surely break, Scipio.'

So it was they reconnoitred in threes.

Cator's voice came through the feed. '*Thracian*, this is *Venetores*. Nothing so far.'

It was followed swiftly by the deep timbre of Brakkius. '*Retiarii* has found something. We are fifty-three metres east of *Thracian's* position.'

Scipio opened up the feed to all three combat squads. 'Converge on *Retiarii*. Confirm.'

A pair of affirmation chimes sounded in the sergeant's ear. Waiting for the last of the necron column to disappear from sight, he waved the others on.

* * *

'ONE OF YOURS?'

They were standing in a shallow valley. The snow blustered overhead but they were well shielded from the wind. A necron lay dismembered in the valley basin. Attached to each of its limbs, skull and torso was a tubular device wrapped in wire. A faint veneer of snow was building on top of the body parts, slowly obscuring it. Scipio looked down at the mechanoid as he addressed his battle-brother.

Crouched next to the corpse, Cator shook his head.

Vermillion Cator was known in the Thunderbolts as an expert at fashioning booby traps. All Space Marines possessed some level of fieldcraft that allowed them to make improvised grenades and other simple snares, but Cator was often described as *gifted*.

Brakkius gave the torso an experimental kick. 'Why hasn't it phased out yet?'

Cator answered. 'Because it's still alive.'

A flurry of movement saw Ortus raise his bolter into an execution position.

Scipio waved him off. 'Easy there, Torias Telion.'

Ortus stood down, but kept his weapon ready.

Scipio looked at Cator. 'How?'

The other Ultramarine was prodding the tubular devices with his combat blade. 'There's an electrical charge running through these wires, attached to a powerful battery.' He tapped the tube itself. 'A strong magnet is keeping it from reforming.'

'It foiled the self-repair system?'

Cator nodded. 'Yes, but it's designed as a form of torture rather than being useful on a military level.'

Scipio pressed further. 'So it can't phase out because it's not sustained critical damage and it can't self-repair on account of the opposing magnetic poles keeping its components apart?'

'Precisely,' Cator said, getting up.

Brakkius shook his head at the meticulousness of it all. 'Who did this?'

'That, my brother,' said Scipio, 'is the *real* question.' He exhaled, thinking. 'I want a deeper spread – a hundred metres.'

Cator cleared his throat. 'Sir, this far into enemy territory – are you sure?'

'Someone or something else is out here with us and I want it flushed out. We can cover more ground separated.'

Showing his obedience with a salute, Cator broke away east. Brakkius went west.

Scipio's combat squad carried on north. When they were moving out, he nodded to Ortus. A single bolt shot, baffled by the wind and the valley depth, rang out a few seconds later as the Ultramarine got his wish.

CHAPTER SIX

Aboard the Valin's Revenge, *forty-seven years*
after the Black Reach Campaign

It HAD BEEN a long time since Scipio had visited the reclu-
siam. The chamber was dark, lit by guttering candles
ensconced in the mouths of votive cyber-skulls. Flickering
firelight seemed to animate their grisly features.

'I have been your Chaplain for over a year and this is the
first time I've seen you in the Emperor's presence.'

Scipio finished his benedictions, stood and turned to
face the speaker.

Elianu Trajan was standing opposite, framed by the reclu-
siam's narthex. The arch was inscribed with holy rubrics
and catechisms, and there was a stylised effigy of the primarch at its apex to bring it all together.

Scipio bowed. 'Brother-Chaplain.'

'Brother Vorolanus.' Trajan, like Scipio, was dressed in a
supplicant's robes. His were black to match the hue of his
battle plate and had a cowl in lieu of a helmet. His crozius

mace hung from a hook attached to a thick leather belt and his Chaplain's rosarius fell to his broad chest suspended from a gilded chain.

Aside from the tools of his office, Trajan did not favour ostentation. Devotion was another matter and his simple power armour was festooned with purity seals and scripture parchment, oaths of moment and votive chains.

He waited in silence, not moving.

Scipio felt suddenly uncomfortable. 'Do you wish to ask me something, Brother-Chaplain?'

Trajan's eyes were penetrating. Embers seemed to smoulder behind the pupils.

'Just this – *why*?'

'Why what?'

The Chaplain's eyes hardened, and the embers became a sharp flame conveying his annoyance.

'I am not one of your battle-brothers, nor am I a fellow sergeant. I am your Chaplain, Brother Vorolanus, and won't tolerate games. Answer the question.'

Scipio's mouth became a hard line. Despite the fact he'd been with the company for over a year, Scipio had not yet found an accord with Trajan. Where Orad had been quiet and reflective, Trajan was direct and exacting. He bullied faith, rather than preached it. A supreme warrior, as fiery and zealous as any Chaplain Scipio had known, but hard to like.

'I have observed the requisite devotions...'

'Just not in my sight. Chaplain Orad served this Chapter with distinction. His death was a tragedy, as are the deaths of all true sons of Guilliman, but I am here now and I alone minister to the purity of this company.'

Scipio's gaze narrowed. He tried not to make a fist.

'What are you suggesting?'

Trajan smacked him hard across the cheek, and the shock of it felled the sergeant to one knee.

'I don't *suggest*. I decree and act,' he snapped.

Scipio found the crozius pressing on his shoulder as he went to rise.

'Stay down,' Trajan warned. 'I am not finished.'

The Chaplain's face glowered behind the shadows of his cowl. 'Your captain and I have known each other for many long years. He speaks highly of your actions on Black Reach, as does Master Telion, so I shall assume you have yet to show me the same qualities that inspired praise in them.'

'If I displease you, I apologise.'

Trajan rapped Scipio hard on the shoulder blade, drawing a scowl from the sergeant's mouth and blood from his body.

'Don't mock or pander to me, Brother Vorolanus. You are already testing my wrath.'

Scipio's teeth were gritted. To strike a fellow son of Guilliman was heinous if done without just cause; to strike a member of the Chaplaincy under any circumstances was unconscionable. He bowed his head, allowing the anger to subside.

Trajan continued. 'Your disaffection has been noted, as has your absence from my ministrations. I will not tolerate it. Orad's ways are not my ways. You will learn to value them and venerate me as your spiritual leader. Are we clear on this, Scipio?' Trajan dug the sharp edge of the crozius into Scipio's flesh to help make his point.

Scipio maintained his position of penitence and nodded.

Trajan nodded back. 'Being a sergeant carries certain *expectations* that you will meet. Now,' he added, lifting the crozius. It left a bloody trail. 'I go to the battle-cages. You should work that anger out. Meet me there once you're done here, if you wish, but regardless, let this be the last time we exchange words.'

Then he was gone, headed to the training deck.

Scipio never joined him.

'WHAT DO YOU think that is?'

Ortus was pointing at something in the distance – a series of large, pyramidal silhouettes.

'Designation: *Monolith*.' Largo had the scopes and was using them to get a closer look. 'And something else.' He handed the magnoculars to his sergeant.

Through the elliptical lens, Scipio saw the three monoliths that Largo had identified. They were moving ponderously, levitating just above the ground on an anti-gravitic energy pulse. Slab-sided, metallic and inscribed with necron runes they looked more like mobile obelisks than battle tanks. Scipio had yet to see one in combat. Given their fearsome weapons array and eldritch crystal power matrix, glowing at the pyramid's summit, he had no wish to. A portal of light shimmered in the front arc of each monolith, emerald like the gauss-technology and rippling as if fluidic. Even without Mechanicus indoctrination, he knew this was some form of energy gate.

The other machinery Largo had pointed out was larger and of a similar design. It was some kind of *alpha*-monolith. Lightning arcs crackled between it and the other lesser pyramids, suggesting it as a sort of power node.

'Looks like a capacitor, something to focus the firepower of the other war machines.' He gave the magnoculars back to Largo.

Ortus's face was grim. 'Moving away from the artillery, too.' His jaw hardened. 'Bound for Kellenport.'

Scipio was already on the move again. 'It gets us no closer to breaching the defensive cordon around the heavy guns. Tigurius can relay a message once we return to camp with better news.'

The comm-feed in his ear crackled.

'*Thracian*, this is *Retiarii*.'

'Go ahead, Brakkius.'

He was whispering. 'A necron static outpost. Forty-two metres north of our position.'

'Status, brother?'

'Hunkered down and undetected. We have eyes on six targets, raider-class construct.'

'Swarms?'

'Negative, sir.'

Scipio muted the link and turned to the others. They were proceeding across a narrow pass and had pressed their bodies against the cliff wall. Heavy snowfall effectively whited-out their armour, forming a natural camouflage.

'Why would the mechanoids garrison an outpost? It makes no sense.'

Largo's broad forehead creased with thought. 'Unless they are defending something.'

'But not artillery,' said Scipio.

Largo smiled and nodded. 'A way into the mountains.'

'Precisely.' He racked his bolt pistol's slide, checking the load. Enough for a skirmish.

'I'm tired of skulking in the ice and wind.' He un-muted the comm-feed, telling Brakkius to observe and wait, then he raised Cator and gave him the coordinates so the Thunderbolts could converge on the outpost's position.

Scipio gave a feral smile before they moved out. 'Brothers, we have our opening.'

SCIPIO CLENCHED HIS fist as he listened to Cator's report over the comm-feed.

'*Venetores* delayed. Route impassable. Doubling back.'

'How long?'

'Approximately twenty-two minutes, brother-sergeant.'

Shaking his head, Scipio eyed the necron garrison. Just as Brakkius had said: six raider constructs, no heavy guns, elites or swarms. Six of Second Company against the mechanoid foot soldier. Scipio didn't want to wait any longer. The outpost could be reinforced or they might miss their assault window.

'Ortus.' Scipio pointed to a shallow ledge behind a cluster of boulders.

The Ultramarines were below the outpost, hiding in the basin of an ice trench. Sharp crags further obscured their vantage point. The ledge was slightly off-centre of a narrow gorge that fed up to the necron bastion – a functional obelisk-like structure with a small chute at the summit, its sides like the petals of a partially open flower – and offered a clear line of sight for Ortus's deadly aim. Rivulets of frozen meltwater swathed the path up to the structure. Scipio thought he saw faces beneath the ice and wondered briefly what it must be like to have human limitations, to be at the mercy of the elements. Slain by the fickle nature of your own world – it was dishonourable.

Ortus got into his firing position immediately and was already sighting his bolter as Scipio outlined the rest of the plan.

He utilised battle-sign. *Retiarii* would attack from the

road, drawing the necrons out and into Ortus's crosshairs. *Thracian* would flank, low and quick, and attack once the garrison was committed.

Telion had often extolled the virtues of 'divide and conquer' as a strategy. It enabled a smaller force to out-manoeuvre and outgun a larger or better defended one. Here, Scipio intended to split the necrons' attention by first having them focus on Brakkius's squad, then Ortus and finally his own.

Scipio reckoned on an estimated total engagement time of thirteen seconds.

He didn't consider another of Telion's maxims, however: 'Always assume the enemy knows something you don't.'

CHAPTER SEVEN

PRAXOR SAW THE Stormcaller a split second after Sicarius.

They had known one of the minor necron lords was present in the vanguard; the further the Ultramarines had forged beyond the Kellenport walls, the more that emerald lightning had cracked the sky open.

It was a harbinger, this one, and a billowing tempest preceded him.

'Twilight falls upon Kellenport and all of Damnos,' uttered Agrippen, his booming voice as deep as the necron thunder.

A stricken tank company, one of the Guard's last few on Damnos, fought valiantly in the wastes but they were alone and engulfed by the eldritch storm. Searchlights mounted to their cupolas strafed the darkness, trying to lock onto targets, but this was no ordinary twilight. There was no way to penetrate it. *Creatures* writhed around in the lightning and the wind, at once solid and incorporeal. Praxor had fought the wraiths before and nearly been killed. What chance did human men have against such things?

He watched with narrowed eyes as the gale overtook the battlefield and pressed in on the Ultramarines. Even the steel plate of a Leman Russ battle tank was no proof against the ghost-like necrons who phased *through* their hulls. Praxor could only imagine the horror of the crews within as they were slain.

The cobalt giants were unmoved, both by the storm and the futile plight of the armoured company. Slowly, the rattle of pintle-mounts subsided and the flash of muzzle flares decreased. Even the churn of turrets and the booming report of their cannons became silenced.

'They are beyond our aid, brother.'

Standing at Praxor's side, Trajan's face was a grim and emotionless mask of sculpted bone as he placed a conciliatory hand on the sergeant's shoulder guard.

Praxor wanted to shrug it off. Elianu Trajan was colder than the Damnos arctic wind. He let it linger, though, using the moment to observe the battlefield.

Kellenport's defences were based on a series of three octagonal walls. Each was punctuated by several towers and fortified bunkers. Each had three gates: south, west and north. The east side of the city – and it was a vast megalopolis – was completely sealed off, its byways filled, its roads mined and razor-wired. Between each wall was a stretch of land. They had once been districts: commercial, residential, military and religious. Now they were ruins; ash and debris flattened in the necron advance, crushed in the sprawl of war.

From his Tactica briefings, Praxor knew the Damnos naval asset, the *Nobilis*, had bombarded some of these outer regions with torpedoes before it was destroyed by the artillery in the Thanatos Hills. The then lord governor had balanced the collateral damage against the severity of the blow it would strike against the necrontyr. No doubt it had bought them some time, and such desperate courage was hard to ignore – without it, the Ultramarines might have landed on a world already subjugated by the soulless machines. But ultimately, it had not saved them and condemned thousands to plasma-death.

Their charred corpses paved the roads and haunted the ruins now, despite the eager snowfall that sought to blanket them with its white veil.

To reach this point, at the threshold of the third defensive wall, Sicarius had led them on a killing spree. Large sections of the necron primary awakeners, as they were designated by Imperial codifiers, had been destroyed but nothing remained as testimony to it. This fact gnawed at Praxor, making him feel the death of Vortigan more acutely.

When we are slain, we stay dead. The necrons merely disappear. How do I know I am not fighting the self same enemy over and again?

Perhaps that's why Trajan had singled him out for benediction first. It was the only reason Sicarius had attacked already – he desired the blessing of his Chaplain. Perhaps Trajan *knew* of Praxor's doubts. He had a gift for it, he of the Black, spotting the chinks in a warrior's armour of faith.

Praxor's expression was firm. 'I am resolved, Brother-Chaplain.'

The armoured company was all but obliterated from sight now. The small pockets of Guard fighting desperately around the vestiges of the city's defences were gradually being eradicated by the meticulous enemy. Once they were

133

finished with the humans, the necrons would focus their full attention on Second Company. Sicarius had been right to strike hard and strike swiftly.

Praxor heard the captain speaking as he was anointed by Trajan.

'We stand as the lonely bastion, the last resistance of an Imperial world.' He stared into the ever-expanding void of necron-fuelled night, his helm in the crook of his arm so his charges could see his noble countenance. His gaze was unswerving like steel, his purpose violent and obvious. 'It was settled in the halcyon days of the Great Crusade, when gods walked amongst us, by our ancestors and the progenitors of our Chapter. Let us not falter in their sight, nor allow the blood they shed for Damnos to be in vain.'

He drew the Tempest Blade – a storm to match a storm – and singled out the necron lord in the midst of the lightning. Replacing his battle-helm, Sicarius growled into the comm-feed.

'Follow me into the stygian night and let no fleshless horrors stay the fury of the Second. *Victoris Ultra!*'

The storm proper had reached them at last. It broke in waves of dense black cloud, roiling in a spectral wind. Lightning cascaded from the sky, emerald green and as unnatural as those who harnessed it. An otherworldly zephyr whipped at the captain's cape and crest. It stirred the purity seals and oath parchments on his armour.

Sicarius charged. The Tempest Blade ignited with a fire redolent of older, greater days.

The others followed, ready to fight and die.

Praxor's doubts, his misgivings about the indestructible foe, vanished in the face of Sicarius's bravura and dauntless courage. Basking in the reflected light of a true hero, he cried out until his lungs burned and the air turned hot with bolter-fury.

They all did, every glorious one of them.

'Victoris Ultra!'

Praxor stayed close to the captain and his Lions, using the resplendent glow of the blade as a beacon. He made to speak but the hellish wind robbed him of his voice. He tried again, bellowing to the Shieldbearers. 'Keep to the sword.'

Upon entering the maelstrom, the comm-feed had died. It wasn't wracked by static interference – it had simply ceased to be. A shroud had been cast over them and all within was deafening silence. Except it wasn't, not quite. The wind whipped and billowed, so loud it shrieked. Voices, cold and mechanical, hollow and pleading, manifested on the chilling breeze. Flecks of earth and pieces of debris churned about in the night-black storm the necron lord had weaved.

A heavy flash overloaded Praxor's retinal display as bolt-lightning forked earthwards in a jagged trajectory. One of the Lions was struck, lit up in cruciform like a human torch. He shuddered, emerald energy wreathing his body, before he crumpled in a smoke-drooling mess and never moved again.

Brother Halnior was dead.

A second bolt arrowed through the night and ripped a ferocious line in the blackness. It cratered the ground then leapt into Etrius.

A flare, magnesium-bright, saturated the storm cloud edging it in white. At its core was Etrius. The Ultramarine was lifted off his feet, the lightning tendrils like a puppet-master's strings animating him jerkily.

A low *foom* battered Praxor's auditory canal and he was pitched into the air with the sudden shockwave. Time slowed in that terrible moment. His arm, going to shield his eyes, moved as if through gelatine. His legs, flung away from the blast, moved with all the purpose of sodden sand struggling through the neck of an hourglass. Belatedly he realised Etrius's spare ammo had exploded. It turned him into a fireball.

Hitting the ground hard jolted Praxor around and time rushed back, urgent and filled with smoke and agony. Hurrying to his feet, he tackled his battle-brother out of the inferno.

Etrius lived, but was barely able to nod as he left his ruined bolter behind. He pulled a bolt pistol from his weapons belt and nodded again to show he was ready to fight on.

But the lightning arc wasn't done. Four more times it struck the earth, tearing holes in the ice and scorching the ground. No one else was felled by the blasts, but it seared battle plate and cut blackened scars into shoulder guards. The Ultramarines' impetus had been slowed.

The wraiths detached themselves from the darkness as if it were an entity and they its cellular defences. Serpentine and sinuous, they advanced on the Ultramarines with a terrifying grace and fluidity.

'Brother-sergeant.' Krixous pointed with his mutilated stump.

Praxor followed it to where Brother Vandius valiantly upheld the company standard. The banner was stilled, heavy as if soaked with rain, though the wind raged around it.

Buffeted by the gale that failed to lift the Second's banner but hammered everything else, Praxor urged, 'Fight on, brother. Courage and honour.'

Something as close to fear as a Space Marine could experience tainted Krixous's voice. 'How is that even possible?'

Trajan's vehement dogma tore through the storm and his doubt. 'Our glory is more than the hallowed cloth of a standard. It is blood and sinew, heritage and valour – virtues these soulless aberrations know nothing of. Wars are not won by cold machination and the calculus of metal. Victory is achieved through heart and flesh-made courage. We are Guilliman's heirs, his noble sons. Honour his legacy!'

He held the crozius aloft and it burst into azure flame, banishing the darkness around it. Three wraiths recoiled from its brilliance, revealed in the shadows. Trajan brought the power mace down upon the skull of one, crushing it and sending the vile thing back to the unholy cradle that spawned it.

Praxor drove at one of the others, swinging his power sword in a lethal arc. It was a master blade, forged by the Chapter artisans, crafted from the purest metals and imbued with an indomitable machine-spirit.

It passed right through the creature as ethereal as smoke. The wraith resolved a moment later and its long talons cut Praxor's bolt pistol in half as the Ultramarine made to fire. He cast the ruined weapon aside as his fist closed on a useless trigger and took his sword in a two-handed grip, feeding more power to its monomolecular edge.

'We are defiant!' he roared, mustering righteous anger. 'The scions of Ultramar!'

The wraith was unmoved and attacked with whipcord, preternatural speed.

An instinctive parry warded one talon strike, a frantic block fended off a lash of the wraith's whip-like tail. He had yet to strike a blow. Hard-pressed, Praxor fell back a step.

'Only forward, brother-sergeant.' It was Daceus. The formidable veteran was leading the line. He bellowed to the Lions, 'Forge a path for the captain!'

Somewhere ahead of the wraiths was the Stormcaller. Sicarius meant to meet him in combat and do what he was born to do – end lives.

Daceus seized a wraith in his power fist, but it squirmed free before he could clamp his fingers together to crush it and was lost to the storm. To his right, obscured by the mist and shadows, Honourable Gaius Prabian fought with sword and shield like the Macraggian battle-kings of old. The Company Champion moved with relentless purpose, a match for any of the serpentine wraiths. He severed necks and sundered bodies, his mind and body as one, his weapons an extension of his martial will. As Daceus and Gaius Prabian drove them, the other Lions sent salvos of fire into the night, tearing the blackness to strips.

Sicarius advanced in the killing ground they made, slaying when he had to, searching for his prey when he didn't.

In those few frantic moments, Praxor's world contracted into microcosm where only his Shieldbearers and the Lions existed, surrounded by the night. Silhouettes ranged in the shadows still, bellowing oaths or yielding screams, but they were indistinct and phantasmal. Somewhere in the dark were Trajan and Agrippen. The faint corona of the Chaplain's crozius was yet visible spitting righteous fire, while the Dreadnought was a hulking nightmare limned emerald against onyx-black with each lightning strike.

Of Brother-Sergeant Solinus and the Indomitable, there was no sign.

Praxor hoped they fought on still. Without his bolt pistol, he drew his gladius and battled with two swords instead. The wraiths still lingered at the edge of his vision, distracted by the march of Sicarius and his Lions. Perhaps the Storm-caller was reacting to an imminent threat to his life, such as it was, and recalling his revenants.

Brandishing his power sword, Praxor roared a challenge. 'Here, machine!'

Twisting its head on a strange, segmented neck, the wraith regarded him as a predator to prey. Coiling first, like a snake, it attacked.

With his gladius Praxor batted away the first talon thrust, following up with the power sword and hacking off the necron's wrist. A burst of shells from Etrius's bolt pistol strafed its torso and skull-face, angering it.

Tartaron impaled it with a thrown spear of rebar he'd found amongst the debris. Somewhere along the line, his meltagun had been rendered inoperative. While the creature was still squirming, Praxor removed its head. Permanent phase-out was instantaneous.

Keeping pace with Sicarius and the Lions was a feat. When a second wraith emerged from the shadows, Praxor lunged – first gladius then power sword – to gain ground. Both blows missed but Krixous hammered it with a bolter salvo, steadying his aim on his ruined stump. Praxor carved the wraith open as it staggered, before Tartaron and Etrius each rammed a gladius into its neck cavity. It jerked once, the balefires in its eyes flaring with impotent fury, before phasing out.

Krixous had his eyes on the sky. 'Emperor's grace...' he breathed, 'Look!'

All eyes went to the heavens where dozens of wraiths swirled and twisted like the denizens of some black infernal sea.

Praxor levelled his gladius in an order to fire. 'Bolters!' he cried, and the air was torn apart by explosive, mass-reactive death.

Some of the wraiths were drawn by the attack, swimming effortlessly in and out of phase, with only the viridian orbs of their eyes a constant.

'Hold them off.' Praxor knew they must give Sicarius time to find and kill their lord. 'By Guilliman's sword!'

The wraiths engulfed the Shieldbearers. Talon-blades and tail-barbs became a ghostly blur as the necrons swept amongst them. Their rending tools cleaved and cut.

Brother Belthonis was dragged into the storm, the hard bangs of his bolter stolen on the air. Skewered through the torso and neck, Brother Galrion crumpled spitting blood. His vambraces shredded, Brother Hexedese screamed the primarch's name as a spear-like tail punctured his plastron and he fell.

'Form a shield around me!' Praxor urged his warriors to rally, and the Shieldbearers closed ranks like an armoured laager, firing in all directions. They were an island of cobalt in a hostile black ocean surrounded by a shoal of pitiless killers. Images flashed before Praxor in the chaos: Daceus crying hell and fury; Gaius Prabian, colder and more clinical in his kills than the machines; Venatio, stooped over the body of Galrion. Through the blood-soaked blur, one resolved brighter than all the rest.

Sicarius…

The Grand Duke of Talassar had found his prey. He angled his blade, energy bleeding off the edge in a pearlescent haze. Answering, the Stormcaller brandished his staff. Alien sigils ran along the haft and it crackled with emerald lightning. Moments later, their weapons clashed in incandescent fusion. Above, the thunder bellowed in empathy. Every emotion, every blow and counter-blow was described in the storm-wracked sky.

For a machine, the necron moved more swiftly than Praxor gave it credit for. He caught only snatches through the frenzy of his own battle, but heard the lightning crack time and again. The duellists became shadows in the harsh light of its afterglow, lit in stark monochrome.

It lasted only seconds. With a shout of triumph, Sicarius cut the Stormcaller's staff in half, sending a backwash of energy through him, and then decapitated the creature with the reverse blow. The necron lord's head didn't even have time to hit the earth before he disappeared, leaving behind the malicious resonance of his passing.

The storm went with him, evaporating as if carried on a strong wind, light replacing dark like a sudden breaking dawn. Lightning ebbed, thunder subsided. Even the wraiths melted away, returned to their master's side. In the centre of it all was Sicarius. He leant on one knee, heaving breath into his body.

The lightning had struck him more than once – the smoke coiling off his scorched armour was testament to that. In spite of the obvious pain, he rose and with straightened back and head held high lifted the Tempest Blade.

'Victoris Ultra!'

Relief and exultation blending as one glorious emotion, the Second – Lions, Shieldbearers, Indomitable and all – gave voice that echoed their captain.

Desolation surrounded them. And more than one of

Guilliman's sons had returned to their primarch's side in the Temple of Correction on Macragge.

Vandius's banner stirred again, rippling on an arctic breeze.

The necron vanguard was defeated.

Though of exultant mood, a small kernel of Praxor felt hollow at the victory. Over half his squad were dead or maimed; Sicarius's maddened rush at the enemy the reason for it. Solinus's squad had suffered too, though not nearly as badly.

As he watched Apothecary Venatio add the gene-seed of Hexedese to that of Galrion and Vortigan, Praxor could not help but question.

'Only in death, Brother-Sergeant Manorian.'

Trajan again, the ever-vigilant shadow of Second Company. 'Duty is all we have, brother.'

Praxor nodded.

'Yes, my Chaplain.'

At least Belthonis had lived, though he was badly wounded. He might walk, but fight? Given their position, he had little choice with either. Venatio would have to patch him up and make him last for however long he could.

Agrippen met the sergeant's gaze, stoic and unreadable within the armour-eternal of his sarcophagus, and within Praxor felt an accord.

Suddenly the presence of the First on Damnos, Agemman's watchmen, seemed all too necessary.

ACT TWO: SALVATION

CHAPTER EIGHT

Macragge, two years before the Damnos Incident

PRAXOR WAS ENRAPT as he listened to the senators' endless debating.

Watching from a seat at the back of the auditorium, Iulus frowned and was glad of the concealing shadows cast in the wake of the late Macraggian sun.

Attired in robes of various hues and ostentation, he found the senators overfond of their own voices, prolix for the sake of it. Their arguments did not interest him. He had come for Praxor.

Helots roamed the hall, plying the officials with drink and sustenance, while lexicographical servitors dictated every spoken word on clacking scriptoria. The debate had been going on for several days. It did not appear as if any resolution were in sight.

Iulus noticed other Adeptus Astartes in the throng, company spokesmen and the aides of captains. Daceus was there. The veteran-sergeant looked strange with a stump of arm instead of his power fist. It was rare to see the Lion without his battle gear. He looked as enthralled as Iulus felt. So too was Helios from the First. His demeanour appeared keener but no less exhausted at the endless procrastination.

Politics was not Iulus's strong suit. He believed in what he could touch and fashion towards war, but the Chapter needed solidity too and so its future was given to the politicians to argue over. Not that their opinions *really* mattered. It was the illusion of diplomacy. Only one man could end the debate with any real authority and finality, and his throne in the auditorium was empty. He wasn't wasting his time listening to this.

Deciding Praxor was too involved to disturb, Iulus headed for the battle-cages alone.

He met Scipio, waiting for him in training fatigues and wielding a blunted rudius.

'I saw Praxor at the senate council again,' he said as he began stripping off his armour. A pair of serfs came to attend him, but Iulus waved them away. 'I am capable of donning my own training garb.' He glowered and sent the serfs scurrying.

Scipio was sketching test swings with his rudius. 'Why do you terrify them, brother?'

The corner of Iulus's mouth twitched as he set down his cuirass. 'Because it's enjoyable.'

Shrugging, Scipio made two arcs, switching from one hand to the other, before ending on a low thrust.

'Serious, eh?' joked Iulus. His armour was stowed and he picked up a rudius himself, gauging the weight and heft.

'I have to be when sparring with you, ox.'

Iulus snorted, mimicking the beast Scipio had likened him to.

Then he swung.

Scipio blocked expertly, moving aside and allowing the blunted blade to roll down and off his own. His riposte was a sharp jab that Iulus swatted down before he backed away and said, 'We have not spoken of it since it happened.'

Scipio leapt and swung an overhead blow that staggered Iulus at first but the sergeant got his footing quickly and rammed his shoulder against his opponent, denying him the room for a follow-up. Scipio grimaced as he tried and failed to match his friend's superior strength. 'Spoken of what?'

Iulus felt Scipio move, turning his momentum against him. He checked his stance, bracing his legs wider, and pivoted on one foot to parry the reverse swipe aimed at his shoulder blade. The rudii *clacked* loudly around the cage.

'Orad.'

A hail of blows rebounded against Iulus's blade and he was hard-pressed to defend against them. He had to back away, fending off each fresh attack, his options for a reply diminishing with every blow. It bordered on frenzied.

Like a pugilist against the ropes, he went in close, seizing Scipio's torso in a wrestling move and heaving him back to reassert some distance. Scipio came back undaunted and swinging. He carved elaborate approach swings in the air and Iulus had to use his full concentration to anticipate his opponent's strike pattern. He blocked and feinted, but could find no counter.

Scipio was relentless. And silent, until saying, 'What is there to speak about? He is dead. That is the likely fate of us all in the end.'

He aimed a punch, which Iulus deflected easily with his meaty forearm. He could sense his battle-brother tiring. Anger, when misused during battle, was as much an enemy as a friend. He asked, 'When did you become so fatalistic, Scipio?'

Their blades locked, one pressing against the other. Scipio's face was a mask of aggression.

'I am merely being realistic.'

He took a two-handed grip. It forced Iulus onto the back foot, but he then rolled on his heel and allowed Scipio to lunge forward into mid-air. Using the flat of his blade, he smacked Scipio hard on the back of his neck.

'I don't think you're angry at me, brother.'

Stung, Scipio turned with murderous eyes and flung his rudius like a throwing dagger. The move almost fooled Iulus, who was forced into a desperate block that sent the weapon spinning loose. It was a hair's breadth from his neck and causing serious injury.

Iulus threw down his rudius a second later and punched Scipio hard in the jaw. He recoiled but didn't retaliate. Shame supplanted anger as he realised he'd broken a sacred trust.

Iulus was breathing hard; they both were. 'You want to fight for real, bring armour and chainblades next time, but don't expect to walk out of this cage.' He moved in close, his voice deep and full of menace. 'You'll need to be carried out.'

Scipio's face was a hard, defiant line.

''Bout over,' he said, and left.

When Scipio was gone, Iulus sagged and wondered at how he had failed to see his friend's degeneration and pain. He slammed his fist into the cage wall, stretching the metal into a perfect mould of his knuckles. Then he picked up the rudius and performed training rotas until he was sore and burning, and all the frustration had vented away.

* * *

The wise say, just before you die, that your life and all its achievements pass before you in a blur of enlightenment.

Iulus recalled the words of the ancient Macraggian philosophers he'd been forced to endure as part of his neophyte training. On his back in the dirt and bloody snow, he found issue with that belief. There was only an encroaching darkness and the dense thunder of pumping blood in his ears. There was no epiphany, no glorious moment when a golden halo beckoned or cherubim sang of his deeds in archaic verse.

It was copper-stink, it was hot fading breath and the futile knowledge that he had been found wanting in the face of his liege lords of old.

As the necron's grip tightened, Iulus railed against his fate, too obstinate to accept it. He wanted to scream his defiance but even that was denied him. He'd pushed the chainblade as deep as it would go, dragged it around organs that were not organs, but still the necron endured.

Then the pressure lifted.

First his sight returned, like a fresh dawn after a moonless night. The blood stopped rushing quite so loudly and mortally after that, and was replaced by a hard insistent *clank*. Something that looked like a spear-tip jabbed out of the necron's left eye socket. Then it happened again and again. Before it phased out, Iulus was dimly aware of a human clinging to the creature's back and hacking for all his worth. The ice-spike's final blow punctured the necron's forehead, dead centre, and it flickered from existence.

The human, a conscript by the look of his uniform, landed heavily but on his feet.

He grinned at Iulus. Behind him, there were other conscripts hacking with blades, picks and axes. 'I have saved an Angel,' he said, and offered his hand.

Iulus got to his feet, ignoring the human's aid because his weight would have toppled him and he didn't want his saviour to suffer that indignity. 'Who are you?' he asked instead.

The necron elites were defeated. The entire war cell had phased out, removed tactically from the battlefield by their masters below and abroad.

'Kolpeck,' said the human. He sketched a salute, but it was awkward and rough. 'Falka Kolpeck.'

Iulus liked him already.

HISTORY WOULD NOT remember the deeds of the Damnos Ark Guard in the liberation of Kellenport. They would fail to record the courageous actions of the four hundred souls who ventured beyond the western gate from the Courtyard of Thor to certain death. Sicarius and his glorious Second would be the heroes and for them alone the laurels of the battle attributed.

But Iulus Fennion would always know the full truth of it.

He regarded the bedraggled remnants of the Ark Guard that had fought and died in the 'wastes' alongside the Ultramarines and felt... *surprise*.

Ever since Ghospora City back on Black Reach, over a century ago, he had known humans had mettle. To fight greenskins from behind barricades and fortified battlements was one thing; to charge headlong into hand-to-hand combat with necrons was something else. Perhaps these hundred or so soldiers before him were suicidal.

They were mainly miners, he decided, Damnosian labourers pressed into service as a last act of a desperate world to shore up its decimated armies. They'd just returned from the Capitolis Administratum bastion with the acting lord governor. With the Deathwinds' payload depleted, it was no longer safe and he was to be secured within Kellenport.

Word had come through Daceus from the front. Sicarius was pressing on into enemy-held territory, to Arcona City and the Zephyr Monastery. He'd requisitioned forces from the rearguard, both squads of Devastators and Brother Ultracius. Kellenport was won, but he wanted to keep it that way.

According to Tactica briefings, Commander Sonne had over fifty thousand Ark Guard at his disposal; a large part of the planet's remaining population. Iulus was given the unenviable job of galvanising them and ensuring they held the line and the ground already won.

Agnathio could not make the long walk. The damage done to his motive functions had reduced the mighty warrior to an undignified shuffle and until a Techmarine could be tasked with conducting the correct rituals and rites to effect repairs, he would remain so. The Dreadnought joined Iulus's command and the brother-sergeant was glad of his presence and his wisdom.

Presently, he had one ear to the recently restored long-range comm-feed.

'Brother.' The return was crackly and broken, but Iulus recognised the voice of Praxor. 'I'm sorry that you've been left behind.'

'It is no matter,' Iulus replied. 'My duty is to the captain and the Emperor whatever form it takes. How goes the battle farther out?'

'Tough.' It was rare for Praxor to be so upfront and honest about the severity of the fight ahead. He was usually possessed of the same vainglory as their captain.

Iulus wondered what had changed.

'You lost battle-brothers?'

The voice that came back over the feed was quieter, almost hushed, 'More than I'm comfortable with. The Shieldbearers are at barely half-strength.'

'We always knew this war would be arduous. Galvia and Urnos were wounded but we are inviolable still.' He was referring to the fact that ever since they'd been formed, the Immortals had yet to sustain a casualty. That feat might be put sorely to the test on Damnos.

'I only wish you were fighting by my side, Iulus,' said Praxor, his mood oddly candid. 'I have need of your counsel and temperance.'

'Guilliman willing, we will all survive this campaign to fight another in the primarch's name.'

'Or die in the prosecution of it.'

Iulus nodded without trace of regret or denial. 'If that is his will, then yes.'

Praxor left a pause as if agreeing with his fellow sergeant then asked, 'Any word from Scipio?'

The activation runes on the portable hololith projector were flashing. Iulus needed to cut this short. 'None, but there is another comm shroud over the Thanatos Hills.'

'May Guilliman watch over him.'

'And all of us. Courage and honour, brother.'

'Courage and honour.'

Iulus cut the feed. Troopers were filing in from the western gate, more Ark Guard. There were twenty thousand men with heavy cannon and servitors. The majority looked like the conscripts arrayed before Iulus in the reclaimed 'wasteland' in front of the first defensive wall.

The hololith unit flickered to life, a grainy blue three-dimensional image suspended in mid-air through a projector node, and Iulus looked away from the marching men.

'Lord Fennion.' It was Commander Sonne, from somewhere within the Kellenport city-bastion. He gave a crisp salute but his eyes appeared haggard, his face drawn and his uniform bedraggled.

'I am a Space Marine sergeant,' Iulus corrected him, nodding in recognition of the salute, 'so you may refer to me as such. I am no one's lord.'

'Duly noted, sergeant. I want to convey my deepest appreciation for your efforts in liberating Kellenport. You have saved many lives with your actions and all of Damnos expresses its gratitude to you, our saviours.'

The words were there, but the belief was not. Sonne did not think his life or the lives of his people were saved, nor did he regard the Ultramarines as saviours. Iulus saw a broken man before him, one that was going through the motions and had all but given in to fatalism.

'Further hard work is needed, commander. We have only stalled the necron advance, not stymied it completely.'

'I am at your disposal, as are my men. I've already sent the twenty thousand requested to the wastes.'

'You might want to reconsider naming that zone,' Iulus advised.

Sonne nodded, mildly chastened. 'Of course… Yes. It was the Courtyard of Chronus before the desolation. So it shall be again.'

'Chronus it is,' said Iulus. 'Our tank commander will be pleased.'

Sonne didn't understand the reference, but acknowledged the remark with another nod anyway.

Iulus went on. 'Your thirty thousand will defend the

city-bastion whilst the other twenty will be split evenly garrisoning the defensive walls. The third wall we mine and give up to the enemy.'

Sonne went to object but Iulus cut him off. 'We're already stretched and defending three walls will spread us too thinly. Our focus shall be on the first two walls, the first as a fall-back point for the second and then Kellenport city-bastion as our last redoubt.'

Sonne looked ashen at that last remark. If they lost Kellenport then it was over. For everyone.

'You push on for the outer territories?' he asked, a rare glimmer of hope in his tired eyes.

'Captain Sicarius is driving the spearhead purposefully, yes.'

As Iulus understood it, the 'spearhead' was actually a series of daring raids. The necron vanguard had been beaten, a tiny respite bought for the Kellenport defenders, but the mechanoids would return as soon as they'd calibrated for fighting against the Ultramarines. Iulus nearly said as much to Sonne but chose to stay his tongue. Perhaps some of Scipio's old empathy was rubbing off on him. But that had been a different version of his friend. Something, the death of Orad he suspected, had hollowed out that optimism and replaced it with a core of ice. He'd half heard of an altercation with Praxor in the past, something prior to Damnos, but had no wish to pry. The business of others was precisely that. Iulus knew his duty and how to do it to the best of his ability. He had gifts, the legacy of his Chapter brothers flowing in his veins, and he meant to honour that with each and every one of his actions.

Iulus only half watched Commander Sonne's salute, his mind on other things as the hololith shrank back into the projector node.

'Don't let it consume you, Scipio,' he said to the wind, shifting his gaze to the Thanatos Hills where the necron barrage continued unabated. 'Don't give in to reckless hate, brother.'

Aristaeus loomed behind him; Iulus could hear the warrior's careful tread.

'Break up the squad,' said the sergeant, 'and distribute it around the separate battalions.' He regarded the one hundred survivors from the battle for the plaza, the renamed Courtyard of Chronus. Falka Kolpeck was standing in the middle, their de facto leader. 'These ones are with me.'

IT HAD BEEN so long since he had hunted.

For a moment he was skin and bone again and it was blood, not oil and circuitry, that flowed through him. The wild lands of his birth stretched as far as he could see and the hooting of cattle and herd-beasts called into the umber evening. The sun was dipping and he felt its warmth fading on his cheek. The coarse grain of his antique phase-rifle was a reassuring presence in his hand. The wind, ghosting through the hills and across the plain, touched his exposed skin with chilling tendrils.

As quickly as they came, the sensations bled away again and left numbness and sorrow in their wake. The sun did not warm him, the wind was as dead as the bloodless arteries of his mechanised body. No rifle identified him as a noble plains hunter. Instead, a pair of gruesome talons betrayed him for what he was – a monster.

Sahtah the Enfleshed groaned inwardly. Even as the tundra rushed by in a blur of greyish white, as his slaves followed his lead, he was not placated. Funnelling into a deep gorge, he paused before the carcass of a dead herd-animal.

Its flesh steamed with recently exposed entrails. Sahtah plunged his talons inside, turning them incarnadine with the beast's spilled viscera, hoping...

'Why can't I feel it?'

He rounded on his slaves in a sudden fury. 'There is no heat from the blood, no kill-stench. Where is it?'

Powerless to answer his demands even if they wanted to, the flayed ones merely stared and waited. Their flesh-cowls were rank with putrefaction but stirred a pang of jealousy in their lord.

'I want my robes!' Sahtah raged. His synthetic voice could only simulate his anger. In a quieter voice, he added: 'I want my body.'

His instincts told him the genebred humans were close.

'Soon I will have it,' he promised. 'Soon I will be enfleshed again.'

CHAPTER NINE

Brakkius led Retiarii up the slope. Brothers Renatus and Herdantes kept low behind their squad leader, weapons up. As soon as they were spotted, a strobe of emerald gauss-fire lit up the snow and ice. It was answered by bolter fire that incapacitated one of the raiders but didn't render it inoperative. Before Brakkius and his troops were retreating, the downed necron had already begun to self-repair.

Despite the lack of lasting damage, their attack provoked the reaction Scipio was hoping for. Three of the six raiders left the obelisk and went after Brakkius.

Two hard *bangs* from Ortus took one of the mechanoids in the side of the skull. It crumpled into a heap, shuddered and phased out. Another shot exploded a raider's shoulder and left it unable to shoot.

The crossfire was working. It drew the other three necrons out. Scipio and Largo had already sneaked into position before Brakkius's attack and were about to flank them when the sniper fire stopped. Scipio was about to give the attack order when he hesitated and looked over to Ortus's vantage point, wondering why he'd stopped firing.

'Brother, report,' he snapped into the comm-feed. Then came the screaming from back down the slope. It sounded like Renatus.

'Brakkius!'

The reply was frantic. 'Under attack, sergeant...'

Scipio had moved out of the gorge and couldn't see back down the path because of the slope's sharp incline. He caught muzzle flashes, though, and knew the weapons that made them were turned away from the obelisk.

'In the ice. Beneath us!'

Largo was ready to move. 'What do we do?'

The raiders were laying down a thickening curtain of fire. Their slow, methodical advance would get them to the edge of the path and looking down on the gorge in a few minutes. Then Brakkius would face enemies to the front and rear. Scipio swore loudly. He still had no sense of what was attacking Brakkius in the gorge but he suspected it was the same foe that had neutralised Ortus.

'We fight!' Scipio came up off his haunches like a jackhammer and thundered half a clip into the nearest raider. Battered, the necron turned and unleashed a swathe of gauss-beams. Scipio took one in the leg that staggered him, but he kept on running. Just behind him, Largo provided support fire and tore the raider's chest open with a series of precise shots. It phased out, leaving four and whatever was in the gorge.

A claw broke through the ice at Scipio's feet, answering that question, and locked onto the sergeant's ankle. Instinctively he shot downwards at his assailant, carving up the ground into jagged chips. Pitiless eyes glowed emerald through the glossy filter of the ice before dying into embers and then voids as the creature phased out.

It was not alone.

Scipio cursed again, realising there *had* been faces beneath their feet but not of Damnosian natives, not any more – they were necrons, flesh-wrapped nightmares that tunnelled and burrowed like mechanical insects. Brakkius fought the same foes. Ortus had been claimed by them. This was a trap, but one of the necrons' making, and Scipio had blundered right into it.

'Sergeant Vorolanus!'

The ice broke apart at Scipio's feet and he was dragged downwards, Largo's warning echoing behind him. He kicked out and made a solid connection, ceramite hitting necron metal. For want of a better strategy, he jabbed his chainsword into the ice-slush where the half-fleshed horrors were slowly emerging. Sparks fizzed and died as they hit the ground, cascading off whatever Scipio's blade was locked against.

Talons. The creatures had long, curved talons just like the ambushers they'd met and destroyed at the Thanatos Refinery. Scipio cursed himself for a fool. He had rushed to engage without properly gauging the lie of the land, but he was an Ultramarine with his brothers beside him – all was not lost. He swung his bolt pistol around, sending two shells into the ice just as a lance of pain shot up his leg where the flayed one had impaled him.

A second broke free of the ice and loomed over him. Scipio yanked his chainsword free and parried a blow that would have slashed open his neck.

'Hell-kite!' Two more shells put down the invisible

aggressor still lodged below, trying to emerge; a swing of the chainblade ripped open the cabling and servos around the other necron's torso. It fell back, stunned, but was self-repairing.

'Brother!'

Largo had his own problems. Three more flayed ones had pulled themselves free of the ground, like corpses come back to life to revenge themselves on the living. Largo sent tightly controlled bolter bursts into their ranks in an attempt to slow them but ammo was low and any damage caused wasn't severe enough to take out the necrons permanently.

The fight in the gorge was fading too. The intensity of fire from *Retiarii* was lessening, which Scipio took to be a bad sign. Brakkius could be dead. When the raiders reached the edge of the gorge, he surely would be.

Time was slowing. Fate had caught up with Scipio Vorolanus. It had witnessed his reckless abandon, his selfish fatalism that had grown like a cancer in the years since Orad's death and decided to make him pay for it.

Scipio railed. 'This is not the end!'

The flayed one he'd maimed was getting up. He swung the bolt pistol around to finish it but the trigger *chanked* empty. Powerless to intervene, still half buried under the ice where his spare clips were pinned against his belt, he watched.

Metal flowed like oil, running on the surface of the tundra. Wires and cables reattached themselves, weaving viperously across the ground, re-establishing function to vital systems. The spinal column severed by Scipio's blow caterpillared towards the half-wrecked torso, dragging abdomen and legs with it. Metallic fusion occurred quickly and vigorously – only the necron's cape of skin showed any lasting damage.

'Breath of Guilliman,' he spat through clenched teeth, looking heavenwards for divine intervention. 'Can't they just stay dead?'

Largo had run out of room and ammunition. He hauled Scipio from the ambush-pit and onto his feet. Back-to-back, they faced six flayed ones, a match for any warrior of the Second. The raiders had their own mission and closed on whatever was left of Brakkius and *Retiarii*.

Scipio slammed his last clip into his bolt pistol; Largo let his spent bolter sag on its strap and drew a combat blade.

'If I had known, Largo…'

'We would have still followed you, brother-sergeant. Only in death.'

Scipio nodded grimly. 'Only in death.'

A smoke contrail *foomed* across the Ultramarines eye-line, making them turn. It lit up the closest flayed one in an incendiary burst, tearing the creature into fragments. A pair of grenades followed in its wake. They emitted a low hum before attaching magnetically to a second necron. The explosion was hot and deafening. Frag showered the Space Marines' armour. Disregarding this new element to the skirmish for now, Scipio and Largo broke apart and were about to engage the enemy when a bola whipped around a mechanoid's neck and took off its head in the resulting firestorm.

Three necrons phased out in under a minute. The raiders were turning, reacting to the change in engagement dynamics. Three las-beams pinned one, shredding leg joints and the chamber on its gauss-flayer; a thrown axe embedded in a second. Laced with explosives, it was blasted apart like the flayed ones.

Sensing the swing in their favour, Scipio cut down another mechanoid with Largo applying the killing stroke with his combat blade. The two raiders and flayed ones that remained, their forces so brutally punished, phased out.

In their wake, Scipio observed their saviours. His enhanced eyesight picked out their shadows in the snow-kissed crags above. They wore ice camouflage and had powder beneath their eyes. Even their guns were swathed in bleached-white rags and painted to blend in with their surroundings.

'Show yourselves,' Scipio addressed the half-darkness. 'In the name of the Emperor's Adeptus Astartes.'

Slowly, the hunters, or whoever they were, came down from their vantage points. They were well-armed. Scipio saw a tube launcher, heavy-gauge lascarbines, grenade lanyards and several improvised explosives amongst their battlegear. Every one of them carried an ice-pick too. It was this, and not an axe, that had been utilised earlier.

As they emerged into the light at last, though it was a fuliginous twilight that shadowed the gorge and the plateau at its summit now, a band of grizzled men were revealed standing amongst the Ultramarines. Scarred and as hard as the permafrost beneath their feet, Scipio knew guerrilla fighters when he saw them.

He nodded to the one who looked like their leader. A thick beard covered the lower half of his face and there were strange tattoos marking his cheeks and forehead. He wore several ragged scarves and his nose, ears and around the eyes were red with overexposure to the cold. Bandages, several layers thick, served as gloves. A tattered cloak that might once have been a storm coat fluttered on a solemn breeze.

Though Scipio towered over the man, he didn't flinch or appear intimidated.

He looked down, extending a hand. 'We are in your debt.'

Besides taking a firmer grip on his lascarbine, the man didn't respond.

'The trap wasn't meant for you,' said a confident voice from higher up in the crags. It was a woman, moving slowly but expertly through the rocks. She was attired like the others but Scipio noticed a ribbed bodyglove beneath her scarves and cloaks. It reminded him of some kind of environment suit, albeit non-functional. Reddish hair, dried out and rough with the cold, peeked from beneath a furred hat. A pair of goggles, their lenses tinged a pinkish hue, hung around her neck.

Piercing jade eyes appraised the Ultramarine, taking in the curves of his armour, his sheer size and power, as she approached him.

'They're after me.' Stopping a few metres away from Scipio, she spread her arms wide. 'All of us.'

Pointing to the obelisk, she added, 'Communication tower, Emperor knows how it works. The Herald uses it to speak to us.'

Scipio frowned. 'Herald?' He recalled Tigurius's traumatic connection with a creature of the same name.

'He is their voice,' she explained. 'Don't see many towers this far out. Must be expanding.' The woman came closer, deciding she could trust the warrior, and held out her hand. 'Jynn Evvers.'

Scipio took it out of politeness, being careful not to crush her delicate fingers, and was surprised to feel some iron there. 'You're hunting them.'

'Why do you think they want to catch us? Got close too until you Angels arrived from on high.' She turned in profile, revealing a string of the self-same tattoos down

163

her neck as on the bearded man. They weaved like a strand of chromosomes. 'This is my crew: Densk, Farge, Makker…'

The names were unimportant to Scipio, though this Jynn related all eighteen of them. Each man and woman nodded, smiled or returned grim indifference to the Ultramarine sergeant. Densk was the bearded one. He later discovered the man had no tongue – he'd lost it due to frostbite. He also later found out that there had once been more of them… lots more.

'We should move,' she concluded at the end of the introductions. 'The metal-heads will be back soon.'

Scipio exchanged a glance with Largo – this must be the guerrilla's term for the necrons. Out the corner of his eye, he noticed Brakkius emerging from the gorge. He was limping. Herdantes cradled a wounded arm. Between them they dragged Renatus.

Largo went to go to them when Scipio placed a hand on his shoulder. 'Find Ortus,' he murmured.

'Captain Evvers!' One of the guerrillas, a woman called Sia, was watching the perimeter. Her warning was met by the priming of lascarbines and an immediate dispersal of the human forces amongst the crags.

Scipio was mildly impressed – he'd seen squads of storm troopers that were only a little better disciplined. He didn't move, though. An auspex chime revealed the identity of the new arrivals to him.

'Stand down,' he said, seeing *Venetores* led by Cator run into view. 'They're with me.'

The guerrilla fighters eased off but only when Evvers gave the signal. Scipio's opinion of them improved further. He surreptitiously battle-signed to Cator that the humans were allies. *Venetores* were back amongst the others in short order after that.

'I'm sorry, brother-sergeant,' said Cator, speaking for his combat squad. 'Doubling back cost us a lot of time.'

Scipio waved away his contrition. 'I should have waited, brother. And now...' He gestured to the carnage that had hurt the Thunderbolts.

'What happened?'

Brakkius and the rest of *Retiarii* joined them.

'We were ambushed,' said Scipio. 'In the gorge and up here.'

Largo returned but shook his head when he met his sergeant's gaze. Ortus was gone.

'Venatio is back with Captain Sicarius. His legacy is lost to us,' he said.

Scipio gritted his teeth, not liking the options. 'We can't get him back across the mountains.'

Largo was shaking his head again. 'It doesn't matter. There's nothing left of him.'

Now Scipio made a fist. He was trying hard to rein in his anger. He turned to the woman, Evvers.

'How close is your camp to here?'

'Not far.'

'Do you have medical supplies?'

'Some.' She looked worried, as perturbed about unfolding events as Scipio was.

'Take us there.'

Largo put a hand on Scipio's vambrace. His eyes counselled caution.

'What choice do we have? What else would you have me do, Largo?'

He let it go, but wasn't quite done. 'What about the mission?'

'Without a way through the mountains, there is no mission. Ortus is dead already, so too Naceon.' Scipio looked to Brakkius and his men. 'I won't lose another. Not senselessly, not like this.'

Largo nodded.

'So, your camp.' Scipio asked Evvers. 'Where is it?'

IN THE END, Jynn had no choice. She didn't want to bring the Space Marines to the encampment, for one thing their presence would attract the metal-heads, but how could she refuse? It had been a close call whether to intervene on the Ultramarines' behalf, and as they wended through the mountains a part of her had begun to regret that decision.

Of course, the superhuman warriors would make excellent protectors but the humans had survived so far without them and Jynn had no desire to change that, plus she couldn't be sure that protection was the Space Marines' primary objective. They were death incarnate and being close to such beings would only invite the very spectre of mortality into their ranks.

As they climbed higher, up the steep ice-daggered slopes and brittle crags thick with snow, she wondered about their leader. From listening in on the Space Marines' hushed exchanges, she gathered his name was Scipio and he was a sergeant. Jynn knew about as much as most Imperial citizens did about Space Marines, which was precious little. To her, they were warriors of myth, Angels sent on wings of fire and wielding fists of thunder and lightning.

Such impressions were romanticised, of course, little more than cultural extrapolations from tapestries, statues and galleria. The truth was there before her. These were super-men, for sure, but they were fallible and could be killed; they weren't the untouchable immortals that some claimed them to be. Jynn would have been in awe of them, she felt, if her spirit had not been so embittered by the war.

The memory of Korve, her long-dead husband, came into her mind as they crested another high and the drifts thickened. What started out as a light dappling of snow upon her shoulder and head became a deluge that swathed Jynn's entire body. She slipped on a patch of ice and nearly fell. Reaching out, she braced herself on a rocky spur that felt smooth to the touch and realised it was Scipio.

'Be careful, Captain Evvers,' he warned, setting her upright again.

She nodded a curt thanks. 'It's Jynn,' she said. 'My name, I mean. It doesn't seem right that an Angel of the Emperor should call me "captain". It doesn't seem right that any-one should.'

'You carry the rank well… *Jynn.*'

She prodded the Ultramarine's plastron. 'And you are Scipio?'

Scipio looked down at her pointing finger, debating what to do about it. In the end he merely answered the question. 'I am Brother-Sergeant Vorolanus, yes, but you may call me Scipio. You very probably saved my life and that of my squad, so you've earned the right.'

She snorted derisively, echoing, '*Earned the right*, eh? Come on.' She turned and moved on. 'We're close.'

THEY REACHED THE encampment in a few more minutes. It was high up and well shielded from the necrons' attention. The guerrillas must have had engineers and technicians amongst their group, for they'd erected bafflers to thwart the mechanoids' sensors.

Scipio counted six more men at the camp; one was a medic, the other looked like the individual responsible for the sensor jamming array.

Largo appeared at his sergeant's shoulder and spoke in a low voice, 'Our comm-feed is down, should we…?' He indicated the bafflers: slim, flanged antennae jabbed into the ground like a spear. Looking at them, Scipio realised the entire encampment, even its rough tents and boxy generators, was portable. He wondered how many times the guerrillas had been forced to move since the occupation and how long it had taken them to realise they needed to.

'No.' He held up his hand, flat with the palm down. 'Leave it. The comm-feed is no use to us out here, anyway.'

They followed Jynn Evvers, the guerrillas bleeding off from the main group to talk with their comrades and help explain why cobalt-blue Angels were in their midst. Scipio ignored their awed glances. Only the medic seemed unmoved.

'Medical tent,' Jynn supplied as they passed it.

Scipio gestured for Brakkius and the injured to peel off and get some attention. He held Brakkius's forearm as he was leaving and looked to Renatus. 'How bad is he?'

'Sus-an membrane coma. Only Venatio can bring him out of it.'

'Get him inside and see what can be done for his wounds.'

Brakkius tried to mask his shock. 'We're leaving him?'

'Better that than drag him through the mountains. He's safer with the humans. We will come back for him, brother.'

Satisfied that Brakkius understood, Scipio let him go and caught up to Largo, who was waiting a little way ahead. Cator, Garrik and Auris had stayed behind to watch the entrance. The humans had sentries but they were not

Space Marines and Scipio trusted his Thunderbolts above all others.

Defensively, the guerrilla camp left a lot to be desired, amounting to little more than a few clustered tents, some razor-wire barricades and a handful of tripod-mounted heavy stubbers. Not enough to seriously deter a necron attack but then he supposed that was why they had the bafflers. It was meant as a place of shelter, somewhere to regroup and rest, not a fortress.

'In here,' said Jynn, without looking back.

Scipio left Largo outside. He was alone with the female guerrilla leader in what he assumed was her operational base. There were hanging charts and maps, a simple sleeping bag in one corner and a butane lamp kit turned off in the centre of the space. Low burning lumen rods dangled from the tent's internal guy ropes and provided the only light source. The blowing breeze that had started to pick up nudged the rods. As the shadows moved, more makeshift bomb and grenade combinations were revealed here and there. Someone had set up an improvised table and there were more maps and charts on it.

'Found a lot of patrols on our forays inland,' Jynn explained. She turned on the lamp kit and rubbed her hands next to the warmth. She looked over her shoulder at Scipio. 'You generate a lot of heat, don't you?'

The Ultramarine shrugged, as much as he could whilst wearing full power armour. He knew she was right but heat or cold was of no concern to one such as him.

'We could have used some of your generators in the early days.' She started to unbuckle her kit and peel off the body-glove. 'Certainly makes doing this a lot easier.'

Jynn had her naked back to him as she changed out

169

of the sodden kit into something dry. 'Good thing about having fewer mouths to feed,' she said ruefully. 'It means there's plenty of extra rags to go around too.'

The tattoos on her neck went down her shoulder and across her back, all the way to the base of her spine. Despite her nakedness, Scipio didn't avert his gaze. Jynn seemed unconcerned about it.

She called. 'Densk!'

The bearded one from earlier came in, silent on account of his missing tongue. He stalled a little when he saw the Space Marine but moved around him to Jynn's side.

'Lamp's hot,' she said. 'Three marks.'

There was a metal prong next to the lamp. Densk took it and proceeded to burn the three marks Jynn had requested. To her credit, she barely flinched.

When he was done, Densk dabbed some gauze with counter-septic on the wounds and left the tent just as he'd arrived.

'Those scars,' Scipio ventured when Densk had gone. 'What do they represent?'

She arched her neck to look, touching one of the higher tattoos. 'Kill-marks,' she said. 'One for each metal-head I've ganked. Everyone alive in this camp has them.'

Scipio counted at least seventeen kill-marks. He'd seen Chapter veterans do something similar on their armour.

'Three from the ambush. Yours is the highest tally, am I right?'

Jynn taped fresh pads of gauze over the burns. She struggled to reach the lowest one. 'Could you assist me?'

'I'm no Apothecary,' Scipio replied, but came forward and applied the last of the tape. He had to be careful; his gauntlets were ill-suited to delicate work, especially field medicine.

'Thank you.' Jynn stepped away, shrugged on a fresh bodyglove then an overcoat, and faced him. Her eyes were like shards of glass. 'Yes, mine is the highest tally. And I'll see it doubled, tripled until everyone one of those mechanical bastards is dead.'

Scipio recognised something in her demeanour. It was like looking into a mirror. The bitterness, the impotent anger. He wondered whom she had lost to make her this way.

'You've buried many comrades-in-arms?'

'No, but I've seen friends and colleagues die. And I've lost family too – my husband, but not to the necrons.'

'My condolences,' he said, even though he didn't really feel the compassion of the words. He eyed the maps and charts, particularly the ones on the table. 'You know these mountains?'

Jynn laughed but it was without humour. 'We've been dying and surviving in these crags for over a year. Yes, we know the mountains intimately.'

Scipio walked up to the table. There was a marker to one side and Scipio used it to circle the Thanatos Hills. 'And here,' he added, drawing an arrow to represent the Ultramarines' desired angle of attack on the necron artillery that would bypass their defensive cordon. 'Do you know of an approach through to this region from this heading?'

Jynn studied the map for a minute. She smiled at Scipio. 'Now you'll owe me two.'

He eyed her curiously. 'You are not like most humans I have met.'

'Most humans haven't seen the things I have or endured what I've had to.' Sitting down on a crate, she started to field strip her weapons. 'Do you know how many times I've died out here in this arctic hell. Well, almost died?' Jynn held up four fingers. 'Makes you think about your existence a little differently.'

Though his expression was neutral, Scipio marvelled at her confidence. There was something about this woman, something great and indefatigable. Whatever her attire or current disposition, she was much more than she appeared to be. It wasn't disrespect, Scipio didn't feel that. It was fearlessness and a determination that made Jynn Evvers stand out amongst the human flock. Such a thing was rare and usually reserved for generals and great war-leaders with names like Macharius, Creed and Yarrick. She was just a miner turned guerrilla fighter but her charisma and presence were undeniable.

'Two? How so?' Scipio asked eventually, willing to play along.

Jynn took the marker and jabbed it into the centre of the Ultramarine's circle. 'We're the answer to your prayers, Angel.'

CHAPTER TEN

THOUGH HIS MORTAL faculties had long since been surrendered, Sahtah the Enfleshed could still find prey. Other senses guided him now and though he didn't fully understand the instincts of his machine brain, he learned to embrace them.

Ice and snow were forming on his body, masking it against the all-consuming white. Scraps of delusion impaired his emerald vision. Images from a past he no longer fully remembered flicked back and forth like visual interference. The arctic mountains became high dunes; the tundra below, a desert plain stretching for leagues. There were cities, so small they were just specks, and carrion birds wheeled in flocks framed against the hot afternoon sun.

Sahtah longed to bask, to feel the sun's warmth against his neck and back, but his nerves were dead, his form cool and aberrant. Ever since biotransference it had been that way. Somewhere in the process, perhaps during the *long*

173

sleep, his engrammic circuitry had been damaged. It was difficult to discern present from past, old from new. It hurt Sahtah's mind and made him want to scream.

The encampment had first appeared as an enemy village with high stockade walls and a wooden gatehouse. Now he saw it for what it was: a cluster of tents and the promise of new 'robes'.

He crouched and let the arctic storm smother him and his wretched companions. There were chunks of half-chewed flesh, the rime of dried blood around the flayed ones' mouths where they'd gorged themselves.

'We are ghouls...' Sahtah told them, though they didn't answer.

They would circle the camp and avoid the genebred warriors at first.

Sahtah wanted blood. He wanted skin.

Oh, how I hunger...

FUGE CLAPPED HIS arms around his body for what must have been the fiftieth time. It was doing no good. Even the many layers of storm cloak, his padded jacket and bodyglove, couldn't keep the cold out – it was insidious. The storm had worsened. Visibility was almost nothing. He looked at the magnoculars, sitting next to his freezing feet in the tent, and decided to ignore them. Captain Evvers was quite strict – scan the perimeter every fifteen minutes – but Fuge was too numb to move. What good would they do anyway? The Space Marines were protecting them now. He'd seen them, walking back and forth like animated statues, unperturbed by the cold. Not everyone was so hardy. Fuge didn't see why he couldn't just find a warmer tent and a sleeping bag to crawl into.

The sentry was still bemoaning his poor luck when he noticed something outside the tent, maybe fifty metres away. It was hard to tell – the snow was thick and the wind was tossing it around like a maelstrom. Fuge reached for the magnoculars.

His goggles were fogged with an icy sheen, but he didn't bother clearing them when he pulled them down off his face so he could peer through the scopes. Training the magnoculars fifty metres distant, he tried to discern what he thought he'd seen earlier.

'Definitely something…'

His voice trembled, teeth chattering as he spoke.

The wind was really howling now, making even thoughts hard to hear. It tugged at Fuge's thermal layers, slipping in through the gaps, chilling him.

Through the greenish resolution of the scopes, he thought he saw something… *burrowing*. He knew of ice-worms that roamed the northern tundra – it was the closest thing he could think of to describe what he was seeing. But this was the mountains. No ice-worms up here.

Fuge zoomed in and worked the focus. Thirty metres out now. Just as he was about to raise someone on the vox, the wind kicked in, tearing his coat loose, and he dropped the magnoculars.

Scrambling at his feet – the fear was on him now for some reason – Fuge picked them up but only got the scopes halfway to his face when he felt a hot burn in his chest. He looked down and saw a metre of sharp metal jutting from his body. Lifting his head was an effort but when he managed it he met the gaze of his killer. Two emerald green orbs regarded him as a god would an insect. They flared, ignited by an infernal desire.

'*Your flesh is mine*,' the thing promised.

So frozen was he with terror, poor Fuge didn't even scream as he was flayed alive.

ANKH WATCHED AS the last of the Undying's limbs were finally attached to his body. The venerable necron shone with an unearthly lustre, gilded and ochroid as befitted his station as overlord.

It had taken time and many repair constructs to revivify his master.

As if a sudden power surge had granted him life, the Undying's eyes flared brilliant and terrible.

'Stormcaller is dead,' he uttered.

'He has returned to us, my lord,' Ankh replied. 'All must return in the end.'

'Architect,' said the Undying. His mental functions were still slightly addled by his aeons of slumber. 'I am whole and desire to exact vengeance.'

'Our forces have resorted to retreat protocols. It may be some time before Stormcaller and his vanguard can be resurrected.'

'I have the means of resurrection,' the Undying assured him, 'and the tools of death.' In his hand he clutched a brutal war-scythe, its blade coruscating with energy.

He exhaled breathlessly as the last of the scarab swarms reknitting his body retreated into the hidden alcoves of the chamber. The Undying's revivification casket opened and the overlord strode out imperiously. His heavy footfalls *clanked* as they hit the metal floor.

Ankh bowed deeply in the manner of the old courts. 'You are resplendent, my liege.'

The Undying glowered at him. 'Send your drones, Architect. Retake the ground that the Stormcaller lost.'

Wrong-footed, Ankh stumbled a little. 'I... My lord, our war cells are still reviving. All our repair constructs are needed to bring them online. It will only be a matter of–'

'No. Send them now. Activate the monoliths and bring our legions into the city of the fleshed. I am awake and will not suffer the degradations of these interlopers any further.'

It was pointless to protest. The Undying was all and everything; Ankh was a mere cryptek at his whim and command. True, he had dominion over the scarabs and the tomb spyders. He could make them all cease with but a simple command, but the Undying was not an overlord to deny. His wrath might see Ankh destroyed and another set in his place. He had worked too long, too hard as Architect to allow that to happen. 'As you wish, overlord.'

The Undying did not wait for confirmation. At some invisible, mechanised signal an aperture opened in the ceiling of the resurrection chamber. At the same time a band of light delineated a circular disc in the floor that began to rise. The overlord rode the levitating disc all the way out of the chamber, bound for the surface.

Ankh was linked to the tomb like no other in the hierarchy. He felt its movements, knew the position and condition of every scarab, tomb spyder and wraith that made up its dedicated cohorts. Through them, he was interfaced with the hundreds of thousands still slumbering, still self-repairing and gradually coming online, that made up the necron war cells.

With the repair constructs occupied elsewhere that process would take exponentially more time to complete. Ankh made the calculations in a nanosecond. In the next he retasked the swarms to attack the city above.

Izarvaah was not a subtle creature; he shared many traits

with Tahek. He would gladly march his immortals and his warriors into the jaws of enemy guns, convinced of his own inviolability. Cloaked by lightning, his eldritch darkness swarming with wraiths, he assumed he was untouchable. At least one amongst the genebred saviours had disproved that belief.

Ankh was not so foolish or arrogant. His ways were cunning. He resolved to use a different method of attack.

But first he would chill their hearts and make their mortal bodies tremble. The Herald of Dismay extended his skeletal fingers and summoned the invocation node.

Unlike the Stormcaller, he would not fail.

SICARIUS SURVEYED THE battlefield ahead. Just like at Telrendar, Selonopolis and Ghospora, he looked every inch the hero. Cape flapping in the breeze, his patrician face open to the elements, he was Invictus, Cestus, Galatan – a true inheritor of Guilliman.

The forces from Kellenport Plaza had joined his spearhead. Sicarius had summoned their sergeants. Standing amidst the ruins of an Imperial temple, Praxor was amongst them.

This was an ill-fated place, he decided. It had none of the glory or culture of Macragge. Even Calth, its upper atmosphere wretched with poisonous fumes, had spirit. These were a broken people. Damnos should be defiant, yet the humans cowered in their last remaining city, their lord governor in hiding and their military commander unwilling to leave the safety of his walls. Praxor thought of the sacrifices already made and wondered if the Damnosians were a people worth saving.

Daceus intruded on Praxor's dark thoughts and he was

glad of the interruption. Never far from his captain's side, the veteran had a pict-slate clutched in his hand and showed it to Sicarius. It was a geographical map of the immediate area, radiating several kilometres from the Ultramarines position.

'Since the defeat of their vanguard, several necron phalanxes have started to converge on us,' said Daceus.

The initial defeat of the Stormcaller had immobilised the necrons under the lord's immediate command. The Ultramarines found them holding their ground where they stood, unwilling or unable to press. It made them much easier to neutralise. At first, it seemed as if the necrons were in retreat but soon other forces, those attacking distant areas of the city, were rerouted. Another necron command node had taken over. It regarded the Ultramarines as a threat it could not ignore, or tolerate.

Sicarius glanced at the slate, but only cursorily. His attention was on the horizon where the necrons could be seen in the distance manoeuvring and amassing. There were thousands.

'A cut from the gladius's blade has got their attention, then.' He smiled, but Praxor thought it had an indulgent, ugly quality about it.

A storm was rolling in, coming off the mountains. Low drifts were already curling across the tundra. Soon it would develop into a blizzard.

'Even if Guilliman were still with us,' offered Daceus, 'we cannot fight them all.'

Sicarius stepped down from a rocky plinth where he'd taken vantage.

'And yet, we shall still engage them. The weather turns, worsening still. We'll use it to our advantage.'

His sergeants were arrayed before him in a semi-circle. The Lions, along with Daceus, stood apart. Trajan stuck to the shadows, divorced from the rest but ever watchful. In the background, towering over them all, was Agrippen. The other Dreadnought, Ultracius, was with the squads waiting outside the temple ruins.

The venerable one's modulated voice rumbled, 'Our odds of victory against such a force are miniscule, brother-captain.'

Sicarius bowed to Agrippen's obvious wisdom. 'We are still the gladius, Ancient, and our thrust has barely pierced our enemy's armour. With the application of greater force, we will penetrate flesh and organs.'

Agrippen shifted and his servos churned as he moved his massive bulk. A few of the sergeants stepped out of the way to avoid being crushed. 'You mean to strike the heart.'

Sicarius was pugnacious. 'I mean to cut it out. The necrons come for us. We are a threat that they must neutralise. I shall turn that mechanised response against them.' He pointed to the silvered legions mobilising in the Ultramarines' direction. Pyramidal structures shadowed the horizon too, but they seemed to be locked on a less direct route. 'These are creatures of cause and effect. Whatever we do to them, they react accordingly.' He clenched his fist. 'It is a *weakness* that we can use against them. Force is met with greater force. Apply it in the correct place and the enemy will render its heart to us. That is when they are vulnerable.'

Brother-Sergeant Solinus spoke up. 'Tell us where you wish us to strike, captain, and it shall be done.'

Nodding approvingly at his commanders, Sicarius pointed to the slate at the core of the necron force. 'Here, right in the middle. With everything we've got.' He pointed the fingers of his left hand, making them into a blade. 'This,' he said, 'is the necron line. It is predictable, industrious. Here,' he added, making a fist with his right hand, 'we are. Our heavy guns will get their attention. We'll emulate their tactics and hold the line. The necrons, realising they possess overwhelming firepower, will simply advance towards us.' The bladed hand moved closer to the fist. 'When the storm rolls in it will obscure our positions and mask our true intent.'

'What is our *true* intent, captain?' Praxor asked, not yet seeing the wisdom of this plan.

Sicarius smiled and made the fist into two fingers, which he then proceeded to move around his other hand to the tips of the fingers. 'While our Devastators and Dreadnoughts hold their attention, you and I, brother, and the Indomitable–' Sergeant Solinus nodded humbly '–will attack their flank, cutting a hole through to their very heart.'

Praxor was unconvinced but chose to keep his misgivings private. He was not Sicarius and did not see battles as his captain did. It was his duty to obey and fight to his utmost, for the Second, for the Chapter and Lord Calgar.

Sicarius picked up his battle-helm from a broken stone tablet nearby, indicating that the tactical briefing was over. He faced Trajan, clasping the crested helm under his arm. Sinking to one knee, he said, 'Chaplain, bless us as we go to war.'

Behind Sicarius, the other sergeants followed their captain's example and kneeled before Trajan. Praxor was amongst the last. Agrippen met his pensive gaze before the Dreadnought too bowed, as much as he was able, to the Chaplain.

It was a deadly gambit that Sicarius proposed. The Second had already lost so many.

Praxor's slain battle-brothers rose foremost into his mind. As the Shieldbearers, they had been at the forefront of countless engagements for company and Chapter but they had never been as badly mauled in any action as they had on Damnos.

I am my captain's sword, Praxor reminded himself of the oath he had sworn upon elevation to the Second and the rank of sergeant. *I am his will and blood, his fury and his courage.*

But as Trajan's shadow fell over him and he closed his eyes to receive benediction, Praxor couldn't banish his doubts entirely. All of the catechisms and liturgies known to the Chapter couldn't do that.

AFTER BENEDICTION, SICARIUS dismissed the other officers. Ahead were the ruins where he planned to make their stand. By the time the Ultramarines had reached them, he reasoned that the storm would have already begun to impede visibility. Once in position, the attack would have to come swiftly.

The Lions were already moving to the centre of the battle line. Daceus was the last to leave.

Sicarius called out, 'Brother.'

Daceus stopped and turned. Like no other in the Second he wore his veteran status with the pride of a hard-won battle-scar. He had lost his left eye in a previous engagement – a bionic one replaced it – and his left arm was gloved by a formidable power fist, another relic earned during an earlier campaign. His face was a knotwork of scars and scabbed flesh. His laurels and purity seals were as abundant as the chips and grooves in his well-worn armour.

He had always been at Sicarius's side and the captain trusted Daceus above all others. He also confided in him.

'Back aboard the *Valin's Revenge*, just before planetfall, I was wrong.'

'Sir?'

'I said our chance of victory here was almost none. I was wrong.'

Daceus frowned, wondering what had changed.

'They are automatons, brother. They cannot function properly without leadership. When I struck down the leader of their vanguard, the others capitulated. It affected them, *tactically*.'

Daceus nodded, remembering. 'And unlike greenskins, these revenants are all cast into specific roles. One does not simply supplant the other.'

'Exactly. If I can incapacitate their principal command node, it will send shockwaves throughout their war infrastructure. They will be crippled.'

Daceus's eye narrowed as he thought about it. 'An impossible victory.'

'Attributed to the Second,' Sicarius concluded for him.

'Agemman's position would be tenuous after this.'

Sicarius's demeanour hardened instantly and he straightened as if insulted. 'I serve the Chapter and its glory, Daceus, as do we all.'

The veteran-sergeant bowed, reprimanded. 'Of course, captain. We are the inheritors of Guilliman. His legacy is the torch by which we light the darkness of the galaxy.'

'You sound like Elianu.'

'It is one of his sermons, or a part at least.' Several affirmation runes flashed up on Daceus's retinal display. 'The battle company is in position. We move out on your order.'

Sicarius donned his helmet. It clamped to his battle plate with a hiss of pressurisation. His voice was full of grit as it came through the vox-grille. 'Then make ready. Glory awaits us, brother. Guilliman is watching.'

CHAPTER ELEVEN

THE WATER FELT cold but it did nothing to revive Adanar as he splashed his face.

He was in the bombed-out ruins of ex-Commander Tarn's operations chamber. It looked quite different now from how it had been less than a year ago. Much of its super-structure was exposed, like the metal innards of some dying beast. The wounds from the necron gauss-artillery went deep. Parts of the chamber were little more than rubble. Blank map screens, thick with dust, reflected Adanar's grim face. He had aged twenty years since the invasion, or at least that was how it appeared to him.

Fresh water from the ice caverns below Kellenport's bed-rock was still being pumped into the facility and Adanar stood bent-backed over a dirty basin in the corner of the room. He surveyed it despairingly. Tarn's old desk was bro-ken, the two halves slumped in the centre where a chunk of debris from the ceiling had cracked it. Occasionally the walls shook – most of the paintings and tapestries had fallen and been crushed underfoot by the incessant necron bombardment. Statues of former nobles and Ark Guard officers, once standing proudly in alcoves around the chamber, lay shattered and discarded. *So much for glory now.*

An overwhelming weariness overtook him. The weight of it sank Adanar to the ground, one hand limply grasping the edge of the basin when he fell. Fumbling around in his uniform jacket, he found his service pistol and set it down on the floor. Then he unwound the chain from around his wrist and took the locket-charm in the palm of his left hand.

'How much more must I give?' he asked.

The two picts inside of his wife and child couldn't answer.

'Why didn't I flee? Why didn't I send you away?' The fingers of his right hand brushed against the laspistol's grip. 'Say I've done enough…'

He was abruptly aware of someone watching from the broken archway into the room. An ashen-faced Corporal Besseque was standing there staring.

'Commander Sonne?'

'What is it, Besseque?'

The corporal ventured a few steps into the chamber. 'Sir, the– Are you all right?'

Adanar growled at him, tucking his possessions away again and getting to his feet. 'Make your report.'

'The Space Marines have signalled they are in position.' He pulled a data-slate from the folds of his padded jacket. Besseque shivered as he did it – the water was still being piped in to the city but the heating was out. It was almost as cold as it was on the wall in the operations chamber. 'I have the dispositions here. Our defences are ready, sir.'

Adanar ignored the proffered data-slate. 'What good do you think they will do us, corporal?'

Besseque was genuinely confused. 'The Space Marines, sir. They are a cause for hope.'

'They cannot protect us.' Adanar's bile was really flowing now. All his grief, his sense of impotence and futility, it came out toxically. 'We cannot even protect ourselves.' The chamber was rocked by a close artillery impact outside but both men managed to keep their feet. Adanar slapped the wall where the dust and debris were still rolling downwards. 'What use are defences if our enemy can merely pass through them? What good are guns if our foes stand up again after we've killed them? What use is hope, Besseque, tell me that!'

Another tremor hit the chamber as the necron bombardment increased. A chunk of debris parted from the ceiling and struck Besseque across the forehead, preventing his reply.

As the corporal fell in a heap, Adanar picked himself up and ran to him.

'Besseque!'

A heavy contusion marred the corporal's forehead, spreading like a bloom of purple ink across his skin. The cut was only shallow. It left a thin trail of blood but Besseque was dead. An internal haemorrhage had killed him instantly. The data-slate he'd been carrying slipped tamely from his lifeless grasp.

Exasperated, Adanar sat down cross-legged next to the corpse. He laid one hand on Besseque's still chest. It was ridiculous. The horrors of the invasion, the bombardment – all the things the corporal had survived only to be killed by a chunk of rock, and not even a large chunk at that.

Adanar threw back his head and laughed. He laughed uproariously until his throat was dry and his eyes stung from the tears. All the while, the room shook and the necron guns thundered.

ADANAR MET RANCOURT on the stairwell. The acting lord governor was shadowed by Sergeant Kador, who looked less than thrilled with his posting.

'Commander Sonne,' he said, slightly tremulously, 'I am glad I've found you.'

Adanar moved past him and Rancourt went with him, walking at the commander's shoulder. 'What is it?'

'I have been trying to get a meeting with you. Your aide – Becket, is it? – was supposed to inform you.'

Adanar took the stairs two at a time. They led up to the battlements. He was making it deliberately difficult for the Imperial official. 'He's dead.'

Rancourt let out a little gasp. Adanar had to begrudgingly give him credit – he was keeping pace. 'Dead? The necrons killed him? Are they inside our defences?'

Adanar stopped halfway up the stairs and glared straight ahead. 'No, acting governor, he's back there.' He thumbed over his shoulder. 'A rock killed him.'

'A ro– A what?'

Adanar faced him. 'A piece of debris fell from the ceiling and he died.'

Rancourt peered upwards, as if expecting a similar fate.

'What did you want?' Adanar pressed.

When Rancourt saw the undisguised contempt in the commander's eyes, he reacted. 'Respect, firstly. I am an agent of the Imperium, the highest authority on this world. And I–'

'No,' Adanar replied flatly. 'You are not.'

Rancourt practically screeched at him, '*I am the lord governor!* I demand–'

Shaking his head, Adanar interjected. 'You are not. You are acting governor and your authority at this time is meaningless. I will grant you a guard detail, but your demands will not be met.'

Kador's face darkened further at the news.

Rancourt grasped the commander's lapels. 'Let the Adeptus Astartes fight. That is what they were made for. We should make all haste to the Crastia Shipyards and evacuate.'

Adanar looked down at Rancourt's scrawny fingers. He let the commander go.

'Secure your evacuation, you mean.'

Rancourt made a plaintive expression. 'As the lord gov– As the *acting* lord governor,' he corrected, 'I should, by Imperial dictate, be amongst the first, yes. But–'

'Look around you, Rancourt. Look at the skies. What do you think those tremors are that shake the walls? What are you listening to when the air booms? It's not thunder, not in any natural sense, anyway.' Adanar leaned in close. His alcohol breath wafted back at him. 'The necrons control the skies. They fill it with emerald death. Even if we could reach the Crastia Shipyards, even if they were still standing, we would not get off the ground. Our vessels would be destroyed before they even breached the upper atmosphere.'

Rancourt knew this. Despite his actions to the contrary, he wasn't a stupid man, just a desperate one. He seemed to shrink with the realisation that Adanar was telling the truth. His voice quivered like a child's. 'But I'm afraid...'

At first, Adanar regarded him with disgust – this was the

lord governor of Damnos, the one the people looked to for leadership – but then he only felt pity.

'We all are,' said the commander and carried on up the stairs.

'I HAVE NEVER fought beside an Angel before.'

Iulus's attention was focused on the battlements. His command was the second wall, the one farthest from Kellenport bastion, the heart of the last city on Damnos. The third was well mined and booby-trapped. He credited Commander Sonne – he had drilled his men well. They had marched from the western gate and assumed the positions on and around the walls as Iulus had instructed.

His keen eye for tactical dispositions picked out gunnery nests, heavy stubbers on pintle-mounts, bolter emplacements and lascannon at enfilading points around the wall. The lines of Ark Guard were not thick but they were steady and every man, woman and child capable of doing so carried a lascarbine, autogun or shotgun. The Damnosian armouries were bare. Everything they had was on the walls or in the courtyards and it was pointed at the killing-fields where the necrons would come. He had named the courtyard below Xiphos, on account of the fact he liked the weapon. It was a cutting, thrusting blade and in the Terran dialect meant 'penetrating light' or something close to that – he was no expert in translation. There had been overly much darkness and not enough light on Damnos. The name was a fitting one, he decided.

As if only just realising he'd spoken, Iulus raised an eyebrow at Falka. 'What did you say?'

The trooper was alongside him, part of the Ultramarine's retinue, his 'One Hundred'. 'I said: I've never fought beside an Angel before.'

Iulus returned to surveying the defences. 'I am not an Angel. I am a soldier, like you. Why must you humans constantly over-venerate?'

Falka laughed. It was a deep and wholly honest sound. 'Me, a soldier? No. I'm a rig-hand, a miner. Have been all my life.'

Iulus looked at him askance. 'Then you do a convincing impression of a soldier. I had not thought humans capable of such reckless courage as you showed. Do you crave death? I have witnessed men commit suicide in battle in similar circumstances to this.'

Falka shook his head. 'No. I want to live but think I will probably not, at least not for much longer. I lost... a friend, and I want my death to mean something so that her sacrifice will too.'

Iulus considered that before resuming his vigil.

'Those studs in your head,' said Falka a few seconds later. 'What are they for?'

Iulus touched the tips of the platinum studs with his gauntlet. He was almost reverent. 'They signify a century's service to the Chapter.'

Falka whistled. 'So, you're over two hundred years old?'

'Yes, though I have not really thought about it before.'

'Are you immortal, then?'

'No, I don't think so. Long-lived certainly, thanks to the gene-science of the Emperor, but not immortal.' Iulus kept his gaze ahead, as if drawing inspiration from the silent desolation of the killing-field. 'Ours is a violent calling. Death is an inevitable fact of our existence. I'm not sure if an Adeptus Astartes's mortality has ever been put to the test. I cannot think of one who has ever died of old age. That would be a failure of our warrior purpose, I think.'

Iulus angled his neck to look at him. 'You ask a lot of questions, human.'

'Just nervous, that's all,' Falka replied. 'We all are.'

Iulus took a moment to look around the battlements and the Courtyard of Xiphos below. Haunted faces came back at him, with hollow eyes and empty hearts. A revelation struck him. The defenders were not merely guns and bodies, they were people and within they had already lost the battle. He had mistaken fatalism for fortitude, acceptance for resolve.

'Trooper Kolpeck,' he said, still scanning the frightened crowds. 'How can I galvanise these men so they will fight for me as you did in the Courtyard of Chronus?'

Falka followed the Ultramarine's gaze as it swept the walls and ground below.

'Inspire them,' he said. 'Give them something to fight for.'

Now Iulus stared at the trooper, nonplussed. 'There is no greater honour than to serve the Emperor in battle, and die in His name.'

'We are a courageous people, proud too, but we have long been without hope.' Falka rubbed the hard stubble on his chin, seeking the right words. 'Tell a man enough times that all is lost and his world is doomed, and he'll start to believe it.'

As if prompted, the image of the Herald of Dismay flickered in the sky over Kellenport.

Heed the edicts of the necrontyr, your doom is at hand. Your efforts are in vain. Abandon this futile defence, abandon hope and the—

The heinous image vanished, consumed by an explosion that destroyed the invocation node from which it was being broadcast. There were dozens of others erected throughout Damnos but this one was the closest to Kellenport, within sight of its walls. A stunned silence greeted its demise.

Iulus handed the rocket-tube back to one of the conscripts on the battlements. They had precious little ammunition and a part of him, an old part, regretted the waste of materiel, but it was worth it.

'That's enough negative propaganda for one war,' he told Falka. 'Hand me the vox.'

A trooper carrying a boxy vox-caster scurried over to the cobalt giant who had turned to address the stunned masses. It crackled loudly and there was a squeal of static before Iulus's voice came through.

'I am Brother-Sergeant Iulus Fennion, of the Ultramarines Second Company. I am warrior-born, clad in the Emperor's metal, bearer of his wrath. You have been under the boot of your oppressors for too long. It ends. Here. Now. On these very walls. In this very courtyard. My brothers and I will bleed with you, and through blood will buy back your freedom. Do not surrender this world without a fight. Show these horrors that you wear the Emperor's metal too. Show them our faith will not be daunted.'

Iulus drew his chainsword. All of Kellenport, the warriors on the walls and in the Courtyard of Xiphos – his battle-brothers included – were listening.

'Damnos shall not yield.' His voice grew in stature and power. 'We shall not yield!' He thrust the blade aloft and everyone who heard him cheered. Their fear and anxiety, their long-held despair and heart-gnawing grief came out in a cathartic flood of noise. It resounded off the walls and the barricades. It was a call to arms, an affirmation of belief that they all had needed to hear.

'How was that?' he asked Falka when the noise had finally subsided.

He took the receiver-cup – a little dumbstruck – and gave it back to the trooper with the vox-caster. 'Stirring.'

Iulus looked stern as he about-turned to face the battle-field again. 'Good. Now I expect them to fight.'

WORDS, JUST WORDS. That was all they were. Even when spoken aloud and with purpose by an Angel of the Emperor, Adanar could not deny the fact. His faith had been crushed long ago under the tenement rubble that killed his wife and daughter.

He wanted to be uplifted, to believe there was anything else but death for the people of Damnos, but he couldn't.

Corporal Humis, his new aide, stepped into his peripheral vision. 'I can hear cheering.' He was standing at Adanar's shoulder and turned towards the commander. His face was full of hope. It could get a man killed, hope. It could hollow him from the inside out and he wouldn't realise he was dead until he dared to hope again. By then it was too late, he was already a walking corpse, a shadow waiting for some hell to claim him.

'It is just a false dawn, Humis, that's all.'

The corporal licked his lips. He'd been Adanar's aide for less than an hour. 'Perhaps a few words would steel the troops on this side of the wall. Perhaps a rousing speech–'

'There'll be no speeches. There'll be no hollow words.'

'But, commander... Why not?'

Adanar fixed him with a withering gaze, and as Humis looked into his dead eyes he understood.

'Because I won't lie to them, corporal. I won't lie.'

CHAPTER TWELVE

I<small>T HAD BEEN</small> aeons since the throne room had enjoyed attendance. It was a dust-clogged ruin now, its lustre dulled, its ostentation tarnished and decrepit.

Old statues lined the alcoves, clutching ancient glaives, their appearance skeletal and overly regal. Sickly luminescence emanated from the geometric sigils carved into the floor and walls, the chamber's only light source. Their emerald glow limned the throne. It was immense, set upon an oval dais and wrought of gold or some superior mineral compound that looked like gold. Rune-sigils marked its every surface.

Ankh toured the dilapidated halls and anterooms with an air of detachment. It did not surprise him that the Undying avoided this place now. It was a reminder of a long-dead age, of a former life. Sahtah bemoaned his loss of skin and blood like a crazed, hungry dog but he was not alone in that malady. It was an affliction that clawed at every

necron, at least those whose memory engrams still functioned with lucidity.

He flickered out of time for a moment, bending the
chronology of the universe and mocking its laws with
his advanced science. Ankh was back in the revivification
chambers again, the lowest catacombs this time.

Malady.

The forming of the word in his subconscious had brought
something to mind, something aberrant. He regarded the
humming caskets of the destroyers. This cancer, the one
which the destroyers represented, was everywhere amongst
the necrontyr. Ankh would have pitied them if he were
still capable of such an emotion. Nihilistic, fatalistic and
possessed of the conviction that their sole purpose was to
eradicate, the destroyers were a breed apart.

Madness flowed through their mechanised arteries, fed
the electric impulses of their cables and hard-wiring. This
was the fate of all necrons. They butchered their bodies,
removing limbs and replacing them with repulsor platforms, tesla beams and gauss-cannons – all the better to
destroy, all in the service of the destroyers' only creed:
annihilation.

Delusion was common, as was a false sense of pre-eminence.

It was at times like these, when confronted with the real-
ities of their existence and its potential corruptions, that
Ankh felt the necrontyr's fall most keenly.

Virus plagued them, more insidious than any disease
of mortal flesh. They had exchanged their humanity for
bodies of metal, their sinews for servos, their individual-
ity for servitude and base sentience. They had done all of
that and still they were not immune to corruption. Little
wonder that so many of Ankh's kind were angry or insane.

He would revive the destroyers soon.

Tens of thousands of caskets lined the catacombs. The tomb went deep into the world's heart and many levels were surrendered to the revivification chambers. Of all the constructs, the destroyers numbered the greatest. A dull glow emanated from every runic archway to every sarcophagus. To a non-machine mind the vista would be incomprehensible, stretching into infinity in all dimensions.

The role of the destroyers in this conflict was assured and predestined – he had already witnessed it with his own cold, dead eyes. Ankh just wanted to look upon them and remember the shared doom of his damned race.

Another flicker of chrono-dislocation brought him back to the throne room. His true business was here, now that he'd satisfied idle curiosity. The effect of translocating was disconcerting. It pulled at the strands of Ankh's sense of reality. For a moment, he tried to recall what this place was like before biotransference. But the images in his subconscious mind were far from vivid.

Despite the stability of his memory engrams, he found recollection a little difficult to come by sometimes. He was a master of the elements, a chronomancer, a phantasmal manipulator, a walker between universes, but still he could not always grasp the thread of his former existence. In fact, the more he tried the more it unravelled until he realised his grip on the days before the long sleep was eroding, inexorably.

He regarded a cracked mirror of polished jet along one of the walls. Faces swarmed in and out of focus within its reflective surface. It was not Ankh, nor was it several beings. Rather, it was just one, trapped inside the stone a fraction out of time like the cryptek in his speculum. Ankh liked this particular torture most of all.

He uttered, 'Awaken.' It was more than just a word; it was a command, a mechanical imperative that put balefires in the eyes of the statue-guardians. The lych-like creatures arrayed through the hall came jerkily to life. Rimes of filth cracked open as their slow-moving joints stirred. Dust motes spilled from their servos and webs of gossamer parted from their cabling like torn funerary shrouds.

'We serve the royarch,' they chimed as one.

Standing in the centre of the hall, within the protective cordon of a ceramic sigil-totem inscribed in the floor, Ankh was surrounded.

He bowed. 'I am the Architect, the royarch's vassal and extension of his will.'

The guards did not react. Instead they stood with their pole-armed glaives straight against their armoured bodies, pommel down against the floor.

'Your apotheosis is at hand,' Ankh declared. He drew a portal with his staff in which a vision of Damnos was projected. It showed the walls of Kellenport, occupied by the fleshed and their genebred saviours. 'Our world is overrun and the royarch calls you to war.'

One of the lych-like guards stepped forward. He wore a circlet of tarnished gold around his forehead and his shoulder guards were cracked pieces of super-hardened ceramic – this was the leader. He raised his war-glaive and cut through the portal-image, banishing it.

His eyes flared with millennia-old anger. 'We obey.'

LARGO LISTENED TO the wind as he kept vigil over Renatus. His wounded battle-brother was deep into sus-an membrane coma now and would not easily be revived. It was a regenerative measure, triggered in extremis when a Space Marine was so badly injured that he could fight no further. Much of Renatus's armour had been removed so he could be examined properly. His power generator, helmet and plastron were nearby, laid out reverently by Herdantes. There were blade marks in the ceramite, as long and thick as one of Largo's gauntleted fingers. They were a killer's marks, aimed for the weak points and targeting vital organs. Renatus had survived by virtue of being Adeptus Astartes, but only barely.

Largo hadn't witnessed what happened in the gorge but suspected it was bad. Herdantes was on the other side of the tent, lost in shadow and catalepsean sleep. Another hour and it would be Largo's turn. The other Ultramarine hadn't spoken about the ambush. There'd been little time and too much blood. Brakkius had left the tent earlier, in need of air and an opportunity to stretch his injured leg.

Outside the medi-tent, the storm was building. Largo didn't like it. He didn't like being stuck in this camp with the humans and so far away from the rest of their battle group. He didn't blame Scipio. He was Largo's sergeant, as brave and resourceful a Space Marine as he'd ever known, but there was no denying the necrons had them reeling. He wanted, bitterly, to strike a blow.

'I will watch him,' said the medic. His name was Holdst, a man of middling human years but with a world-weary air that made him hunch. 'If you need to rest, like your comrade.' He glanced at Herdantes.

'I need no rest. I am a Space Marine.' It came out harder than Largo had intended, but he wasn't sufficiently moved to apologise.

'Of course,' said Holdst. He'd been washing the blood off his hands and carried a pinkish rag that he used to dry his fingers. 'There's nothing further I can do for him, though.'

'I understand. The Chapter thanks you for doing your duty to the Emperor.'

Holdst lingered and set down the rag.

Largo looked at him.

'There is more?'

'This was my world that has become a wasteland. I had a family, a life. I am angry too.'

For a human, Holdst was remarkably perceptive. Largo was about to respond when Holdst turned around at a noise behind him. It was hard to see what had got the medic's attention, the tent was poorly lit and his body was in the way.

'Fuge?' he said at first, then, 'Merciful Thro–'

Four blades punched through Holdst's back and lifted the medic off his feet. His legs were already spasming as the thing wearing Fuge's face stepped into the tent and the light. Largo was up, his bolter loose.

'Herdantes!'

The other Ultramarine snapped awake and armed himself.

Twin muzzle flares tore open the darkness, filling it with fire and noise.

Poor Holdst was shredded. The man was already dead when Largo and Herdantes opened up at the ghoul inside the tent with them. Bolter shells exploded against its tough carapace but failed to slow it. The creature sprang, its body swathed in bloodied flesh flayed from one of the sentries, and landed on the bench supporting Renatus.

Largo drew his gladius, afraid he'd hit Renatus if he kept on shooting. In his peripheral vision, he saw Herdantes turn and spray wide as another flayed one ripped through the tent lining and came scurrying inside. The blast pitched the necron off its feet but it was followed by another and another.

Largo kept going. Renatus was in danger. A fifth creature emerged on his flank and he was forced to engage. A swipe of his gladius parried its talons wide of the mark, leaving them to scrape the ceramite of his greave, before Largo triggered his bolter point-blank and blew a hole in the flayed one's torso.

'Herdantes. Our brother!'

Seeing the danger, Herdantes was moving. He punched one necron in the jaw, stunning it, before bounding onto the slab where Renatus slumbered. The necron crouching over the wounded Ultramarine was different to the others. There was a gleam of malicious sentience in its eyes and its trappings were more elaborate.

'*Fleeessshhh…*'

It hissed at Herdantes. Its teeth were gummed with blood and viscera. There wasn't time to lift a gladius as a swipe of the necron's talons ripped Herdantes's armour open and sent him sprawling.

Largo reacted to his brother's cry of pain and converged on Renatus. But he was too late to stop the creature lopping off Renatus's head and bathing in the bloody fountain projected from his neck stump.

'No!'

A flayed one tried to stop him, but Largo rammed his gladius into its neck all the way to the hilt. A second he gunned down with the last of his ammunition, before discarding both weapons and leaping for Renatus's slayer, his hands curled into strangling claws.

The creature wearing Fuge's face punched both talons into Renatus's lifeless body, hoisted the dead Space Marine onto its back and, pumping its legs, sprang through the roof and out into the night.

Largo's fingers closed on air and he cursed again.

Herdantes had been finishing off the last of the flayed ones in the medi-tent but saw what happened. There was something akin to fear in his voice. 'It will defile him...'

Largo roared through clenched teeth, took up his fallen bolter and ran outside into the storm.

THE CAMP WAS in chaos. Screaming merged with sporadic las-fire, half heard through the wind, as Scipio rushed from Jynn's command tent and realised they were under attack.

He tapped the comm-feed in his ear, scanning the darkness for threats. 'Brothers! Thunderbolts! Report!'

Cator's voice, crackling with the weather interference, came through first. 'Something got through the gate... went under... everywhere... Engaging!' Percussive bolter fire cut him off. Scipio saw the muzzle flashes in the distance. Several more came from the direction of the medi-tent and he was torn.

'Largo!' he shouted down the feed. Silhouettes crossed his vision, the guerrillas were running back and forth as they struggled to fight an enemy they couldn't see. Scipio almost shot one of them on reflex. 'Captain Evvers,' he called behind him. 'Marshal your troops before my brothers and I cut them down by mistake.' She was on the vox in her tent, trying to find out what was happening.

Her reply was cut off by the voice of Largo, loud and urgent in Scipio's ear. 'It's got Renatus! It cut off his head, sergeant. It took him.'

First Naceon then Ortus and now Renatus – this war is exacting a heavy toll.

Scipio crouched in the lee of another tent. The tripod

guns had started rattling. Someone was panicking. 'Largo, repeat. You're not making sense.'

'It took him,' said Largo – his breathing was hard, he was running and angry. 'I'm getting him back.'

A skin-draped horror emerged from the gloom before him and Scipio realised at last what was attacking the camp.

He ran at the flayed one, thumbing the activation rune of his chainsword.

There was a hollow *prang* and a cascade of sparks rained down onto the snow as blade met talon but Scipio would not be denied. He aimed a punch at the creature's neck, followed by a blow that cut through its clavicle and severed a clutch of cabling. It crumpled and Scipio finished it. Instant phase-out told him he'd done it right.

Jynn Evvers came running up beside him. She was armed and kitted out for a sudden departure. 'We're overrun.'

Scipio's eyes were on the darkness. 'They're here for us.' Shadows cast in the camp's portable floodlights swivelled in all directions. It was like trying to catch smoke. A dozen gun battles were happening at once but most of the guerrillas were firing at shadows. Or each other.

Jynn sounded rueful. 'I know.'

Before Scipio could respond, Brakkius joined them. His cooling meltagun suggested he'd had a recent encounter.

'Necrons have tunnelled into the camp and bypassed the sentries.'

'How many?'

Brakkius shook his head. 'Hard to tell. Could be as many as twenty, possibly more.' He clapped the stock of his weapon. 'I took out two, but there are skirmishes breaking out everywhere.'

'Have you seen Largo or Herdantes?'

'No. I went back to the medi-tent but they were already gone.' He met Jynn's questioning gaze. 'I'm sorry, but your medic is dead.'

Her face tightened into a hard line as she suppressed the grief. That wouldn't serve her now.

Brakkius focused his attention back on his sergeant.

'We can't mount an effective counter-attack in these conditions. What are your orders, sir?'

Nodding, Scipio said, 'Signal the squad, all Thunderbolts to regroup at the command tent.' He turned to Jynn. 'Your men, too, Captain Evvers. Bring them all here, what's left of them. We're falling back.'

Scipio broke into a run, away from the command tent.

'Sir, where are you going?' asked Brakkius.

He looked over his shoulder, his face determined. 'After Largo. He'll ignore the order. He wants revenge for Renatus.'

'How do you know?'

'Because it's what I'd do.'

'Wait!' Brakkius pulled a spare bolt clip from his belt and threw it over.

Scipio caught it, nodded and ran off into the night. The snowfall thickened in his wake, smothering him from sight as if he'd never even been there.

Brakkius raised the others on the comm-feed.

SCIPIO'S BLOOD WAS up. He was crouched low against the wind, using the falling snow to mask his advance through the camp, but all he really wanted to do was unleash his anger. One clip, given up by Brakkius, was all he had – that, his chainsword and his gladius – he'd need to make every one count.

He headed for the medi-tent, hoping to pick up on

Largo's trail. The camp was relatively small and should have been easy to navigate but the battle was spilling over its borders into the mountains beyond and the weather conditions were impeding even his superhuman senses. The guerrilla fighters had trained in this arctic waste, they'd fought and survived the environs but even so they would be blind in this blizzard. Their screaming punctuated Scipio's every thought. He blocked it out, focused on finding Largo.

Can't lose another. Not this way.

The medi-tent was empty, aside from the carnage. Even the medic's corpse was gone, though Scipio discerned bloody drag marks in the snow.

What kind of automatons are these things?

He found Herdantes a few metres away. He was slumped against a rock, veiled in snow and holding his ruined chest so his organs stayed inside.

'Brother-sergeant,' he rasped. The frozen air from Herdantes's mouth was blood-flecked, suggesting internal bleeding. Even his Larraman cells were struggling to form clots. 'Opened me up,' he continued, moving his hand for a few seconds to show the red crater in his torso. 'But I killed it, sent it back to whatever hell spawned it.'

Scipio wasn't sure what that place was or if the necrons could even *be* killed. He knelt beside Herdantes, assessing the damage. 'Where's Largo?'

Herdantes went to speak but the blood in his throat only gurgled. He pointed to the darkness just outside the camp instead. It was north, deeper into the mountain range. Scipio narrowed his gaze and made out the jagged silhouette of a frozen peak.

'Are you armed?'

Herdantes nodded wearily. His breath was coming out

205

in ragged gasps. Patting the bolter on his lap was difficult.
'Half a clip.'

'Use them wisely. I'll return,' Scipio promised. A group of
guerrilla fighters appeared out of the blizzard and he waved
them over. 'Get him up, regroup at the command tent.'

The storm was so loud, the humans just nodded.

Scipio left them and headed for the jagged peak.

LARGO WAS HUNKERED down behind a cluster of snow-caked
boulders, staring into a sheer-sided rock face above. He
glanced over at Scipio as he crouched next to him.

'It's up there,' he whispered, nodding to the fathomless
darkness.

The blizzard was getting worse. It made following Largo's gesture almost impossible.

'I see nothing,' Scipio hissed.

'It's there. It's got Renatus. Look...' Largo unclasped his
bolter's targeter and gave it to the sergeant.

Scipio lined the crosshairs over a plateau above. The
night-vision scope picked out the shoulders and spines of
massive rocks in the darkness. He tweaked a dial on the
sight to heat-tracking. A muffled red shape resolved as the
image went from hazy green to grainy blue. It was moving. There was another shape in front of it, though its red
glow was less vibrant.

Renatus. Scipio suspected the dead Ultramarine's generator was providing most of the heat trace.

'It took his head, brother-sergeant. Tore it off in front
of me.'

Scipio scanned the area through the targeter. A chasm
fell away a few metres beyond the boulders, explaining
why Largo had given up pursuit. A fragile ice escarpment

led to the edge of the precipice which was thorned with dagger-like crags.

He brought the crosshairs back up to the plateau again, gauging the distance the necron had climbed. The fact they were capable of such feats surprised him. 'Where is your squad, brother?' Scipio asked.

Largo was nonplussed.

'Where are your brothers?'

Largo looked behind at the snow-shrouded encampment.

Scipio still had his eye on the plateau. Something was happening. 'We cannot indulge in personal vengeance, Largo.'

'Renatus–'

The sergeant cut him off. 'Is dead. But the rest of your battle-brothers still live. We're– *Move!*'

Scipio dropped the targeter and thrust Largo aside as the necron landed between them. It had vaulted the chasm.

Both Space Marines were on their feet quickly with weapons drawn.

'Circle it!' Scipio shouted. He began strafing along the necron's flank, drawing its gaze, as Largo went the other way to blindside the monster.

It tracked Scipio's movements, like an alpha predator tracks a threat. Scipio levelled his chainsword, but kept the movement slow. His bolt pistol was at his side, ready.

It was a *ghoul*, this thing. Ropes of skin clung to its skeletal form and great tranches of flesh swathed its back, fashioned into a cape or robes. Blood crusted its muzzle and thicker visceral fluids drooled through the cavities in its structure, hanging off cables and congealing over wires. Its face was the most disturbing aspect of its appearance, for it was a mask of flesh. The human called Fuge had been butchered for his skin and this creature had taken his face whole, robbed the man of the only thing left to him in death – his identity. Even so, the mask was breaking, stretched too thinly across the necron's gruesome visage, and patches of gore-streaked metal showed through. As the flayed one glared at him, Scipio saw a piece of chewed skin tear and fall to the ground.

'A *face*...' It spoke with sepulchral madness, trembling with anguish. '*I had a face. Give me my face*...'

Scipio realised it wanted *his* face or anyone's. It was the only reason it had jumped from its perch. It had decapitated Renatus and lost his face. Now the wretched creature wanted another.

Only Scipio's psycho-conditioning stopped him balking in terror.

Largo could wait no longer. He'd drawn his gladius – with only the necron between them, he might hit Scipio with his bolter – and leapt at the creature.

With viperous dexterity, the flayed one parried the blow and stabbed Largo in the shoulder. It drew a shout of pain from the Ultramarine.

Scipio launched his attack a second later before the necron could injure Largo further.

Again, the creature moved with preternatural swiftness, coiling its body around to slash at the brother-sergeant. The talons missed Scipio's neck by a finger-width and he stepped back, warding off the monster with a chainsword thrust. It smacked the weapon aside, chain-teeth spitting sparks but doing little else.

Largo attacked again, slowed by his wound. He managed to land a blow on the necron's shoulder but it *pranged* off as if striking adamantium. The resulting shockwave ran up Largo's arm and into his shoulder, numbing it.

'*Flesh…*' A jagged wound ripped open Largo's face, drooling blood.

The blizzard was worsening and enveloped the combatants in a swirling maelstrom.

Scipio's shout was almost robbed by the wind. 'It's not working. Follow me, brother.' He peeled off from the attack, making for the escarpment.

'What are you doing?' asked Largo, taking off after Scipio.

'Do you trust my judgement, brother?'

'You are my sergeant.'

That was all the answer Scipio needed.

Behind them, the necron turned. Despite its fluidity in combat, when not under imminent threat its insanity seemed to slow it down. It took a few seconds to realise its prey was running, then it sprang into the air with a dense crunch of servos and landed on the boulders, squat like a skeletal gargoyle.

'*Flesh…*' it hissed, filled with a terrible yearning. '*I need it…*'

Backing slowly towards the escarpment, Scipio could feel the ice cracking under his weight. This was no ordinary necron, he realised. It was one of the masters, a superior construct. Within a few seconds of the engagement, Scipio knew the chances of the two of them defeating it were slight.

'*When an enemy seems unbeatable, do not attack it head-on.*' The sage words of Telion came back to him. '*Instead, devise another strategy that turns its strength into a weakness and balances the odds.*'

It was massive, a hulking monster of a necron. Judging by its size and the strength behind its blows, Scipio reasoned it probably weighed more than him and Largo combined. He remembered how it had leapt from the plateau, the power in its servos, and saw the raw need in its eyes to take their skin.

'Are you ready, Largo?'

They were barely a half-metre from the edge where the escarpment curled like a clenched finger and was at its weakest.

Largo nodded.

The flayed lord's shoulders were heaving up and down with the movement of its chest. It had no lungs, no way of dragging air into its body even if it needed to. It was emulating a remembered behaviour.

Scipio was reminded of a rabid dog. He'd holstered his bolt pistol, and pulled out his gladius as he called to it. 'You want our faces,' he said, drawing a shallow cut across his cheek with the blade. 'Come and take them.'

The flayed lord threw back its head, emitting a shriek of machine-noise, and sprang off the boulders.

Scipio waited until it reached the apex of its jump and then shouted to Largo. 'Now!'

The Ultramarines threw themselves aside a split second before the necron crashed down in their wake. It whirled around when it realised its prey had gone, skin-robes flecking the snow with blood and matter.

Cracks veined the ice, but the escarpment held.

Largo had rolled onto his back. 'It's not breaking!'

'Give it some encouragement,' Scipio bellowed.

Largo unleashed his bolter against the cracking ice. The effect was instantaneous.

A massive chunk of the escarpment sheared away from the rock face and took the flayed lord with it. Their last image of the creature was its hellish eyes, blazing, thwarted.

Largo got up and punched the air. 'Ha! Bastard!'

Scipio grabbed his shoulder. 'Now we go.'

Both gave a last look to the plateau where Renatus's head-less corpse was lying unmourned, without honour. The destruction of the flayed lord would have to do as tribute.

Then they ran back towards the camp and the command tent where Scipio hoped the rest of his squad were waiting.

THE SUN WAS warm against his tanned skin. It felt good to be out in the mountains, alone and unshadowed. Sahtah couldn't remember the last time he'd been climbing, he couldn't remember…

He couldn't remember…

…*Anything.*

Reality came crashing back like a cold wave. The sensory illusion faded and he was clinging to the rock face again, his talons lodged in the sheer-sided wall of the mountain. Sahtah had been broken for a moment, but his mechor-ganic body had healed him. He blinked, though it was an android interface rather than a physical one – he had long since surrendered his eyelids. Even during the long sleep he had not closed them. His awareness during those aeons had been fleeting, confusing, as if he were only partially alive and a passenger in someone else's body.

He didn't know how far he'd fallen but the ice-gorge was dark and deep. The spines of rocks scraped and broke against his body. His robes were being torn. Sahtah moaned, climbing faster, but the damage only worsened. A false sense of urgency filled him. He wanted to be out of the chasm and back amongst the peaks. Reaching the lip of rocky plateau, he pulled himself up and found the feast he had left behind.

It had no face.

Sahtah wanted a face. The one he wore now was virtually gone; his robes were in tatters too. He regarded the semi-armoured carcass lying in front of him.

It would have to do.

When he saw the glistening ribbons that bound it, the redness inside, the pallor of its succulent organs, he was overcome. Like the ghoul he knew he was but inwardly reviled, Sahtah sprang onto the corpse and continued to feed. And as the red matter inside splashed across his borrowed face and drizzled down the cage of his ribs and amassed in his joints, he was visited by such horrific visions.

Flesh palaces resolved in his ancient mind, infinite realms devoted to the skin. Corpses hung from hooks and ringed the vaulted ceilings on chains like gruesome chandeliers. Blood ran in rivers, thick with viscera and carrying chunks of bone. Piles of offal, threads of muscle and intestine formed incarnadine sculptures that decked the stinking halls. And everywhere the feast of the flayers went on indefinitely, lost to madness, lost to flesh.

Sahtah threw back his head and emitted a keening that reverberated around the mountains. It signalled his desire, his terrible anguish and the certain knowledge that he was damned.

In the distance his slaves heard the call of the master and echoed it.

'WHY HAVE THEY stopped fighting?'

Across the encampment, the flayed ones had shuddered to an abrupt halt. As one, they squatted in the dirt and growled – a dirge of machine-noise that hurt Jynn's ears.

Only the Space Marines seemed unaffected. The one

Scipio had called Brakkius was standing stock-still and peering into the darkness. He moved at some unseen disturbance ahead – Jynn had no idea what – and signalled to the others who had recently joined them.

'Is it Scipio?' she asked.

Brakkius regarded her as a disapproving mentor would his student. His eyes were two ovals of blood-red. '*Brother-Sergeant* Vorolanus is still absent.'

Clearly the cobalt giant didn't approve of first name familiarity.

'Who then?'

Jynn's question was answered when three of her guerrillas emerged from the blizzard supporting one of the Ultramarines. His injuries looked bad but he was walking, albeit with help.

'Herdantes…' There was an edge to Brakkius's voice, an undercurrent of suppressed anger that frightened her. She also felt something else at the sight of the stricken Space Marine.

She realised it was anxiety.

For Scipio.

At Brakkius's command, two Ultramarines went to their wounded comrade and took his weight off Jynn's men. The three guerrillas looked exhausted when they finally reached her.

'The metal-heads are no longer killing us,' said Sia. She had a small cut on her forehead and the arm of her jacket was slashed, but otherwise she was unharmed.

'Glad you made it,' said Jynn, exchanging a brief embrace with all three of them. Of the twenty-four guerrillas she'd started with at sun-up that day, only nine remained before the night was out. Doc Holdst was amongst the tally of the dead. It was hard to be grateful for anything when confronted with such wasteful loss.

Jynn turned to Brakkius. His attention was on the Space Marines dragging the one called Herdantes to the command tent. 'We need to move. My people, or what's left of them, are all here.'

Brakkius didn't bother to look at her. 'Mine are not.'

She tugged on his vambrace to get his attention. It was like trying to move a mountain. Brakkius didn't shift. Jynn went on anyway. 'Look, those monsters have stopped for whatever reason. Maybe they're fallible after all and there's a malfunction in their wiring or something – I don't care. I've lost nearly two-thirds of my people and the rest of us won't last much longer once those metal-heads come around again. We have to move!'

This time Brakkius met her gaze. It was impossible to tell through the lenses of his battle-helm but she hoped there might have been a measure of respect in his eyes. He held her gaze for a few seconds before looking back at the darkness.

Another Space Marine approached him and stopped by his side. 'Herdantes is badly wounded.' He glanced at Jynn. 'The human is right, we must leave this place.'

'I won't leave him, Cator. You go – lead the others back to Lord Tigurius if you can. I'm staying.'

Brakkius resumed his vigil.

In the end, Cator didn't have to decide. Two more cobalt giants came running through the blizzard.

Jynn recognised Scipio – the other one she'd heard him call Largo.

Now they could go.

'I'm pleased you're alive, Jynn Evvers,' said Scipio upon reaching the command tent.

'So am I.' It was a truthful answer at least. She was about to say more when the low growl emitted by the dormant flayed ones grew into a shrieking cacophony. Several of Jynn's men were sick, some wept openly. It took all of her resolve not to break down too.

'What is it?' she asked, her hands pressed to her ears.

Scipio exchanged a knowing look with Largo and said, 'Time for us to leave.'

He recognised that sound and as they fled back down the mountain, headed for what she assumed was an army of Space Marines somewhere below, she heard Largo mutter to himself.

'It's not dead.'

CHAPTER THIRTEEN

FEAR SATURATED DAMNOS. It permeated its air, its rock and ate away at its people like a cancer. Their screams, their plaintive moaning, their abject grief was an urgent throb at the back of the Librarian's mind.

Tigurius was a supreme psyker, the most accomplished of his Chapter, perhaps of any Chapter. There were others with power, of course: hooded Ezekiel, enigmatic Vel'cona, dreaded Mephiston. All were masters of their art but Tigurius was of the Ultramarines, the purest of all Space Marines, and his abilities were prodigious. Even so, he struggled to find a path through the necron shroud and the fear they propagated.

His mind had touched that of the necrons. It found only infinite darkness and endless hate. There was something buried in that well of nothingness, a warning; he felt certain of it. Without knowing why, he realised it was important and that by not seeking the truth of that vision he would be allowing some heinous evil to pass. Tigurius had fortified himself, performed the many rituals and psychic mantras designed to steel his mind against any potential aggressors. The Herald was strong, far more potent than he had first realised. Tigurius resolved that this time he would be prepared.

Inscribed in the ice with the pommel of his force staff were three concentric rings. Double-banded, he had also wrought sigils of warding and aversion to bind them together. Tigurius crouched down in the centre, his eyes closed, and tried to ride the darkling waves of his subconscious.

Everlasting night filled his mind, the fearful voices of the humans pushed to the fringes and no longer a distraction. He went deeper and fashioned a psychic beacon that he attached around the Hood of Hellfire like a halo. Still, the darkness would not yield. Landscapes resolved below him as he soared across Damnos as a mental projection of himself. It was grey and bland, the life had left it.

Was this a vision of the future? Was he witnessing their ultimate failure?

Something glowed up ahead and Tigurius soared towards it. Psychic winds buffeted him, tried to throw him off course and dash him against the rising mountains on either side. He renewed his efforts, making his body into an arrow that sliced the air apart and cut through the tempest.

For a moment, a tiny light shone below him but it was fleeting and quickly snuffed out. The glow ahead intensified, turning from a phosphorescent white into a sickly emerald. Too late, Tigurius realised the danger he was in and tried to flee. The light became a blazing green orb that reached for him with the tendrils of its light.

One caressed the Librarian's arm and pain, hot and incandescent, fed into his body. His heart was thundering, a dull ache filled his head and a keening wail deafened his thoughts.

Must return…

All his efforts were focused on getting back but something was stretching the psychic landscape below, reshaping it so the distance became light years instead of leagues. Behind him, the baleful sun rose further and its tendrils grew with its influence.

They lashed at the Librarian like the appendages of some ocean-borne beast, a kraken or leviathan of old. Tigurius was forced to weave and pinwheel and dart as the sparrow eludes the eagle. Though he had not moved from his chosen spot since the vigil began, he still felt the physical exertion of his efforts. Mind and body were concomitant aspects of most beings – one affected the other. At that moment as he angled through the mental sky, his mind was being put to the sternest test and it visited that self-same tension upon his body.

Back at his vigil point, Tigurius had blood in his mouth and a tremor in his limbs.

Maintain focus…

Below, grey mountains and cities became monuments of emerald and obelisks of necron devotion and servitude.

Death…

The wind promised a certain end should he let the green light touch him.

Only light can outrun light and in so doing bend the laws of time. That revelation prompted a response. Tigurius fashioned his arrowing form into a beam, pure and focused and so thin it left the baleful sun in its wake. The crouching form of his physical body loomed before him, solace for his mind at last.

Tigurius came to swathed in a feverish sweat. It took a moment to regulate his breathing, another to ensure he had awakened in the physical world and this reality he inhabited was not merely verisimilitude.

The vision was beyond his grasp. It lay behind the emerald sun and the Herald was preventing him from seeing it. With that obstacle alone, Tigurius might have triumphed but, combined with the darkness shroud, it was near impossible. He did witness something, however. The snuffed-out light – it was a glimpse of the future. Prescience was guiding him to something, some event yet to transpire. It must be close; otherwise he would not have seen it. Somehow, the keening he had heard was a component of that possible future.

Like the vision, he knew deep down that it was important. That he must act. Though his limbs protested, Tigurius got to his feet and let his instincts pull him. The mountains beckoned. Drifts that had yet to fall upon the lower regions swathed the peaks in a storm. He headed upwards, leaving his battle-brothers behind. They were deep in the valley, monitoring the Thanatos Hills. Urgency governed the Librarian's step – there was no time to summon the other Ultramarines, no time at all.

PRAXOR ADVANCED THROUGH the ruins slowly and carefully. He crushed something underfoot and looked down.

It was a bent piece of flat metal, frozen solid and cracked down the middle. Frost-edged letters were described on it in Gothic script.

'Arcona City,' said Etrius. His voice was low and sombre as if he were touring a mausoleum.

In many respects, he was.

Praxor assembled the fractured letters into a more mean-ingful arrangement and nodded. Kellenport really was the last human bastion on Damnos.

The Ultramarines line was well dispersed. Each of the cobalt giants kept a wary eye on the way ahead, watching the ruins for hidden threats. According to reports, too many had already fallen to necron ambush. Sicarius led from the front, as he always did, his Lions of Macragge alongside him. The stretched battle line was a deliberate strategy from the captain. Not only did it make it easier for the Ultramarines to pick their way through the rough ground, they'd also present a harder target for the mass fire of the necrons. Once the storm hit, it would present the illusion that a larger force was arrayed against them too. Engagement would happen soon, but they kept the pace even so Atavian and Tirian could keep up.

The Devastator squads occupied one end of the line. Heavy bolters and plasma cannons were low-slung on their cumbersome rigs. Too weighty for a human to bear alone, the Space Marines hefted them with relative ease. The missile launchers and lascannons, being shoulder-mounted, were pointed down and steadied by the gunner's other hand. Ponderous but implacable, the Dreadnoughts marched with the Devastators. Their cannons were simply a part of their bodies, whirring and auto-targeting as they scanned the immediate area. As soon as battle was joined, these heavy guns would close ranks and present a concentrated volley of fire to hold the necrons' attention.

Just as Sicarius had predicted, the storm was rolling in. It began a half-kilometre back, the incessant ice flurries getting thicker and faster by the minute. There came a sweeping veil of finer snow in their wake, fogging the air and veneering the forlorn ruins still further.

Praxor moved on. 'Tactica briefings suggest there was a garrison here at the start of the war,' he said to Aristaeus down the comm-feed.

'There was... before the city was left to rot in the wake of necron victory. Look at the earth banks around the ruins, brother-sergeant.'

Praxor did. What he had initially mistaken for emplacements and earthworks, he now saw for what they truly were. Fused by ice to the very bulwarks they were sworn to protect were hundreds upon hundreds of Guardsmen, frozen forever in the moments of their deaths.

The necrons had turned this once proud Imperial city into a bombed-out mess. It was a grim place now, inhabited by ghosts and their terrified memories. Had he been anything other than Adeptus Astartes, Praxor might have quailed at this realisation.

'Apparently, Arcona was once a key city on Damnos,' added Aristaeus.

Praxor's mood was as cold as the weather. 'Looks like every other ruin on this hollow world.'

They were making steady progress across a roadway that had suffered least in the bombardment. Only part of its surface was cratered and it was still navigable. The quiet gave Praxor too much time with his thoughts. Even the thickening snowfall failed to smother them and he railed against the doubts plaguing him.

I am Adeptus Astartes. I am without fear, unaffected by doubt!

His misgivings weren't so easily silenced, though. Captain Sicarius was an incredible warrior, the greatest Praxor had known. In his presence, a warrior of Ultramar felt invincible, became capable of feats even a Space Marine would think impossible. He had... an *aura* about him that was undeniable. Yet he was relentless, even reckless. Heedless of casualties or cost, he would pursue his plans and vendettas until they were achieved or he was dead. In a perverse way, it was this obsessive, mercurial nature that made him the hero he was. It was also why he garnered voices of dissent within the Chapter.

Praxor was torn. He had not believed he'd ever think this way, but here on Damnos... this was beyond what the Second had ever faced before. He was not superstitious but Praxor couldn't deny the sense of foreboding that was building steadily within him. He didn't like the sensation; it felt almost treasonous.

Less able to pick their way through the denser rubble, the Dreadnoughts had shifted position in the battle line to walk along the roadway. It brought Agrippen close to Praxor and he nodded to the ancient warrior when he joined them.

Ahead, the Lions grew distant as they forged off with their captain. Sicarius was ever eager to be the first to battle and kept a close counsel with his command squad. Save for Argonan, who had died in the landings, he had yet to lose a single one of his chosen Ultramarines.

'They are a breed apart from the rest of us.' It came out more ruefully than Praxor had intended.

'And yet you aspire to join their ranks.'

Praxor glanced at Agrippen but the hulking Dreadnought was unreadable. The words simply emerged from his vox-speakers as fact. 'No. I am proud to serve as the sergeant of the Shieldbearers. It is my honour and oath to the Chapter.'

'I don't doubt it, brother. But I know your service record. You and the Shieldbearers are almost always leading the line, the first into any engagement, always at the forefront of our assaults. Some of a more cynical nature might suggest you were trying to prove something.'

Insulted, Praxor's voice took on a hard edge that he was careful to monitor in the face of the venerable Agrippen. 'Only my unswerving loyalty and dedication to the Ultramarines.'

'Do you think that is in question, brother?'

'Is this really the time for such a conversation, on the cusp of battle as we are?'

'Tell me of a better time to discuss honour and courage than before going into war against our enemies,' said Agrippen. 'But you are avoiding my question.'

Praxor left a long pause. He did not find the answer easy. 'Perhaps. There are times when I have questioned.'

'At Ghospora, a campaign over a century old.' It was a statement, not a suggestion.

'You of all of us, venerable one, should know that time is immaterial when concerning matters of honour.'

'Aye, I do. It displeased you that your captain left you behind?'

'It stunned and humbled me,' Praxor admitted. 'It felt as if I were being punished, though I did not know why.'

'Humility is as important a lesson as learning how to wield a gladius properly or fight in a squad with your brothers.'

Praxor nodded and saw the wisdom in the Dreadnought's words.

The roadway was coming to an end. They were deep into Arcona City now and the drifts were coming down in swathes. Even through the blizzard, Praxor could see the necron phalanxes manoeuvring to intercept them. It wouldn't be long.

'Before we go to battle, I must ask you something, Agrippen,' Praxor said, voicing his mind as he had wanted to since they'd made planetfall.

'Speak. I shall answer if I can, brother.'

'Are you here to watch for Agemman's interests? Is what they say in the senate true?'

'As all should do, I serve the Chapter alone and my Lord Calgar.' Agrippen was stern but there was no hint of reproach in his modulated diction. 'I possess the wisdom of centuries and all I see are two great heroes, dissimilar in method but equal in courage and honour.'

'In the senate, I have heard talk from Agemman's ambassadors of Sicarius overreaching himself.'

'He is daring and innovative,' Agrippen conceded.

'But there is concern that this will go too far and of the consequences when it does.'

'And how does our Lord Calgar respond to such concerns?'

'He is not present. His voice is absent from proceedings.'

'And what does that tell you, brother?'

Humbled again in the time it takes to field-strip a bolter, Praxor decided he would speak less to Dreadnoughts in future. Their logic was as redoubtable as their armoured bodies. 'That I should not listen to Chapter politics.'

'And what do you think, Praxor Manorian? Do you think Cato Sicarius, your captain, overreaches himself?'

Praxor's gaze went to the Lions out of reflex. Sicarius was as fine a warrior and a captain as there was in the Chapter. Perhaps he was even the best they had.

'Until now, no.'

'And now?'

'He does things, formulates tactics and executes plans that I could never even conceive of.'

'That is why he is captain of the Second. It's why his legend will endure long after he is dust. But you haven't answered my question again.'

Praxor bowed his head. His answer was forestalled by Sicarius's voice blasting over the comm-feed.

'Ultramarines! We are engaging!'

CHAPTER FOURTEEN

SPORADIC GAUSS-FIRE ERUPTED across the ruins, forcing the Space Marines to hunch over. It kicked up snow and fragmented rubble but missed the Ultramarines who advanced steadily, returning fire. Bolter flashes lit up the icy gloom in retaliatory bursts and spread the necrons' aim across the line so that no one part of it was ever under heavy barrage.

A blanket of snow and ice rolled over the battlefield, carried by a biting wind. Neither necron nor Ultramarine felt it, their metal bodies and their armour protecting them, but it made targeting more difficult.

'Holding positions!' shouted Praxor, prompted by a rune-signal on his retinal display. The Shieldbearers adopted firing postures. Farther up the roadway, the Lions had slowed to allow the rest of the company to catch up.

Sustained bolter fire came from the more advanced tactical squads, punctuated by plasma bursts and missile expulsions. At the end of the line, the Devastators unleashed their guns. A heavy bolter salvo filled the air with the dense *chug-chank* of high-velocity shells. Missiles boomed from their tubes. Plasma and lascannons spat incandescent death in a series of bright lances. The storm made it difficult to tell easily, but the necron frontliners were being torn apart by the fusillade.

'Keep it up,' ordered Daceus, shouting between bolter bursts. 'Make them pay for every damned step.'

It was as intense as any battlefield Praxor had fought on. His warrior-spirit soared. The line was dug in well, spread thin and hurting the necron phalanxes. But they were not like most enemies and could absorb a lot of punishment. Even obscured by the fog, their numbers were staggering too.

'Seems we have poked the nest,' offered Krixous.

'And they respond to the threat,' Praxor replied, pointing. He opened the comm-feed. 'Captain, monolith rerouting on our position.'

He saw Sicarius turn towards the floating pyramid of living metal moving slowly into a flanking position.

'Maintain fire,' he said. 'We need to draw them on.'

But the necrons had stopped advancing and occupied static positions. A small cohort of elites had joined the raider constructs, their heavier fire swelling the barrage.

Praxor registered a couple of hits on his tactical display but so far no red icons. Several Space Marines were at amber status – injured but still effective.

Elianu Trajan added his voice to the battle, 'Repel them, brothers. Bring down the soulless xenos, hated in all its forms. Do not relent. There is no forgiveness, no quarter. Guilliman is watching!'

He couldn't see the Chaplain – the fog was too thick now – but Praxor noted his position on the tactical map, accompanying Atavian's Devastators. He was advancing swiftly: soon he'd be with the tactical squads. Praxor could almost feel his wrath already.

'Pour it on!' yelled Daceus. All the while the shadow of the monolith was getting closer. Still the necrons took the hammering, refusing to move, refusing to commit their command nodes to the fight.

'Do they know our plan, captain?' he asked over the clangour.

Sicarius was adamant. 'Impossible. They are not engaging because of the monolith.' Daceus heard the snarl behind his captain's battle-helm. So far, the captain's objectives were eluding him. The storm was worsening, though. Visibility was weak to poor. If they were going to break off then now was the time.

'We need to destroy that thing. Do you still have your melta bombs, sergeant?'

Daceus let off a burst of bolter fire then nodded.

Sicarius holstered his plasma pistol. 'Give them up.'

Handing them over, Daceus said, 'What are you going to do?'

Mag-locking the additional melta bombs to his armour, Sicarius replied, 'Take out that monolith. Gaius, I'll need your blade.'

The company champion bowed his head. 'I am yours to command, my lord.'

'Captain–' Daceus began.

'It is my duty, sergeant,' he said, and his posture took on a nurturing look. 'I know you would throw yourself into the hells of the warp for me, Daceus. You are more than merely my sergeant – you are my ally, my friend.'

Daceus saluted by slamming his fist against his chest-plate. 'Courage and honour, Cato.'

'Courage and honour, Retius.' It had been many years since the two had exchanged first-name greetings, and never before on the battlefield. There was something about it, and this war, that Daceus did not like. It felt significant in a way, an ending of sorts. It did not portend well.

Sicarius showed none of his sergeant's misgivings. 'You have command. See the plan out.'

Then, together with Gaius, he ran into the fog.

PRAXOR SAW TWO cobalt figures running from the Lions' position. With the adverse weather, he couldn't be sure who they were.

'Brother-sergeant?'

'I don't know, Etrius. Maintain fire.'

Sergeant Daceus's voice crackled over the feed. 'All flanking forces, converge on the Lions' lead. We move now!'

The rest of the command squad broke off from the battle line, headed in the opposite direction to the pair of Ultramarines.

'Temple of Hera,' breathed Praxor. 'It was Captain Sicarius.'

'Guilliman's breath, what is he doing?' asked Krixous.

Though he was saying it, Praxor could still not quite believe it. 'He is living up to his legend, and going to destroy the monolith.'

Etrius was incredulous. 'Alone?'

The reply sounded hollow even to Praxor. 'Gaius Prabian is with him.'

'Make their sacrifice a deed of honour!' boomed Agrippen, plasma cannon pulsing. 'He is Cato Sicarius, High Suzerain, Captain of the Second and Master of the Watch.

On this field, he is Guilliman's sword; we are *all* Guilliman's sword.' The Dreadnought had regrouped with the Devastators and was intensifying fire along with Ultracius.

Praxor found his purpose refocused after the ancient warrior's words. Sicarius's reckless bravery would not be in vain. In his retinal display, he saw Indomitable was moving. Not to be outdone by Sergeant Solinus, Praxor led the Shieldbearers after them. As they joined up with the Lions, his gaze met Trajan's.

'He has the courage of Invictus and the guile of Galatan. Banish your doubts, brother-sergeant.'

They were moving too swiftly for a long reply, so Praxor merely nodded. Still the necron phalanxes weren't moving, content to hold and defend while their ponderous war engine got into position. If the monolith managed to open up its power matrix in a singular beam-pulse, the plan was finished. Broken off from its phalanx, the machine was fairly isolated but attacking such a thing beggared belief.

'Stay on me! Move as one!' Daceus was keeping the line intact, marshalling the tactical squads into position so they could prosecute Sicarius's plan.

They deviated far from the roadway, which was now wholly occupied by the Devastators and Dreadnoughts. The necrons' reaction to the barrage was feeding more mechanoids into the grinder. Their supplies were endless, their sense of self-preservation obsolete, despite the strange cries that came from each mechanoid as it was struck down. Phase-outs were happening constantly but just as many of the creatures self-repaired and returned to the fight.

The Ultramarines couldn't win by sheer weight of arms – they didn't have enough battle-brothers.

'Any eyes on the command node, yet?' Daceus had drawn

them to halt, out of the firing line and approaching the flank of a necron phalanx exchanging fire with the Space Marine heavy guns. The storm was so thick now, they could only see through their retinal senses or magnoculars.

Solinus was at the scopes, scanning the silver horde. 'Nothing from here.'

On the opposite side, Praxor also returned a negative.

'We need to get into them, force their hand,' said Daceus. He opened the feed. 'All heavies advance and resume fire.'

Praxor watched the line move up through the fog. Agrippen and Ultracius anchored it with Tirian and Atavian's Devastators in the middle. The necron casualties intensified. And with slow inevitability they started to shift.

Daceus grinned ferally. 'That's it, you xenos scum...'

But the attack would still be stalled if the monolith couldn't be destroyed, and without Sicarius they would have little chance of eliminating a necron overlord.

Praxor looked to the looming pyramid. Its capacitors were wreathed with emerald lightning, preparing to fire. It would need to be soon.

'KEEP LOW, BROTHER.' Gauss-beams flashed overhead, forcing Sicarius into a stooping run.

Gaius Prabian kept his combat shield up and close to his body. Several blasts had already skimmed off its surface.

The power armour of both Ultramarines was pitted and scored from where they'd run the necron gauntlet. Ahead, the shadow of the monolith finally reached them.

It was immense, a horrifying testament to the mechanoids' power. In truth, Sicarius believed the necrons to be much more than mere robots. They were something else entirely. Something ancient.

Although Arcona City had been pummelled into dust during the necron invasion, some ruined structures were still standing. Using the fog to cover their movements, the two Ultramarines skirted around to the monolith's flank. Its gauss-arc projectors were patrolling the immediate vicinity but looked incapable of firing whilst the machine was feeding energy to its crystal power matrix. Close up, they got a chance to see the shimmering unreality of the monolith's surface and the eldritch sigils engraved upon it. Truly, this was an engine of evil.

Sicarius noticed the crystal at the pyramid's summit start to glow brighter as the capacitors fed it power from their lightning field. Its power matrix was coming on-line.

A small retinue of raider constructs protected the monolith, moving in step with it, their weapons ready but not yet firing. In his time as a warrior of Ultramar, Sicarius had prosecuted many tank ambushes. An armoured column was a fearsome force in battle; its guns were powerful and its resilience potent against all but the heaviest weapons. But it was also relatively slow and cumbersome. Surgical strikes by squads bearing armour-busting grenades were deadly to tank formations. This monolith was no tank, and Sicarius suspected its strange surface would be resistant to most weapons, but he was determined to at least neutralise if not destroy it utterly.

A commando move such as the one he was about to attempt didn't exactly follow the strictures of the Codex but then Sicarius had his own way of interpreting Guilliman's writings. He hoped the primarch would approve of his ingenuity and bravura.

'Champion,' he said, resting a hand on Gaius's shoulder guard as they crouched in the ruins and peered out at the passing monolith, 'you are my unsheathed sword.'

Gaius nodded slowly, his eyes on the raiders. There were only five of them. He ignited the blade of his power sword and it hummed hungrily.

Before he let him go, Sicarius added, 'Beware that portal at the front. Only Hera knows where it might lead you. Courage and honour.'

Gaius growled back through the vox-grille of his ornate helm. 'Courage and honour, my lord.'

The two then split apart, Sicarius headed around what appeared to be the rear of the monolith and Gaius engaging from the front.

The Champion vaulted the ruins and cried, 'For Ultramar!'

TURNING AS ONE, the raider screen opened fire with their gauss-weapons. Gaius Prabian was an experienced warrior. As Champion he had slain countless warlords, alien potentates and demagogues. Before Damnos, he had never engaged necrons. Held in an aggressive gladiatorial position, his combat shield absorbed much of the mechanoids' fire and enabled him to run and defend at the same time. Several beams lanced his shoulder guard and greaves, but he ignored the damage runes flashing on his retinal display. Perhaps realising hand-to-hand combat was inevitable, the closest of the raiders stopped firing. Instead, it brandished its gauss-flayer like a club, intending to cut the Ultramarines Champion apart with its barrel-blade.

Gaius's shield broke skeletal teeth and snapped the necron's corded neck as he thrust it into the creature's face. The head was hanging by a piece of cabling at an odd angle when the mechanoid crumpled. A second creature Gaius cut down with his power sword, slicing through a weapon barrel and then the necron itself. The wound was catastrophic and it phased out. The third and fourth were dispatched by fierce sweeps of his blade – the air hummed and crackled as the weapon bisected it. The fifth he battered with the shield. He was a force of will, a deadly guardian intent on his mission. All three necrons phased out. He stalked over to the last, the one he'd injured but not quite enough. Already, the necron's broken neck was repairing itself. Gaius slammed the edge of his shield against the cabling that was holding the mechanoid's head to its body, severing it.

'Stay dead,' he spat, and the last of the retinue phased out…

…Only to return, or so it appeared, through the portal – five more raider constructs, carbon copies of the first. They moved slowly, resolving first as dark shadows in the pooling emerald light, then as actual beings of metal and hate.

Gaius Prabian faced them down and, touching the blade of his power weapon to his forehead, saluted.

No, he had never fought necrons before. It was to be a challenge.

'I am the unsheathed sword,' he vowed, and charged.

A BATTLE TANK had flanks, it had hatches and tracks, it possessed weak points and was forged of metal in a foundry – this monolith was something else. It had no aspects, save perhaps the front and that was only because the emerald portal suggested it together with the direction it moved in. The flanks or rear were merely faces of the pyramid, constructed of some dark pseudo-metal, a substance that didn't appear entirely corporeal or, at least, constant. Looking carefully, Sicarius could see that the sides of the monolith rippled, their hue changing in the light like oil upon water. He wasn't even certain that an explosive charge could be attached to its surface, let alone destroy it. Priming a melta bomb, he eyed the gauss-arc projectors. The cannons protruding from the machine swivelled and turned to draw a bead on him and Gaius Prabian, but they were powerless as a defensive measure whilst all the monolith's energy was being used to unleash the crystal power matrix.

That situation wouldn't last. Sicarius slammed the first charge against the flank of the machine. It took hold and stuck there. Then he attached another. And another. He planted four melta bombs in total, all of his and Daceus's supply.

A pulse rippled down the side of the monolith as they went off, expelling intense microwaves that the machine seemed to absorb and nullify. Ordinary metal would slough and corrode against a melta bomb, but the material comprising the monolith was much more resistant.

Despite its alien resilience, the combined explosive fury of Sicarius's melta bombs would not be denied and the captain shouted his approval as something in the machine died and it floated slowly to the ground. At its peak, the crystal faded as the charging of the power matrix was forcibly aborted.

'Brother Gaius.' Sicarius ran around to the front of the machine in time to see his Champion destroying the last of the retinue. Even the emerald portal was dormant, revealing bare metal behind it. With its structural integrity damaged, the necron monolith became nothing more than a monument, inert and powerless. At least for now.

'Should we enter?' Gaius pointed his sword at the area where the portal had been. It seemed he intended on cutting their way inside.

'No. We return to the others. We don't know how long the war machine will be offline. Let's make the most of it.'

Mission achieved, they headed back to the line.

Behind his battle-helm Sicarius smiled. Perhaps there was glory to be had on Damnos after all.

SICARIUS'S RETURN WAS heralded with restrained joy. There was no time for celebration. The Devastators and Dreadnoughts were taking a lot of fire. With the monolith neutralised, at least for a time, the others had to press the attack from the flank and cut into the necron horde.

The captain of Second Company lifted his Tempest Blade into the air as the mechanoids advanced into a position where the edge of their formation was exposed.

'There is still no sign of the command node,' Daceus warned.

Sicarius was not about to be denied. 'We can wait no longer.' He slashed his sword down. 'Ultramarines, attack!'

IT WAS INFECTIOUS. Praxor felt the groundswell of strength and righteous anger first in his feet, then his legs until it infused his entire body. Sicarius was the source of that power, he was certain of it. In his presence, it was as if a halo of inner fortitude surrounded them and made them capable of the deeds of legend.

'I am my captain's sword!' he swore, power sword tearing open the first necron in his path even as his bolt pistol shattered a second. All of his doubts, his notions of Sicarius's vainglory, were banished from his mind in that single attack. In their place came an utter certainty that they would triumph, that Cato Sicarius would lead them to glory.

He had never fought harder, neither had the warriors

around him. Together with the Lions of Macragge, the Shieldbearers and the Indomitable ripped into the necron flank and sundered it. They were several ranks deep, mechanised limbs and appendages tossed like metal refuse, before the Ultramarines slowed.

'Come to me,' he heard Sicarius rage at the heart of the battle. 'Face me now!'

The captain searched the silver horde for the command node but still it would not present itself. Row upon row of endless necron warriors did instead. The Tempest Blade was reaping a heavy tally, but it could not slay them all. Even the mighty Cato Sicarius could not achieve that feat.

Praxor glanced behind him. They were slowly being surrounded. Even now, some of his warriors had formed a rearguard with battle-brothers from Solinus's squad. In a matter of moments, they would be enveloped.

Trajan was at the front with the Lions, spitting curses and litanies. He would never surrender – he was, in every way, Sicarius's Chaplain. But it occurred to Praxor that there was now a certain futility to this plan. Without sight of the necron overlord the Ultramarines were effectively attacking an infinite production line of necrons. In that, there could be no victory.

In the end, it was Solinus that was the first to break.

'We should retreat,' he said, defending against a flurry of attacks before replying with one of his own. 'There is no glory in this, for Damnos or the Second.'

Smashing necrons with his crozius, Trajan was quick to silence him. 'Hold to your purpose and the orders of your captain. Fight for the glory of Ul–'

A necron blade in his gorget cut the diatribe short. Trajan blasted the creature with his bolt pistol, before dismembering it with his crozius, but could not remove the metal wedged in his neck armour.

The circle of Ultramarines was getting tighter. They were back-to-back now, their gallant charge stalled by the sheer amount of resistance facing them.

Sicarius turned to Daceus. 'Signal the other squads, close and concentrate fire on this part of the line.'

'Our brothers might be hit also, lord,' suggested Venatio. The Apothecary was holding his own, as gifted a warrior as any of the Lions.

Sicarius was quick to counter. 'It's worth the risk. Daceus, give the order.'

'Should I order the Dreadnoughts to engage, also?' came the veteran's gruff reply.

'Negative, they won't reach us in time.' Sicarius sounded angry. 'This isn't working. We're disengaging.' It wasn't an easy decision but the captain of Second didn't like lost causes, nor did he like admitting to them. He opened up the comm-feed to the flanking force. 'Cut a hole through them. Fall back.'

DESPITE HIS DARING actions that neutralised the monolith, despite goading the necron horde into being outflanked, despite everything the plan had failed. Sicarius needed something to strike; something to attack and kill that might make a difference. He could not do that slaying endless hordes of mechanoid warriors. Though it was difficult to admit, he had underestimated the necrons and their forces. He resolved not to do so again. He needed greater numbers.

Victory was possible; he felt it in his heart. It could be won at the tip of his Tempest Blade, but for now it eluded him.

Cutting his way back through the necron ranks, one hand dragging an injured Brother Samnite of the Lions, an unpleasant taste filled Sicarius's mouth. It was at once acerbic and unfamiliar.

It was defeat.

IN THE CHAOS of the melee there is little time for thought. Instinct takes over. It is a part of every Space Marine's genetic coding; it is the reason for his existence, his purpose and God-Emperor given duty. War is not just their craft, it is their sacred calling.

So it was for Praxor as he fought his way back through the horde that had slammed around the Ultramarines like a vice. The warriors of Ultramar had sprung the ambush but they were the ones caught in the necrons' trap. These things, with their cold logic, their calculating processes, could not be fought like an ordinary foe. And they were endless; at least, it felt that way as Praxor's shoulder burned with the continuous hacking through living metal.

Trajan punctuated his every blow with grating vitriol. The Chaplain had removed the metal sliver from his neck, or rather it had phased out along with the necron it belonged to, but it had left him with a razored harshness to his voice. If anything, it only made his wrath even more imposing. These realisations would come upon Praxor later, after the maddened fight to break out of the necron phalanx was done.

Punching through the other side, mechanoids exploding dangerously around them with the heavies' suppressing fire, an ordered retreat was put into effect. Veteran-Sergeant Daceus was first out, battering his way through with his power fist. He marshalled the line, setting up a fire base of bolters to open the gate of the trap for the others. Slowly, the Ultramarines emerged. Mercifully none fell, but Samnite was injured and so too were three of Solinus's men. Praxor had been spared more casualties.

The mist thickened further still, enabling the Ultramarines to make a tactical retreat without pursuit. Sicarius was the last to leave the fight. His reticence to do so and his rage were almost palpable.

In truth, all of the Ultramarines felt it.

'Retreat to the line,' he snarled when they'd put some distance between the phalanx. He caught Daceus up. 'Have the Devastators and Dreadnoughts begin a staggered retreat. We're withdrawing from Arcona City.'

Snow and fog swallowed the Ultramarines. It took the necrons too, who merely continued their implacable advance. They already had forces headed to Kellenport, a phalanx of monoliths. Some of the other phalanxes would reroute there too.

'Are we regrouping with the others?' asked Daceus. In the background, Venatio supported Brother Samnite. Gaius Prabian kept a wary eye on the fog as if expecting a necron to spring forth at any moment, but none did. The mechanoids had even ceased the gauss-barrage.

Sicarius sheathed his blade. He took a while to do it and for a moment Praxor thought he might plunge back into the fog and seek his prey anew. 'No, the necron artillery *must* be destroyed. I want heavy armour and the guns of the *Valin's Revenge* on these metal heretics. But the assault squads should be reappropriated. We need to attack and withdraw, disrupt their formations, strike at the weakest points. Heavy punishment hasn't worked, so we sting them with punitive raids instead.'

'Lord Tigurius won't be pleased, captain.'

Sicarius was remorseless. 'He will submit to my orders. The Librarian's pleasure is not my concern. Make it so, Daceus.'

The veteran-sergeant saluted, opening up the long-range feed as they began the march back towards Kellenport. He only got a few footsteps when Agrippen spoke up.

'Are we still trying to win this war?'

All eyes went to Sicarius who'd turned at the Dreadnought's voice to face him. He removed his battle-helm so the venerable warrior could see his eyes. 'Of course. If victory is possible then we must strive to achieve it.'

'Though I serve the Chapter eternal and would glorify it with every deed, I can see no victory here.'

It was a bold statement. Only Agrippen as one of the First and a revered Ultramarines veteran could have made it. The old and wise had ever had the right to challenge the decisions of the young and reckless.

'There is,' said Sicarius with finality. He replaced his battle-helm, the last part of his statement grating through the vox-grille. 'I will make it thus.'

Agrippen bowed. If he had any further doubts, he did not voice them but merely continued the march instead. Praxor had no idea if the Dreadnought was assuaged. When Agrippen had spoken up, he'd at first thought this was the moment when Agemman, through his venerable champion, would make his feelings known about the captain of Second. In the middle of a campaign, the timing would have been inauspicious but seldom were the moments when Sicarius could be brought to task.

The words, though not as inflammatory as they might have been, lingered. They resonated inside Praxor's skull, kindling the sparks of his own uncertainty. He wished they were not on the battlefield, though perhaps that was where the instincts to follow and obey were simplest to adhere to. Trajan was an iron-hard bastard but he was their Chaplain. His counsel would be greatly appreciated. In lieu of that, Praxor opted to be pragmatic. He organised his squad into the march, silently proud at their battle-conduct. It was a defeat, but the Shieldbearers had acquitted themselves well. Even still, it was hard fought for little to no gain. Heading out, he rotated his shoulder to work out some of the muscle ache.

'Should I summon Apothecary Venatio?'

Praxor winced as he snapped his dislocated shoulder into place. 'No, Krixous,' he said. 'It's just been a long time since I hurt this much after a fight.'

CHAPTER FIFTEEN

Aboard the Valin's Revenge, *two years and nine months before the Damnos Incident*

BY THE TIME Praxor left the battle-cages, most of his brothers had gone to their cells for nocturnal meditation. True, some still trained on the shooting ranges or otherwise occupied their minds towards the betterment of making war in the Emperor's name, but the way back to his dormitory was largely empty.

The Cullinar Suppression had gone well. A task force of Ultramarines, on direct orders from Lord Calgar himself, had been sent to the little known planetoid of Balthar IV to eradicate an uprising of the tau in one of its principal cities. Cullinar was wretched with xenos, who'd managed to sway a significant amount of the human population with their lies including much of the noble family that ruled it. All efforts by the Vardia Imperial Guard 15th and 18th battalions had failed to break the will of the xenos, whose influence had spread to neighbouring enclaves. Allow them to go unchallenged for much longer and a planet-wide secession from the Imperium was in danger of becoming a reality.

The arrival of the Ultramarines put a stop to that. Breaking into fire-teams, they cleansed the avenues and excised the root of alien taint within three days. Not all of the Second had been chosen for the duty, which had also included elements of the First Company veterans and Tenth Company Scouts. Praxor had neither seen nor heard Torias Telion at the battle, but knew the Master Scout was behind enemy lines pulling the strings and blowing things up. He suspected the explosion that had swept in a firestorm through the sewer lines where Praxor had then led the Shieldbearers to kill the tau ambassador was caused by the invisible hand of Torias Telion.

Scipio had fought with the Master Scout at Black Reach. Most only glimpsed him in shadows or on the training fields, for Telion was a supreme mentor within the Chapter. Praxor admitted, shamefully, to a pang of jealousy on that account. He had bled with the Master Scout on Cullinar, but had never seen him. He had seen the Terminators, led by Helios, and was as impressed as he'd been on Black Reach when they'd joined bolter and blade together.

Sicarius had not led the assault; rather it was Agemman that had captained the battle force in a methodical cleanse and burn approach. It was painstaking and exacting, where Sicarius would have been direct and brutal. The war had taken longer, Praxor suspected, than it would have with Sicarius but the risks were less and the results almost guaranteed. He would have preferred to serve his liege-lord, but Praxor was still ebullient after their victory and celebrated by performing seven hours of training katas upon return to the *Valin's Revenge*. Agemman's strategy was utterly unlike Sicarius's, though adherence to the Codex ensured certain basic similarities, but these were almost unnoticeable due to the way they were applied. The experience had led Praxor to consider observing some of the senate sessions when afforded the opportunity. They were headed back to Macragge for an official ceremony: Mikael Fabian, the captain of Third, and Master of the Arsenal, was to be honoured.

Ultramarines vaunted the successes of their Chapter; they did so proudly and in full voice. All who could attend would be expected to be there.

On his way across the flight deck where the Thunderhawks slumbered, their landing stanchions mag-locked to the ground, and mindless servitors toiled, Praxor saw another Space Marine.

He was also not wearing his power armour, but instead had a blue surplice with a cowl to hide his face. His bulk and manner marked him out as one of the Chapter.

'Brother,' he began in idle greeting.

When the Ultramarine looked up, he realised it was Scipio.

Praxor's mood hardened to steel in an instant. He had witnessed first hand lately Scipio's disregard in battle. To Praxor's mind, there was a difference between insane bravery and just plain insanity. 'You are no longer in Venatio's care, then.'

Scipio stopped in front of his old friend. 'I left the apothecarion a few hours ago.' He looked Praxor up and down, noting the training fatigues and half-carapace he was wearing. 'I see you still live in the battle-cages when not at war.'

Praxor raised an eyebrow. He felt a challenge in his brother's tone. 'And is that something to frown upon? Does it not make me a better warrior in the eyes of my captain and my Chapter Master?'

'It depends on your motives, brother.'

'And you suspect them to be less than admirable, do you, Scipio? It sounds as if you have decided my reason already and deemed it an unworthy one.'

'A selfish one, perhaps.'

Praxor licked his lips. It took all of his self-control not to unsheathe his rudius and smack Scipio around the head with it. 'You were in that sus-an membrane coma for several weeks so I shall allow for your behaviour. Do not forget your place, brother.'

'I am of sound mind, I can assure you, Praxor.' Scipio drew back the hood. His eyes were diamond-hard. He wasn't about to back down. 'And we are both sergeants. *You* perhaps have loftier designs.'

Now Praxor let his anger show. 'What is your issue, brother? Ever since Karthax you have carried your aggression like a clenched fist aimed at whoever or whatever displeases you. Is that anger now focused on me?'

'Seekers of personal glory will only ever find the means to undo themselves,' Scipio spat.

'What is that supposed to mean?'

'They are the words of Orad. You should know them, brother.'

'What? What are you even doing here, Scipio? Were you awaiting my arrival so you could pick a fight?'

Scipio's mouth was a hard line. He gave nothing away, so Praxor was forced to continue without his participation.

He leaned in close. 'Do you know why I go to the battle-cages, why I seek to perfect my warrior-self? I shall tell you, Scipio, I shall do so because you and I are brothers, we are friends. I do it to become strong, in mind and in body. You cannot blame yourself for what happened. It was frailty that Karthax exposed. It was a tragedy, but one brought about through weakness.'

'So I have heard you claim… *several* times.'

Praxor frowned, incredulous.

'I awoke from my coma days ago.' There was a grating undercurrent to Scipio's voice. Whether it was caused by his ire or his injuries, Praxor didn't know. He went on. 'Venatio had me confined to the apothecarion while my wounds healed–'

'A pity whatever damage was done to your head and humours was not also allowed convalescence,' Praxor interrupted. He was in no mood for Scipio's misplaced anger, but when he went to move around him the other Ultramarine stepped in his path. 'You are rash, brother. That's why you spent time on the Apothecary's table. I would counsel caution in your future actions.' He was no longer referring to campaigning, Praxor made that much obvious with his tone.

Scipio's blood was up, though. He would not be denied this reckoning. 'While my wounds healed,' he said again, 'I heard talk of Karthax and Orad.'

'I did not speak ill of him, brother.' There was a warning in Praxor's voice, one that suggested he did not enjoy the inference Scipio was making.

'Weakness, was it? Is that why he fell?'

Praxor clenched his fists. There was no avoiding this now. Tensions had run high between them for months. It had to come out; this was as good a way as any.

'You know the answer to that. Now,' he added levelly, 'do what you came here to do.'

Scipio roared and threw himself at Praxor. Anger fuelled a rain of blows that battered the other Ultramarine before he could reply or throw up any defence. Still pumped and alert from the battle-cages, Praxor blocked a frenzied punch to the side of the head, deflecting it with his forearm before planting a jab in Scipio's stomach. An elbow-smash to follow crunched Scipio's shoulder blade and the combination was finished by a blade-kick to the ribs.

Scipio tumbled and rolled, grunting in pain, but got his footing quickly.

'You're still weak from the apothecarion,' said Praxor, wheeling around Scipio's flank, forcing him to rotate. 'Let your wounds heal and we'll settle this in the battle-cages in the proper manner.'

Scipio shook his head. 'We do it now.'

Praxor scowled. 'You are a fool, Scipio. A slave to your emotions and your anger.'

'Are you afraid, brother?' The curled lip made Scipio's face ugly in the half-light. There was something dark inside his eyes.

Praxor shook his head – it *was* inevitable then – drew the rudius and tossed it aside. This was a fist fight. He would not dishonour it further by using a weapon, even a blunted one, against an unarmed combatant. 'You want me to break you, brother, I *will* break you!'

Scipio charged, but Praxor was quick to avoid his battering ram of an attack.

'Reckless…' He slammed a fist into Scipio's flank. A chop to the side of his brother's neck paralysed the nerves and sent pain sparks into his eyes. 'And ill-considered.'

They faced off, circling one another. Despite the inappropriate setting, the hangar deck made for a perfect arena. Their audience, the servitors, continued their labours without pause or regard. The long shadows of the Thunderhawks bathed the combatants in darkness. Scipio was breathing hard, belaboured by his injuries. Praxor had yet to break sweat.

'Where is the warrior Torias Telion has spoken so highly of?' he goaded.

Scipio came on again. He feinted, drawing Praxor's guard, and landed a heavy blow on the other sergeant's cheek. A headbutt brought white dagger-flashes to Praxor's eyes and he staggered.

'He's right here,' Scipio promised and hit him again.

Despite his earlier advantage, Praxor was being worn down by his brother's fury and was forced back a step. Sensing his superiority, Scipio leapt and came at Praxor with his fists linked in an overhead smash. Had the blow connected it would have probably shattered his clavicle but Praxor sidestepped out of harm's way, punching Scipio hard in the gut with the same motion. The other sergeant grunted then choked as the air blasted from his lungs.

Expecting that to be the end of it, Praxor relented but Scipio whirled around and caught him with a wild haymaker. He felt the bone crack and reeled at the force of the impact. An uppercut from Scipio's other hand glanced Praxor's chin. He had enough presence of mind to retreat defensively, so the blow was telling. Throwing up his arms, Praxor hit the side of Scipio's head with the flat of his hands, stunning him. Dizziness made the other sergeant sluggish and Praxor used it to his gain, blocking another all-or-nothing swing and driving a knee into his brother's stomach. Seizing Scipio's wrist, he bent it around and used his weight to push him down to his knees. The other arm he wrapped around his neck and squeezed.

'Yield!' He was breathing hard, partly from exertion, partly from anger.

Scipio still struggled.

'You've lost, brother. Give it up.'

Still Scipio fought. He made enough room for an elbow strike to Praxor's gut and drove it back hard.

Praxor grunted, hurt, but held on.

'Weakness,' he hissed between clenched teeth, spitting phlegm. 'Yes, you're right, brother. It was weakness.'

Scipio roared, anger lending him strength, but Praxor didn't let up. Rather, he pressed further.

'But who is weak, now?' He wrenched Scipio's neck when he tried to move. By now the air was being cut off to his lungs, though a Space Marine could last much longer than an ordinary man in a choke-hold – even one made by another Space Marine.

Praxor leaned in so he could speak directly into Scipio's ear. 'You are a patrician son of Ultramar, an inheritor of Guilliman,' he said, almost pleading. 'This does not befit your Chapter or your heritage. Don't dishonour that any further.' His grip lessened, allowing Scipio to speak, albeit in a rasp.

'I have no honour left.'

Praxor loosened his arm further. Scipio had stopped struggling now and hung like dead weight in his arms. 'What are you talking about?'

'Do you know what happened on Karthax?'

Praxor's eyes narrowed in confusion. 'A tragedy, the death of a hero – we lost Orad.'

'It was more than that. No one else knows… No one but the captain and maybe Daceus.'

'What happened?' A strange sensation was working its

way up Praxor's spine as he asked the question. He couldn't quite place it; it had been a long time since he'd experienced the emotion or one similar.

Scipio's confession was delivered with sobs for a fallen brother. 'I killed him, Praxor. I killed Orad.'

'WE NEED TO move, now!'

Scipio was waving the human guerrilla fighters farther down the mountain pass, but his attention was fixed on the upper slopes behind them.

It was Largo who had spotted it, skulking in the peaks, concealed by the drifts. Not content with its feast, it still craved their skin and had come to claim it. What was more, the flayed lord was not alone – it had brought its cohorts with it. Like slavering dogs, ruddy with the life-blood of others, they galloped down through the icy crags on all fours. A wave of sheer terror had swept through the humans upon the first sighting. Men and women, those who were left of Captain Evvers's group, had fled wildly. One had even pitched off the side of the mountain in his haste to escape. The scream only lasted a few seconds before it was lost to the wind or snuffed by the razored flanks of rocks.

'What do we do?' asked Brakkius. He was kneeling down by the edge of the pass, bolter aimed at the peaks where the silhouettes of necrons were steadily gaining ground on them.

'Look how it moves,' added Cator, a little incredulously. These things were not merely the automatons the Ultramarines had first suspected them to be; they were so much more than that. 'An automaton should not be that agile.'

'We can't outrun them,' said Scipio, once all of the humans had passed him. 'So we fight.' He turned to Cator.

'Have Garrik and Auris get Herdantes back to the camp. Brakkius, Largo and I will hold back the necrons for as long as we can.'

Brakkius went to protest, as did Cator, but Scipio silenced them with a glance. 'See it done,' he said.

Neither Ultramarine would see their sergeant endangered but they were dutiful soldiers and followed orders.

Only Largo made no reaction. He still had unfinished business with the flayed lord – the blood of Renatus was on the fiend's talons and he would make it pay for that. He eyed the storm intently, tracking each shadow as it moved through the drift, a patch of grey on white.

'I'll return as soon as Garrik and Auris are on their way,' promised Cator. The others were at the front of the column, scouting the way ahead, all except Herdantes who was only able to limp alongside the guerrillas. His wounds were healing but it would take time. A ready bolter filled his grasp and Scipio didn't doubt his purpose, only his combat effectiveness.

'See that you do,' said Scipio, clapping a hand on his brother's shoulder. 'We'll need all the bolters and blades we can get.'

Cator saluted and set off down the pass in search of the others.

'That leaves the three of us for now,' said Brakkius, somewhat redundantly. He checked the load of his weapon – the ammunition count was low. Scipio saw it flash red in the darkness. He had a similar number of shells remaining in his pistol.

Largo wasn't watching, but breathed deeply. 'The air is crisp and clean. I like it up here,' he added. 'I think I will be happy to lay my gladius down in this place.'

Scipio didn't bother to reprimand him. It wasn't fatalism. Largo had simply come to terms with his probable death and embraced it. If anything, Scipio admired him for it. He racked the slide of his bolt pistol. 'Hold them off for as long as you can,' he said, the whipping wind adding drama and sorrow to his words. 'Let's give our brothers every chance to reach the sanctuary of the camp.'

Brakkius nodded. His weapon was already primed.

'Brother-sergeant,' he said. 'It has been an honour to cross blades and shed blood with you.'

'I could not be prouder of the Thunderbolts,' Scipio replied. 'You are my warriors, my brothers.'

'Courage and honour,' added Largo in a level voice.

Brakkius echoed him.

'And to the hells of the warp if we fail in this task,' said Scipio at the end.

Shoulder-to-shoulder, bolters ready, they waited for the flayed lord to come. There'd be no precipice to send it over this time, no cunning ploy to trap or destroy it. Scipio was as proud as any warrior of Guilliman. He was one of his patrician sons, something a friend had told him long ago – a shame it took his imminent demise to realise that. But he was not dragged down by hubris, either. He knew this creature had the beating of them. He avowed he would make it work for its feast. While there was blood still pumping in his veins and the veins of his brothers, there was hope. A keening cry split the rushing of the wind, giving it a sharp edge that felt as if it could shear steel. Death was coming.

It would reach them soon.

ANGER AND SHAME warred with excitement in the mind of the Enfleshed. Since his apotheosis, a need had arisen in his jagged psyche. It was a wholly unnatural hunger. He had railed against it at first, but now he embraced it and let it consume him.

If I am damned then so be it…

His slaves scurried on all fours like pack hounds on the hunt. He resisted the urge to prostrate himself like that; he was still a noble lord of the necrontyr despite how debased his form had become. He was not an animal yet, not quite.

He revelled in his agility, leaping rocks, darting around crags and racing down the icy slopes towards his prey. Flashes boomed in the darkness below, framing the gene-bred humans in orange, as they unleashed their weapons.

The Enfleshed felt no fear, only anticipation of the kill, of the skinning to come. His talons clacked and scraped of their own volition at the prospect.

Flesh…

It was as if his mind was being pulled apart, stretched taut in many directions at once – loathing, self-pity, feral abandon, ennui, self-satisfying sadism. He was Sahtah no longer; only the Enfleshed existed now.

One of the slaves was struck in the chest. The Enfleshed lost sight of it as it fell with a pseudo-scream. The storm of hot metal was intensifying the closer he came to the end of the slope. Something chipped his armoured shoulder, but he paid it no heed. To his left, another slave was destroyed. The Enfleshed smiled, or at least he did so in his mind – his rictus jaw was incapable of such expression – it meant more skin for him.

I shall devour you all…

He imagined hot blood coursing down his gullet, the succulence of ripe flesh rolling around in his mouth. It was intoxicating. A final thought penetrated the shattered remnants of his memory engrams as he leapt the final few metres to the kill.

I am lost…

The heavy shells burst hot and hard against his chest as the prey tried in vain to stop him, but the Enfleshed was not to be denied. His talons fanned in a killing arc, eager to eviscerate…

…when another figure emerged through the storm.

The light surrounding him was painful to the Enfleshed's dead eyes. The aura seemed to expand, washing over the others in a wave of azure. It was fringed by crackling bolts of power, coursing over a growing energy dome like vipers. It struck the Enfleshed mid-flight and threw him back.

A scream tore from the Enfleshed's throat and was echoed by his slaves, who felt it sympathetically. Pain snapped at his nerves, some real, some imagined – though he couldn't tell one from the other. Blood, dried hard by the frost, cooked off his joints and servos in a ruddy haze. He tried to stand, poised to attack this newcomer and rend his face from his skull, but another bolt arced from the figure's fingertips – his eyes were alive with power – and now the Enfleshed felt fear.

His chest was torn apart, his living metal body sloughing into slag. Sahtah, the Enfleshed – his head was so scrambled, he couldn't tell who or what he was any more – felt his memory engrams exploding one by one. Though he grasped at it with his melted talons, he could not seize his fading identity. Sentience shrivelled and turned to dust like bones upon a pyre. Slumping to his knees, Sahtah felt oblivion approaching. It stirred a final thought in his destroyed consciousness, one that would echo for aeons.

Peace…

* * *

TIGURIUS REGARDED THE steaming remains of the necron lord with contempt as it phased out. His storm had vanquished the other flayed ones too and the mountainside was disturbingly empty barring where his psychic lightning had scorched it.

He allowed the aura around him to fade and with the absence of the light, darkness swarmed in around them again.

'Your intervention is timely and most welcome, Lord Tigurius.'

The Chief Librarian turned at the sound of Scipio's voice. As he nodded, it took a moment longer for the fire in his eyes to die.

'I was travelling the Sea of Souls when I witnessed you in peril, Sergeant Vorolanus,' he said, motes of power still drifting from his lips and an unearthly resonance in his timbre.

Scipio bowed. 'We are glad of it.'

Tigurius looked beyond the brother-sergeant and his warriors. 'Who are these people?'

Drawn by the lightning storm, the human guerrillas and their Ultramarine escorts were standing a little farther down the path.

Scipio glanced over his shoulder where the humans had sunk to their knees before the Librarian.

'They are our saviours, Brother-Librarian.'

Tigurius eyed them curiously, unconvinced. 'Get up, all of you.' He turned back to Scipio. 'How so?'

'One amongst them can lead us through the mountains, bypassing the necron picket lines.'

Tigurius considered this for a moment, before answering, 'Bring the scout with us, the others we must leave behind.'

Scipio opened his mouth to protest, but the Librarian's steady gaze, latent with psychic power, stopped him. He nodded then gestured to the humans. 'Captain Evvers.'

A woman, the farthest forward in the group, who had now all got to their feet, looked up.

'You're with us. The others–'

'Are coming with me,' she said firmly, shaking her head. 'I won't leave them, not now.'

Tigurius glowered at her impudence. He released a little of his power into his eyes, which crackled with tiny lightning sparks. 'You will obey. This is not a negotiation.'

The one Scipio had called Evvers cowered a little but stood her ground. 'I need them. To get through the mountains. I need their skill. So do you.'

Tigurius didn't like it. Being beholden to one human was bad enough. To be argued down as well bordered on intolerable. 'I am tempted to ignite you like a flare, little human,' he said. Evvers looked like she might shrink from the threat but stayed steady. Despite her obvious frailty, she impressed the Librarian.

He laughed, as alien and unusual a sound as Varro Tigurius was ever likely to make. 'You have some courage in you.' He slammed his staff into the ground. 'Stay close. None of the Ultramarines here will be responsible if you fall behind.'

Evvers nodded. He could tell she was shaking and eager to be away from his penetrating gaze. 'Same goes for you,' she said, by way of rejoinder and went to marshal her troops.

'She is… *forthright*, brother-sergeant.'

Scipio nodded in agreement. 'I have never met a human like her.'

259

The drifts were lessening. Winds still howled around the peaks, chill and desolate. The storm wasn't done, it would come again.

Tigurius watched Evvers leading her troops down the slope. 'I saw into her mind. She carries much grief and anger, but believes she can master it and do what is asked of her.' He turned his gaze on Scipio. 'Do you believe it, too, Brother Vorolanus?'

Scipio's eyes narrowed. 'Do I believe what, my lord?'

'Exactly as I asked.'

'She will do her duty, as will I.'

Tigurius's expression was neutral, he gave nothing away. 'Then that is all any of us can be asked to do.'

'What else did you see, my lord, in the Sea of Souls?'

Scipio had been there when Tigurius had tried and failed to identify the darkness plucking at the edges of his prescience. He knew it had disturbed the sergeant and now he wanted assurances. But the Librarian couldn't provide them.

'Nothing.'

'There is no doom in our future, then?'

'No, there is a tragedy to come but I cannot see it. A terrible will is blocking my prescience. For now, my eyes are blind, Scipio.'

The expression on the sergeant's face told Tigurius he had only enhanced his misgivings. That could not be helped. A lie would not serve him, either.

They left the slopes after that. The valley where the rest of the Ultramarines waited was not far. If what Scipio said was true and the humans could indeed find a way through the mountains and the necron defence line then victory was possible. The artillery could be destroyed and a foothold gained on Damnos all in the same move. Tigurius only wished he could grasp the thread of his disquiet. A sense of foreboding weighed upon him still. His psychic flight had done nothing to dispel it. The dark shroud over his thoughts was heavy and obscuring. Perhaps when the mission was done and the Voidbringer vanquished that veil would be lifted. He only hoped that by then it wouldn't be too late.

CHAPTER SIXTEEN

AFTER MONTHS OF continuous bombardment Adanar Sonne was used to the sound of the necron guns. They were a constant throb against the inside of his skull, a heavy-handed passenger demanding his attention. At the moment, the artillery was silent and it was the absence of their din that was unsettling him.

'It's like a lullaby, don't you think?'

Corporal Humis frowned. Not long after the Ultramarines had defeated the necron vanguard, a curious stillness had descended on Kellenport. The silence of the guns in the Thanatos Hills could mean anything. Perhaps the Emperor's Angels had destroyed them somehow and salvation would come from the stars in the form of an evacuation boat, or perhaps the necrons were merely preparing to unleash some greater horror. For now, the air was quiet... except for the screams.

'I don't understand, sir.'

'Of course you don't,' Adanar replied. He was using the lull to tour the battlements, to check on their defences. Even if they were fated to die – and Adanar was certain this was the case – he would ensure they would go down fighting, in blood and fire. 'You haven't been on the wall as long as I have.' He turned to look at him. 'You don't come from Kellenport, do you, Humis?'

'I was stationed at the Zephyr Monastery, sir.'

Adanar smiled thinly. 'Ah, protecting the priests and their relics.' He carried on down the wall, saluting the officers blindly as he went. Humis followed in lockstep with his commander. 'Well, your piety has got you this far, I suppose.'

Humis had no reply to that.

'So, what's left?' Adanar was all business again as he regarded the fire-blackened remains of the Kellenport artillery.

Consulting a data-slate, Humis said, 'Three *uber*-mortars and three long-nosed cannon, sir.'

'Earthshakers?'

'Yes, sir.'

'And what of the *Hel-handed*?'

'Still functional.'

Adanar nodded, satisfied. He already knew that the rail guns, cannon nests and emplacements were below thirty-five per cent. They were useful against infantry, but it was the really big guns that mattered – and they didn't come much bigger than the *Hel-handed*.

'Raise Sergeant Letzger on the vox,' he said. 'I want to see through the eyes of his god-engine.'

IT TOOK A further eighteen minutes to cross the battlements and meet with Sergeant Letzger. They passed strung-out

squads of Ark Guard and conscripts on the way. All of
Damnos, the remains of its entire population, had mus-
tered in one last act of defence. The officers saluted, some
even muttered greetings – many were just silent, contem-
plative of their fates. It seemed to Adanar that the army
had thinned greatly since he'd last been around the wall.

A broad-shouldered, stocky man, Letzger was one of
the few original officers to have survived the siege of Kellenport thus far and was the city's, and the Ark Guard's,
gunnery master. Sweat-stained breeches, a pitted helmet
strung with webbing and a flak jacket riddled with cigar
burns painted a dishevelled picture of a man that Adanar
trusted with his life.

'Commander Sonne.' Letzger saluted when he saw Adanar approach. His bare arms were covered in wiry black
hair that failed to stop the Guard tattoos from showing
through. His leather gloves were cut off at the ends, revealing oil-stained fingers. It didn't stop Adanar from shaking
the man's hand after he returned his salute.

He appraised the cannon. 'How does she fare?'

The *Hel-handed* was a massive artillery piece. It was so big
that it had to be built into the very foundations of the city
wall and had immense recoil dampeners and impact compensators wrought into its leg stanchions. The column-like
barrel was telescopic and segmented in four places. It
required a crew of six men to fire it. A team of three was
needed to rotate the barrel. Its firing platform was large
enough for half a platoon of Ark Guard to stand on. Kill
markings ran down the barrel, a source of pride as well as
an illustration of Letzger's vengeance against the necrons
that had invaded his world and murdered his friends.

Such engines were described as 'Ordinatus' by the Adeptus

Mechanicus. This one had been fashioned and anointed by Karnak, but the tech-priest was no longer able to perform the rites of the machine – he had died in the early weeks of the invasion. The fact that *Hel-handed* had kept firing without pause or complaint was a testament to the fortitude of its machine-spirit. There was not a day went by that Letzger did not thank it for that.

'Still operational, sir. The break in the bombardment has given us a little time to effect some minor repairs.' Letzger nodded to the work crews halfway up the barrel reaffixing plates and the servitors welding sections back together. 'She's holding.'

There was a tang of ozone in the air. Adanar tasted it on the back of his tongue. The smell was in his nostrils. It was preferable to the stink of death, at least.

'And the shield?'

Letzger breathed in. He genuinely enjoyed the acrid taste in his mouth.

'Still burning out my nose hairs, commander.' He smiled and his entire face seemed to crease up like an old rag. The stubble on his face was patchy and clumped with the movement of his features. Letzger really was an ugly brute.

Because of its size and importance, the *Hel-handed* was protected by a void shield. Such measures were usually only afforded for Titan god-machines but certain static installations like defence lasers and macro cannons also possessed them. With its sheer mass and destructive potential, the *Hel-handed* easily fell into that distinction. The void shield was the only reason it had not been rendered to scrap by the necron guns months ago.

'You've come to sample the view, I take it?' Letzger added.

Magnoculars only penetrated so far through the fog, but

looking through the sights of *Hel-handed* was like peering through the eyes of a god.

'Only if it won't interrupt your labours.'

Letzger gestured to the machine behind him with a wide arm. 'Go ahead, sir. Her gaze hasn't wavered since the killing and death began.'

Humis balked a little at the gunnery master's words. Adanar allowed himself some private amusement – Letzger's pragmatism was infinitely preferable to the desperate hope of most of his officers. At least it was honest.

Mounting the platform, nodding to the crews who saluted him crisply, Adanar took up a position in the sighter's chair and looked through the *Hel-handed's* crosshairs.

Unsurprisingly, the view was fixed on the Thanatos Hills where the necron artillery was based. It was something of an unfair fire exchange but Adanar sensed the challenge was relished by Letzger's old girl. The arc of pylons and heavy gauss-cannons blighted the rugged horizon line. Several years ago, when his family was still alive, Adanar had trained in the Thanatos Hills. His barracks were based at the old refinery. That too was in ruins now, little more than a blast scar on the ground. So much was gone, never to return.

He squinted through the sighting lens, careful not to alter any of the gunnery master's measurements. He couldn't tell why the necron artillery had stopped firing but he did see something moving to the west. It was on the fringes of his vision through the scope. Adanar turned to Letzger.

'There's something out there.'

Letzger gave the reports back to his chief engineer and took up the secondary sighter's seat. He peered through the lens.

'Eighteen degrees west,' he bellowed into the vox-horn. Several metres above him, a trio of crewmen rotated the barrel precisely.

Letzger adjusted the scope, tweaking it for focus. 'Clever bastards.'

Adanar had the same view but wasn't seeing whatever the gunnery master was.

'See the hill line?' asked Letzger.

Adanar nodded.

'Watch the peaks.'

Adanar stared. The drifts were blowing themselves out but despite that and the incredible range of the *Hel-handed* it was still hard to discern detail. He *had* seen something earlier, though, so he tried to focus on that. His eyes narrowed and he smiled.

'They're moving.'

'Aye, it's no hill line out there.'

'Necron pyramids,' Adanar asserted.

'Trying to sneak up on us. Hoping we'd think the barrage was over and relax our guard.'

'How close do you think they are?'

Letzger made some adjustments, consulted instruments. He also lit a cigar and puffed on it enthusiastically.

'Too close.' He started yelling orders at the crews, shouting out coordinates. There was a flurry of action as his men reacted. Letzger left the sighter's seat and looked at Adanar.

'We need to get you off the platform now, sir,' he said politely.

Adanar matched the gunnery master's salute and left with Humis. They were heading back down the wall when he noticed something else that gave him immense displeasure.

'What is *he* doing on the battlements?'

Humis didn't catch on immediately. Adanar had to point him out before the corporal understood.

Rancourt was on the walls, his guard detail with him. It looked like he was trying to inspire the men, but was getting strange looks and wary salutes instead.

Adanar scowled and thrust out his hand. 'Get me Kador on the vox, right now.'

SERGEANT KADOR KEPT his voice low; the acting lord governor was only a few steps ahead of him and he didn't want to be overheard. 'He insisted, commander. I believe he wanted to do his part to galvanise the men.'

A stream of invective made Kador wince ever so slightly. 'I understand, sir.'

There was more, and the sergeant could see by Commander Sonne's hand gestures, as far away as he was on the battlements, that he was extremely displeased.

'I will do so immediately.'

The vox link was cut abruptly and Kador gave the receiver cup back to his comms-officer. His face was as hard as Damnos ice. 'Bring Governor Rancourt to me. Now.'

'NEVER LET IT be said that Lord Governor Zeph Rancourt sat idle while his people suffered.'

Kador thought he looked knowingly officious in his robes and suspected the only reason the lord governor had ventured from his quarters was in fear of the ceiling falling in on him. Upon hearing of Corporal Besseque's death, he'd been especially paranoid about that.

'Commander Sonne has ordered me to escort you from the wall, sire.'

Rancourt looked genuinely nonplussed. 'But who will inspire the men?'

'He assures me they are well steeled already, sire.'

'Yes, of course…' His gaze drifted to the southern gate. 'The Crastia Shipyards,' he said. 'They are a short march in that direction. With the cessation of bombardment, an evacuation might be possible.'

'Commander Sonne has ordered that no one is to leave the safety of the city.' Rancourt returned his gaze to Kador. His expression was distinctly conspiratorial.

'A small mission from the city gates would likely go unnoticed.'

The sergeant's face was like stone. 'What are you suggesting, sire?'

'Nothing. Only that an enterprising officer might be well rewarded should he deliver an Imperial official from certain peril.'

Kador leaned in close, just to be sure there was no misunderstanding. The relish in the lord governor's eyes made him want to clench his fists. 'No one leaves the city. *No. One.* These are my orders, sire. The Crastia Shipyards have been taken. Even if there were a vessel capable of taking us to orbit, the area is likely to be swarming with the enemy. Necrons employ hidden snares. They have troops able to bore through earth. There's no telling what hazards we would encounter.'

The lord governor looked as if he might argue but Kador's glare placated him.

'Yes, of course. I was merely speaking hypothetically.'

'Hypothetically, sire, indeed.' Kador stepped aside, indicating the lord governor should make for the battlement stairs.

'You are a dutiful servant, sergeant,' he said as he passed.

'Thank you, sire.' Kador watched him go. Perhaps Governor Rancourt was right, perhaps the ceiling would fall on his head. He could but hope.

CHAPTER SEVENTEEN

A LOW RUMBLE ran through the earth below the newly christened Courtyard of Xiphos. Iulus felt it through his armoured boots, his greaved legs. In his core, he knew the necrons had found some fresh way to attack Kellenport.

He expected to see lumbering war machines, bipedal walkers, arachnid constructs or a host of other mechanical horrors pounding towards the walls. But no emerald beams scorched through the snow-fog that had rolled down off the mountains and swathed the world in dirty white. There were no ranks of blinking, soulless orbs as the phalanxes marched on the city. Even the necron communication-nodes were silent. It was something else.

Iulus scanned the third wall, the one that was mined with as much explosive as he could spare. The rumble beneath his feet grew deeper and heavier. Some of the men had to steady themselves on the battlements to stop from falling.

'Battle positions,' he bellowed. The order was relayed

through the other Immortals. The entire defensive line, including the troops in the courtyards, tensed.

A Space Marine can exist in a state of heightened battle-tension for hours, even days. Their enhanced physiologies are genetically engineered to cope with even the most arduous mental extremes. For a human it is unbearable. Like a sinew pulled taut across a muscle it can only be strained for so long. Over-tense it and it will snap.

Still the tremors persisted.

The men looked fit to break.

Despite the absence of a vox-caster, Iulus's voice reverberated around the wall. 'Hold positions!'

Again, he searched the third wall. The proximity triggers were rigged throughout the ruins. There was no way the necrons could have bypassed them all. He searched the killing-field on which their guns were aimed and primed, despite the fact he knew no enemy could set foot there without first coming through the third wall. Where was the fire? Where were the explosions and the shrapnel storm he had laid for them? *Come on, come on… We shall unleash death upon you.*

'Where are they?' hissed Kolpeck, the normally stoic conscript showing signs he was on edge.

Iulus silenced him. 'They are close. Be ready, brother.'

He'd said it without thinking, by rote. Iulus didn't take it back. He could see instantly the effect it had on Kolpeck's resolve. He was emboldened. In another life he would have made a fine Space Marine, Iulus was sure.

'I am at your side, brother-Angel.'

'And I yours,' Iulus muttered. Breaking up his squad had felt unnatural at first. Iulus would still have preferred his brothers by his side but Kolpeck was a good soldier and a fine companion. He had never really thought much of humans before. This enemy they faced was enough to push an Ultramarine's resolve and strength to the limit and yet here these men stood, in defence of their homes, defiant to the last. Yes, Iulus was proud to stand with them and learn an important lesson about the depth of the human spirit.

Small motes of debris were shaking loose from the defences now. The Ark Guard in the gun nests had to hold onto their pintle-mounts and tripods to prevent them moving and fouling their aim. Several troopers knelt, leaning against the wall for stability. Some prayed, making the sign of the aquila. Others locked arms with their comrades for mutual support.

'Like ice in your veins,' Iulus said to them, his abyssal voice carrying on the wind. 'Your spine and will as steel.'

A conscript with a rocket tube gestured into the whiteout fearfully. 'What if we cannot see them? What if they are already upon us?'

Iulus growled at him. 'Get hold of your fear, seize it and lock it fast. *I* will see them coming.'

Except he couldn't see them. Iulus saw no more than the frightened conscripts on the wall. How quickly a man's insane courage could corrode in the face of inaction when confronted with the unknown. There were no horrors in the universe that could compare to what a man harboured in his own mind. It was a place where daemons and monsters reigned, where blades and guns were no protection. And it was here that a Space Marine was armoured the most.

But still, the humans held.

A cry echoed across the battlements. It was followed by the crack of splitting stone as part of the wall collapsed. Huge plumes of dust, grit and snow spewed up into the air like a frozen geyser just under fifty metres from Iulus's position. Men and materiel were swallowed in the cloud, their screams dampened by the crash of sundered stone.

In the other direction, another section of the wall fell, broken in two as if its foundations had rotted through or succumbed to rapid erosion.

Uncertain where best to turn first, Iulus reached for the vox. He was scanning the dust cloud for some clue of a necron attack, when Kolpeck left his position and raced for the ladder to the lower level.

Iulus shouted, 'Trooper, stand and fight!' He had no time to go after him. Something was happening to the wall but he was still ignorant of the cause. He eyed the third wall again, but the mines and explosives were intact. He heard no las-fire, no bolter bursts. Kolpeck had fled, climbed down the ladder and was racing down the stairs to the Courtyard of Xiphos.

So much for human courage, Iulus thought bitterly. Perhaps the war had broken the man. Cracks were usually hard to see until it was too late to shore them up.

At least the rest of the One Hundred were holding firm. He'd glared at them all when Kolpeck had run, defying them to move with sheer force of will. None did.

Putting the thought aside as he would a spent clip or blunted gladius, Iulus barked down the vox. 'Aristaeus.'

He was the closest Ultramarine to the site of the second collapse. Iulus himself was in command of the wall section where the first collapse had taken place.

Aristaeus's reply was riddled with static, the dust and grit muddying the signal even at close range. 'Nothing, brother-sergeant. I see...' The vox-return crackled.

'Repeat. I cannot make you out, brother.'

'A hole, brother-sergeant. There is a vast hole opened up in the wall right down into the earth.'

Iulus heard screaming over the vox-return and could imagine the fates of those on the section when it collapsed. Aristaeus continued.

'I can see into its depths. There is…'

There was a pause as Aristaeus consulted his autosenses and cycled through his retinal spectra.

Iulus's patience was threadbare. They were under attack but he still had no idea by what or from where the next assault would come. 'Speak, brother. What do you see?'

'Darkness, only darkness.'

Crouched at the battlements, one eye on the dissipating dust cloud ahead of him, Iulus frowned. 'Is your retinal display malfunctioning? Tell me what you see through infra-red and night vision.'

'Nothing, brother-sergeant. It's just black, like oily cloud. Visual filters have no effect.'

'That can't be good,' said Kolpeck. The grizzled rig-hand was out of breath and clutching a strange device in one hand. He'd obviously gone to retrieve it after the attack. It was based on a long metal spike with some kind of data-slate at the top. Iulus had never seen one before but its design suggested some kind of seismological mining tool.

'A soldier does not desert his post, Trooper Kolpeck.' His voice was stern but now was not the time for a long reprimand. He wanted to know what Kolpeck had found.

'I'm sorry, brother-Angel, but I was acting on a hunch,' he replied with a little less contrition than Iulus had expected. 'I told you, I am a miner not a soldier.' He brandished the seismological device. The data-screen was grubby with dirt and hoarfrost but a series of undulating lines were visible along three horizontal axis. 'They are *beneath* us.'

The three lines were depth markers. The last, therefore the deepest, was jagged with activity. Iulus saw what the necrons were doing. Undermining was a common siege tactic, well-used and perfected over millennia of war. Here the necrons had added a fresh element – they were using the darkness as a way to conceal themselves.

Iulus seized the vox, nearly crushing it in his gauntlet as urgency overtook him. 'Aristaeus, burn it! Burn the hole. The mechanoids have tunnelled underneath us!

'Pour everything you've got into that bore hole,' he shouted, running the battlements in long, metre-eating strides. 'Turn the cannon emplacements, fill it with hell and frag!'

Iulus got halfway to the site of the first collapse when the ground beneath him gave way and he was falling. Another bore hole had opened up in his path. Several of the One Hundred plunged to their deaths, unable to move in time. It was a dishonourable end for such brave men. Iulus reached out, his survival instinct impelling him to grab a chunk of rock jutting from the broken rampart.

He stared down into the abyss below and saw the darkness there that Aristaeus had described. Unhooking his weapon, he could almost sense the presence of alien minds regarding him and fired.

The bolt pistol scream resonated inside the bore hole, magnified as it rebounded off its sides. With the darkness cloaking the advancing scarabs, Iulus didn't realise he couldn't miss. As soon as the first creature was hit, the illusion faded and the blackness receded to reveal a chittering host of the things. They scurried up the walls, which were ridged with the burrowing action of whatever monster or device had hewn them, in a swarm. Their eyes glinted like tiny emeralds in the natural shadows of the circular cavern, mandibles champing.

When Iulus's bolt fire struck them, a stream of the scarabs exploded, leaving burning contrails in their wake as they fell. He panned the pistol around, finger tight on the trigger, and left a muzzle scar across the open air. Still holding on one-handed to the piece of broken rampart, Iulus gave a wordless cry.

He could not kill them all. Even with the las-fire flashing down from above, the scarabs would soon breach the surface. He estimated there were hundreds of the things and for every one he destroyed, another four replaced it. His ammunition counter was burning to zero when Iulus noticed a large mound ripple through the undulating mass. Down to his last rounds, he switched targets and fired a close burst into the mound. The scarabs outside it were blasted apart like a piece of ablative armour revealing a much larger construct beneath. It moved slower than the others but its carapace was thick and absorbed the impact of the explosive bolt shells without pause. Iulus was debating whether to draw his chainsword and drop into the bore hole to kill the monster personally when it swung a gauss-blaster arm in his direction and fired.

The beam cut into the Ultramarine's battle plate and he cried out. Armour shed like snake skin as the flaying effect of necron technology went to work and Iulus's greave was reduced to half-corroded mesh.

The pain was so severe he dropped his pistol. For a moment his grip wavered. Several more of the larger mounds were moving through the scarab swarm, which had almost reached him. Dangling off the edge of the precipice, Iulus realised it would mean his death to fall now. Eternal night reigned in the depths of those bore holes, as cold and unnatural as the creatures emerging from it.

A hand clasped around his wrist. Then another and another. Iulus looked up to see Kolpeck's straining face above him.

'Heave!' he yelled to the other conscripts – all from the One Hundred – who were trying to rescue their captain.

'At your side, brother-Angel,' Kolpeck said again through gritted teeth.

It took the combined efforts of four men to lift the Ultramarine even a small amount. They were all rig-hands, all strong men used to back-breaking labour in the Imperial mines beneath the Damnos ice, but none had ever worked so hard to lift something such a short distance.

It was enough for Iulus to swing his free arm around and grip the battlements with both hands. He pulled himself up as another gauss-blast speared the rock where he'd been hanging a moment earlier. The conscripts fell back as he emerged back over the top.

'Back! Fall back!'

Iulus turned towards the bore hole even as the conscripts started to retreat. He unclamped a pair of frag grenades from his belt just as the first wave of scarabs was spilling over the edge of the wall. Ignoring the smaller creatures, he tossed the explosives over the shiny bodies. A low boom came from beyond and below. The mechanoid spyder did not emerge and Iulus thanked the Emperor that his grenades had done their work.

He contemplated staying and trying to hold off the scarab swarm coming at him – he had already drawn his chainsword – but decided to fall back with the others.

Kolpeck was just behind him, waiting for his captain.

'We need to get off the wall,' he said, bringing his lasgun to bear on the smaller mechanoids.

Iulus pushed the barrel down. 'Then do it. Marshal the One Hundred. Every man is to head for the Courtyard of Xiphos. We'll stand a better chance of holding them there.'

Kolpeck nodded and ran. He was already shouting orders at the men, ushering them downwards, organising them into groups.

Unclamping his last pair of grenades, Iulus tossed them towards the scarab swarm and jumped from the wall.

The explosion blossomed behind him, kicking up debris and broken scarabs as the Ultramarine landed hard on the Courtyard of Xiphos. From there he could see the wall was breached in no fewer than six areas, each sunken by a bore hole and now swarming with scarabs. Gauss-fire cracked from the spyders, stripping men to bone and ash.

'Heavy weapons, target the larger mechanoids. Bring them down!'

From across the courtyard, rocket tubes and heavy stubbers hammered into the spyders. They were tough and took a lot of killing, but they were falling. So too were the Ark Guard. A mass retreat was in effect. Even done in good order, the humans were still pressed on all sides. The walls were empty, apart from the dead. Several squads had been overwhelmed completely in the first few seconds of the breach, swallowed beneath the necron wave. Even their bodies were no longer there, the scarabs had stripped them from existence.

The first wall was behind him, and Iulus knew they would need to fall back to here if they had any chance of surviving, let alone repelling, the attack. A massive bore hole opened in the Courtyard of Xiphos, splitting flag-stones and toppling shattered monuments. Men went with it, whole swathes of Ark Guard lost with a tortured scream. Iulus thought he saw something gargantuan surface from the depths. It looked segmented, almost centipedal, but was quickly swallowed by the unnatural darkness. Scarabs and spyders spilled forth in its wake.

'Incendiaries into the bore holes,' Iulus bellowed, point-ing to the fresh attack point. 'Burn it down. Cleanse their route of assault.'

He saw Aristaeus, a rack of three promethium flamer tanks rattling on his back. He reached the circular crevice in the courtyard and threw the tanks in. Bringing up his boltgun in the same motion, he fired off a single round and a jet of liquid flame as thick as the pillars of Hera's Temple shot up from the bore hole.

The blast wave took Aristaeus off his feet but he was quick to recover and head for his sergeant. The other Immor-tals were doing the same, marshalling their troops with them, converging on Iulus as they sought to consolidate their forces.

Slowly, the squads came together. Stragglers were picked off easily by the scarab swarm but a concentrated wall of fire was ripping steadily from the Ark Guard now. At the orders of their Space Marine captains, they formed firing ranks and bathed the courtyard in hot las.

'Brother-sergeant.' Aristaeus reached Iulus's side and held out his sidearm. 'You seem to be without the Emperor's wrath.'

Iulus punched his chest, the air filling with las-beams around him. 'Here is where I keep it, brother,' he said, but then smiled as he took the bolt pistol.

More Ark Guard joined the others massing outside the gates to the first wall – even the troops on the battlements had opened up with their weapons – and the rate of fire intensified. The scarabs and their larger, monstrous cousins had seemed infinite at first but now they were withering. None of them could penetrate the slowly retreating Imperial cordon. Even the spyders were pinioned by lascannon beams from the first wall battlements. But the necrons were tenacious and fed even greater numbers into the meatgrinder. Like a river of mercury swollen at its banks, they began to lap at the sides of the Imperial defences.

Several soldiers at the outer edge where the Ultramarines presence was weakest were dragged screaming into the swarm.

Iulus tightened the cordon further still but his troops were already shoulder-to-shoulder with their backs against the gate of the first wall. He sensed the tide turning, the sheer overwhelming force of the necron constructs tipping the balance. What had started out as an organised defence of hold and repulse was turning into a desperate last stand.

Behind him, there came the churning of gears as the mechanism to the gate was activated. It did not open wide but it was enough to admit a towering war machine into the Courtyard of Xiphos.

'The walls of Chundrabad shall never fall!' Agnathio's multi-melta tore a hot line through the scarabs. Men of the Ark Guard hurried from the Dreadnought's path as he bullied his way to the front rank. 'I serve the Chapter eternally!'

Though he moved slowly, his motive servos still spitting oil and steam, when Agnathio reached the necron horde it reeled. So indomitable, so utterly relentless, the venerable warrior's example was followed by all. Together, they threw the scarabs back.

Agnathio had been joined by the rest of the Immortals and several platoons of Ark Guard who lent their fire to the Imperial barrage.

As if sensing the futility of their attack, the necron machines retreated like ants from a fire and withdrew to their bore holes.

The shooting from the Ark Guard was slow to relent. In the end it took all of the Ultramarines to bring the humans back down again. They had survived a terrifying ordeal and fear did not give up its hold on lasgun triggers easily. When the noise of the barrage died, a wintry silence swept through the Courtyard of Xiphos. Already, the drifts were covering the evidence that a battle even took place. There were only the half-flayed remains of dead Ark Guard, anyway; all of the destroyed necrons had phased out. It made for an eerie scene.

Iulus rested his hand on the still-hot shoulder casing of Agnathio's multi-melta. 'We owe you a debt, honoured one.'

Pride was not really amongst a Dreadnought's limited emotional responses. Agnathio was typically matter-of-fact. 'I am my Chapter's servant. I seek only the glory of Ultramar.'

'Well spoken, brother,' Iulus murmured, humbled by such stalwart courage and loyalty.

Brother Galvia had been one of the Space Marines from the first wall to come and bolster the beleaguered defenders. 'Do we return to the second wall and try to regarrison it?' he asked.

Iulus shook his head. The second wall was all but rubble now, the bore holes had seen to that. It would be indefensible. He turned to Kolpeck who was crouching nearby, breathing hard while some of the men around him were puking out their nerves.

'Find as many of those seismographic staves as you can,' said Iulus. 'Plant them around this cordon, ten metres out.'

'I could take them as far as the second wall,' Kolpeck suggested.

'No. Ten metres, no farther. Do it quickly.'

Kolpeck saluted, gathering up some men he trusted, and went about his orders.

Iulus's face was grim as he surveyed the ruins in front of them. Aristaeus was by his side and must have seen his expression.

'Something wrong, brother-sergeant?'

'That was just a probing attack to test our strength,' he said. 'This isn't over.'

Iulus did not intend his words to be prophetic but as he said them there was a flash of emerald light around the rubble of the second wall. A crack had opened in the air itself. The drifts did not fall there. It was as if something had interrupted the very ebb and flow of nature. The crack widened and became a pool of light that expanded again into roughly the size of a large doorway. Within it, the emerald light rippled as if something very deep down beneath the pool was attempting to surface. Shadows loomed there. Iulus could not be certain but he thought he could make out a long, glowing corridor with the shapes of necrons marching down it, growing more distinct with every step.

Another portal opened up a few metres away. A third followed swiftly after that. Down inside the bore holes a chittering clangour arose as the scarabs returned.

On the battlements, some of the Ark Guard were pointing beyond Kellenport's walls. Officers were looking through scopes. Iulus could hear the larger guns rotating to fresh trajectories.

Some of the men were muttering amongst themselves. A few in the front ranks who could see the enemy emerging had turned and were trying to reach the gap in the gate, but it had already closed.

'Hold to your positions!' Iulus bellowed, revving the teeth of his chainsword. He levelled it at the trio of portals and the shadows coming through them. 'Death comes for us. It comes clad in metal and with engines instead of organs. We shall hurl it back, back into the abyss. Faith in the Emperor.'

The rallying cry was taken up by his brothers; some of the One Hundred, including Kolpeck, echoed it too.

'Faith in the Emperor!'

Emboldened, perhaps even shamed by the ragged band of conscripts, the rest of the Ark Guard stopped trying to flee and gave voice.

'Faith in the Emperor!'

As the shout of defiance echoed to nothing, Kolpeck, alone, could be heard.

'And in the name of our brother-Angel, Iulus Fennion!'

Iulus wanted to rebuke him, but then the Ark Guard and the conscripts resounded with, 'Iulus Fennion! Brother-Angel!'

Despite himself, Iulus felt a slight swell of pride. It lasted but a moment as the shadow of the monoliths loomed through the gaps in the wall and the necrons emerged at last.

'Keep your courage steady,' he told Kolpeck as gunfire filled the Courtyard of Xiphos.

LETZGER SWEATED LIKE a stuck pig. The gunnery crews had worked well; *Hel-handed* was ready to unleash her first salvo.

'Let 'em have it!' he cried into the vox-horn.

Even with the dampeners and compensators, the recoil from the cannon was immense. It shook its staging platform like the hand of an angry god, while the explosive shell fell like its clenched fist.

A huge cloud of dust and debris rose up from the strike point, obscuring the slow-moving phalanx of monoliths from view. It looked like a direct hit. Certainly, Letzger had made no mistake in his calculations. That heavy a missile payload… Nothing in human creation could survive that.

Some of the gunnery crew were already celebrating. It was as much fear as it was exultation that fed their shouts and angry cheers.

Letzger stayed at the scopes, sweating. He was wearing plugs, but his ears still rang from the report of *Hel-handed*. She was a noisy bitch, all right, sometimes capricious, but he loved her and he loved what she could do.

Through the scope the smoke and dust was clearing. Ice and snow around the blast site had melted away to steam, adding to the obfuscation.

'Let me see it,' he murmured. 'Let me see your broken carcass.' He'd never fired on monoliths before; he didn't know what happened to them when they were destroyed. Perhaps they phased out too; perhaps he was looking for a ghost he'd never see.

The image resolved. Letzger sagged at his post and the men groaned in despair. It was still there. Three of the necron pyramids advanced towards Kellenport. Somehow, impossibly, he had missed. The crater was so large, its effect so awesomely powerful, he didn't know how. But *Hel-handed* had been fouled somehow.

Wiping away the perspiration on his forehead and lips, the cigar cinched between them no more than a smouldering nub, Letzger peered through the scopes more intently for an answer. He saw tendrils of darkness, coiling and twisting between the triumvirate of war machines. They appeared in synch, feeding off one another, boosting the terrible shroud that had somehow saved them.

The only mercy was that, for now at least, the monoliths were not firing their weapons. They had phased forces into the vicinity, but otherwise their power matrices were dormant.

For an experienced crew, it took six minutes to load, prime and fire an Ordinatus like the *Hel-handed*. Letzger prided himself that his men were the best. As he bellowed the orders to reload, he knew the old girl would be spitting fury in less than five.

As he watched the monoliths float towards them, in defiance of all natural laws of physics, he clutched the aquila bracelet on his wrist.

'Come on, sweetheart,' he said, patting the gun. 'This time...'

ADANAR WAS RUNNING the battlements when the first shot from the *Hel-handed* rang out. He'd not got far, and even though he knew he was out of position, stopped to watch the magnificent weapon in action. The blast wave, felt even where he was standing on the wall, was invigorating. His heart sank to a cold and pitiless place when he looked through Corporal Humis's magnoculars and saw the monoliths were untouched. He'd always thought nothing would survive a blow like that.

From the Courtyard of Thor behind him, the *uber*-mortars

and long-nose cannons churned out shells as if on a production line. With their subterfuge revealed, the necrons
recommenced their barrage from the Thanatos Hills. As
the emerald beams from pylons and gauss siege-cannon
started up, Kellenport was under siege once more.

This time, however, the mechanoids were aiming for the
walls.

A chunk of crenellation spumed into the air, trailing dust,
grit and snow. Men went with it, broken and half-flayed.

Adanar ducked, grabbing Humis's jacket before he fell
off the battlement like several others. The screams of the
falling men didn't last long as they cracked against the
ice-hardened flagstones of the square below.

'I've lost one aide today,' he said through gritted teeth,
dragging the corporal bodily against part of the wall that
was still intact. 'I don't intend on losing another.'

Humis was a little shell-shocked but otherwise grateful.
He gestured to the blast-scarred section of wall. It gaped
like an old wound, still festering. 'We are dead men out
here on the wall.'

Adanar nodded. 'Agreed. All except the heavy cannon
and gunnery nests are to drop below the wall to the lower
level. The emplacements are dug in harder, that should
give them some protection. For the rest: heads down and
hunker down,' he added, as Humis got on the vox and
started relaying orders to the officers spread throughout
the defences.

The corporal put his hand over the receiver cup, though
he scarcely needed to – the combined barrage from both
sides was deafening. 'What about the troops in the Courtyard of Xiphos? They'll lose the support fire from the
platoons.'

Adanar thought for a second. He ducked again, as did Humis, when another explosion rocked the wall. More screaming followed.

'Tell Sergeant Fennion he's losing his support and offer to open up the gates. He's a warrior-knight, so I doubt he'll retreat easily, but at least the Ark Guard can get behind shelter if the Ultramarines want a glorious death.'

Adanar could tell by Humis's expression that he'd shocked the corporal. 'I'm sorry, Humis. It's hard to see any hope amongst all this death.' Subconsciously, he rubbed at the locket-charm strung around his wrist. 'It's been too long since I've seen anything else.' Another blast shook Adanar from his reverie. 'Give the order. The Angels are not immortal, they'll either fall back or they'll die like heroes.'

CHAPTER EIGHTEEN

IT FELT STRANGE to be above the ground. So long he had dwelled in darkness, his thoughts lost in a timeless miasma without meaning. The long sleep had gnawed at the Undying. Even his name, his true name, was denied to him. He was only the Undying now, an immortal king upon a decayed throne. Eternity was not the paradise he had hoped for. With every waking moment, as his lucidity returned to him, it became a terror instead.

How can I exist for all the long aeons of the galaxy? Will I not atrophy? Will my mind not erode to oblivion?

As a member of one of the necrontyr's royal houses, he enjoyed certain privileges. No servitude as an automaton for him. Though the Undying had lost part of his identity, he knew that much. Plebeians and nobles were separated by a gulf. Since the necrons had embraced metal over flesh, that divide had increased exponentially. Not only was freedom denied to the lower classes, so too now was true sentience.

Though tarnished and tattered, the Undying's vestments looked regal enough. As he'd left the tomb, eager to dispense death and annihilation, his lych-like guardians had found him.

Like their lord, they carried long war-scythes in silvered fists. As they bowed, he saw the flare of recognition in their eyes and knew these were no ordinary slaves.

'Retinue,' he had proclaimed. 'Summon my phalanx to war.'

Immortals had filed from the bowels of the tomb, rank upon rank recently armed and revivified. They were the Undying's honour guard. In the lowest levels, the very catacombs, the reviled spilled forth. Held aloft on humming repulsor platforms, the destroyers were a blend of necron and something else. Nihilism burned coldly in the depths of their eye sockets. Fused with gauss technologies, boasting cannons not limbs, they were amongst the tomb's deadliest servants.

The Undying felt an instant kinship with them, despite the fact that the house shunned such creatures. Their curse, the slow descent into madness and destructive desire, was a fate shared by all. The destroyers' presence was merely a reminder of that.

Lesser creatures joined the hovering gun platforms in legion, raider constructs and the flickering shadows of tomb wraiths. The latter were an obvious bribe. The Architect was trying to make certain of his position and influence.

That might have amused the Undying once but now, as he gazed out upon the frozen city of the humans, he only craved to vanquish. There was one out in the wastes who had defied him. He had led an attack and slain lords of his royal court. As the killing urge boiled up within him, the Undying vowed he would humble this worm. An arc of emerald fire raced up the war-scythe's blade in empathy of its master's rage, as he willed his forces onwards in the snow and ice.

They marched, their royarch at the forefront, and together their footfalls shook the earth. There were no war cries, no banners held aloft, none of the pomp and ceremony of other armies. The necrons were silent and implacable, their advance unstoppable. Nothing except total annihilation would do. And even then, the Undying's lust for carnage would not be sated.

'Let it all burn,' he growled, and in the balefires of his eyes it did.

ANKH SURVEYED THE cold black metal of the necron artillery approvingly.

Rows of pylons, once held in stasis and now dredged from the very earth, stood alongside static gauss siege-cannons. The latter were long, multi-barrelled monstrosities. Their flanks were wrought from the living metal of the necrontyr and pulsed fluidly in the half-light. The former were sickle-shaped turrets that spat death from their gauss-annihilators. A wash of emerald light bathed the ordnance with every discharge of their power. Lances of energy scored the sky, cutting into it with harsh green jags of light. Where the pylons fed continuous beams into the heavens, the siege-cannons throbbed with the drumming staccato of their salvos.

The earth trembled. Far into the distance, the human city was slowly rendered to dust.

Ankh joined another of his noble brethren, who was watching the barrage from the same icy ridge but with prideful eyes.

'Impressive,' the cryptek conceded.

Tahek, the Voidbringer as he demanded to be known, turned on the other necron lord like a jackal scenting prey. 'It is irresistible, world-slaying,' he snarled.

Black vapours surrounded the Voidbringer, the reason for his name. They roamed and twisted about his metal form, seething through the gaps in his ribcage, spilling over his skeletal fingers and out of the sockets of his aeons-dead eyes.

This was the Night Shroud, a piece of ancient necron technology that had existed since before the long sleep. Not only did it swathe the Voidbringer, it encircled his dominion too. Like some unnatural fog it rolled over the ground and between the artillery emplacements, foiling the efforts of the humans to target them with any certainty. It was not foolproof, some of the weapons had been destroyed in the ordnance exchange, but the Voidbringer's technology kept the damage to a minimum.

Effective as protection, it was when deployed as a weapon of terror that the Night Shroud truly excelled. During the taking of the Thanatos Refinery, Voidbringer had sent the darkness snaking through corridors, seeping into ante-rooms, infiltrating the hearts and minds of the crude human soldiery. Mortal fears amused him greatly. So primal, so instinctive, the horrors of the dark would ever plague the souls of the fleshed.

Tahek Voidbringer was powerful, Ankh knew this and it was the reason for his visit. He also knew of the Undying's malady. Despite his status, the long sleep had not been kind to him. Tahek was aware of that too and had set his ambitions to becoming royarch.

'The Night Shroud proved extremely useful,' said Ankh,

showing his appreciation with a slight bow. 'The humans are trapped inside their stone cage.'

'Did you doubt it?' Voidbringer snapped. A crackle of energy was fed down the haft of his staff but dissipated quickly.

Ankh went on, unperturbed. 'Your shadows blinded them to the machine host until it was too late. Their outer defences are in ruins, their forces driven back.'

'Yeeesss.' A fire burned in Voidbringer's eyes. It was as if he had discovered something in the cryptek's penitent demeanour. 'I know why you are here, *Ankh*.'

'To return your gracious favour, my lord.' Ankh bowed lower.

'*My lord*? Yes, that's right. I am of noble heritage and you...' Voidbringer's tone expressed his disdain. 'You are little better than a plebeian with certain... *gifts*.'

'I live to serve the necrontyr,' answered Ankh, carefully politic. Away from the tomb he was vulnerable. Although very unlikely, Tahek could decide to destroy him here and he'd be able to do little to stop him.

'You will serve me,' Voidbringer asserted. 'The Destroyer curse has him, does it not?'

'As lord, I bow to your wisdom. I am merely–'

Voidbringer seized Ankh by the chin, clamping his mouth shut and halting his reply.

'This pact we have made is a wise one for you, *Ankh*. The Undying is mad. He has succumbed, hasn't he?'

Ankh did not need to move his jaw to speak but the sound emanating from his vocal emitters was tinny and dull as it resonated through his metallic frame.

'As will we all.'

Voidbringer nodded slowly. 'The tomb is awakening,' he said, 'and other crypteks can be put to the task of weapon-making and revivification. Yours are not the only tomb spyders and scarabs, Ankh.'

There was a pause as Voidbringer allowed the threat to sink in, before Ankh was released.

'Now,' said the lord, holding out a skeletal hand. 'Honour me with what you came here to give.'

Bowing again, Ankh produced a shiny black orb from within the folds of his robes.

As he took it, Voidbringer's emerald eyes flashed with hunger and desire.

'A resurrection orb?'

'The very same,' Ankh replied, taking a humble step backwards.

Waving the cryptek away, his gaze still locked upon the orb, Voidbringer said, 'You may leave. Your favour will not be forgotten.'

A portal opened in reality, a long chamber stretching away from a green doorway of light that led back to the tomb and sanctuary. Ankh was pleased to be going. As he was about to go, the falsehood of Tahek's promise still ringing hollow in his mind, he stopped. He had his back to the noble but spoke anyway.

'A word of warning before I take my leave.'

'You warn me?' Voidbringer's tone betrayed his anger. The mad dog was straining for the kill.

'The Enfleshed is gone, so too are his cohorts.'

'And? He was a wretch and a ghoul. I am glad to be rid of his presence.'

Ankh turned briefly. 'The genebred ones destroyed him. There is one amongst their ranks who has power.'

Voidbringer scoffed. 'I have felt his presence. He is nothing, less than an insect.'

'He comes for you.'

Now the flames of wrath truly flared along the Voidbringer's staff. He was easy to rile and Ankh amused himself at his impotent rage.

'I fear nothing,' Voidbringer told him. 'I am invincible.'

As he disappeared through the portal, Ankh's gaze lingered on the orb and he whispered, 'Of course you are…'

ACT THREE: SACRIFICE

CHAPTER NINETEEN

SCIPIO RETURNED TO the camp to find Squads Ixion and Strabo already gone.

It fell to Sergeant Vandar of the Victors to relate the news of Captain Sicarius's orders and the redeployment of the assault squads. He stepped forward from the defensive ring of cobalt the Ultramarines had made whilst stationed in the valley and approached Tigurius.

The Chief Librarian masked his anger well as he stopped to hear Vandar's report and survey the forces he did have left at his disposal.

'Did our brother-captain mention why he was recalling the assault squads?' he asked.

To his credit, Vandar kept his eyes up and his answers brief. 'The orders were relayed through Veteran-Sergeant Daceus, my lord, and no he did not.'

'I see.' Tigurius's face was carefully neutral but the air around him visibly crackled.

Just as they had found a way to sabotage and destroy the necron heavy guns bombarding Kellenport, Sicarius had taken away from them their chief asset in that attack. From the encounters he'd survived so far, Scipio knew it would have been tough enough to assault the Thanatos Hills. Without Ixion and Strabo, the odds of mission success had narrowed considerably. If the necron forces were led by a lord too...

Withdrawal of the assault squads left three tactical squads, including Brother-Sergeant Octavian's. They carried the honorific Swords of Judgement and were amongst the best marksmen in the Second, possibly the Chapter. Ortus had matched his skill against their best many times. The record sheet was well-balanced. With the Ultramarine's death it would forever be so.

Scipio put such maudlin thoughts from his mind as he greeted his fellow Space Marines. Despite everything, it was good to be back amongst his brothers again.

Tigurius was not done addressing the battle force. 'Fortunate, then, that we bring good news.' He gestured to Scipio, inviting him to elaborate. 'Brother-sergeant?'

Several of the battle-brothers, including their sergeants, had been eyeing the humans that had joined them in the camp. For their part, the guerrillas looked wary and afraid. Only Jynn seemed unperturbed by the cobalt giants in their midst. She came forward.

'I am Captain Evvers, and these are my men... What's left of them, anyway,' she added ruefully. 'We are your salvation.'

Sergeant Vandar was looking down on the woman when he raised his gaze to lock eyes with Scipio. 'Why does this human speak for you, Brother Vorolanus?'

'She is bold,' added Octavian. It was hard to tell through his battle-helm but he sounded mildly amused at the woman's outburst. 'And what is this "salvation" she boasts of? Are we in need of rescue?'

Scipio shot Jynn a reproachful look, before bringing his attention back to Vandar. 'She does not speak for me,' he said, before addressing Octavian, 'but she does possess some useful information, a route into the mountains behind the necron's defences.'

'Through the defensive circle?' asked Vandar, suddenly interested in the human now. Vandar was known for his tactical brilliance, yet even he could not devise a strategy that would allow the battle force to bypass the necron defences around the artillery. He wanted to know more.

'We have a way to breach the impenetrable mountain ridge, yes,' said Tigurius, 'but a plan is needed if we're to make the most of this opportunity.' His gaze fell on the three sergeants as he was walking away.

'My lord?' asked Scipio.

Tigurius didn't look back. He was heading towards an isolated promontory of rock. Much like the Librarian's thoughts, it was swathed in snow and ice. 'I must consult the Sea of Souls,' he muttered, his mind already drifting elsewhere. 'The future is uncertain.'

'Brother-Librarian,' Scipio called, risking censure for using such familiar language.

Tigurius turned. His eyes were ablaze with actinic fire.

'Are you sure that is wise, given your last attempts?'

'Experience matters not, Sergeant Vorolanus,' he replied solemnly. 'Need drives us. I must *know*.' A swell of snow spiralled up from the ground and the Librarian disappeared into it.

Scipio regarded his fellow sergeants. 'Vandar, make the most of our reduced forces.'

Vandar nodded. 'I shall bring victory to our cause, brother.'

The three departed to marshal their squads and prepare for imminent departure to the Thanatos Hills. Scipio left Brakkius to organise the Thunderbolts, while he spoke to the humans.

Jynn returned a steely expression as he regarded her.

'Accompanying Space Marines into battle is no small thing,' Scipio told her. 'It is dangerous beyond imagining. For one, you are not equipped as we–'

'Look at us,' said Jynn, interrupting.

Scipio stayed his anger as he waited for what she was about to say. He took in the guerrillas. They were a sorry, but war-hardened sight.

'What do you see?' she asked, turning to her troops. When she looked back, there was a proud glint in her eye. 'I see survivors. I see men and women who have lost their homes, their families, everything they have ever known or will know, and have only vengeance to drive them. We are aware of the dangers and we are not Space Marines, it is true, but do not say that we're not equipped for this fight; months scrapping for our survival against these bloody things in the ice wastes says otherwise. We will fight, and we will die, but don't expect us to slow you down – we won't. We know these hills, this land. Dead or alive, I'll get you through that cordon. Promise me one thing: make those soulless bastards pay for what they've done.'

Scipio met her fearless eyes and his anger ebbed in the face of Jynn's glorious pride. 'By Guilliman's blood, I swear it,' he said. He held out his massive gauntleted hand and uttered in a quieter voice, 'For I desire revenge too.'

She nodded. Her tiny hand was engulfed by his but the gesture was all-important. A compact had been struck, a swearing of an oath that only death could break. In that moment, Scipio saw the grief in her eyes at her loss, and recognised it instantly.

Karthax, forty-five years after the Black Reach Campaign

THE LAST REMNANTS of the cultist army were being driven back from their walls by the guns of Helios's Terminators. Enfilading storm bolter fire cut the wretches to fleshy ribbons, whilst bursts of heavy flamer cleansed any lingering heretics from the roadside bunkers.

The Fortress of Ardant had once been a bastion to the Imperial faith; now it was an abomination. Filth caked its walls, hell ruled its halls. Blood and flesh, not mortar, held its bricks together. The emblems of the aquila, soaring proudly from its minarets and looking on imperiously from its crenellations, were defaced. It was rotten with cracked timbers and pitted stone, rusted metal and moth-eaten banners – yet it stood. Somehow this festering palace was more resilient than a bunker, in spite of its obvious decay.

With a thundercrack, the incendiary charges placed by Tenth ignited and the gates to the Chaos bastion were blasted open. Severed from the fortress itself they quickly crumbled to dust. From within the gaping maw behind the gates, a swarm of mutated cultists emerged in a frothing frenzy. Other beings came with them, once flesh but now something else, something terrible. They stretched the skin of their hosts, manifesting in the corporeal world as disgusting horrors dredged from man's worst imaginings.

'Warp creatures!' bellowed Helios, a statement of damnation as much as a warning. The First unleashed their weapons. The horde withered as assault cannons and cyclone missile launchers cycled up and let rip. Explosive payloads ruptured the throng, painting bloody welts across the smoke-blackened roadway. Half-putrefied cultists, little more than the walking dead, were blasted explosively apart.

Guard units from the Mordian VI, the Stygian Hounds, were ordered into the breach. Armoured formations began the slow grind towards the bastion: Leman Russ to pound, Hellhounds to burn and purify. In a single day, the Ultramarines had cracked open the enemy resistance, a feat the Imperial Guard couldn't manage after over three months of continuous siege. But it wasn't over yet. The broken gate led into a deeper heart of evil. It had to be excised.

Helios waved on the Ultramarines waiting by the Rhino transports on his right.

'Advance, brothers. In the name of Agemman and the Chapter Master!'

Orad gave the signal to embark. The black-clad Chaplain was last aboard the transport, the access hatch still closing as he stepped inside and the tank drove off at speed.

Nine Ultramarines met him inside, down on one knee with their heads bowed as he entered the troop hold.

Scipio Vorolanus was amongst them.

Outside the patter of small-arms resonated through the hull. The Chaplain hardly noticed it.

'Reject the taint in all its perfidy,' Orad began, spitting vitriol against the inner surface of his skull-mask. 'Resist and crush those who worship Chaos. Know in your hearts you are pure of purpose and that the Emperor walks with you. His light will vanquish the traitor and the daemon.'

As the engines thrashed, the sound reverberated and inten-sified around the hold. Orad fought it, his oratory rising from a shout to a scream. An explosion nearby rocked the Rhino on its tracks, but he kept his feet. 'The Ultramarines fight with clenched fist around bolter and blade. We are the inheritors of Guilliman, the heirs of Ultramar. They know our names and they quail as we recite them with bolters as our voice.'

The engine slowed as the Rhino struck the enemy. A lethal rank of spikes gave the hard nose of the tank a kill-ing edge. Crunching bone, the spatter of blood and the screams of the dead came dully through the hull. A body rolled under the tracks – something big – and the Rhino lurched up and over it before landing square.

'For the glory of Ultramar, we shall know no fear!'

Screeching to a halt, the tank's hatch slammed open and the Ultramarines charged out with Orad at their head.

Blood and death greeted their arrival. Cultists clad in rags, wrapped in pus-soaked bandages pressed in, a horde of the unwashed. The Chaplain cut through them, his cro-zius blooded, leaving a string of enemy corpses in his wake.

Scipio was behind him, he had a perfect view of Orad's back. His shoulder plates compensated for the movement allowing his arm to rise and fall like a piston as he bludg-eoned. Rancid flesh gummed the brunt of his crozius. He flicked it off with a desultory gesture as a sporadic muz-zle flare lit the end of his bolt pistol. Punished heretics exploded as the mass-reactive shells did their holy work. He'd engraved every one with a litany of hate and purg-ing. Orad knew their order in the weapon's chamber and spoke each and every one as it killed a traitor. Nothing stayed his wrath.

It was… *inspiring*.

Chainsword chugging on the flesh of a dying cultist, Scipio forged himself a little space and briefly examined the battlefield.

Across the roadway, on the opposite side of the gate, a second squad of Ultramarines had deployed. Like Scipio's Thunderbolts, they were swarmed by enemies. He recognised Sergeant Solinus immediately and felt an urge to breach the gatehouse before him. Given Orad's fervour, the Chaplain wanted that honour too.

'Repel them!' he roared. 'Smite them! Become the Angels of Death!'

He was locked in battle with a ferocious warp-thing, a possessed flesh puppet of some daemon from the abyss. Tentacled appendages spewed from the creature's distended maw. Several fizzed and burned against the Chaplain's rosarius field impelled from the icon chained around his gorget, but at least one got through and bit into his power armour.

Pressed by his own opponents, Scipio thought he heard Orad grunt and saw the protective energy field flicker for but a moment when the Chaplain dispatched the bloated hell-beast with a hate-filled curse.

Sensing a shift in momentum, Scipio ordered his warriors with even more aggressive tactics. Bolters were slung in favour of gladius and pistol as the Thunderbolts closed hand-to-hand. Brakkius snapped a cultist in two across his armoured knee, whilst Ortus stabbed another in the throat and crushed the skull of a second in his gauntlet.

Cator unleashed a ragged line of fiery promethium into the decaying ranks from his flamer and they burned. Combined with the furious blade assault it tore enough of a gap for the Thunderbolts to advance, gaining precious ground into the gatehouse and the inner citadel beyond.

The horde of traitors that had sallied forth was slowly being cut down. Helios kept up a furious but disciplined barrage from the edge of the Ultramarines battle line, withering the enemy troops that had sought to flee the fighting.

Nothing must survive. Those were Calgar's orders.

Ground under the tracks of tanks, eviscerated by blades or crushed underfoot, it didn't matter – the only sure way to cleanse the fortress was to systematically eradicate everything inside.

Once the tactical squads were in, the Terminators would begin their implacable march to the gates. The Mordians would follow, bringing tanks and more flamers for the purge.

Elsewhere on the battlefield the Tenth were taking down gun towers, cutting off supply points and collapsing defences under Master Telion's expert direction. Several weapon emplacements had already been sabotaged, leaving behind twisted metal and blast-scarred sandbags.

A plasma cannon turret, protected inside a mobile bunker, slowly turned to draw a bead on the Thunderbolts. Its rotational axle was slicked with pus instead of oil and the bulbous maw of the weapon that extruded from the firing slit was malformed with corrosion. The weapon had almost built to expulsion when an explosive typhoon engulfed it – more of the Scouts' unseen work. Shrapnel and flesh-parts pattered against Scipio's armour as the Ultramarines fought through the last of the cultists and entered the courtyard behind them.

'Glory to the Thunderbolts,' said Scipio quickly but good-naturedly to Solinus.

'It is for the Chapter, Brother-Sergeant Vorolanus,' Orad said before Solinus could reply.

Both sergeants bowed to the Chaplain's wisdom before moving into a slow run towards the inner citadel, a craggy, gore-stained structure that poked out of the centre of the bastion like a diseased talon.

It was the briefest of respites as they crossed the courtyard, which was littered with the dead but otherwise empty of threat, and reached the portal to the inner citadel. The door was like an open wound, festering with decay. Veins pulsed in the marblesque rock, like arteries swollen with plague. But it was unbarred.

Orad held the others back with his outstretched arm as he stood at the threshold of the inner citadel, staring. 'It is dark as sin, but the way is open to us,' he said. As he led them onwards down a shallow set of steps, Scipio thought he heard Orad's sharp intake of breath. It sounded like pain.

'Brother-Chaplain?'

'It's nothing,' said Orad, though the timbre of his voice suggested he was injured. It had a faint gurgling quality, like there was blood or mucus in his throat.

One of the warp-thing's barbs had got past his rosarius field and penetrated his power armour too. Scipio noticed crusting around the wound and some of the ceramite had even started to corrode.

Scipio paused, uncertain what to do.

'It's nothing,' Orad said more vehemently and just for the sergeant this time. 'Our enemy is close. We must destroy it. I will seek out an Apothecary later.'

He turned, signalling an end to it, and beckoned the Ultramarines on, closer to the nest of evil.

There was a stink upon the air, copper-blood and the reek of putrefaction. Corpse-fattened spiders and bloated flies skittered from the light as the Ultramarines switched on their lamp-packs. Grainy lances of magnesium white stabbed into the blackness in all directions. There were alcoves where more corpses lingered, slumped against columns or strewn over debris from the fallen ceiling. The only route further into the citadel was ahead, over a stinking carpet of mould that stuck to the Ultramarines boots and led to a temple of horrors.

'Steel yourselves,' hissed Orad as they arrived at the entrance, the oleaginous glow of rancid lanterns spilling sticky light ahead of it.

As he touched the rim of the light, Scipio could almost feel it coating his armour in a film of decay. He suppressed the urge to remove his trappings and be free of the taint, wanting nothing more than to experience the cleansing fury of his ritual ablutions.

The foetid temple was no better.

Rusted chains hung lankly from a pitted ceiling, strung with flayed corpses and gossamer-thin webs of flesh-dust. Filth-streaked columns were inscribed with ruinous sigils and contained alcoves bearing cadaverous, half-fleshed skulls. A pit was hewn in the centre of the room, which had once been some kind of great hall but was now divested of its former use and put towards corruption. Something boiled within it, wallowing in a soup of pestilence. Noxious bubbles belched to the surface as the creature moved, disturbing bleached skulls and half-digested viscera.

So it wasn't only a temple, it was also the abomination's feasting chamber. It was the very root of evil on Karthax.

Orad had seen enough.

'Destroy it!'

Squads Scipio and Solinus unleashed their weapons in a terrifying storm at the loathsome spawn in the filth-pool. For a moment, it was utterly obscured from view by the Ultramarines blistering salvo.

After a full minute of the hell-storm, the reports of bolters and the hiss of flamers slowly echoed away around the circular room. Smoke and fire trailed from the pit afterwards. Most of its disgusting contents had been splattered around the walls or flecked the Ultramarines power armour.

As the smoke cleared, Orad ordered Solinus forward. The sergeant acknowledged, and approached the edge of the pit warily. He used his boot to nudge something within it, leaning back from the sight suddenly repulsed.

'There is a body.' Solinus waved the others forward.

Scipio crouched by the ragged corpse of a man. He was wearing robes and his flesh and bones had been utterly sundered. Bolt impacts marked his body. His exploded limbs and innards, the shattered bones and scorched skin were testament to the effectiveness of the Ultramarines weapons.

'A sanctioned psyker of some sort,' he decided, noting sigil-marks on the skin the fusillade hadn't obliterated. 'Cursed by Nurgle.'

'So where is it?' asked Solinus.

Scipio met his gaze, questioning.

'Where is the beast?' the other sergeant clarified.

'That was not the creature I burned,' offered Cator.

His battle-brothers were right. This thing was a puppet; no more than a vessel for whatever entity had claimed this place and transformed it into its own wretched domain. Where was the plaguebearer that had claimed the soul of this man?

Scipio turned around at the sound of ceramite clattering against stone behind them.

'Brother-Chaplain, replace your battle-helm. This place is unclean!'

He went to go to Orad but was held back by the Chaplain's warding hand. The wound in his power armour was seeping gore and pus. It crusted his entire forearm and was spreading.

His words were thick with phlegm. 'Stay back.'

'Lords of Ultramar,' Solinus gasped and reached for his bolt pistol. 'It has taken him, it has taken our Chaplain.'

Scipio pushed down his aim. 'Wait!'

Orad went to speak again but bent double and vomited a stream of corruption. Chin drooling with sick, he spat a last gobbet of the stuff from his mouth. His eyes were sunken in his skull, the old wounds on his face throbbing, raw and reopened. He sank down, knee deep in the filth. His crozius fell from his grasp.

'What are you doing?' snapped Solinus. 'He has the taint – we must end him now!' He shook off Scipio's grasp and brought up the weapon again.

Scipio stepped into his line of sight. 'He is our Chaplain. Of us all, his faith is the most devout. How can this be?'

'It matters not. Stand aside, now.'

Ever since Scipio had been a Scout, Orad had been his Chaplain. He had counselled his doubts on Black Reach, had instilled the power of his faith in him. And now he was damned, reduced to no more than a vessel for an insidious terror. The taint of Chaos had claimed him. It had breached his aegis through the smallest of cracks, widened it and rotted him from within.

Scipio drew his own sidearm. His voice was low and solemn. 'I will do it.'

Nodding, Solinus lowered his aim. 'Then do it quickly, before it is too late.'

Orad had wrapped his arms around his torso and was convulsing violently in the pool of filth he had created. There was no sentience in his eyes any more. He was a gibbering wreck, a once proud servant of Ultramar brought low.

But when Scipio drew a bead upon the Chaplain he hesitated.

There must be a way. Orad can repulse it.

In eerie synchronicity with the sergeant's thoughts, the Chaplain's neck snapped up and his dead eyes fixed onto Scipio's pitiless retinal lenses.

'Mercy...'

The trigger squeezed a little tighter in Scipio's grasp, but he couldn't do it. Orad shook with a sudden palsy. Something within the Chaplain was changing.

The sergeant felt a hand on his pauldron. The world was slowing as if mired in the very foul stuff that pervaded the temple. The reek of death and decay overtook the chamber, more noisome than ever.

'Kill it! Do it now!'

Scipio was only dimly aware of Solinus's urgent voice, of the slow *chank* of bolter shells filling their chambers, of the bounds of Orad's armour bursting apart like an overfilled lung.

Too late the first shell spat from Scipio's pistol, its burning contrails flashing in the air. The sheer lassitude of its trajectory brought on by the hell-transformation unfolding before him allowed Scipio to appreciate every spark, every mote of flame.

Too late, other shells joined it from the battle-brothers

around him; nascent spits of flamer too and the glowing coruscation from a plasma gun.

Too late, Scipio realised what his hesitancy had cost them and shouted a warning to Brother Naius.

The husk of Orad's armour broke apart under the barrage but the creature that had stolen the Chaplain's flesh was no longer there. It had leapt onto the ceiling, latching to the rock with the acid-slime on its claws, spewing out barbed tendrils from a distended maw.

Three of the tendrils punched through Naius's chestplate and he fell, bolter loosing off wild rounds as he died and his death grip clenched.

Scipio reached him a fraction too late. He bundled Naius over with the barbs still hooked in him. They stretched and ripped free as he went down, breaking open ceramite and taking chunks of flesh into the darkness above as the beast retracted them. Then it was gone.

'Naius!' Scipio unleashed a burst into the gloom but hit only rockcrete. It was a pointless act, save for the fact of venting his anger. Resting a hand over the neck where Naius's only intact progenoid was still harboured, Scipio got to his feet. He had been one of Solinus's squad and now his legacy had ended – all because Scipio had hesitated. The Ultramarines were on the offensive, searching the vaults in the temple above, throwing out random bursts of fire as someone saw a shadow or detected the insidious scuttling of the daemon.

Avoiding Solinus's furious gaze, Scipio went on the hunt for the thing too, determined to avenge Naius. It was Orad no longer. Trapped for a moment in the lurid glare of a pestilential lantern, the Ultramarines saw an abomination where once had been their Chaplain. Gelid-skinned, surrounded by flies, it was more corpse than man. A horn had sprouted from the daemon's head; claws replaced hands; it had hooves instead of feet. It was emaciated, its innards showing through diaphanous skin. Pustules and boils puckered flesh that sagged like melted wax and a grotesque hump bent the monster's back.

Seeing the Ultramarines' obvious disgust, it chuckled.

'What's wrong... *brothers*?' Its hideous voice was a slurred parody of Orad's.

Bolter impacts riddled the wall where it was clinging like some human spider, but went wide of the mark. For such a diseased beast it was quick, racing up pillars and skittering through the shadows too fast for the Space Marines to bring it down.

'Keep it pinned,' shouted Solinus, directing warriors left and right in pairs. Three battle-brothers guarded the temple entrance and were primed to release a deadly salvo if the creature came within range and sight.

Scipio did the same and was about to give chase, determined the beast that had killed Orad would not escape, when something seized his arm. At first, he thought it might be Solinus and he turned with defiance on his lips. That emotion turned to horror when he realised it was Brother Naius. His armour was corroding from the inside out. A bloodshot eye, rampant with pestilence, glared madly from a wound in his eye socket. The point where the tendrils had pierced his chest bulged, cracking his plastron.

Swinging round his chainsword, Scipio cut Naius down – the second son of Ultramar he had condemned by his inaction – finishing him with a blast from his pistol.

Or so he thought.

Partially exploded, a huge cavity in his stomach yawning

open with pustulant debris, the undead-Naius rose on twisted limbs. The chainsword had chewed off part of his helmet. Blackened nubs of teeth bared in a snarl as the creature came at Scipio.

'Brother!' The sergeant ducked when he recognised Cator's voice. A *whoosh* of rapidly expelled promethium followed, sending heat spikes registering on Scipio's retinal display when the flamer burst just missed him. It engulfed the undead-Naius, though, eliciting a scream that was no longer wrenched from his former brother's lips.

'Don't let the mouth barbs touch you,' Scipio warned, backing up and searching the shadows. Behind him, Naius burned away to ash, leaving rotten armour in his wake.

Seven grotesque pillars supported the vaulted ceiling of the plague temple. The daemon weaved and scuttled between them, using the darkness to thwart the Ultramarines.

'Herd it!' Solinus bellowed, his voice echoing from somewhere deeper in the vast room. Sporadic bolter fire followed and Scipio thought he saw the silhouette of something unholy coming his way. He pressed his body against one of the pillars and waited. He couldn't see the daemon but he could sense it. Not in a psychic way, Scipio was no Librarian. But it was in his nose, despite his olfactory filters; it veneered his skin, though he wore power armour over a mesh bodyglove; it buzzed in his ears like the droning of flies.

Scipio shut his eyes and focused on his instincts. The creature was fast but not impossibly so. He owed it to Orad, to Naius, to kill it.

Close now. The shouting of his battle-brothers was getting nearer. They were operating in a dispersed formation in order to cover the most ground. He heard Cator and Brakkius, the clipped shots of Ortus in the vicinity.

Not yet. He pressed against the pillar, denying the urge to engage, to wreak bloody havoc as an avenging Angel of Death. He needed for it to come closer.

When the moment arrived it almost took him by surprise, but Scipio's body was honed, conditioned to preternatural levels and it reacted out of instinct. He opened his eyes. Springing from cover, his chainsword was already swinging. The mouth tendrils spilled like dead worms as the blade-teeth cut through them. The blade continued its buzzing trajectory, embedding in the rib bone all the way to the base of the sternum. Face-to-face with the daemon, Scipio levelled his bolt pistol and for a split second it was Orad there and not a plaguebearer.

'Brother–' it began to mouth, a look of anguish on its diseased face.

'Get back to the abyss!' The bolt pistol fired and the shell struck the daemon in the eye, turning the creature back to its true form. It still wore Orad's flesh, strips of body-mesh clung tenaciously to his enhanced musculature, but it was not him.

It isn't him…

The plaguebearer's visage exploded in a bloom of viscera and bone-chips as the mass-reactive shell detonated, leaving it without a head. It sagged, deflated almost, as a keening wail ripped the air like a fat blade. Ichor exuded from the orifice in the neck, pooling about the dead Chaplain's shoulders. The daemon was banished; its meat puppet was Orad again. A dead and decapitated Orad, but it was him.

Scipio nearly sank to his knees at the sight. Solinus steadied him. His voice was stern but genuine. 'That thing would have killed us all. You had no choice, brother.'

But Scipio felt differently. His inaction had caused Naius's demise; his bolter hand had slain what was left of Orad.

'I made my choice too late,' he breathed, avowing silently never to do so again. 'And it killed Orad. It killed them both.'

DAMNOS

ULTRAMARINES

2ND COMPANY

PICT DATA 22833/00/35
NECRON WARRIOR
ACCESSING DATA:
DATA RUNE N244 ACTIVE//
PROCESSING....DISPLAYING
THREAT STATUS: HIGH
WEAPON DATA: UNKOWN GAUSS TEK
ADVISORY: DISENGAGE/DELTA TEK

Thought for the day:
Harken not to the
whispers of the warp

DAMNOS
PLANETARY MAP

Mandos Prime – Geothermic fusion stations under the purview of Mechanicus Magos Karnak suffer critical failure after increased seismic activity, heralding the xenos invasion.

Damnos Prime – Several manufactorum sites of Damnos Prime are utterly destroyed by the necron advance. Ark-Guard forces are unable to meet the threat and swiftly eradicated.

Tyrrean Ocean – Upon crossing the largest water mass on Damnos, the necrons drain much of the ocean into an extra-dimensional sinkhole, turning it into a barren wasteland. All fighting vessels still operational are beached, their crews slaughtered.

Halaheim – All hands at Dagoth Station at Halaheim are massacred. A pict-cast caught by a servitor drone escapes ahead of the comm shroud but only foments greater anxiety in the surviving Imperial resistance.

Damnos Secundus, Tertius, Southern Polar Bastions, Fourth-Bloc Mining Station – Attacks break out across multiple locations. As the necron comm shroud moves southwards, military coordination between Imperial Guard regiments is rendered impossible. Resistance is quickly crushed.

Zephyr Monastery – All priests, serfs and helots, together with relics, basilica and all religious icons, are lost in a single necron energy pulse.

Arcona City – Secondary Damnosian settlement is subdued, its army decimated, within hours of the necrons' arrival. Scattered damage reports indicate heavy and sustained bombardment.

Thanatos Refinery – Total destruction of refinery complex by a necron splinter force moving into the Thanatos Hills for purposes unknown. Area suffers from a total comms blackout more pervasive than experienced previously.

Kellenport – The last major city of Damnos is besieged by an immense necron force. Despite the presence of the battleship *Nobilis,* the city is swiftly overrun and Imperial forces retreat into the inner bastion walls.

Crastia Shipyards – Remaining starport is rendered 'out of commission' and overrun by subterranean necron forces. All efforts to retake ended with failure. Fate of garrison stationed at Crastia: unknown.

COMMANDER ANTARO CHRONUS

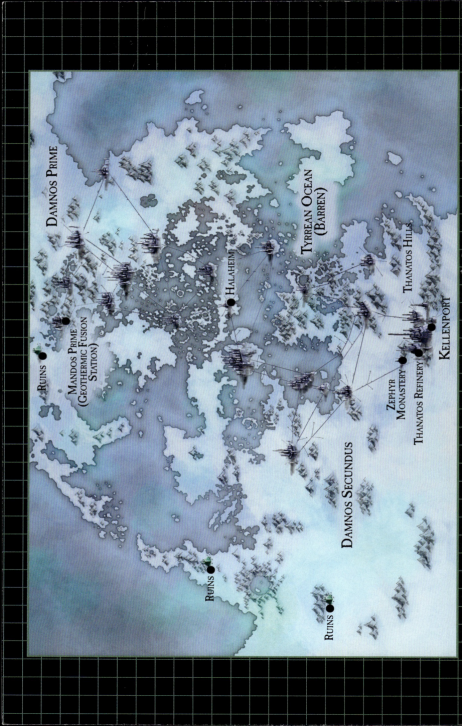

DAMNOS PRIME

TYRREAN OCEAN
(BARREN)

HALAHEIM

THANATOS HILLS

MANDOS PRIME
(GEOTHERMIC FUSION
STATION)

RUINS

KELLENPORT

ZEPHYR
MONASTERY

THANATOS REFINERY

DAMNOS SECUNDUS

RUINS

RUINS

CHAPTER TWENTY

Sicarius signalled the retreat. He'd cut a path through the necrons, dispatching one with every blow of the Tempest Blade. The air was thick with the stench of phasal shift. At their captain's command, the Ultramarines bled back into the ice-fog, their forms lit by the star-flash of bolter muzzle flares. Slow to react to the lightning assault, the necrons didn't even attempt to give chase. They settled for a desultory salvo of gauss-fire and then continued their advance towards Kellenport.

'Does this seem too easy to you, brother-captain?' asked Daceus when they were clear. He reaped a heavy toll with his power fist and was sweating with the effort of killing, but they'd barely dented the enemy's forces.

Sicarius's initial silence betrayed his anger. 'It's ineffective, sergeant,' he replied at last. 'Our attacks are of no consequence.' He opened up the battle-force-wide comms-feed. Though the necrons were blocking most vox-signals, it was only long distance communication that was affected.

The leaders of the attack groups he'd deployed to harry the necron phalanxes returned with similar replies. The mechanoids were defending themselves but otherwise had ignored them. Since their first foray, this was the fifth engagement. No one had, as of yet, managed to get close enough to the core of the force to ascertain if a high-level lord was present.

Sicarius clenched his fist, his rage impotent for now. 'Regroup, all squads.'

'Sir?' asked Daceus when his captain didn't make any move.

'This isn't working. I have to draw it out, Daceus.'

'My lord,' the voice of Sergeant Manorian crackled over the feed.

Sicarius was brusque. 'Speak.'

'The necrons have stopped moving.'

Sicarius acknowledged then cut the link. 'Something has changed.'

'A new weapon in their arsenal? Perhaps they're consolidating after our raids? They might be having an effect after all,' suggested Daceus.

'No, I don't think it's that.' Sicarius eyed the fog, as if searching it for the answer he wanted. 'But I will know the answer before we're done.'

SICARIUS STARED THROUGH Praxor's magnoculars, waiting for the rest of the force to join them. The Ultramarines would regroup in an area of sparse ruins, part of one of Arcona City's commercia districts. Most of the megalopolis had been levelled by necron heavy artillery. These blackened nubs of debris were a rare feature on an otherwise bland and flattened landscape. The squads filtered in from the north and south; west was where the necron advance was coming from – though, in truth, they dominated most of the planet – and east led back to Kellenport. Ixion and Strabo, redeployed from the Thanatos Operation, arrived first on contrails of fire. Several of their number were wounded but they'd sustained no casualties.

Venatio was patching up the injured and stopped in front of his captain.

'I'll need to see that,' he said.

Lowering the scopes, Sicarius glared at him. 'Why do you think they've stalled their advance, Brother-Apothecary?'

'That's not my concern at this time. The injury to your shoulder is, however.'

A long cleft split part of the captain's pauldron and there was blood gumming the wound. It looked deep. Praxor had been taken aback at first when he'd seen it. He'd never known Sicarius to bleed. He knew he was flesh and blood, but Sicarius was such a peerless warrior, he had never witnessed more than a scratch against his armour. Praxor hoped it wasn't an omen.

The captain was about to protest again but Venatio's resolve was unwavering; so too was his stare. Sicarius passed the scopes back to Praxor and seated himself on a chunk of ruin for the Apothecary to examine him.

'The shoulder: how is it?' Venatio was removing the cracked pauldron and was probing the mesh layer beneath to get at the wound.

'Stiff,' admitted Sicarius, rotating the blade once the armour was removed. Acutely aware he was being observed, he turned to Praxor.

'Watch them, brother-sergeant,' he said. 'I want to know the moment anything changes.'

Praxor nodded and continued where Sicarius had left off. There was a ridge of blackened stone just ahead of the Ultramarines position. It was a better vantage point to observe the necrons so he made for it.

Agrippen met him there.

'How do you defeat an endless foe?' Praxor asked after a few moments as he looked through the scopes.

'The same as any, with courage and honour,' the Dreadnought replied.

The ridge was little more than a spur of rock, a collapsed column or statue – the damage and the ice made it hard to tell – and could just about provide enough room for Praxor and the ancient.

'Our forces are battered, though. I would follow my captain into battle until I could no longer wield bolter and blade, but it is hard to see how we will prevail.'

'The Chapter has been bloodied before. Some wars are merely harder than others. It is here that we truly test ourselves and prove our strength.'

Praxor tried not to think of the remark as facile. So much of what he knew, or thought he knew, had been tested on Damnos. Not all of it had survived the journey.

He looked below and saw that the rest of the battle force had returned. Sicarius was gathering them for something big, some fresh assault as he sought his prize.

Praxor chastened himself – such thoughts were unfitting for a Space Marine. He resolved to speak to Trajan at the earliest opportunity. He returned to the scopes.

'They are like statues. What are they waiting for?

'Perhaps they seek to gauge our next course of action,' suggested Agrippen.

Praxor lowered the magnoculars again and looked at the

Dreadnought. 'Tell me, brother: how would Agemman have prosecuted this war?'

Agrippen's reply was emphatic but neutral. 'He would not have.'

'Damnos would have been left to burn?' Praxor was incredulous.

The Dreadnought fixed him with a glare from the vision slit in his sarcophagus. 'It would have been *made* to burn.'

'You think that Damnos is already lost?'

'It doesn't matter what I think. I serve the Chapter. On this field of war, on this campaign, I serve Captain Sicarius. What I believe or what I know is immaterial; duty is what matters most.'

'I am unworthy of that honour,' Praxor admitted. 'I do not see my captain's mind and I doubt our purpose on this world.'

'What do you doubt about it, brother?'

Praxor paused, weighing up his next words carefully, 'These are a broken people. Imperial citizens, yes, but unworthy of that honour. It is hard to find accord with saving a people that does not want to save itself.'

'Are you so sure they are without defiance? Courage?'

'It is what I have seen, yes.'

Agrippen considered that for a moment, before saying, 'Answer me this, brother: do you believe you are above these humans in some way?'

'In all ways,' Praxor said flatly.

'Then is it not the duty of those lofty individuals to inspire and lift those beneath them so that they too might achieve some measure of greatness?'

Praxor wasn't expecting that. The Dreadnought's logic

was hard to refute, so he didn't try. Instead, he bowed his head. 'Of course it is.'

'There is more?' Agrippen pressed. Praxor's shame was not only at his discarding of the Damnosians' right to protection and life.

He lifted his head. 'I had thought you here to press Agemman's interests and secure the pre-eminence of the First by undermining Sicarius. It was an unworthy belief.'

Agrippen was sanguine. 'Your faith has been tested, that is all. It must be if it is to remain strong.' There was no hint of reproach in his rumbling sepulchral voice. 'As to the matter of Agemman, too much is made of this supposed rivalry. I trust in the wisdom and leadership of our Lord Calgar. Do you know why that is so?'

Praxor's silence bade him to continue.

'Because I have witnessed his courage and heard his words. Victory or death – one or the other awaits us on Damnos. I do not fear it. I do not let it concern me. It merely *is*. This is our duty. It is what makes us Emperor's Angels. He will protect us and He will grant Sicarius the wisdom and guile to lead us.'

Praxor bowed his head again that such a noble warrior had deigned to share his wisdom with him. '*Victoris Ultra*, venerable one.'

'*Victoris Ultra*.'

Servos whirring, gears grinding, Agrippen dismounted from the rocky spur and went to find Ultracius. He left Praxor to his thoughts and his duty.

'What do you see, brother-sergeant?' Sicarius asked a few moments later. He was done with the Apothecary and had come for a status report.

Praxor was looking through magnoculars at the distant

enemy formations but the ice-fog was still thick. They'd reached the edge of Arcona City and were about to pass over its borders, if they ever moved again.

'They are waiting.' In spite of the weather, Praxor could see the massive phalanxes standing shoulder-to-shoulder. Their utter stillness was unnatural. Skeletal-faced, their eye sockets aglow, they reminded him of revenants. 'Do we attack?'

Sicarius shook his head, ignoring the proffered scopes. Daceus was with him, carrying his captain's battle-helm.

'We will fall back.'

'We continue to flee?' asked Praxor.

'A Space Marine does not flee, brother-sergeant,' interjected Daceus. His bionic eye seemed to burn with indignation. 'When met by an implacable enemy, he does not throw his strength at it until he is spent. He finds a way to bring the battle to his advantage.'

'We need to level the scales, Sergeant Manorian,' asserted Sicarius. 'A warrior has many weapons in his arsenal. This–' he brandished his plasma pistol. 'And this.' He tapped the hilt of his sheathed Tempest Blade before gesturing to their surroundings, 'but he must also use his mind and mould the battlefield into a weapon too.'

He paused, peering into the mists. 'How close are they now, brother?'

'Two kilometres and static. My lord, what are they waiting for?'

'What else?' Sicarius answered, and there was a hint of a smile in his voice as his eyes narrowed. 'For their potentate, the one who wields power.'

Sicarius was right. Praxor looked back through the magnoculars and found the necron lord who commanded the army. He had just emerged in the throng. It was an ancient, terrible creature with age-tarnished trappings and a body of shimmering gold.

'I think the wait is over, sire.' He handed his captain the scopes and this time Sicarius took them.

'So it seems. Tell me something, Brother Manorian, have you heard of the Battle of Thermapylon?'

'I know a myth, from the days of the Terran battle-kings.'

'Go on.'

'Seven hundred men of warrior blood held the pass of Thermapylon against the numberless hordes of Xeruclese from across the sea. Their sacrifice allowed the army of King Vidus to muster and throw back the enemy, harrying them all the way back to the beaches where they made their berths, and burn their ships at anchor.'

'*And the seas ran red with their blood and the sand became as crimson night,*' added Sicarius, reciting from the epic poem that recalled the legend.

Praxor was briefly wrong-footed; he didn't know his captain had studied the arts. But then it was military history, mythic or not, and Sicarius was an arch-student of war. It made a certain sense.

'Do you know how they triumphed?'

'With blood and steel, I presume.'

'Oh, their blades were red as the dawn, brother, but that wasn't how they engaged an army of five hundred thousand with seven hundred men. No, they achieved their goal because they knew the lay of the land. Every death was paid for by a hundred enemy soldiers. It was a battle of attrition that could only end in suicide but it wrested time from the hands of fate and used it to the king's advantage. His army was ocean-borne and won a great naval victory against Xeruclese's allies. Much of the details are lost to time but the message remains true and relevant.'

'I am ready to die for my Chapter, brother-captain,' said Praxor.

'That is not what I mean.' Sicarius returned the magnoculars. 'This war *can* be won. But we need time. We need our tanks – Antaro would relish this theatre of war – and the *Valin's Revenge*. I plan to get us that time and cut down the necron overlord into the bargain. But I do not plan on dying to achieve it.' He turned, fixing Praxor in a gimlet glare. 'My legacy is not yet at its end, and I would add more laurels to my banner.'

Praxor nodded. Sicarius's defiance was stirring, even if he found his arrogance a little bitter with the casualties they'd already sustained.

'Outside Kellenport, at the edges of the city wall, we will funnel the necrons into our own pass and there they will fall to our fury. Tigurius will have destroyed the Thanatos guns by then and Antaro can unleash his armoured fists.'

'The necrons are formidable, my lord. They are not the hordes of Xeruclese, nor do they merely wield spears or travel in wooden boats.'

'Indeed, but we carry bolters and are Adeptus Astartes.' He turned to Daceus. 'We make for the Kellenport outer marker,' he said. 'Signal Sergeants Ixion and Strabo to range ahead of us there and tell them to make haste. The necrons are moving.'

Both Strabo and Ixion came back to Daceus swiftly. The speed of the reply sent a tremor of unease through Praxor as did the veteran-sergeant's grim face as he related the reply to Sicarius.

'Request denied, sir.'

'Explain, brother-sergeant.'

'They cannot. There are forces coming from the east, from Kellenport. The necrons have us blocked in.'

Sicarius took his battle-helm without response. When he slammed it down against his gorget, there was a *clang* not unlike a death knell across the frozen quietude of the wastes. When the captain did finally speak it was with the grating cadence of his vox-grille.

'Gather your battle-brothers, and have the other sergeants do likewise. We make our stand here.' His tone turned belligerent as he drew the Tempest Blade and pointed towards the advancing horde and the necron overlord in its ranks. 'Death or glory awaits us – I will welcome both.'

CHAPTER
TWENTY-ONE

ANKH WAS CONNECTED to all the mechanoids of the tomb. They were his workers, his messengers, his eyes and ears. Truly, he was the Architect. Most creatures of the universe – he had come to think of them as simpleton children when compared to the majesty and intellect of the necrontyr – beheld the necrons and saw only machines. They were so much more than that. Their science had fundamentally changed their race. It was so advanced that to look upon it would be to perceive what primitive cultures called magic. These humans, a race of barely evolved primates, were one such culture.

To serve the machinations of his lord, he would unleash 'magic' of a terrifying magnitude. He had activated a dooms-day phalanx of monoliths. Through the multi-faceted eyes of one of his drones, Ankh had witnessed the destruction of one of his pyramidal engines. It had surprised him. Per-haps it was why the Undying wanted so desperately to kill

this one. Was the genebred warrior really any different from
the rest of his species? Certainly, he attired himself more
ostentatiously than any of the other armour-clad savages.
Immobilising the monolith was also a feat worthy of note,
especially done single-handed.

Ankh had moved the others at his overlord's command.
The Undying wanted to see annihilation; the talons of the
Destroyer curse had made their first incisions into his fragile engrammic sanity. Pre-eminent amongst these weapons
of war was the Doomsday Monolith.

'You desire destruction, my lord,' Ankh said to the quietude of the tomb. Through the eyes of his creations he
could see the trio of monoliths gliding into position; the
nexus of energy between them had almost reached critical
mass. 'Then you shall have it.'

Ankh unleashed his 'magic'.

'GIVE ME MORE. Break your backs if you have to, but bring
those things down!' Letzger was hoarse from all the shouting. Above the roaring thunder of the guns, he had to
bellow to be heard.

His gun crews knew the drill, though. They knew that
sweating blood was necessary and that their lives and the
lives of their people depended on it.

Hel-handed boomed again, shaking dust from its foundations and sluicing debris down to the lower levels with
every seismic explosion from its barrel. From the Thanatos
Hills to the monoliths converging on the meagre defenders
in the Courtyard of Xiphos, Letzger had changed targets. So
far, his efforts to bring down one of the necron pyramids
had been in vain. There was some kind of ethereal veil protecting them all. Shots that weren't lost to the black void

coiling around the machineries were otherwise absorbed by the living metal from which the monoliths were constructed.

The view down the *Hel-handed's* crosshairs was not an encouraging one.

Letzger seized the vox-horn. 'Leave 'em be and send a shell into the square.' He rattled off a series of measurements, amending the cannon's aim and trajectory. 'And give those metal bastards a half-shell. Don't want to crucify our Angels in the blast.'

Slamming the speaker cup down, Letzger was about to get settled on the scopes and watch the show when something bright blazed on the horizon.

Emerald light burned from some unseen source, forcing him to look away. He felt the heat against his skin and smelled his hair smouldering before the beam hit.

'*Merciful Emperor,*' he breathed as a green fire hit the *Hel-handed* and a god-weapon died.

ADANAR FELT THE explosion before he saw it. He felt it even before the beam hit the Kellenport wall and tore the *Hel-handed* open. Letzger had been on that platform, the ornery old dog. After the emerald flash faded he simply wasn't there any more; neither were his gun crews. The weapon was a twisted mess. There was little of it left. Most of the wall and the troops nearby, even those who had hunkered down on the lower level, had also been obliterated.

He turned to Humis, who had ducked behind the barricade. Part of the corporal's uniform was on fire, ignited by the heat wave. Adanar was patting it down when he realised his own face was burned raw. It stung to the touch.

'Throne of Earth,' mewled the corporal. 'We are all dead men.'

Adanar was getting to his feet. He'd only realised belatedly that he'd been knocked down – must have been from the void shields breaking. 'We were dead men before now,' he said, snarling at the pain in his face. 'Yet here we are.' He pulled his pistol. Something was materialising on the wrecked battlements amidst the fire-blackened debris of the *Hel-handed*.

Necrons.

The first of the men inside Kellenport died without realising what killed them. Their faces were still etched in terror as they turned to ash.

Adanar loosed off a shot that struck a steel skull in the jaw, making the mechanoid jerk its neck. It didn't stop it from flaying the Ark Guardsmen in front of it.

'Turn and fight!' the commander raged. He was further away than he remembered and his right leg hurt with all the fires of the warp.

Slowly, the troopers below the battlements started to fight back. A sergeant was even shouting for order before a gauss-blast reduced his head to a greasy memory. He toppled, his neck wound cauterised, before someone else took his place.

Humis was running alongside Adanar, dodging the stray emerald beams and vaulting chunks of rubble. The platform wasn't that far, the enemy even less so. 'They must have used a weapon on us,' he said. There was a hollow sound in his breathing, as if he had a punctured lung. Perhaps he had. Humis didn't complain, though. 'It must have been powerful to cut through the shield.'

How were they even functioning? Adanar had no clue. They'd been punched across the battlements, caught in the blast wave – he knew that now. Somehow they'd stayed on the wall instead of being pitched to their doom, but they were both hurt.

Following their commander's example, more of the Ark Guard got up from their posts and joined Adanar and Humis. There weren't that many necrons on the wall yet; there was still time to block the attack.

'And now they're phasing in their raiders to finish the job.'

Adanar didn't talk. He assumed Humis needed to or he'd realise what they were doing and flee, or lose what scrap of sanity he had left.

A half-glance below revealed the Space Marines and some of the conscripts were exchanging fire with the mechanoids assaulting the square. The necrons obviously didn't possess the capacity to phase all of their troops onto the walls or they'd already be overrun. Silently, he wished the Angels luck. It seemed an odd thing to have to do. Over the last few hours, the Emperor's avengers had seemed altogether more human than Adanar had ever given them credit for. It was to the good and the bad, he supposed.

He was running past a vox-officer when a gauss-beam jagged out and took the poor swine in the gut. His innards were dissolved to atoms and he slumped with a gurgle. Adanar crouched behind a broken crenellation, taking cover for the first time since the surge towards the gun platform. Hot, green energy flashed overhead as he stooped for the fallen vox-cup. A few seconds later, Humis was right there with him. The man had blood on his collar from where he'd been coughing. Adanar boosted the vox-signal as high as it would go and yelled into the cup.

'This is Commander Adanar Sonne. All forces to the gun platform on the east wall. Repel the enemy at all costs.'

The barrage lessened as more troops joined the effort of

dislodging the necron invaders, and Adanar was on his feet again. He patted Humis on the shoulder, indicating they needed to get going, but the corporal didn't move. When he looked back, Adanar saw the pallor of his face and the glass in his eyes. Humis was dead.

He carried on.

Las-beams were hammering the necrons now, who didn't bother to seek cover or retreat. They merely advanced, implacable as death.

Something was happening up ahead. He thought he recognised a desperate figure fleeing from the mechanoids, taking several squads with him. Adanar's fists clenched when he realised it was Rancourt. The cowardly worm was trying to save his own skin but had opened the trap the Ark Guard had forged around the raiders.

He wanted to shout, to tell them to turn back, but he was too far away and the din of gunfire was too loud. Instead, Adanar carried on. He was racing to his doom, and he knew it. He didn't care. This was the moment he had been waiting for. At last he would know peace. He couldn't just throw his life away, *she* wouldn't like that. But this was different. Adanar's sacrifice might save the lives of those Rancourt had endangered. His only regret was he wouldn't get to see the bastard suffer for it.

Just a few more metres and he'd be on them. He nearly tripped on a corpse. The poor wretch had been sliced in two by a necron beam. Though hard to tell, Adanar knew it was Kador and that Rancourt had bolted when his bodyguard was slain.

The locket-charm around his wrist dug into his skin where his arm was blistered by the terrible emerald flash. Adanar tore it free and gripped it in his hand.

I'm coming… The words echoed inside his head, meant for those who had waited long enough already. Leaping the half-flayed wreckage of a gun crew, Adanar made it onto the platform and was ready to meet his end.

THE COURTYARD OF Xiphos had lit up like some infernal flare. Snow and ice melted instantly before evaporating into steam as the beam struck the wall and fire washed over those below.

Some of the men closer to the impact point were flattened. Their uniforms caught alight and there was screaming. Other conscript squads were fleeing; some stayed to help the injured but Iulus waved them on.

'Forward as one, bolter and blade!'

Except these men didn't carry bolters, nor did they wear power amour or possess the strength and skill of a Space Marine. For more times than he needed to count, Iulus was impressed by the fortitude of men. The conscripts took up their weapons and kept up the fight.

The beam that slew the god-weapon on the wall hadn't come from the Thanatos Hills. That barrage, as potent as it was and still persisting even now, was unable to knock out the void shields. The range was too far. No, the killing blow that ruptured the massive cannon's aegis came from the monoliths. The pyramids had fired as a collective, unleashing a beam of such potency that it had overloaded a void shield.

'We will die in this hellstorm,' shouted Kolpeck beside him. It brought Iulus from his thoughts.

The two sides traded intense fire across the Courtyard of Xiphos. Most of the Imperials had found cover and this mitigated the fact that their armour paled in comparison to that of the necrons. As each force advanced, the carnage only intensified.

Iulus nodded, 'Glory or death,' he cried to the rig-hand turned soldier. 'Embrace it and the Emperor will take you to his side when it is done.'

This *was* death. Iulus had a mind for tactical acumen, just like any Space Marine. He knew odds and strategy, and he could recognise a last stand. With the Ordinatus on the wall destroyed, so too went their final chance of survival. A sense of inevitability had crept into the ebb and flow of the fight. Iulus meant to sell his life dearly.

'Brothers!' he bellowed as the roar of bolters and heavy weapons pummelled the air.

Around him, the last of the Immortals gathered.

Aristaeus gave a nod. Galvia held up a clenched fist. Wherever he looked, Iulus saw his warriors proud and defiant in the face of certain destruction. Since he had been instated the squad's sergeant, they had never lost a battle-brother and had become dubbed the 'Immortals' on that account. It was fitting then that if that honorific was to be broken now they would die as one.

'Immortals to the end!' said Brother Pention and the cry was taken up by them all, the conscripts and Ark Guard too.

A beam took Uklidese in the shoulder and chest. He fell but was dragged up by Illion and Menalus. Venkelius was the next to drop, clutching at his gorget.

Then Aristaeus. Iulus reacted quickly, supporting him under the arm.

'Stand, brother,' he growled. 'We'll meet them on our feet.'

Agnathio was punctured by a dozen beams, the Dreadnought lanced through and spewing fire, smoke and fluids.

The venerable warrior ground to a halt and his weapons cycled down to dormancy.

'Ultramar!' Iulus wanted it to be the last word on his lips. He spat it at the necrons, as if his will and vitriol could destroy them in an all-consuming wave. 'Ultramar!'

The Ultramarines took up the call, even those who were injured, even Venkelius who could barely speak at all.

'Ultramar!'

It was an end worthy of note. Iulus found the admission of that strange. He had never considered death before or what it meant. He had always only thought in terms of function and need.

I am a warrior and my function is to kill in the Emperor's name.

He had not believed his legacy was important, save to pass on to the next Ultramarine who succeeded him; that his deeds and actions really mattered. Faced with the imminence of mortality, he found his opinion changed. Dying well mattered and this was a manner of death that Iulus could be proud of.

'Stand with me, Kolpeck,' he said, using his body to protect the rig-hand, 'and let us die well together.'

'While I have breath, I will,' Kolpeck replied. 'For her, for Jynn.'

Iulus didn't know who this person was but he understood the sentiment. Men were more than just materiel that could wield a gun, throw a grenade or drive a tank. They were flesh and blood, with hearts and minds. And it hadn't been an honoured warrior, a stern-faced veteran consigned to the lectorum or even a Chaplain that had taught the sergeant this. It had merely been a man, a miner at that. The Ultramarine felt humbled and wished it could end differently for Falka Kolpeck.

Abruptly, at no outward or fathomable sign, the necrons stopped. A radiant emerald flash filled the Courtyard of Xiphos again but not from some doomsday weapon, it was translocation. Iulus detected the scent of phasal shift and as he opened his eyes saw that the raiders were gone. All of the necron cohorts had simply vanished.

A reprieve. He felt slightly robbed. The practical side of his character exerted its will over his emotions quickly though – they were alive. Most of the humans, too, had survived. For Agnathio, they mourned. The Dreadnought was a steaming husk of blast-scarred armour. His life had left him.

'Where did they go?' Aristaeus asked the question as dumbstruck Guardsmen gazed around the walls or the square. They lived, but they didn't know how or why. Even the tunnellers had fled, leaving nothing but rubble in their wake.

Iulus looked around too, trying to reason what had just happened.

Snow was forming, laying a fresh patina across the courtyard. Ice already crusted the wall as the bitter cold reasserted itself after the fire storm. Soon the scene would be virginal again, a chilling graveyard where the dead do not sleep.

Why does a force retreat? Either they are on the brink of defeat or they've found a better fight elsewhere.

Clearly it was the latter.

He uttered one word. 'Sicarius.'

ADANAR WASN'T DEAD and the revelation weighed upon him like an anvil around his neck. He should be dead. This was supposed to be his moment; this was when he was to be reunited with them. But the Emperor – damn his capricious will – wasn't done with Adanar Sonne, it seemed.

Relief, not despair, washed off the other men on the wall. He could feel it almost palpably, see it in their surprised faces. They hugged each other; some even cheered, though the gesture was only half indulged. Fatigue seized them now that the adrenaline of trying to stay breathing faded. Life for another few minutes at least. Adanar half expected the necron artillery to release such a blistering barrage from some other *uber*-weapon that it obliterated the entire city and everything in it, but they didn't. The necrons had retreated.

He was about to ask Humis to contact the army's officers for a report when he remembered the corporal was dead. A screeching sound arrested his attention. His despair and confusion turned to anger as he was confronted by Rancourt.

'Blessed Emperor, we are saved!' He was ebullient, but on the point of hysteria. 'Our saviours are victorious.' Rancourt looked at Adanar nonplussed. 'Why aren't you cheering, commander? We have won. Damnos is saved.'

Adanar slapped him hard across the face with the back of his gloved hand. The blow drew blood from the acting governor's lip.

'Shut up, you idiot. They are not defeated. There is no victory to be had here.'

A group of officers and troopers had gathered around the altercation, drawn by the raised voices.

Now it was Rancourt's turn to be incensed. He touched his chin, but it wasn't just his skin that had been stung by the commander's reprimand. 'How dare you strike a member of the Administratum?' He looked around for an ally in the throng and pointed at a trooper. 'You,' he said. 'Shoot him, shoot Commander Sonne at once.'

At first the Ark Guard trooper looked shocked and distinctly uncomfortable that he'd been singled out. He held up his hands, wanting no part of it.

Frustrated, Rancourt's attention went to someone else. 'You then,' he bawled. 'Shoot them both. I command you to execute them in the name of the Emperor and the Imperium.'

'No.'

Rancourt was looking around rapidly, his gaze flitting from one soldier to the next. 'You're all in on it.' He spat at Adanar's feet. 'Your personal guard, no doubt.' Pointing a finger that he swept around the onlookers, he added, 'You'll all be shot for this. Disobedience, dissension–'

Adanar hit him again and this time put the administrator on the floor. Seizing him by the scruff of the neck, he lifted Rancourt up so he could glare into his eyes. He saw fear in them.

'You are a loathsome worm, Zeph Rancourt,' he declared, 'and your cowardice nearly killed us all. I suspect it may have killed Sergeant Kador, a good man and a good soldier.'

'Kador was a traitor,' spat Rancourt. 'He tried to leave my side.'

Adanar's eyes widened when he saw the butt of a pistol sticking out of the administrator's robes. 'What did you do?' he rasped.

'I didn't kill him if that's what you mean. It was a warning shot. I only winged him.' Rancourt saw the change come over Adanar's face and quailed. 'What are you going to do?'

'Did you hit him in the leg, slow him down and lower his guard? Eh? Is that when the beam hit him?' Adanar tightened his grip around the other man's collar.

Rancourt's feet were almost dangling off the ground. 'Let me go, let me go,' he pleaded.

Adanar brought him closer, eye-to-eye. 'Oh, I'll let you go,' he whispered. With a grunt of effort, he lifted the administrator above his head.

'Unhand me!' Rancourt shrieked.

Adanar had him poised at the edge of the battlements. 'As you wish,' he said, and threw him off.

There was a wet crunch as the ex-governor hit the ground. Blood pooled in the snow, turning it crimson. Not one of the men on the wall emitted so much as a gasp, let alone tried to arrest their commander for murdering an Imperial official. But they all turned as the massive shadow drew over them.

One of the cobalt giants was walking up the steps and had reached the battlements.

Adanar nodded. 'Sergeant Fennion.'

Iulus nodded back as the man went down on one knee.

'Execute me if you must. I would have gladly done it again.'

The Ultramarine growled. 'Get up. I've not come for your life nor do I care about what you've done. We are at war. There is no time for bureaucracy.'

Adanar got to his feet, frowning. 'Then what is it you need?'

'Your men,' replied the cobalt giant. 'Enough to make a difference.'

CHAPTER TWENTY-TWO

THREE GROUPS TRACKED through the mountains. Scipio was up front, just behind Captain Evvers. He could see now why the Ultramarines had struggled to find a way through. She took them on a winding route, through almost invisible canyons, secret passes and sunken valleys. It was treacherous but no one fell to their deaths, the humans more sure-footed than their armoured protectors.

Scipio activated the comm-feed. 'Brothers. Vox-silence from this point.'

They'd reached an outer marker of five hundred metres. Both Vandar and Octavian, who were in the other two assault groups, replied with affirmation runes that lit up Scipio's retinal display.

'What's wrong?' he called ahead.

Evvers, with three of her kinsmen arrayed around her, held up a hand. They were making certain of the route. Snow-shawled crags surrounded them, barely visible against the high mountain drifts. A wicked wind was howling in from the north and the humans had to keep low to avoid being blown off the peaks. Scipio approved of their caution; one false step could be terminal in this white-out.

Tigurius joined him, the inner glow of his eyes only just fading.

'The truth is still veiled to me,' said the Librarian.

'What of our endeavours here? Can your prescience divine a path, my lord?'

He shook his head. 'I cannot breach the veil. Something is blocking my sight.' Tigurius looked down into the impenetrable fog and gloom. 'Below,' he added.

Although he could not see them, Scipio knew that a small army of the necrons awaited them there. The route through the mountains would allow them the element of surprise and they would need to make the most of it. Outnumbered and likely outgunned, the Ultramarines' plan was predicated on causing as much damage to the artillery as possible before the defenders roused into action. There was a lord amongst the mechanoids, too, the one Tigurius called the 'Voidbringer'. From their encounter with the ghoulish necron commander at camp, Scipio was well aware of their power. He wondered briefly what abilities this one would possess.

Evvers was waving them on.

Scipio would find out soon enough.

VOIDBRINGER WAS FRUSTRATED. By attaching him to the artillery in the Thanatos Hills, the royarch had effectively leashed him. He wanted to cow these worms, eradicate them from the face of the earth and reclaim it for the necrontyr.

'I am a conqueror,' he decided, visions of conquest flashing across his memory engrams in a blur, 'not a custodian.'

It only convinced him further that the Undying had submitted to the Destroyer curse and his sanity was all but eroded. The long sleep had taken a heavy toll and as such he would not be able to lead the tomb. Cast out by the other lords he would be reduced to a king of madmen, those who would butcher their metal bodies to the cause of annihilation.

Voidbringer wanted to annihilate but he also wanted to rule. He felt the pull of the infinite, time-eternal stretching before him like an endless conduit, but he did not fear it. He embraced it. His glory would be everlasting.

The orb given unto him by Ankh hummed with power. He regarded it idly as the gauss-obliterators thundered all around him. He did not pretend to understand the arcane science of the crypteks; his own technologies were esoteric and well guarded by just a few of the royal cohort. Energy whorls shimmered inside it, like trapped event horizons collapsing and coalescing in microcosm. If he stared long enough, Voidbringer fancied he could unravel the inner secrets of the universe, unlock the vagaries of chronomancy and the manipulation of living metal. Such things didn't interest him. Let the crypteks be distracted by such petty diversions. Rulership required action, not contemplation.

Even still, the resurrection orb was fascinating. With it his ascendancy would be assured. A subliminal command, like a muscle reflex, opened a chamber in his metal breastbone. The chest cavity opened wide enough to accommodate the orb and Voidbringer placed it carefully within. It glowed briefly, connecting with the necron's systems and enhanced physiology. The surge of power it radiated through him made Voidbringer shudder. His staff of light crackled in sympathetic symbiosis. The cryptek could be useful, he supposed, but he also didn't trust him. Voidbringer also hated the fact he referred to him by his old name. *That* appellation was no longer fitting. None whose memory engrams still functioned remembered the royarch's name, he was just the Undying. It gave him power, a resonance that elevated him above the other nobles.

Voidbringer wanted that. He also wanted an advisor who was more pliable and less likely to betray him. The pact with Ankh was ended; Voidbringer resolved to destroy him once they had achieved victory on this world.

If he could have smiled, he would have.

'Soon,' he whispered to himself, the thought caressing his ego, 'I will rise above all.'

Cocooned by images of his ambition, the Voidbringer failed to notice the figures creeping closer. Perhaps his awareness had been dulled by some outside agent, perhaps the dulcetly throbbing orb embedded in his chest played a part…

ANKH SAW ALL. His tiny burrowing machines kept close to the genebred humans, followed them through the pass and into the mountainous peaks. They kept out of sight; the Architect ensured they remained undetected. Tahek had activated the orb, or at least begun its cycle – Ankh felt this too.

Multiple futures played out across his synapses, each one a subtle variation of the last. The attack of the artillery would cripple the necrontyr and cause a chain reaction throughout the royal court. Nobles would be destroyed, their memory engrams forever degraded. But then Ankh was not a noble, he was merely an elevated servant with certain skills. The rule of law in the tomb was about to change and he, in part, would bring about its apotheosis. His actions, or inactions, had helped to bring this about. The war on Damnos was about to take a debilitating turn.

Ankh was a necron, his loyalties were unquestionable in that regard, but he was also a survivor.

THE RAIDER SENTRIES patrolled the perimeter with predictable regularity. Like automatons, they marched back and forth, gauss-flayers at rest, their fell eyes aglow. A blizzard was rolling down off the mountain, bringing with it a shrieking wind and veiling snow. It built up on their joints, settled on their vast shoulder plates. They betrayed no signs of discomfort. Essentially they were dead things, barely sentient and moving only through the borrowed will and animus of other more powerful beings.

Three pairs performed sentry rotations on the small section of the perimeter that abutted the sheer-sided cliffs of the Thanatos mountain range. One of the necrons paused in its cycle, alerted to something in the icy mists. Its sockets flared with baleful energy as its twin also stopped, a few metres away. The inquisitive raider took two steps forward – at this sector of the perimeter they were largely isolated until the other sentry pairs crossed them again – before its head jerked violently to the side. It raised a hand, releasing its grip on the barrel of the gauss-flayer, to touch the brass shell lodged in its cranium. Emitting a low-pitched whine the shell exploded, taking the necron's head and most of its torso with it.

Realising it was under attack, the other raider switched to defensive protocols and was about to unleash its gauss-flayer in a spread firing pattern before a second shell punched through its eye socket to similar effect. Both mechanoids phased out instantly.

Seconds later, Sergeant Octavian and his Swords of Judgement were tracking low across the rugged hill line. The heat from the capacitors on the artillery was turning the snow into a thick, obscuring mist. It was above waist height and utterly occluded the Ultramarines from view. Reaching the site of the sentries' demise, Octavian opened the closed comm-feed by tapping the side of his helmet, red against the starkness of the ice-fog – with the first kills, vox-silence was no longer necessary.

'Attack group "Iron Sights": Hellfires away and mission achieved.'

THE AFFIRMATIONS FROM the other sergeants came swiftly through Scipio's comm-feed. The sentries were down and all Ultramarines were in position. With the perimeter breached, the way to the necron artillery was open. It was a minute aperture for a small commando force to enter and Scipio meant to exploit it to the full.

The necrons had used machineries, perhaps tunnellers and other large mechanoids to reshape and flatten a section of the Thanatos Hills. He'd taken vantage from the cliff top, just before they'd descended to the base. Thermal-imaging through the scopes revealed a roughly diamond-shaped area, with the artillery pieces arranged around it, one at each point and another weapon in the centre. Five targets for three assault groups – they'd miss Strabo and Ixion, but it couldn't be helped. Evvers and her guerrillas would have to do their part.

He regarded her through the uncompromising slits of his

retinal lenses. She was watching the route ahead through a pair of infra-goggles, and seemed tense – her heart rate and breathing were elevated. Only Adeptus Astartes could undertake a mission of this magnitude and hope to survive. Some might consider it reckless for Scipio to throw the humans into it without consideration for their safety. He cast any lingering doubts aside as he felt an iron fist clench around his heart. Orad had paid the price for his lack of resolve. It would not happen again. They would do their part or they would die in the attempt.

Tigurius emerged out of the fog next to him. He kept low, just like the rest. The Ultramarines were crouching, whereas the humans only had to stoop to become invisible. If the Librarian knew what Scipio was thinking, it didn't show. He seemed preoccupied.

'I must seek out the veil across my sight and cut it loose,' he said, as if penetrating Scipio's mind after all. 'Lead them in, Sergeant Vorolanus, but wait for my signal. Courage and honour.'

The Librarian moved off into the fog on his own private mission.

Scipio watched him go until he was lost to the mist. He opened up the comm-feed again, 'All Ultramarines: close on targets.'

A TREMOR OF unease rippled through the aeons-old consciousness of Voidbringer. It niggled insistently at the edge of his awareness but he allowed the reassuring drone of the orb to comfort him and eclipse it.

TIGURIUS HUNTED THROUGH the mist. He stayed clear of the places where the necron forces were most concentrated, guided psychically. They were little more than unmoving shadows, statues in the ice-fog. Emerald fire in their eyes was the only evidence of unnatural animation in the necrons and even that was dampened by the mist. Not that he truly needed to see. The Librarian's witch-sight might be temporarily blinded, the strands of fate shut to him, but he could still feel…

It was close, the void blanketing his thoughts, that which had almost destroyed him with its malice when he had ridden the Sea of Souls as a psychic avatar. The hulking silhouettes of the pylons and massive gauss-cannons loomed here and there in the ice-fog, rising above the artificial white tide. In part of his mind, that which was largely committed to his subconscious for now, he was aware of his battle-brothers closing swiftly on the structures. Before they committed fully to the attack, he needed to find the one called 'Voidbringer'.

Emotions were easy things for a psyker to detect, even a nascent one. Hatred bled off this monster, as hot and acerbic as acid. Tigurius followed it, a jagged trail of red in his mind. At the end of it he knew he'd find his nemesis.

WITHOUT ANY SCOUTS, the attack force's best chance of making stealth an effective option was through the Thunderbolts. Scipio had drilled his warriors in the arts of subterfuge and operating behind enemy lines, much of his skill imparted by Torias Telion. They were not even close to matching the Master Scout's abilities but the blizzard and the fog were useful tools he could exploit, as was the fact the necrons seemed uncharacteristically sluggish.

Hugging close to the ground and sticking to the channels where the ice-fog was thickest, Scipio and his battle-brothers had crossed almost half the distance to their target without raising an alarm. The stillness of the necron defenders, eerie as it was, made the task of avoiding them easier. If they possessed some kind of sensors or form of auspex that didn't require visual confirmation they were either fouled by the weather or simply not attuned to the presence of the Space Marines.

A strange, preternatural darkness lapped at the edges of the artillery zone. Tigurius had described it as the 'Night Shroud', some piece of necron technology and part of the reason for his psychic blindness. Scipio tried not to look at the darkness too long. They'd penetrated it easily enough at the perimeter and once through the veil, it was just the ice-fog in front of them.

The Thunderbolts' target was a pylon, situated at the farthest apex of the diamond. He checked the melta bombs mag-locked to his armour. Upon returning to the encampment after the encounter with the flayed ones, they'd re-equipped and resupplied. The original plan was a lightning attack, spearheaded by the assault squads and supported by tactical squads, but without Ixion and Strabo that strategy was no longer viable. They'd stealth their way to the objectives instead, attach incendiaries and ignite them at once in a single hammer-strike. Whatever the explosives only managed to cripple, the heavy weapons would finish.

For their part, the guerrilla fighters were well tooled. Carrying improvised bombs and grenades, as well as some of the magnetic foiling devices they'd used to prevent necron phase-out, they were capable of delivering a significant punch of their own. It was insanely dangerous, but Scipio had no compunction about throwing them into the battle just like his brothers.

He stopped a second to interrogate his retinal display. A series of runic indicators were making their way across his plane of vision. Distance notifiers expressed formation and proximity to the targets. All were making solid progress but a further engagement was nearing.

Each of the artillery pieces, pylon or heavy gauss-cannon, were manned by a small group of raider constructs. Scipio doubted the machineries needed crew to function. He didn't understand necron technology but he had discerned enough to realise that much of it was autonomous or controlled by the lords. Whatever their role, the raiders would need to be dispatched first before incendiaries could be deployed. The attack also had to be simultaneous. Wits dulled as they appeared to be, the necrons would still activate with defensive protocols as soon as they realised their perimeter was breached and they were under fire.

A rune flashed silently on Scipio's retinal display. Vandar was already in position. He judged Octavian wasn't far either. Casting caution aside he increased the pace, not realising he'd attracted the attention of something dwelling in the Night Shroud.

As the force rod grew hot in his gauntleted fist, Tigurius knew he was getting close to his prey. The crimson energies he'd been following sparked and forked with almost palpable expression. Briefly, he portioned out a small part of his mind to check on the situation of his battle-brothers – they were nearing final positions.

Perfect synchronicity was needed, but the slow-returning threads of his prescience told him that would be so. Satisfied, Tigurius shut them out and focused all of his thought on finding the Voidbringer. Though he didn't know why, the veil was thinning. Visions swirled in his psychic eye, the fragments of those he'd tried to grasp before slowly coming together.

Marshal your thoughts.

Now was not the time to seek out the elusive truth and uncover the forbidding threat that had dogged him since the mission began; now was destruction and the unleashing of his psychic might. At last, he caught his prey, surrounded by a hot corona of red light. It was standing alone on a desolate ridge, surveying its majesty.

Inside his mind, Tigurius coaxed a ball of lightning into being.

SCIPIO BECAME AWARE they were under attack when Densk was lifted off his feet as if a set of invisible hooks had caught him and begun reeling the guerrilla fighter in.

Jynn screamed, swinging her gun around to try and draw a bead on his attacker, but it was as if the fog had come alive to take him. Blood was spewing down Densk's beard, his cries of pain muffled by the fact he had no tongue. It was an odd, discordant sound. When a slash of crimson washed the ground like the insouciant sweep of a painter's brush, Densk fell apart. His body disintegrated into shreds as his assailant revealed itself through the red haze.

Serpentine, with a necron's torso and a set of wicked talon-blades on each hand; it was a wraith. Only partially corporeal, the thing was half blended into the ice-fog. Its eyes blazed with a yearning for further carnage.

Jynn's snap-shot went wild. She half fell, backing up because the monster was so close. Scipio pushed her down as the necron's tail whipped out and the barbed tip missed her head by the smallest margin. He roared, weighing in with his chainsword. Like an adder, the wraith jinked aside and the blade-teeth bit ice-frozen earth. It flicked out a talon, which Scipio fended off with his forearm. Gouges raked down his vambrace but they weren't deep enough to penetrate.

Cator appeared behind it and thrust his gladius between its neck and collarbone. The wraith emitted a sort of part-scream, part machine-whine and twisted to slash at the Ultramarine. Scipio took his chance and cut off the monster's head with his chainsword. Critically damaged, it phased out, leaving only blood in its wake.

Jynn knelt by Densk's remains, sobbing. Scipio seized her by the shoulder and pulled her up. Their subterfuge was exposed. They had to act.

Furious at his impatience, for sealing Densk's death warrant on account of it, Scipio snarled down the comm-feed. 'All Ultramarines, attack now!'

PSYCHIC LIGHTNING ARCED from Tigurius's force rod. It struck Voidbringer's staff as he turned, breaking his strange torpor. A serpent of light and energy, the discharged psychics roiled down the haft of the weapon. He wrestled with it, trapping the force as it coursed across the staff and asserting dominance.

Tigurius's eyes widened. That bolt should have ripped the creature apart.

Energies dissipating from the psychic attack, Voidbringer turned his attention to the Librarian facing off against him on the ridge. A nimbus of power was playing across the psychic hood the Ultramarine wore and his eyes were alive with actinic force. He held the rod out in front of him, so it formed a cross with his body as the spine.

'Fell creature of the void, oblivion awaits you.'

Unmoved by the threat, Voidbringer only glared. The necron lord appeared... curious.

Again, Tigurius was surprised and horrified at the ancient intelligence in that gaze. It was like the mechanoid was appraising a laboratorium specimen. The sensation was unsettling. Tigurius knew enough of the galaxy and its species to realise mankind's pre-eminence was far from assured. Alien races clamoured to devour, usurp or study humans. It was part of the reason the Emperor had created Space Marines. But the necrontyr were something different, something so old and enduring that even an Adeptus Astartes as powerful as Tigurius was given pause.

Victory against this aeons-old culture with all their knowledge of the universe, their advanced technology, it was... *impossible*. They should give in now, submit to the will of the necrons and accept annihilation. They should–

Stop! The psychic echo was as much a command to his own subconscious as it was to the metal monster. Reasserting his composure, Tigurius smiled mirthlessly at the Voidbringer. 'I thought the other one was the Herald of Dismay.'

Though his jaw didn't move, a metallic voice, edged with the bitterness of millennia and abyssal deep, droned from the Voidbringer. '*You are the one who tried to penetrate the veil.*'

Tigurius nodded slowly. He felt like an insect being studied beneath a slide, but his resolve was as steel now.

'I am your doom, creature.'

A tinny, grating sound rattled from the necron's mouth. It was laughter, or what passed for it at least.

Describing arcane sigils of warding that lingered in the air in fire, Tigurius beckoned the monster on.

Voidbringer's eyes narrowed. '*Are you a pyromancer, worm?*'

A flash of light burst from the staff before the Librarian could stop it and hit him square in the chest. Tigurius was spun off his feet and sent sprawling from the ridge.

'*Not a very good one,*' he heard the necron lord remark.

Picking himself up, the Librarian scowled. 'I think I loathed your race less when I assumed you were humourless machines.' Fire sprang from his fingertips, reaching up towards the ridge line above and forcing the Voidbringer to retreat. Earth blackened and cracked as the flames lapped at the edge of the spur, spilling over the lip of rock rising higher and growing hotter. Snow condensed into steam in an eyeblink, scalding the air.

The necron's withdrawal didn't last. A hazy silhouette resolved through the conflagration and the Voidbringer leapt through it, fire trailing on his ancient vestments.

Ice cracked under the impact as the necron lord landed next to Tigurius. He threw out an arm, bodily catching the Librarian who was smashed aside and scraped across the ground. Blood was drooling down his lip as he rose; he could taste the tang of it in his mouth too.

Voidbringer was strong, much more unyielding than the lesser constructs. And he possessed cunning beyond mere programmed response to attack and external stimulus. The necrons, especially these noble castes, were far from machines. Even artificial intelligence didn't describe them accurately. They were something else, something vengeful and terrible. Spite, hatred, malice – the emotions were raw and tangible. Tigurius could feel them like tiny blades rubbing against his skin, like acid-edged pins in his mind.

Though the creature was not a psyker – it bore no warp-aura that the Librarian could detect – the artefacts he wielded were formidable.

As the Voidbringer rose, energy crackled the length of its arcane staff. It coruscated around the tip, a strange pronged sigil Tigurius had seen emblazoned on the carapace of some of the larger constructs. Darkness exuded from his body. Tendrils of night coiled around his limbs and weaved through the necron's skeletal frame.

The monster was well named. Casting about, the Voidbringer assessed the level of infiltration by the Ultramarines and acted accordingly. Shadows stirred in the mist around Tigurius as the necron constructs guarding the artillery began to animate.

'You are no warp sorcerer,' said the Librarian, his voice echoing with gathering power.

The Voidbringer's eye sockets flared emerald-bright and Tigurius was transported back to his narrow escape in the world-between-worlds. *'I am more than you could ever comprehend, human. I am eternal!'* A cascade of magnesium fire coursed from the necron's staff.

Tigurius was ready for the attack and quickly fashioned a defensive sigil in the air. The arc of flame spilled against it, dispersing around the edges of a cerulean shield. It struck again, the necron throwing more force behind the blow. Staggered, Tigurius struggled to maintain his footing but repelled the energies. Sweat froze upon his brow as quickly as it formed, only to melt into hot steam a moment later. He needed to assert dominance in the duel and threw a bolt of chained lightning.

Voidbringer's body became as incorporeal as mist as the darkling mantle he wore engulfed him, rendering the psychic attack ineffective. The Night Shroud expanded, drawing strength from the blackness surrounding the artillery. Shreds of shadow became as hard as onyx as they wrapped themselves around Tigurius and all light was eclipsed. As the baleful gaze of the Voidbringer filled his vision, the Librarian felt his armour contract.

Seals cracked, ancient parchments and votive charms tore and broke apart as the necron lord exerted his cruel will.

'All is night. All is black at the end of days…'

Tigurius was fading. His mind was awash with endless darkness. It filled his senses, overwhelmed his thoughts and in that moment of near-destruction he achieved a mote of clarity. The visions, those that had dogged the Librarian since he'd made landfall on Damnos, became as clear as crystal. Death, it was death that he saw. Not the death of a world but the death of a hero. At first he believed it was him and this was, now, the instant of his demise. But the visions sharpened, just as the real world dimmed, and became more lucid. The truth was opened to him, a final torment before the end.

Tigurius saw…

SCIPIO HACKED THE last of the sentries apart. Its spinal column shattered and the necron phased out, but more were coming.

'Attach explosives.' He slammed the melta bomb against the base of the pylon, mag-locking to the strange metal. Cator and Herdantes provided covering fire. Bolt shells and incandescent plasma chopped into the ice-fog and the advancing silhouettes were blasted apart. Gauss-fire answered from the reinforcements coming in their wake as the damaged necrons reassembled and rejoined the attack.

'Will this even work?'

Scipio turned at Jynn's voice. She was hunkered down with Sia, returning fire when they could. She looked afraid.

Densk's death had clearly rocked her, but she remained determined to fight.

'I don't know,' said Scipio. 'That's why we need to use everything.' He glanced briefly at the tactical display in his retinal lens. All attack groups were in position. Then he saw Tigurius's rune.

It was amber. The Librarian's vitals were weakening. Scipio looked across the ice-shrouded plateau and found Tigurius locked in battle with a necron lord. He was slowly being crushed, enveloped by a veil of darkness.

'Cator, bring your plasma gun and follow me.'

Scipio ran off towards the Librarian, his brother in tow.

'Wait!' shouted Jynn. 'Don't leave us!'

Brakkius, Herdantes and the others were engaging the necrons closing on the pylon. They were stretched and more wraiths were moving sinuously on the undefended humans.

Scipio paused, torn. He had brought them into this fight. After they'd penetrated the mountains, he could have left Jynn and her guerrilla fighters behind. They could have watched from a safe distance. But he wanted to destroy the necrons utterly, smash their artillery and grab glory for gaining the Thanatos Hills. It was too late to turn back. The humans had chosen their fate. He ran to Tigurius.

'Scipio!' Jynn's impassioned cries followed him all the way like a curse.

CHAPTER TWENTY-THREE

Ever since becoming a battle-brother, Sergeant Atavian had been in the Second Company Devastators. It was a full-fledged Ultramarine's first calling in the Chapter proper – Maxima Atavian had simply never left. His squad were known as the Titan Slayers, a name which they'd earned for obvious reasons. As a heavy weapon trooper, Atavian had principally been responsible for the lascannon. It was his favoured weapon. Tank-killer, it was also called. Atavian's motto had always been, 'Why stop at tanks?'

The honour of carrying the Slayers' lascannon went to Brothers Hektar and Ulius. Sergeant Atavian had to satisfy himself with guiding their destructive fury. During his century of service, he had seen many monsters and machineries felled by the hot beams of a lascannon. Tyranid bio-forms, daemonic engines of the Great Enemy, ramshackle ork battle-fortresses – Atavian had seen them all undone by this stalwart weapon. For a Space Marine on foot and at range, there was nothing so powerful. But here on Damnos, he had seen such technologies that he wondered if even a lascannon would prevail against them. Floating obelisks of living metal, skeletal warriors utterly destroyed only to rise as if unscathed, small beetle-like creatures capable of twisting a weapon's machine-spirit and turning it on its wielder – this was what the Second were up against, the necrontyr.

On bended knee and with their heads bowed, Atavian and his brothers recited the litanies of accuracy and function. They had formed a half-circle, heavies in the middle either side of their sergeant and bolters at the ends. A flattened column offered them little cover but a good vantage point to overlook the wasteland tundra between the edge of Arcona City and Kellenport.

Across from the Titan Slayers were their brother Devastators, led by Sergeant Tirian. Atavian gave him a curt salute when he'd finished the litanies and was on his feet again, to which Tirian replied by holding his power fist aloft and giving a slow nod. His squad, Guilliman's Hammer, occupied a staggered platform of rock. It might once have been the tiered steps of a temple but was all but obliterated now. Heavy bolters took the first level, the missile launchers behind them crouched down and pointing eastwards towards the advancing necrons.

The shadows of the monoliths were easy to pick out as the sun faded quickly on the horizon. These would be Atavian's principal targets, the living metal pyramids that fired death from the crystals at their zeniths. There was a larger monstrosity moving amongst the still-gargantuan smaller ones. It was taller, a tower of long tubular crystal attached to a conventional monolith base. Energies crackled between this one and the other two surrounding it. A node of some sort, Atavian decided. He put the targeting scope back on the stock of his bolter and addressed his warriors.

'Steel and death! Meltas and plasma to the fore, tank-killers with me at the rear. Remember how we took the *Soulmauler* apart, a renegade Titan, no less! Remind me why we earned the Principex Maxima that day and why our name shall pass in to legend when we are dead.'

Shouts of approval and affirmation met the sergeant's words. These were campaign veterans, despite their role as Devastators. He trusted each and every one.

'Glory to the Titan Slayers and may the God-Emperor revel in our furious thunder!'

A collective roar belted from the Ultramarines mouths.

Sergeant Atavian had never been prouder. The cries of his Titan Slayers echoed into silence, as did the shouts of Tirian's warriors across from them. One last look down the targeter revealed the necron hordes were coming within range. Emerald energy was building between the phalanx of monoliths. Everything depended on their incapacitation. Atavian prepared to give the order to fire.

'PINION', THE TUTORS of the Chapter, Praxor's old masters, had called it. 'When one force manages to outflank and surround another.'

To the west, the necrons from the tomb itself, amongst them their overlord and the one Sicarius wanted to bring to single combat. To the east, the forces that had got around them to assault Kellenport, recently recalled to close the Ultramarines in a trap they might not escape from.

Knowing he faced a foe on two fronts, Sicarius had arranged his forces in two semi-circles each facing an aspect of where a threat was coming from. To the rear he positioned the Devastators. The necrons had brought machineries: the hulking monoliths Praxor had seen the captain take on single-handedly. Through sheer bravura, he had destroyed one of them, or at least immobilised it. If only they had three more Sicariuses with the same fortune, the same skill to achieve that feat three more times. Tactical Squad Solinus completed the rearguard, ready to wade in once the heavy guns had done all they could.

Praxor was amongst the force facing the brunt of the necron infantry as well as its command echelon. The Dreadnoughts Ultracius and Agrippen joined them, stoic alongside the Lions of Macragge. At either flank, Sicarius had used the assault squads as anchor. They would strike at the heart of the phalanxes, cutting a way through so that the captain of Second might get his opportunity to kill the necron overlord.

Chaplain Trajan knelt in the centre, between the two semi-circles of Ultramarines. Their last stand was apparently on top of the remains of some ancient basilica. The Chaplain had discovered a large stone aquila buried under all the fallen snow. He performed a final blessing on top of the ruins, beseeching the Emperor to protect and grant them courage.

In his heart, Praxor knew this would be the single biggest and hardest battle he would ever fight as an Ultramarine. Making the sign of the Imperial eagle over his breast, he hoped it would not be his last. His gaze fell on Sicarius.

The captain was looking to the north, towards the Thanatos Hills.

'It's quiet,' he said underneath his breath. His Lions, including Daceus, stood by silently.

Praxor spoke up. 'A cessation to the barrage could mean that Scipio…' He paused to correct himself. 'Sergeant Vorolanus and Lord Tigurius have been successful in their mission.'

Sicarius turned. His eyes were hard like granite as they appraised Praxor. He hadn't realised he'd intruded on the captain's private thoughts.

'*Scipio?*'

'He is – was – my friend, brother-captain.'

Sicarius looked to the west. Battle was approaching rapidly.

'We are, all of us, linked by a shared brotherhood. Our blood is the distilled life essence of our primarch, may he one day stir from slumber in the Temple of Correction. But some bonds are stronger than others. Do you understand?'

Praxor nodded humbly.

Satisfied he was understood, Sicarius drew his Tempest Blade and levelled it at the oncoming necrons. It was a gesture he was overfond of making.

'Do you know what I see out there, brother-sergeant?' he said. 'I see destiny. I see our names alongside the legends of our Chapter's greatest heroes, inscribed for all time on the walls of the Temple of Hera. Are you ready to embrace it?'

He didn't wait for an answer. Instead, Sicarius summoned his Lions and advanced to the front of the line. Agrippen was close by.

'You wish to share in the glory of this moment, venerable one?' asked the captain.

'It is only fitting that I am by my liege-lord's right hand. It is the Chapter's will.'

Sicarius laughed, loud and belligerent, before putting on his helmet. So close now, the necrons seemed endless.

The Lions appeared unfazed, their demeanour stoic. It had been Praxor's desire to join them, to be like Gaius Prabian or Daceus. In these last moments before the final clash, he found himself questioning whether he could stare into the void and not blink.

He caught Vandius looking at him. Perhaps the Company Banner Bearer could guess what was on his mind. What he thought of Praxor's ambitions was unknown; he merely nodded to the sergeant and fixed his standard high. The gilded twin-headed eagle perched upon the Ultima symbol around a deathless skull stared down upon the Space Marines as if measuring them. 'Guardians of the Temple', warriors of the Second – if they survived, even achieved victory here, it would be spoken about for hundreds of years to come.

Sicarius seemed attuned to the magnitude of the moment.

'Destiny!' His voice echoed around the shattered basilica like a clarion call. 'Sons of Ultramar, if you seek renown eternal then it is before you. Ours is a proud line, it is cobalt and steel, it is unbreakable, it is spirit as adamantium. We are kings, you and I, like the old lords of Macragge in bygone days. On this soil, this frozen earth, we will make our stand and live forever in the annals of our brothers. Fight for the fallen, fight for the Second and the legacy left by those who came before us. Honour them with your deeds, your sacrifice.' He extended his open hand and clenched it tight. 'Reach out for immortality with your gauntleted fist and seize it!' The Tempest Blade was held aloft. Its edge shimmered in the fading sunlight, casting it in visceral red. 'In the name of Roboute Guilliman, *Victoris Ultra!*'

The call to arms resonated throughout the ruins, repeated

by every Ultramarine who was about to give his blood to war. As the roar of it slowly faded, the sound was replaced by the merciless, clanking march of the necrons.

Sicarius turned away from the hordes for a moment to look at Praxor. 'Sergeant Manorian, you and your Shield-bearers will be at my side.'

'It is our honour, my lord,' Praxor replied. Yet after everything he'd seen on Damnos, it didn't feel as glorious as he'd expected.

ONLY THE LIONS were listening. Only they, his honour guard and inner circle knights, could hear what Sicarius had to say next.

'No battle cries for them, no rousing speeches,' he murmured. The Lions maintained their silence. 'They are devoid of humanity, these necrons. They have no capacity for compassion or pity, or any notions of glory or comradeship.' He spat the words, repulsed at such hollow creatures. Sicarius shook his head slowly. 'I will need to get into the heart of their ranks. Your blades and bolters will open the way.'

'We are your unsheathed swords, sire,' snarled Gaius Prabian with a vertical blade salute. He was eager for battle.

'When it comes, Gaius, you must lower your sword and allow me to fight it alone.'

The Champion assented but did so reluctantly.

'Daceus, you will lead them once I am engaged. Vandius, the banner must not fall.'

Both nodding, the veteran-sergeant clanged his power fist against his right pauldron, whilst the Second Company's standard bearer replied, 'To my dying breath, lord.'

'And you, Apothecary,' Sicarius turned his head to look at Venatio. 'You know what your duty is.'

'I hope not to have to perform it, but the legacy of Ultramar will be preserved, rest assured of that, my captain.'

Lastly, Sicarius spoke to them all again as one. 'You are my brothers, my equals and peers. I expect of you what I expect from myself – duty unflinching, courage unwavering, blade unswerving. These soulless automatons will drown the galaxy in darkness if they are left unchecked. I care not for Damnos, I care that this foe is taught to fear the Adeptus Astartes. Mankind will not be destroyed without a fight. Let it begin here, on these frozen wastes. Whatever else, the Ultramarines must not fail. The necrons have to be stopped, one way or another.'

VAST PHALANXES OF raiders had been roused from the tomb. The Architect had done well, but the Undying was finding it increasingly difficult to keep hold of that thought. His mind was awash with visions of destruction and annihilation. The cold emptiness of eternity clawed at his resolve. Far from being an unfeeling golem of metal and machinery, he was deeply afraid of the long dark. He had already slept, it had seemed endlessly, and now awake he was confronted by oblivion of an altogether different stripe.

Destroyers glided on their repulsor platforms, moving slowly into formation at either end of the necron battle line. Abhorred by those who could still comprehend such an emotion, simply avoided by those with simpler engrams left to them after the long sleep, the destroyers were both loathsome and terrifying at the same time. Unlike most of the necrontyr, even those of the basest level, the destroyers had abandoned all hope of returning to *fleshtime*. Their bodies were... amended, given over to the pursuit of decimation. Though it scared him to admit it, the Undying liked the idea. He could imagine repulsors where his legs now were, a gauss-cannon to replace his arm; perhaps his war-scythe could be merged with the other limb too.

Such carnage I will reap… All the souls of this world.

Out in front, ahead of his bodyguard who crowded around him with glaives crackling with eldritch light, were the immortals. Stoic and implacable, these superior constructs would spearhead the advance. Anything that survived them was obviously worthy indeed and something the Undying should test his prowess against. Hubris then, and arrogance, still stirred in his cruel machine heart.

He surveyed the metal multitudes of skeletal warriors, each the same as the last, without need for banners or laurels of any kind, and knew the days of humankind were finite. These warriors were but a fraction of the cohorts still slumbering within the tomb. With a wordless command, the Undying impelled his army forward and imagined the slaughter to come.

CHAPTER
TWENTY-FOUR

JYNN EVVERS WAS strong-willed, some might even say fear-less. She'd had to be. After losing her husband to the quakes – it seemed longer than a couple of years, more like lifetimes – she'd needed courage and had dug down into herself to find it. For a while, during the darkest days, Jynn had wondered if she'd come back from that insular place at all. Buried so deeply, she'd returned a different person when she'd finally emerged. The prospect of living her life alone, without Korve, terrified her. She would have gladly spent all of eternity with that man. Even the ice and the long, relentless days didn't seem so bad when he was still there. When Korve died, a part of Jynn died too. She became as hard and unyielding as the rock face she laboured over for the greater glories of the Imperium.

She saw the same sense of disconnection in Scipio. He was a Space Marine, as far from humankind as was possible without actually being a different species. Jynn was in awe of these warriors from beyond the stars, they all were, but she also pitied them. Never at peace, incapable of love. Bonds of duty bound them to their purpose. It was a noble one, and they valued honour, like any soldier, but had little else. Bred without fear, without compassion and only the will to act, they were the warriors that mankind needed. But why then did they feel grief? Perhaps it was to separate them, however thinly, from the unliving automatons that were trying to eradicate the people of Damnos? Perhaps it was some anachronism of humanity that had endured whatever process it took to become a Space Marine?

There was a hardness to Scipio. Jynn had once believed she was devoid of emotion too and then the attack on the Thanatos Hills came and all of that changed. Guerrilla warfare was one thing, striking from the dark, ambushing small groups – it was dangerous but doable. This was insane. Out here in the open, Jynn felt exposed. She felt threatened. Most of all, she felt fear. She'd believed she'd given up on life, that it didn't matter if she died. She was wrong and it took mortality staring her in the face for her to realise that.

'Sia, get down!'

Though the Space Marines bore the brunt of the fighting, there were too many necrons for them to repel at once. Without Scipio and the others, the humans were in tremendous danger. If they died here, their names would not be put on a plaque and venerated in some dusty temple. Their legacy would not live on for future generations. They would be dead and that would be an end to it.

Jynn grabbed Sia by the collar of her jacket and dragged her down behind the massive platform supporting the necron weapon. She'd heard Scipio call it a 'pylon'. It was huge and terrifying, an arc of black metal spitting emerald-tinged death into the sky. The noise of it hurt her ears. Jynn had gritted her teeth so long that when she'd shouted to Sia she'd found it hard to dislodge them.

Sia went down with a grunt. She was clutching a pack filled with explosive. 'We need to get this attached to the gun, bring it down. It's what Densk, Holdst – what all the others – would have wanted.'

Gauss-fire flashed overhead, burning the air with its acrid stench. Below the fog line everything else was hazy white. Necron silhouettes were moving in the mist, though. Their eyes were the first things that became visible. Jynn saw them everywhere. Lucky for her and Sia, they had yet to turn in their direction.

'You can't avenge them if you're dead. We have to stay down for a while.'

Sia shook her head. There was a wildness in her eyes, a sense of abandon that said she'd cracked under the pressure of it all.

'It's now or never, captain.'

Jynn reaffirmed her grip. 'Sia, no.'

'I can't stay like this. Ever since the camp, ever since…' She was crying. Sia threw off Jynn's hand and was on her feet. She got a couple of metres with the pack and was unclasping it when the beam caught her in the chest.

Jynn cried out but Sia was gone, her torso vaporised by the flayer blast. She slumped, gurgling blood, and died.

Holding her breath, Jynn was waiting to see if the necron would follow up on its kill. The hard bang of bolter fire caught its attention and it moved away. Sia was right, even if her attempt at completing the mission was suicidal – they needed to attach the bombs. Jynn got down on her belly – even through the thermal layers, the icy ground felt cold – and started to elbow her way towards the fallen pack. She had explosives of her own, tied up in webbing around her back, but they'd need Sia's too.

Screaming came through the fog, perversely crystal clear despite the hammering artillery. Jynn recognised the voices and knew they were getting slaughtered. It could have only been minutes, but it felt like hours. For the fifth time, she inwardly cursed Scipio. A means to an end, that's all she and her men were to him.

Fear closed in again when she reached the pack. Her fingers were shaking almost uncontrollably, and not from the cold, as she tried to remove the improvised bomb. Jynn breathed deeply, trying to master her terror, and achieved a small amount of calm. It was just enough to remove the explosive payload from the pack, arm it and attach the whole thing to the pylon. She wanted to detonate it immediately, but the resulting firestorm would kill her if she didn't get clear. Instead, she pulled out her pistol and made for the next artillery piece.

One down, one more to go.

SCIPIO WAS RUNNING. The sound of Jynn's voice still echoed on the air, but he banished it from his mind. Necrons were flooding the artillery now, summoned by their lord. The Ultramarines had nearly run out of time.

A glance at his retinal display showed that Vandar and Octavian had attached explosives and were ready to proceed. Scipio opened up the comm-feed to them both. 'Execute now!'

Plumes of fire erupted from locations around the plateau a few seconds later. In the distance, one of the pylons collapsed. Its weapon-arc crumpled as it struck the base, severed by the explosion. Emerald energy rippled across the remains frenziedly.

Scipio drove on, Cator just behind him.

The sergeant dispatched a necron warrior that loomed in their path with his chainsword. It came out of the mist late and Scipio had to react quickly. Instinct and urgency were guiding him. Consequence became secondary. All that mattered was Tigurius.

Cator blasted another off its feet with a quick burst from his plasma gun. The blue beam cut through its spinal column, ate up some of the torso and the mechanisms within. It was enough damage to make it phase out. But the necrons didn't stop. The Ultramarines were being overrun. Scipio shut off the urgent pleas for reinforcement from Brakkius. A blow-by-blow report was unfolding from the other Thunderbolts. He was pulling back, along with Herdantes. Largo too, together with Garrik and Auris, were trying to retreat. Scipio wasn't listening any more. He had to get to Tigurius. With a single act of bravura, he could save them all and atone for Orad's death.

Cutting down another of the advancing necrons, he yelled, 'Brother, are you still with me?'

Cator was resolute. 'Heading straight into the jaws of death, sergeant.'

An explosion tore up the ground nearby as another of the necron guns was ripped apart. It rocked Scipio and Cator on their feet and pushed away the ice-fog with a belt of emerald-tinged smoke. The Ultramarines let it roll over them.

The pall of smoke and debris was thick. They had to fight just to be free of it.

Largo was shouting down the comm-feed, 'Necron artillery sixty per cent effective, damaged but still operational. Our incendiaries haven't worked.'

Grey cloud was everywhere, a directionless void without end.

Largo was insistent. 'Your orders, brother-sergeant.'

Checking the retinal display, knowing they were close to Tigurius but not yet within striking distance, Scipio found similar reports coming from Octavian and Vandar. Two of the artillery pieces were down, but the others were still functional.

'Get heavies and whatever grenades you have left on those guns, brother.'

'Negative, sir. We are no longer in control of the strike area. Necron aggression is too heavy. Falling back to the centre.'

Scipio cursed. Without the assault squads there was no backup plan, no route of egress should the mission fail. His voice was bitter. 'I've led us to our deaths.'

He felt something seize his wrist and was about to lash out when he saw it was Cator. 'We're not done yet, Scipio. Courage and honour.'

Scipio clapped him on the shoulder and nodded once.

The smoke cleared. As the two Ultramarines emerged from the cloud, their objective came into sight – they'd reached Tigurius. At least they could achieve something.

Another necron was coming at them out of the ice-fog and Scipio was forced to meet it. He only had time to point at the darkness crushing Tigurius.

'Shoot it!'

Cator hesitated. 'I might hit Lord Tigurius.'

'Do it now, brother!' The shriek of chainblade teeth striking metal sounded close by.

Muttering an oath to the primarch, Cator took aim into the dark veil and fired.

PAIN WAS AN outmoded concept in the experiential range of the Voidbringer. He had long ago outgrown the capacity to feel the sensation. Even so, he knew he was injured and the desire for self-preservation still influenced his actions. In order to find his attacker, he had to release the pyromancer. He was nearly dead, anyway. Voidbringer resolved to eradicate this new threat and then finish what he had started. Darkness billowing about him, withdrawn from crushing the pyromancer, the necron lord searched the battlefield. He unleashed the power of his staff and the hot beam found Voidbringer's enemy and pitched him off his feet.

'Insect!'

The brief moment of pique cost him. When he turned his attention back to the pyromancer he saw his enemy was far from defeated, he was glowing.

AN AURA OF power surrounded Tigurius, chasing away the darkness from the necron lord's unnatural veil. It was a magnesium-bright sun, banishing the shadow with the Librarian as its focus. Jagged forks of lightning peeled off from the aura around his body. His eyes were alive with a captured storm, mirroring the tumultuous thunderhead surging into being around him.

The air cracked with the sound of his voice. 'Now you die, machine.'

Bolt after bolt of psychic lightning hammered into the Voidbringer, who reeled beneath the blows. A crack split the monster's chest, tore off an arm. His arcane staff spilled away on the eldritch wind summoned by the

Librarian. Harsh and metallic, the necron lord roared as if in agony. Tigurius doubted it could feel, it was merely railing against its imminent demise. Even when the Void-bringer was nearly sundered, he didn't stop – Tigurius poured it on, opening his mind to the warp and releasing its terrible power.

PSYCHIC LIGHTNING WAS ripping into his body, tearing away strips, burning mechanisms so old and complex that no human mind could ever hope to understand them. It was happening too fast – even the Voidbringer's enhanced regenerative abilities couldn't self-repair quickly enough. A mote of something cold and unpleasant flickered in his engrammic circuitry. Something akin to anxiety seized his aeons-old mind for just a moment as the necron lord contemplated the long dark.

I am the master of darkness, not its slave...

The self-declaration seemed pointless in the circumstances. Escape was still possible. He would not submit yet. Voidbringer *would* be royarch. He would self-repair, kill this worm that had stung him and assume the throne. Ankh, the self-aggrandising plebeian, had given him the means to do it. Before he was lost, Voidbringer activated the resurrection orb.

THE MONSTER WAS almost destroyed. Scipio watched from a safe distance, the broken body of Cator in his arms. A long burn marred the Imperial eagle on his plastron, but at least Cator was still alive. He glared, willing retribution on the necron lord. Leaking fluids, machine parts crackling and fizzing in his skeletal armature, the Voidbringer was done. Tigurius was relentless and so too was the storm blazing from his fingertips. It lit up the plateau, searing away the ice-fog.

Scipio's eyes narrowed. Something was happening amidst the storm. Impossibly, the necron lord was self-repairing. Despite the fact his form was being stripped apart by psychic fire, the Voidbringer was regenerating! Living metal pooled together, running in rivulets over his shattered body, and started to form fresh carapace. Seemingly terminal wounds in the necron were reknitting, sealing. Scipio noticed the orb in the monster's chest. It was black like onyx and shimmered as the regeneration process perpetuated itself.

Thumbing the activation stud on his chainsword, Scipio knew what he had to do. To step into that lightning meant certain death. It was a small price. He only hoped his sacrifice would be enough.

Voidbringer was laughing. He glared down at the pyromancer who forced more of his crude sorcery into being.

It is to no avail, worm. I am eternal. I am–

He stopped laughing. Voidbringer's savage joy turned to anguish and horror. His wounds were reopening, his body was disintegrating. The pull of the long dark returned, teasing at his consciousness.

No, no…

An inner chill swept over him. The scent of the tomb and the dust of the long sleep filled his olfactory sensors. It was simulation, he was sure of it. His memory engrams were reacting to his approaching destruction. Voidbringer tried to engage with the resurrection orb, to shut off the process, but it was too late. Instead of healing him, it was disassembling his body, unravelling systems and the technology of his entire being. As the genebred ones closed with their weapons, sensing his demise, Voidbringer cursed Ankh. The Architect had tricked him.

TIGURIUS HELD UP a warding hand.

'Wait!'

The lightning was ebbing as he recalled the power of the warp back into check, marshalling the destructive forces he'd called upon by using his psychic hood as a cerebral dampener. It was a complex procedure and he created sigils of temperance and control in the air to focus his thoughts. Instead of a conduit, the Librarian's force rod became a vacuum channelling the psychic energies away to dissipate harmlessly.

'Wait,' he breathed, feeling the pull on his physical strength as he asserted mastery of his mental power. Light gave way to dark, the ice-fog came back and the plateau was stilled. An intense fatigue washed over the Librarian, as if his entire body was a tensed muscle allowed to relax. He staggered and fell, but waved Scipio away as he came to help him.

He scarcely had the breath to command: 'Finish it. Do it now.'

CHAPTER
TWENTY-FIVE

ATAVIAN SAW THE energy lances cut into the hard metal of the monoliths only for the damage to be absorbed and nullified a second later.

'Mercy of Hera, are they impervious to all harm?'

Tirian's voice came over the feed – Sergeant Atavian hadn't realised he'd broadcast his words to the other Devastators. They were on an open channel, in order to better coordinate their fire. In the fury of the barrage, that fact had slipped Atavian's mind. 'I heard that Captain Sicarius destroyed one single-handedly,' said Tirian.

'I don't doubt it, brother. Perhaps he'd be willing to come over from the front line, run the three hundred or so metres between us and it, and show us how he did the first time.'

Tirian's booming laughter was at odds with the seriousness of the situation, but it made Atavian smile.

A few hundred metres was no distance at all. It was optimum range for lascannons but then most decent distances were – Atavian had never known a more accurate, more relentlessly deadly weapon. Hektar and Ulius hammered the advancing monoliths that were using their energies to transport necron phalanxes from outside Kellenport to the force attacking the Ultramarine rearguard in the ruins of Arcona City.

Tirian's squad drilled the infantry. The muzzle flashes of the heavy bolters were almost constant, burning through their belt-feeds in seconds rather than minutes. It was testament to the sergeant's skill and preparation as well as that of his gunners that not one of the heavies had jammed. He was no Techmarine, but Atavian muttered a blessing to the Omnissiah for that. Explosions blossomed in the packed necron ranks as high-velocity bolt shells smashed into the front ranks. It was like throwing rocks into the ocean. There was a ripple as some of the mechanoids were destroyed but then the sea of metal subsided again, the casualties swallowed into the horde or simply redeployed through the monolith portals.

The floating pyramids had to go, Atavian decided. By crippling the enemy's ability to recycle its fallen troops directly into the battle the Ultramarines at least stood a chance of slowing them down. As things stood, they couldn't even do that.

'Aim for the crystal nodes,' Atavian told his heavies. 'All weapons.'

As the Titan Slayers lifted their aim, a shadow fell across them. The whine of repulsor engines promoted Atavian to shout, 'Down!'

A pair of necron gun-platforms hovered overhead at speed.

'I can vanquish them!' It was Brother Ikus – he'd stayed on his feet. 'In the Emperor's name!' The burst from his plasma cannon engulfed the lead gun-platform, turning it into a mass of plummeting fire-wreathed wreckage. The second jinked out of the plasma bolt's path, avoiding the worst of its fury, and returned fire.

Ikus swung the heavy weapon around, grunting with the effort. The plasma coils on his back-mounted generator were still cycling. The necron's heavy gauss-cannon sent out a pulse of emerald light that bored through the Ultramarine's armour, transfixing him. Ikus shook as most of his internal organs were flayed to atoms and then crashed head-first down the steps.

'Neutralise it!' Atavian was pointing towards the gun-platform, which was wheeling around for another pass until one of Tirian's missile launchers tore it open in mid-air. The necron plummeted to the earth just in front of the other Devastators, twisted and on fire.

Brother Korvus of the Titan Slayers slung his bolter as he went to take up Ikus's fallen plasma cannon. Meanwhile, one of Tirian's warriors had made it to the gun-platform's crash site to execute the stricken necron in the debris.

'Still alive,' said Korvus, checking Ikus's vitals.

'Put that cannon on the monoliths,' ordered Atavian, sending another of the bolter-armed battle-brothers to drag Ikus to relative safety. He turned his attention back to the monoliths. In the distance, they were turning their energy to something new. A web of light was growing between the three hovering structures, the larger one at its nexus.

'That can't be good,' Atavian muttered, before ordering the lascannons to intensify fire on the middle monolith. The tactics had changed. Rather than overwhelm the Ultramarines with infantry, the necrons would scour their bodies from the very earth with hellish firepower.

Watching their implacable advance, knowing there was little else he could do to resist the monoliths, Atavian wished he had more lascannons.

ULLYIOUS IXION CURSED as the necron gun-platforms escaped his wrath. He was still shaking loose the wreckage of the last machine he had crushed when he landed. The end of his jump took him into a phalanx of raiders and he immediately set about them with a deadly arsenal of plasma pistol and power fist. Alongside their sergeant, Macragge's Avengers were imperious and brutal. A spew of flame ripped through the packed necron ranks from Ptolon's flamer. His brothers leapt on the burning mechanoids and cut them apart with chainswords. It was tough work; the necrons were hard, but the raiders fell back before the assault squad's onslaught.

More gun-platforms, a different group, were coming around again as Ixion looked to the skies. Engage, destroy, manoeuvre and repeat: these were the tactical rotas of an Assault Marine. At their sergeant's sub-vocal command, Macragge's Avengers boosted into the air leaving scorched earth behind them.

Near the apex of the jump, Ixion asked, 'How does Strabo fare?'

The other assault squad, the self-dubbed Heroes of Selonopolis, were on the opposite flank to the Macragge's Avengers and focused on similar targets. Ixion had instructed Brother Ptolon to keep a tally.

'They outstrip us by a single gun-platform, sergeant.'

Targets, urgent and red, were coming into view through Ixion's retinal lenses. He took aim down the small barrel of his plasma pistol. 'Then let us even the score.'

Even in desperate battle, squad rivalry was evident. Sicarius liked it that way – it kept his warrior-brothers sharp. So did Ixion.

The necrons were everywhere. It was a battle without end. Ixion revelled in it.

'Death from the heavens, fire and wrath! For Ultramar!'

BELOW THE AERIAL duelling between the assault squads and the necron gun-platforms, Praxor was cutting apart the last of a raider group sent to blunt his attack. The Shieldbearers were rampant through the mechanoids' ranks; Praxor had never fought beside his warriors this fired-up. He, too, was at the peak of his prowess. Deep within the thick of the necrons, they needed to be.

He saw Sicarius just ahead of him through the melee. It was close-up work, bolters and blades, just what Space Marines were made for. Though tough, the raiders were not as adept at close combat as the Space Marines – it put them at a disadvantage despite their regenerative capability. In hand-to-hand, or at close range, it was easier to ensure a necron was badly damaged enough that they phased out; at distance, where the Ultramarines had first engaged, too many were self-repairing and getting back up.

Though not equipped specifically for assault, Praxor had ordered his squad to switch to gladius and bolt pistols as soon as the necrons were within range. Advancing in a 'V' formation with the sergeant at the tip, the Shieldbearers were brutal and shredded the mechanoids' ranks.

Agrippen was merciless.

Both he and Ultracius had waded into the enemy throng a few seconds behind Sicarius. They ranged at either flank of the captain and his Lions, crushing bodies with their power fists and unleashing close-proximity barrages with their main weapons.

Against the Dreadnoughts, the necrons had no answer. Their flying gun-platforms couldn't get close; Ixion and Strabo were marshalling the skies. Nothing else could touch them. Unable to draw significant firepower against the venerable warriors, the necrons were getting slaughtered. But where one raider fell, another three replaced it. And these were just the rank and file; the elites would be a much tougher prospect. Sicarius's plan was a risky one. If he didn't draw the necron overlord into battle soon, all of the Dreadnoughts' efforts, the efforts of all the Ultramarines, would be for nothing.

A moment of calm descended over Praxor, his closest foes all dispatched for now. It enabled him to take stock of the battle. The Ultramarines had ventured quite far from the ruined basilica and driven a small wedge of cobalt into the necron sea of metal. As it got further, the wedge narrowed like a slow-moving lance seeking out the heart of its foes – in this case, the necron overlord. Another phalanx was moving around to try and stymie the daring Ultramarines' attack.

Its machine-spirit humming for further death, Praxor pressed his power sword up to his battle-helm to beseech the blessing of the Emperor and the primarch before thrusting back into the fray.

THE GILDED NECRON overlord was not easy to miss. Sicarius had the creature target-locked in his left retinal lens. Schemata scrolled across the right, overlaying his vision. Weaknesses were hard to identify in the monster's metal armature. He was plated like the other necrons, but bigger, the same size as the elites pressing ahead of him in a tight warrior-cohort.

They were of a different caste, these mechanoids; just as implacable but better drilled. The elites stayed close to their lord, just in front of a tight ring of bodyguards. The latter wielded shimmering war-glaives that looked like they'd shear straight through power armour. Much like the elites, these too would need to be broken open in order to reach the overlord.

He had gambled with the Ultramarines under his command, allowed them to fall into the necron lord's web, all so he could draw the monster out.

'You have me, creature,' he whispered to the confines of his battle-helm. 'Now come and claim me.'

Sicarius's mind was set: one way or another this war would end between him and the gilded necron. Even if he had to kill every one of the elites and then destroy the honour guard, he would do it. To the death.

The comm-feed in the captain's ear crackled, indicating long-range interference. He severed a raider's torso with his Tempest Blade, immolating another with a close burst from his plasma pistol.

'This is Sicarius. Proceed,' he growled.

The voice that answered was not who he expected but the news it brought allowed another plan to form in the captain's mind.

Cato Sicarius smiled.

'Daceus,' he said, turning to his second-in-command. 'Prepare the force to withdraw.'

The veteran-sergeant was pummelling a raider with his power fist as he looked up. 'Sir?'

'We fall back to Kellenport as originally planned.'

'Our forces are boxed in, brother-captain. We have no route of retreat.'

'Not yet. Defensive postures for all troops. Do it now, brother-sergeant.'

The order was relayed. The Ultramarines who'd fought the necrons back this far were told to give up the ground they'd won and consolidate at the ruins.

'I HAVE AN attack vector to the elites. We can engage. I repeat, we can engage.'

Ixion was soaring on the flaming pillars of his jump pack, locking onto his next target, when Daceus's voice brought his imagined glory crashing down to earth.

'Negative. Pull back to the ruins, all squads.'

The feed was cut. Ixion pulled up short, landing in a patch of no-man's-land with his squad.

Brother Ptolon thundered down alongside him. 'Sergeant?'

'We're falling back to the basilica ruins, all of us.'

Ixion looked heavenwards and saw Strabo was already on his way. He did not question, he did not doubt – he merely obeyed. But Ullyious Ixion did feel his wrath magnified at the denial of his warrior-urge.

He craned his neck, looking up into the stars appearing in the sky, and ignited his jump-jets in a stream of fire. 'Fly, Avengers!' .

'BRING IT DOWN!'

Hektar and Ulius struck the lead monolith time and again but every blazing bolt was simply absorbed by the machine. Inexorably, it came forward with the other two monoliths moving behind it in perfect unison. Slow and ponderous, whatever the triumvirate was about to unleash would be terrible. As he shouted the order, Atavian knew they had to stop it. But as the energy nexus strung between the crystal nodes of each of the pyramids grew into a blazing coruscation, the sergeant was struck by a solemn truth.

We are going to fail.

Emerald lightning crackled around the lead monolith's apex as the energy tendrils were drawn up its tubular conduits and into its crystal matrix. A corona of light built around the crystal, increasing in intensity with the passing of each second.

Atavian gave the only order he could think of that would make any difference. 'Get into cover!'

A thick beam of power pulsed from the lead monolith's crystal. It struck the steps just below the Titan Slayers' position, turning the air to steam and the world to fire around them. The shockwave lifted the Ultramarines off their feet. Motes of dust and debris were suspended briefly in the blast radius. It resonated outwards like an earthquake, splitting the ground with a web of cracks centred at the origin point.

Despite the dampeners built into his helmet's systems, Atavian's auditory canal was overloaded with sound. Blood vessels burst in his nose and ears, nulling two of his senses instantly. Retinal lenses couldn't process the sudden influx of intense light; excessive heat warnings raced across the internal display before they too capitulated against the sheer strength of the blast. He remembered crouching down before the blast hit and the section of wall disintegrating in front of him. It was what he imagined an atomic explosion to be like. A sense of weightlessness overtook his body as Atavian realised he'd been lifted off his feet.

Propelled backwards he slammed into a still-standing column and slumped, knocked onto his backside.

Ultramarines lay scattered around him, some Tirian's, some his own. They were thrown like debris before a storm – the deadly emerald beam showed no respect for the heirs of Guilliman. It was death. Pure and undistilled. Despite himself, Atavian couldn't help but feel awed by its incredible power. It didn't stop him from wanting to destroy it.

Cobalt-armoured bodies were stirring. Smoke and fire wafted and flickered between them. The stone steps were levelled, most of what was left of the ruins too. The sound of scraping battle plate came from all around him as Atavian's battle-brothers got up and tried to regroup. Defeat was not a word in an Ultramarine's vocabulary, or so the sergeant believed. Pain-suppressing drugs were already flooding his nervous system and Larraman cells began the process of rapid blood-clotting as Atavian rose to his feet. A pall swathed the atmosphere from the displaced dust and debris. Patches of steam lingered in tiny squalls before crystallising as the cold reasserted dominance.

Atavian's tactical display revealed a lot of amber runes – almost all of the Ultramarines in the rearguard were injured. There were some red icons too, the disabled or dead. Ineffective battle-brothers were not his concern right now; he needed firepower, and quickly. He'd reached the end of the blast zone – perversely, the resulting crater provided some rudimentary cover. Several of his squad and what was left of Tirian's, including the sergeant himself, were already hunkering down.

Tirian handed Atavian his magnoculars.

'Barely even a scratch.'

Atavian had to agree. It was a slow march that brought the necrons and their monoliths to the rear of the Ultramarines lines but for all the damage done to them they could have been advancing one step a minute and they'd still reach the Devastators intact.

He handed the scopes back. 'Its weak point is the crystal power matrix at the machine's apex.'

Tirian nodded. 'An easy enough target.'

Ulius was crouched down next to Atavian and said, 'If something weren't fouling our auto-aiming systems.'

Removing the targeter from Ulius's lascannon, Atavian took a look. 'Trajectory is off.' He made some adjustments, looked again. 'Still off.' He gave the device back to Ulius and glanced around the crater. 'Where is Hektar?'

'Dead, sir.'

'Where is his lascannon?'

'With his body, brother-sergeant.'

Atavian's gaze was on the advancing monoliths.

'Bring it here.'

Ulius did as commanded. He kept his head down as the fire from the Devastators started up again. His caution was unnecessary. The monoliths were recycling, spewing repaired and revivified necrons from their portals and undoing all the damage inflicted by Guilliman's Hammer. Tirian was unimpressed.

'We're wasting ammunition,' he growled, calling for a cease-fire. Missile launchers stayed primed but still; heavy bolters stalled with belts ready-fed. 'The war machines must be neutralised.'

Since the blast, Atavian's Titan Slayers hadn't fired a single shot.

'While they're regenerating infantry, they're not using

those crystal matrices to eradicate us. It's a cycle. Once it's complete, the monoliths will charge those conduits and unleash the beam weapon.'

Ulius returned, hefting Hektar's lascannon and setting it down next to his sergeant.

'What are you seeing, Maxima?' Tirian's use of his first name made Atavian turn to face him.

Tirian's scarred battle-helm was reflected back in his crimson lenses. 'It's what I've *seen*, brother.'

Overhead, stabbing beams of emerald were thickening the air. The necrons were within gauss-flayer range and releasing sporadic bursts as they advanced. Bolter fire answered but it was no more than a perfunctory response.

Atavian continued, 'We cannot trust our auto-targeters. The necrons are machines of a type. Affinity with mechanisms is a component of their xenos construction. We are feeling their influence.'

'The machine-spirits of our weapons are corrupted?' Tirian sounded incensed.

'No, but they've been compromised. The adjustments I made to Ulius's targeter should have corrected the aim – they didn't. Destroying those crystals will take accuracy but it must be done by instinct.' Detaching the seals on his gorget, Atavian removed his battle-helm. Without the voice-augmentation of his armour, he had to shout to be heard. 'By naked eye alone.'

He hefted the lascannon onto his shoulder. The weight of it felt good, almost nostalgic. Atavian side glanced at Ulius. 'Follow my lead, brother.'

Jettisoning his helmet and mag-locking it to his thigh, Ulius tried to gauge his sergeant's aim.

'We are targeting the thirdmost machine?'

'Yes. Wait until they're powering up the main weapon. I will give the order when to shoot.'

It was sniper shooting with a lascannon. Tanks, Dreadnoughts, installations – a lascannon's usual prey was large and relatively static. The monoliths *were* slow but whatever fouling technology the necrons were employing had narrowed the target-window considerably. It required peerless accuracy.

A sniper often prepared for days, scoping out the area, finding optimum position. They would gauge all variables: light, wind speed, weather anomalies, a target's weak points. Though much more powerful, a lascannon lacked the subtlety of a rifle. Instead of days, Atavian had only minutes to prepare his shot. He considered recoil, trajectory, projected impact point. In the end he trusted to two things: instinct and faith.

The last of the repaired raiders emerged from the portals, prompting the crystal nodes on the monoliths to energise again. Frantic lightning arcs sprang from the central machine, creating a link between the other two. Power was fed to the main crystal and the energy coruscation swelled brightly.

'On my signal...' said Atavian, adjusting his position by a fraction. Gauss-fire was chewing up the earth around the Ultramarines, taking chunks off the crater's edge and spitting the debris against their armour. Sergeant Tirian had opened up with his heavies again, trying to give the lascannons some protection.

The glow around the lead monolith's crystal was still growing. Beam release was imminent.

'Make your blow quickly, brother,' warned Tirian.

'It will fall heavily. At my signal...' Atavian muttered,

bringing his cheek to the side of the lascannon and lowering the barrel tip by the smallest fraction.

When trying to disable a fast-moving target, let it come to you.

One of the rubrics of his old masters came to the forefront of his mind.

The monoliths advanced into prime firing position. It also brought them into Atavian's crosshairs. He lifted two fingers from the cannon trigger. That was the signal.

Twin lascannon beams hit the thirdmost monolith as it was feeding the last of its power to the hub-crystal, shattering the node and sending a backwash of energy into the other two.

The struck monolith shuddered as a chain reaction of catastrophic damage rolled through its structure. Cracks formed in its pyramid hull, exuding sickly emerald light. Actinic fire bloomed out of its portal as the vast machine crashed to the ground and stopped. Rampant energy spikes crippled the other two, forcibly aborting the beam projection. Stung and in sudden need of repair, the remaining monoliths began a slow retreat, leaving the shattered war engine behind.

Despite himself, Atavian gave a shout of triumph.

It was echoed by some of the others in the rearguard. The defeat of the monoliths sent a ripple effect through the advancing infantry, who were being chewed up by the combined fire of both Devastator squads. Without the portals they could not immediately repair and redeploy. At last, their numbers were thinning.

A second problem compounded the first for the necrons. Tirian saw it through the magnoculars.

'Brothers, we are reinforced.' The savage joy in his voice was obvious.

Atavian felt it too as he was given the scopes.

'I see conscripts, Guard formations too.' Increasing magnification, he added, 'Iulus Fennion and his Immortals lead them.'

Tirian laughed, surprise and relief colouring his tone. 'I confess I thought the Kellenport defenders vanquished and us an island in a sea of foes.'

Atavian handed off the lascannon to Hektar's replacement. Now the monoliths were neutralised, at least for a time, he resumed his duties as sergeant.

'We are still an island, brother,' he asserted, 'but now we have a channel taking us back to land.'

Orders from Daceus were already coming from the front line.

A full retreat was in effect. All forces were to return to Kellenport. With the concentration of Ultramarines in the area, several necron phalanxes had rerouted to tackle them. Somewhere in their midst, a necron overlord directed their efforts. Sicarius must have irritated them and now baited the trap. Kellenport's walls were as good a staging ground for a pitched battle as any other.

'It's as if he planned it,' said Tirian. The necron infantry was being pressed on both sides.

Before he donned his battle-helm, Atavian met Tirian's gaze. 'What makes you think he didn't?'

BARRING A SKELETON force of defenders, Commander Sonne had virtually emptied Kellenport. Entrenched gun positions were dug out and formed into heavy weapon teams; the troopers from disparate squads were reappropriated into platoons; conscripts were armed and armoured from the dead and forged into their own battalions; and what was left of the Damnosian armour rode out into the wastes led by a small group of cobalt Angels.

Adanar was in the cupola of the lead tank, a Leman Russ with a damaged battle cannon but whose side-sponson heavy bolters worked well enough. Two others followed it in staggered formation, one either side. Both were damaged but still had some firepower left. Sentinel walkers, some without functioning weapons, and Hellhound tanks ranged the flanks. A stoic block of Chimera transports brought up the rear, with one exception. This vehicle was at the head of the slow-moving armoured column. Its roof hatch had been ripped off by a gauss-blast, so too most of the roof. The rest of the Chimera's hull was intact, as were its tracks and engine. It made the perfect transport for Sergeant Fennion and four of his men. The others were amongst the infantry platoons, their presence more galvanising than any tank.

For the first time since the siege had begun, Adanar felt something other than despair. It wasn't hope, only reunion with his dead family could restore that; it was something else, something that at least dulled the fatalism seizing him – it was vengeance.

THE ONE HUNDRED seemed to Falka like a misnomer now. He wasn't sure there'd ever been a hundred poor souls in his improvised regiment in the first place, not exactly. It didn't matter, the name had resonance and the ex-rig-hand turned soldier liked that. What was left of the men marched with him in lockstep alongside the Ultramarines. The Chimera transport of the Space Marines moved slowly so the conscripts could keep up. Sergeant Fennion had initially dismissed the idea of riding aboard the tank, wanting to march the wastes as the humans did, but Falka had convinced him that he needed to be seen. He was a beacon, something for the others to look to, and more inspiring than any banner. Reluctantly, the Ultramarine had agreed.

'What are you thinking, brother-Angel?' Falka asked, looking up in the direction of the Chimera's ragged hull. He caught the last dregs of the sallow sun fading into the horizon. It painted the distant tundra red and rimed the edge of the mountains.

Iulus glared straight ahead as if he beheld destiny. 'That you ask many questions and are impudent in the extreme, Trooper Kolpeck.'

Falka laughed.

'That is why you like me so much.'

Iulus glanced at him askance. There was the shadow of a smile on his lips then it was gone again.

'Are you ready for more war, Brother Kolpeck?'

Falka nodded. 'Aye, my time is almost up I think. I'll be happy to leave my blood here, just as long as I take a few of those metal bastards with me.'

'Fearless and well spoken, brother. You would have made a fine Ultramarine.'

The necron lines were close now. Some of the mechanoids were turning in response to the new threat and sporadic bursts of emerald gauss-fire came rippling their way. It was different to the battle in the courtyard, even the fight to hold the walls. That was desperate, there was no choice but to take up arms or die. This was not like that. A silver sea stretched before the Imperial defenders composed of alien killing machines Falka didn't understand or truly want to face.

Though they moved like skeletal automatons, he saw

the awareness in their eyes and felt their emotions, such as they were. It was hate that burned in their balefire orbs, pure, hollow hate. The necrons would not rest until all of Damnos was gone, its population eradicated like some cancerous plague. It was this chilling fact that made Falka and his men, all of the Damnosians, march to their likely deaths. Better to fight and die, than just to die.

Mortality had never really concerned him. He didn't know if at the end there was anything more than a dark void without feeling. He hoped there would be light, maybe not a Golden Throne in the Eternal Palace of the God-Emperor, but light enough so he could find Jynn and be reunited. That would suit him just fine.

Falka donned his helmet – it carried the markings of a sergeant inscribed with a combat blade by Iulus himself – and hollered to his troops.

'Gather your courage, men. We are the saviours of Damnos, fighting for our native soil. The Emperor is with us. He has sent His Angels to fight by our side. In the name of the Imperium, honour them!'

Las-fire whickered from the Imperial ranks meeting the gauss-beams in a lattice of energy, crisscrossing lethally over the wastes. The shuddering report of heavy bolters joined it as the battle tanks opened up. Pintle-mounts blazing on their cupolas, engines screaming – the last armoured company of Damnos went to war.

An explosion, emerald-tinged and violent, lit up the distance in a viridian flash.

The afterglow still lingered in Falka's vision when he saw two beams of light strike one of the floating necron pyramids and destroy it. Beyond the enemy masses, through the cascade of gauss-flayer death, he saw the beleaguered Ultramarines too, Sergeant Fennion's true brothers.

Even amidst the firefight – seen in cracks between the melee – they were glorious. A figure strode amongst them, his armour gilded and with a white-red crest atop his battle-helm. A cape fastened to his ornate pauldrons via taloned clasps whipped about him as he killed necrons with a glowing blade. This was the personification of a hero. It was valour made flesh. An arch-angel. It was Sicarius.

With the Emperor's name not long passed his lips, Falka wept.

'IMMORTALS, DISMOUNT!' IULUS leapt from the open-topped Chimera, landing squarely with chainsword drawn. In the next breath, he was running, a steady thud of shells spitting from his bolt pistol into the necrons. Four of his battle-brothers were alongside him, charging at full tilt, for the glory of Ultramar and all of Guilliman's heirs.

The clash was fearsome, Iulus and his four battle-brothers weathering a hail of gauss-flayer bursts before they reached the enemy. Necrons responded to force. They had to be overwhelmed, struck such a catastrophic blow that whatever arcane engines animated them would realise destruction was imminent and quit the field for the sanctity of their tomb.

Considering their frailties, the humans showed incredible bravery to be only a few metres behind the Ultramarines. As he severed the spinal column of one of the mechanoids, Iulus felt a swell of pride for these poor doomed souls. In such an intense firestorm, casualties amongst the Guard and conscripts were horrific. Without power armour or an intensely hard armature, they fell quickly and in numbers.

Iulus lost sight of Kolpeck almost immediately. Inwardly, he chastened himself for it but this was war, the great leveller, and it had no use for sentiment. His chainblade growled, eager for the kill, and he fed it. Adopting a semi-circular formation, the five Immortals advanced, laying down an incessant barrage of fire. The necrons had thrown their infantry against them, a horde of raider constructs that the Second had become experts at fighting. Space Marines adapted quickly, learned the weaknesses of an enemy and how best to slay them. The Ultramarines, from Legion to Chapter, had been doing it for over ten thousand years. It was down to a fine art.

'Killing is why we were born.' Iulus recalled the words of his old trainer.

There wasn't much guile to it. The fact that the bulk of the force was conscripted ruled out any intricate tactics. It didn't matter. They would employ the hammer and hope it was enough.

As he cut down a raider trying to rise, Iulus caught sight of the tanks. The one with Commander Sonne was racing in the front.

TWO BATTLE TANKS behind him were burning wrecks. He'd seen them stitched by gauss-beams and then explode. No rifle weapon had any right to be so potent against armour like that. It left a limping Hellhound and a Chimera with its multi-laser still functional to take on the monolith.

Whether reacting to their proximity or merely self-repaired and thrown back into the fray, Adanar didn't know or care, but one of the necron pyramids had turned and was heading for them. Lances of emerald death spat from the cannons arrayed around the machine's flanks. A concentrated burst chewed up the Chimera, riddling it with holes

402

before the fuel reserve cooked off and turned the vehicle into a ball of oily flame. Adanar watched it buck and spin before crashing down on its roof in a smoking, fiery ruin. He let the backwash of heat flow over his face, toss the cape at his back – it was ragged and dirty by now.

The Hellhound slewed to a halt soon after, its axle giving out. The engine screamed hot but it was just grinding metal. Adanar turned. The tank's crew were still fighting to get out of the escape hatches when the monolith found its new target and immolated them. It was the broken axle that killed them. Fate was cruel sometimes.

Heavy bolters on the side-sponsons were throwing out shells, tearing through their belt-feeds with fury. Suddenly one of the guns clunked tight and the fusillade from the right side stopped. Then it was the left. Out of ammunition – they'd run their stockpile dry.

'I want that thing down!' he cried into the darkness of the cupola below.

A stuttering salvo of emerald beams stabbed into the tank's hull before the crew could reply. The tracks slowed almost instantly, engine noise falling from a shriek to a whine to a low hum. Deceleration. It could mean only one thing: the driver was dead.

Leaping down into the tank's hold, Adanar found a scene of bloody carnage. Crimson, though it looked more like black, painted the walls where the crew had been part-flayed by gauss-beams or shredded by internal shrapnel. In such close confines it was worse than a grenade going off. Adanar's position in the cupola had been the only thing that had saved him. Everyone else was dead.

'Can't let it live,' he muttered. Somehow, the locket-charm had found its way into his grasp. He rubbed it idly, though he didn't remember retrieving it. Dragging the driver – or what was left of his half-cooked, cauterised body – out of his seat, Adanar scrambled into the self-same position and hit the accelerator pedal hard. It didn't take a crew of five men to drive a tank. It took one with the will to do what was necessary.

Through the cracked view-slit Adanar made out the bulky form of the monolith. The view was mired by dirt and blood so he wiped it with his sleeve. Collision course set, he gave it everything. Stabs of light perforated the hull as the necron machine opened up again but miraculously he was left unharmed.

Just a few more metres.

The names of his wife and daughter were on Adanar's cracked lips. The sheer side of the monolith loomed, filling the view-slit with black.

'I am coming…' he whispered, and closed his eyes.

AN EXPLOSION LIT up the battlefield. Falka saw wreckage and fire, but he was too busy fighting for his life to make out details. It was the sound more than anything that arrested his attention.

To his right, a conscript pulled a frag grenade and was halfway through a throw when a blast caught him in the neck. He fell and the grenade went off, filling the area around him with noise and hot metal. Falka's vision faded to black. He was dimly aware of being on his back and of a damp sensation over his torso and legs. The dirt was soft and all sound slowly bled away to a soft susurrus. Through the encroaching darkness he thought he could see angels coming through the white mist…

* * *

VICTORY WAS AT hand. Iulus had been in enough battles over his decades of service to realise this. Attacked on both sides, at one a reserve battalion primarily made up of human soldiery, and the other a breakout force of Ultramarines, the necrons were well beaten. Smashed between such desperate and inviolable warriors, the mechanoids phased from the battlefield and left only the bodies of Imperial fallen in their wake.

He held his chainsword aloft, gazing around at the carnage they had reaped. *'Victoris Ultra!'*

Every Space Marine, every conscript and Ark Guard trooper raised their fists.

'Victoris Ultra!'

'And the glory of Damnos!' he added, seeking out Kolpeck amongst the exultant masses. The trooper was nowhere to be seen. Iulus had no time to think further on his ebbing sense of triumph – the captain and his honour guard approached.

Sicarius clasped him in a firm embrace. 'Well met, brother.' He withdrew and held onto Iulus's shoulder guards to help convey his delight at their arrival. 'Well met!'

Humble, Iulus bowed. He saw Praxor just behind the captain and caught his gaze.

'All is in readiness back at Kellenport?' Sicarius pressed, letting the sergeant go.

Iulus confirmed this.

'Then we had best make haste.' Sicarius turned to indicate the larger necron army behind them. The Ultramarines had put ground between them and small longer range skirmishes were still going on between the assault squads and the necron gun-platforms, but the majority of the phalanxes had slowed to a crawl. 'The overlord rebuilds his forces but will continue the advance. We must reach the staging ground before he meets us.' Something flashed behind the captain's helmet lenses; either retribution or anger, but Iulus couldn't tell which. 'I vow this will be our last retreat.'

With that, Sicarius left him. It allowed only the briefest of reunions with Praxor.

'I am pleased to see you still alive, brother,' Iulus said genuinely. The two sergeants clasped forearms.

Where Iulus gave off a reserved ebullience, Praxor's mood was dark. 'Many are not.' From the reduced ranks of the Shieldbearers, it was obvious that his squad had suffered.

'Death or glory, brother,' said Iulus. 'It is our way, our lot.'

'We have chosen death.' Praxor saluted, though the gesture was perfunctory and intended to end the brief discourse, and tramped away with his battered squad.

The Dreadnought, Agrippen, followed in his wake.

'Immortals indeed,' said the venerable warrior, appraising Iulus's men.

'We are too stubborn to die, old one.'

'When we reach the walls of Kellenport to make our stand, that trait will be tested, I feel,' Agrippen replied before walking on.

Iulus looked out into the advancing necron sea, a silver waste bringing ruin to everything in its path. Ixion and Strabo were withdrawing too, having neutralised the vanguard of gun-platforms. The necrons were consolidating their forces. They had time and growing numbers on their side.

'Yes,' his answer came, too late for the Dreadnought to hear. 'Yes, it will.'

Turning, Iulus saw the conscripts and Ark Guard gathering

too. He stopped a corporal on his way. 'You!' The man looked up fearfully at the imposing cobalt warrior-knight. 'Where is Trooper Kolpeck?'

CHAPTER TWENTY-SIX

THEY STOOD SHOULDER-TO-SHOULDER, bolters locked and ready, blades drawn and gleaming with the rising of the moon.

Before them, the third wall, its gates laid open for the sally of the Damnosian defenders. The humans were behind them now, tucked into their firing holes, pressed against their battlements and looking down on their champions arrayed in the Courtyard of Xiphos.

Praxor did not turn to look, he didn't need to. The humans had made their last act of defiance; it was up to the Ultramarines to become the true saviours of Damnos now.

'Do you remember our words about King Vidus?' asked Sicarius. The Shieldbearers were next to the Lions of Macragge in the line.

'A legend of triumph over adversity, my lord,' Praxor replied.

'Indeed, brother-sergeant.' Sicarius pointed to the third

wall and its open gates, an expansive gesture of his sword-arm encompassing the courtyard. 'This is our Thermapylon, and we the seven hundred whose blades and courage blunted the cruel ambition of a tyrant. History repeats itself, Sergeant Manorian, it always does. We stand at the cusp of it now.'

The Lions stood straighter at their liege's words. Vandius thrust the banner of the Second higher and it caught the wind. Daceus sent a crackle of energy through the fingers of his power fist. Gaius Prabian drew the blade of his sword against his shield, making the metal scrape in a wordless challenge.

This was what it meant to be a Lion. It was utter devotion; it was obedience and blind trust without equal. Sicarius only brought those who followed his will without question into his inner circle. Ironically, this was the closest Praxor had ever been to joining them and it was also the moment he knew he never would.

Agrippen was close, on the other side of Sicarius's honour guard. His eternal gaze was on the battlefield ahead. The Dreadnought was not here on Damnos to report on the captain of Second Company's actions, nor was he following any agenda Agemman had set. He was merely here to fight, to honour the Chapter's name and lineage.

'I am my Chapter's unsheathed sword,' said Praxor at last.

'Then make your blade ready, brother,' Sicarius answered, the Tempest Blade held before him, 'for the enemy comes! Courage and honour!'

The Ultramarines took up the bellowed cry, their voices in unison, their purpose as one.

'Courage and honour!'

Necron raiders were the first to breach the wall. As they

did so the charges Iulus had set all those hours ago ignited, filling the Courtyard of Xiphos with rock and fire.

TONNES OF ROCK and plascrete descended on the necrons. Many metres thick, several kilometres long, the third defensive wall of Kellenport was obliterated in the blast, burying everything around it. Dust and dirt rose in a massive pall to blanket the advancing necron forces. It churned across the courtyard, brushing against the assembled Ultramarines and colouring the edges of their armour. The Space Marines let the debris cloud roll over them, unmoving. It only took a few minutes for it to be swept away on the breeze and an echoing silence to eclipse them. Seconds later, green balefire orbs resolved in the gloom as the next line of mechanoids thrust into the rubble.

With much of the vanguard crushed, the necron overlord had little choice but to press his elites into the breach. By now, the phalanxes rerouted to destroy the Ultramarines had been gathered. Necron immortals stumbled over the wreckage of the wall to be met by a stern barrage of bolter fire. They were beyond mere raiders though, and weathered the storm with impunity. Gauss-blasters answered in rapid-fire bursts that shimmered like green pyrotechnic across the snowy courtyard flagstones.

Falka watched it all through his firing slit on the wall. A thick bandage was wrapped around his torso from where the shrapnel had hit him. Despite the cocktail of drugs in his system keeping him upright and battle-worthy, the wound hurt like all the hells. Others weren't so lucky. Pelk lost most of his throat to the blast; Hiiken, an eye and the back of his skull. Men had died, but Falka lived. Perhaps the Emperor had blessed him; perhaps He had blessed them all. He hoped His gaze would fall on His Angels too as the necrons poured into the courtyard.

I AM DOOM. The words echoed inside the Undying's cavernous mind. He had contemplated oblivion, his endless sentence of existence, and decided that all life must be eradicated from the universe. Cities burned, their populations reduced to ash by his wrath; worlds imploded, sucked into a vortex of obliteration; entire systems ignited into endless flame witnessed by his mind's eye.

This is death, this is all… I shall show it to the universe.

The curse was alive in his memory engrams, as pervasive as any flesh-borne contagion. It had condensed his self-awareness down into a singularity – the obsession with total destruction.

Hurl rock and earth, until the world is bare. It is as inconsequential as a speck of dust. Across the debris and the sundered remains of the defensive wall, the Undying found his prey.

This was the one who had defied him.

He glared, imagining the ending of all things, and outstretched a skeletal finger.

'Eradicate them.'

Reacting to the voice of their overlord, the immortals marched into the billowing dust cloud in phalanx. The Undying went with them. His honour guard attempted to close around him, glaives drawn up protectively in the simulated behaviour of aeons past. With a curt gesture, like he was parting the waves of some ancient sea, the Undying broke apart their circle and advanced after the immortals. Obeisant, they followed.

I am no longer flesh. I am abomination. I am destroyer.

The hollow thoughts echoed in his slowly fragmenting

mind. Weapons-fire was coming from beyond the debris. War was joined again. Igniting the blade of his war-scythe, the Undying stared into the storm and felt... nothing.

TWO-HANDED, SCIPIO HAMMERED the necron lord over and again with his chainsword. Whatever the strange orb in the monster's chest had done to it, the Voidbringer was reduced to scrap. With a final cry of anguish, it phased out, seemingly drawn into the artefact only for it then to collapse in on itself in a miniature event horizon.

Scipio sagged a little, his breathing rapid. 'It is done,' he announced, but Tigurius wasn't listening. The aura was still emanating from his body and he focused to control it.

Extending a shaking hand, he uttered in a broken rasp, 'Get me to the ridge, as high as you can.'

Surveying the immediate area, Scipio looked for further threats but the necrons had ceased their advance. In fact, in many instances, they had simply stopped. The effect of the Voidbringer's destruction was potent and debilitating, it seemed. His constructs appeared slower, sluggish even, as if having to recalculate or waiting for the hole in their chain of command to be repaired. Those necrons that had to defend themselves did; those beyond the immediate reach of the battle remained still.

Scipio raised the comm-feed immediately. 'Do not engage. I repeat, do not engage enemy unless necessary. The lesser necron constructs have suffered some kind of catastrophic failure and are reverting to defensive protocols.'

Octavian and Vandar confirmed. There was a clear zone around the artillery. None of the necrons were moving.

'What happened to them?' asked Vandar.

'I don't know, but hold your positions and prime

whatever explosives we have left,' Scipio replied. 'We can level this artillery platform, bury it under the mountain. Make ready.'

The other sergeants issued clipped affirmatives before Scipio was back.

He turned to Cator. 'Are you strong enough to stand?'

The plasma gunner grunted. 'Try and stop me. I'll crawl out of this hell-hole if I have to, brother-sergeant.'

Satisfied, Scipio went to Tigurius. Weakened by his psychic exertions and not entirely lucid, Scipio had to help him up. Temperature spikes throughout his armour's systems filled his retinal display with warning icons from the heat still emanating off the Librarian's psychic aura. Lightning crackled across his arcane battle plate again, ripples and motes at first, but growing in intensity. By the time he and Scipio had staggered to the edge of the ridge, they were developing into jags and forks. Drawn into the foci of his force rod, Tigurius began crafting them into a massive nimbus of psychic energy.

'When we reach the summit,' he said, clambering across the rocks, 'get down. Tell your brothers to do the same and seek cover.'

As soon as they'd mounted the small ridge overlooking the artillery, Scipio jumped back down again and gave the order. Crouched with Cator at his side, he watched.

Tigurius was glowing. A tumult of lightning coursed across the sigils inscribed onto his armour, illuminating their designs, and fed into the force rod. The eye sockets within the skull at its tip were bleeding power ferociously. Arcane instruments – keys, chains, scrolls, all of the Master Librarian's esoteric panoply – rose up with the quickening energies infusing him. It was as if they were partly magnetised and lifted in response to the sudden polarisation.

He lifted. Tigurius levitated off the ground, tiny thunderbolts striking the earth below his feet and leaving burn scars in their wake. A series of runic sigils lit up across the hard features of his face, unseen by the naked eye but visible with the tapping of his power.

'I am a servant of the Chapter Librarius. My body is a conduit. My will is dire and filled with the fire of retribution!'

A split second of silence persisted where all was still and time itself simply ceased. It broke loose the instant the storm was released like a pent-up current rushing through an opened floodgate. Lightning pulsed outwards in a wave, ripping into the artillery, turning their living metal into slag and destroying them utterly. It cooked off the rest of the explosives placed by the Ultramarines and jets of fire leapt from the ground edged with a viridian lustre.

It burned the necrons too, immolating those close enough to the nexus of the storm, banishing wraiths who vanished like frost before the winter sun.

The light died as quickly as it had manifested. Tigurius slumped to his knees, his strength all but spent.

Scipio scrambled up the ridge. The Librarian waved him off.

'I am alive.' But he was also clearly weak. Tigurius's eyes grew penetrating. 'The veil is lifted. I can *see*.'

Ultramarines were emerging through the ice-fog. Brakkius and Garrik, the latter carrying his missile launcher at ease. Largo was just behind him. He carried something too, across both arms, but he was obscured by the others and Scipio didn't see what it was. He was more concerned with Tigurius.

'My lord?'

'The veil is lifted,' the Librarian repeated. His eyes were glassy, trance-like, 'and the future unfolds, like a diamond with all possible roads laid out in its facets.'

Scipio came close, put a hand gently on Tigurius's shoulder. 'My lord,' he whispered, beseeching knowledge.

'A hero will fall, struck down by a fatal blade,' he breathed. 'Futures kaleidoscope, one tumbling into another, fragmenting and resolving again. The images shatter but this is immutable. In all the facets, it is the same.'

'Who will fall, my lord? Whose protection must we look to?' The others had gathered around him, all barring Largo, drawn by Scipio's urgency.

Tigurius's eyes became clear. He seized Scipio's wrist in a fearsome grip. 'It is Sicarius!'

Something cold filled Scipio's chest and made his movements leaden. Prescience was the Master Librarian's greatest psychic talent. He was seldom, if ever, wrong.

Sicarius will fall. The words inside Scipio's mind didn't seem real. He shook off Tigurius's hand, allowing the Librarian to slump, and turned sharply. 'Are we close enough to contact Kellenport?' he asked Brakkius.

'Not while we're in the mountains.'

Scipio looked down at Tigurius. There'd be no psychic communion either.

The comm-feed crackled in Scipio's ear. It was Octavian. 'Last of the charges primed. What is happening, brother?'

'Full evacuation from Thanatos Hills, effective immediately,' he replied.

'Are we under attack?' asked Vandar across the feed.

'Negative, but dire news has reached us. Captain Sicarius is in peril.'

Scipio was on his feet. 'Help him,' he said, and rushed past Brakkius and Garrik as they moved to assist Tigurius.

Cator was up and held out his hand. He looked saddened. 'Wait–'

'There is no time, brother.' Scipio was about to dismiss him when he caught sight of Largo again. This time he saw that the Ultramarine carried a body, a still and inert body.

A second spike of cold jabbed into Scipio. This time it was soured by guilt.

'What?'

Largo bowed his head, looking down on the recumbent form he cradled. 'Most of the guerrillas are dead. The humans simply weren't made for this fight.'

It was a woman in his arms, a cold and lifeless woman.

THE NECRON ELITES were tough, but Praxor's blade would not be denied. His power sword hummed as it cut through the thickened carapace of one, finding the crucial systems that animated it. He plunged the crackling blade deep, until hilt met the simulacrum of metallic bone, and the creature phased out. His Shieldbearers were fighting hard too. Close-range bolter bursts flashed in the encroaching night. A stream of liquid promethium lit a blazing conflagration in the enemy ranks. They moved together, with Sicarius and his Lions as their inspiration.

Despite the dark cloak drawn over his thoughts, Praxor felt uplifted and galvanised by his lord's presence. Before such glory, death would be a lauded thing destined for the annals of eternity. From his advanced position and proximity, Praxor had a good view of his captain.

Sicarius was imperious as he killed. The Tempest Blade flashed like a lightning bolt captured in his fist, unleashed time and again in a storm of righteous anger. It was easy to see why so many followed him, why he was spoken of in the same breath as Agemman and even Lord Calgar. He was ambition and arrogance, he was skill and courage personified, he was guile and reckless bravura. He *was* Ultramar.

Daceus and Gaius Prabian went before him, hewing a route through the necrons in order that Sicarius find his enemy, the one who led the mechanoids. Agrippen applied a similar fervour to his efforts; smashed necron bodies erupted with every swing of the Dreadnought's power fist, phasing out in mid-air before they could land. At such close quarters, he eschewed his plasma cannon and instead utilised the heavy flamer mounted to his armature. It scorched a ruddy line across the silvered necron hordes, burning their armour black. One fell beneath his foot and he crushed it.

'For Macragge and the Lords of Ultramar!'

Overhead, Praxor caught the flaming contrails of Ixion and Strabo as they duelled with the flying necron gun-platforms. One of the Assault Marines fell like a downed comet, wreathed with emerald fire, his armour flaking away before he crashed out of sight into the melee below.

Elsewhere, the Devastators at the back of the line were cutting furrows into the enemy.

Sergeant Atavian punched the air in triumph as his lascannons tore an arachnid construct in half. Bursts from the other heavies scattered the smaller beetle-like creatures, melting their bodies with intense microwaves or engulfing them in bright plasma.

Everywhere the Ultramarines pushed and fought like the Legion warriors of old, those who had trod the same earth as Guilliman. But despite their heroics, more and more necrons were spilling through the sundered defensive wall and into Xiphos. Only one thing would break the deadlock and Praxor saw it.

It stood taller than the others, wreathed in archaic vestments that hinted at a royal heritage. The necron overlord's gilded metal body shimmered, half silvered by the moon, its ochroid nature only revealed in the flash of nearby weapons fire. Encircling its skull-like visage was a crown, a red gemstone in the centre. A blue pectoral hung around its neck and torcs banded its arms. Clenched in its skeletal fist was a rippling pole-arm, glaive-edged and wrought with alien iconography. As its gaze alighted on Sicarius, the overlord's eyes flared.

'I am the Undying, I am doom incarnate...'

SICARIUS HOLSTERED HIS plasma pistol as he faced down the overlord. He wanted to be on even terms with the monster. It was a moment long coming, but now arrived he was ready.

'We are the slayers of kings,' he spat, the words grating through his vox-grille. A crackle of energy coursed up the length of the Tempest Blade.

He would wreak such carnage against this thing.

Sicarius advanced, signalling his Lions to stay back. For a moment he thought he might have to kill the overlord's honour guard too but the Undying ordered them aside.

It was strangely martial, even ritualised.

Sicarius struck the first blow. Chopping with the bluntness of a broadsword, he cut into the overlord's arm. The Undying was fractionally slow to defend itself and a narrow gouge was scraped across its pristine metal. Split torcs cascaded like a fountain of unlocked treasure. A modulated cry was torn from the necron's rictus mouth but its face betrayed no emotion.

The glaive swept out in a wide arc, preventing the Ultramarine's follow-up. He parried, hot sparks dancing off the clashing blades before the combatants parted.

Sicarius came again, aiming a thrust for the necron's midriff which was turned aside by the glaive's long haft. A punch dented the captain's battle-helm and he staggered, before firming up his stance and rolling away a blow heading for his gorget.

He slashed downwards, cutting a jagged furrow in the necron's torso. The glaive's haft smashed against his pauldron before he could properly defend, numbing his shoulder. Sicarius backed up again but the monster would not relent.

The Undying was slow, ponderous even, but tough. Every blow was like being hit by a tank. Sicarius went in again, unleashing a hail of blows against the necron's defences. The monster parried some, took others against its near-impervious body, before replying with a lightning-fast riposte that cut into Sicarius's plastron.

As THE CAPTAIN cried out, Praxor was filled with a terrible sense of foreboding. He moved towards the duel, as did the Lions, but a warning glance from Sicarius held the veterans at bay.

The necron overlord was gathering momentum. The Undying whirled its glaive in a circular arc, spinning it end-over-end. With a viper's speed, it snapped out, clipping Sicarius's shoulder guard. He leapt forward, forging the extra impetus into a double-handed blow that bit into the necron's forearm. Still, the monster came on undaunted. Its cries of pain had turned to laughter.

ENRAGED, SICARIUS THREW himself at the Undying, hacking and cleaving with the Tempest Blade like it was an extension of his inner anger. He fought the Undying back a step and felt the tide turning…

…until a flash of energy from the necron's open palm overloaded his retinal lenses and sent Sicarius reeling. Light, hot and emerald-tinged, filled the captain's world. He backed off, blinded, tearing at the seals connecting his battle-helm to the rest of his armour, and ripped the headgear loose. Blinking away the after-flare, Sicarius had time to parry a blurred attack. The overhead blow *pranged* hard against his sword, forcing him to one knee.

Vision still adjusting, he tore the plasma pistol from its holster and snapped off a quick blast. It struck the Undying beneath the chin, forcing the necron's head upwards and burning off part of its jaw. Staggering back from the kinetic impact, the overlord leavened the press of its glaive and Sicarius stood.

This was it.

He was about to ram the Tempest Blade into the Undying's fleshless skull when something slammed into his side, stopping him.

Agony flared like a thousand burning needles in the captain's flank. As Sicarius looked down, disbelieving, at the glaive embedded there, he felt the world grow cold. A sense of weightlessness overcame him and he realised he was being lifted off his feet. The nerves in his fingers failed him and the Tempest Blade slipped free, clattering on the ground below beside his discarded battle-helm. Blood tanged his mouth, slipped over his swollen tongue like copper filings. He spat a gobbet and it stained the Undying's gilded carapace.

As the war-scythe was driven deeper, the genebred champion gave up a cry of pain. Emotionless, the Undying looked on.

'I am doom,' he rasped as the shouts of others clawed for his attention. More cobalt-armoured warriors were coming for him.

Shucked desultorily off the glaive like a piece of offal, Sicarius crashed earthwards and lay still. Immediately, the Lions surrounded him just as the necron overlord's honour guard closed too.

'No!' The word fell clipped and defiant from Praxor's lips. He drove the Shieldbearers hard into the necron elites, splitting them apart so he could reach the side of his lord. It was to no avail. He lost Sicarius amidst the crowd of bodies, the image of a fallen sword next to a captain's helm imprinted onto his mind.

He saw the banner, upheld defiantly by Vandius. Brother Malican was by his side. Daceus and Gaius Prabian led the line. They struck down two of the honour guard, exchanging a few blows before dispatching them. Stalwart as statues, they stood over Sicarius's body and felled anything that came close. Venatio knelt behind them, working his ministrations. In Praxor's heart, he knew it was too late. Sicarius was dead.

CHAPTER TWENTY-SEVEN

BY THE TIME the Ultramarines reached the edge of the Thanatos Hills and left the mountains for good, Tigurius was
coming back around. Strengthened by the force of his will,
he stood straighter and was able to walk unaided, albeit
by leaning on his staff.

Evacuation from the mountains had been conducted in
silence. Led by Scipio and his Thunderbolts, the Ultramarines were driven by a frustrating sense of urgency. Their
captain was likely in very real danger but until communication was restored they were powerless to do anything.

'Check again,' said Scipio as the icy fells gave way to a
stretch of flat tundra. Perpetual blizzards roamed this part
of Damnos, kicked up in squalls that moved from region
to region on the arctic winds. Weather was still fouling the
connection to their distant brothers.

Brakkius shook his head.

They marched on. Scipio spared a glance for Jynn. She

was being carried on a makeshift stretcher by two of the surviving guerrilla fighters. The rest were dead, left on the plateau where the earth and rock would bury them. Scipio checked the distance from the plateau on his retinal display. A few more kilometres and they could detonate the charges that would obliterate the artillery station.

His thoughts went back to Jynn. He'd left her, abandoned her to this fate. It was the right thing to do, Tigurius was in danger. But he couldn't shake the guilt that she and her troops should never have been there. Scipio was reckless and arrogant, believing they could take the necrons by surprise, sweep in and destroy the guns without casualty. He gave no regard to the potential loss of human life. It made him think of the earlier attack on the outpost and the death of Ortus. Brother Renatus, too, had lost his life on account of injuries suffered during that ill-fated assault. Again, Scipio's lack of temperance had done this.

Iulus's words, spoken long ago on the assembly deck of the *Valin's Revenge*, came back to him.

'You are becoming like him.'

He was right. Orad's death had changed Scipio, although he was only now realising it.

He hoped that Jynn would live.

The comm-feed in his battle-helm crackled. Brakkius had made contact with the others.

AGRIPPEN BARGED THROUGH the silver horde. Scattering the last of the necron immortals in his way, he descended on the honour guard. One he crushed in his fist; the other he burned, pressing the flamer so close it scorched his armature and stripped away the paint.

The necron overlord glared up at the Dreadnought, a

hellish fire ignited in its eyes. Sicarius had wounded it – the Undying's face was caught in the flux of self-repair. Agrippen cared not. He smashed his power fist down upon it brutally, crushing the gilded overlord into ruin.

The destruction of their lord sent a massive shockwave rippling throughout the necron ranks. As one they began to fall back. The Dreadnought was not to be denied, though, and tore apart the mechanoids as they fled.

Assuming command, he drove the Ultramarines forward. Only the Lions remained, surrounding their fallen captain protectively.

They harried the necrons across the rubble and out into the wastes. In disarray, the automatons were easy prey. During the retreat, the warriors of Sicarius exacted their vengeance in a tally of enemies that scoured the earth and cleansed the area around Kellenport completely.

IULUS HEARD A cheer resound behind him as all the men of Damnos witnessed the necrons' defeat. Like his battle-brothers, he was swept up in the moment. When he saw the Lions of Macragge arrayed around the slumped figure of his captain in a protective cordon his exultant mood ebbed. It was replaced by vengeance and the desire to vanquish the enemy utterly.

Stationed in the rear line of the army, alongside the Devastators, Iulus pushed his Immortals forward. He caught Sergeant Atavian's eye.

'Sicarius has fallen.'

Like Iulus, Atavian gave nothing away. 'Is he dead?'

'They watch over him like pallbearers.'

The grating rasp of Chaplain Trajan interjected. 'Rites will be spoken if he is slain. Now we must let our bolters and blades describe our litanies of hatred.'

NICK KYME

He led them into the fleeing masses, crozius swinging. Iulus followed a little way behind. Atavian's advance was slower still with the heavy guns.

A gauntlet reached out and snatched Iulus's arm. He turned about to strike, believing a destroyed mechanoid had self-repaired, but it was Praxor. He wasn't wearing his battle-helm and his eyes were wide.

Iulus said, 'Brother?'

'He is dead. I saw him fall with my own eyes. Captain Sicarius is slain.'

Iulus's expression went from grief to resolution. 'Then we avenge him.'

For over an hour the Ultramarines pursued the retreating necrons, all the way to the far border of Arcona City. Thousands were destroyed in the rout, the mechanoids unable to mount a defence or any kind of useful tactic that might have spared their losses. Without their overlord they were less than automatons, little more than directionless drones. Even the elites appeared locked onto a single course of action – full-scale retreat.

The as-yet unseen phasic generator teleported some of the constructs back to the sunken tomb all the way into the northern polar wastes. No Ultramarine had laid eyes on the device, and it was likely withdrawn upon their arrival.

Only when the last of the necrons had either been teleported or damaged into instant phase-out did Agrippen call a halt, his fury sated. Then the Ultramarines began the long march back to Kellenport.

THE SUN WAS high in the ice-blue Damnos sky when Scipio reached the city. The edges of its walls were veneered in hazy umber from the light.

Led by the Thunderbolts, the Ultramarines from the Thanatos Mission passed through the Kellenport gates just as a viridian explosion lit up the distant hills. So large and destructive, the blast was even visible from the city. The pylons and gauss-obliterators would not return. For one they were buried, for another the Ultramarines had used enough explosive to level the mountainside.

'Sergeant Vorolanus.'

It was Tigurius. Scipio stopped and turned to face the Librarian.

'I will see to our captain,' he said. 'Agrippen has command.'

Scipio bowed, acknowledging.

As they parted ways, Tigurius stopped. 'I saw courage on the Thanatos Hills and a desire for self-sacrifice. Now you know who you are, brother. Remember it.'

The Librarian was heading into the distant hubbub of the city. Already, preparations were being made for the arrival of the Ultramarines armour. Several squads stood watchful upon the battlements, alongside the Damnosian soldiery.

There was no sign of Agrippen or the Lions. Scipio assumed they were in council, planning the strategic defence of the city. At least two other sergeants were not present at that meeting. Leaving Brakkius in charge, Scipio dismissed the Thunderbolts. His gaze lingered on Jynn as she was carried to the nearest medical station. He banished the bleak thoughts from his mind as he went to meet his brothers.

Hugging Scipio firmly, Iulus said, 'I am glad you're alive, brother.'

Scipio laughed mirthlessly. 'You sound like you had your doubts.' He turned to Praxor. 'Brother?'

He looked downcast, his shame obvious in his bearing.

Praxor had believed Sicarius dead and become like the people of Damnos he had thought weren't worth saving on account of that fatalism.

The captain was injured, badly, but lived. The truth of it was revealed later when the courtyard had cleared and Venatio announced to the Lions that their lord still drew breath. He was still in the Apothecary's care, surrounded by his inner circle warriors. But Cato Sicarius would play no further part in the war on Damnos. As soon as possible, he would be ferried to the apothecarion aboard the *Valin's Revenge* and allowed to recover.

Scipio put a hand on Praxor's shoulder. 'Neither of us was there, brother. We didn't witness what you did.'

'I should have known, but instead I gave in to doubt.'

'All three of us have experienced much in this campaign. I confess I never thought this ball of ice would be a place for revelation.'

At this point, Iulus stepped in. 'It's not done yet, either.' He held up a data-slate displaying the planet's northern geography. 'Necron forces are stirring in the north. Scans reveal massive tectonic activity.'

Exhaling, Scipio marshalled his anger. 'So all we have done so far has merely set them back?'

Iulus nodded. 'It would appear so.'

'We have sacrificed much for little.'

'And more is needed.'

Scipio was pensive for a moment before he straightened and clapped his brothers each on the pauldron. 'Then by the glory of Ultramar, it will be given.'

Praxor nodded determinedly. Iulus even cracked a feral smile.

All three looked skywards as a large vessel silhouetted the

upper atmosphere. The sound of the battle-barge's engines was loud, even as far up as it was, and smaller ships were disgorging from it.

Valin's Revenge.

The Ultramarines on the wall, those in the courtyard, all of the Damnosian infantry looked up.

The voice of Antaro Chronus, veteran Ultramarines tank commander, came over the feed. 'The heavens are clear,' he announced, shouting above the sound of heavy machinery in the background. 'We are coming, brothers.'

EPILOGUE

ANKH HAD FORESEEN this outcome. Not through any form of prescience or sixth sense, but rather the cold logic of cause and effect. The Undying's demise was inevitable; the necron retreat likewise. Tahek's death he had engineered purposely – it meant the skies were open for the genebred warriors to bring their vessels and machineries to the surface. It would give them hope, make them believe that victory was even possible.

That thought amused the Architect. In the depths of the tomb his spyders and scarabs were revivifying in thousands, *tens of thousands*. The phalanxes in full retreat on the surface were but a fraction of what lay beneath, and there were things much more terrible in those depths. As the battles raged above, Ankh had been busy waking them.

He felt the touch of an ancient sentience in the emerald gloom of the under-caverns. It was a royal chamber where he stood. As Ankh contemplated the vast catacombs and their slumbering hordes, a pair of eyes ignited in the darkness in front of him.

Ankh took a step back and bowed almost to the floor.

'My lord,' he purred as the royarch's gaze fell upon him.

SPEAR OF MACRAGGE

'They came with the ice, so the natives would later tell us. But the truth was they had always been there, slumbering, waiting. We knew little about them during that first encounter, save that they were ages old and hard to kill. We know precious little more now.

'The dead don't stay dead, not on Damnos. They came back, from up out of the ice, and we shed much blood to put them back beneath it. We are Ultramarines. The exemplars. Our victories are many, but against the enemy on Damnos we tasted that rarest of things, a word I thought lost to our vocabulary – defeat. Few foes have ever claimed that over us, but in the necrons we found a worthy and most terrible one. In the necrons, we found a nemesis, and one which we were destined to meet again.'

– Chapter Master Marneus Calgar, after the so-called 'Damnos Incident'

CHAPTER ONE

FROZEN TRACKS

BENT-BACKED, FROZEN TO the core despite his thermal labour-suit, Engineer Thain swore as he broke the handle of his ice axe.

It was his third one, with only a fourth left in his tool kit. Discarding the broken haft, Thain glared ruefully at the frozen tank track he had failed to loosen. He rubbed his hands together – they were bone-cold, despite his heavy gloves – but got little feeling back into the fingers.

'Use a hand flamer to thaw the hoarfrost, then switch to the ice axe.'

Thain would have started at the voice behind him, but he was too tired, too cold to react.

'It'll fuse the track guards,' he snapped, testy, rising as he turned. 'Make 'em sti–' The word died in his mouth, which was now agape and ghosting air.

He came up to the warrior's armoured chest: a plastron

of cobalt emblazoned with the frost-white Ultima symbol of his Chapter.

The huge warrior had taken a hand flamer from the engineer's kit and offered it to the man in his massive gauntleted hand.

'Not if you tweak the setting, keep the flame low and take it off when the ice starts to melt,' the warrior replied. He was not wearing a helmet, which seemed insane to Thain, given the conditions, and a white rime of frost crusted his hairless brow and sharp cheekbones. There was a platinum stud above his left eye, a record of service, so Thain understood. This one was a veteran, then. The Ultramarine smiled, though the gesture was far from warming. 'You'll break fewer handles that way.'

Thain genuflected awkwardly because of his stiff limbs. 'Gratitude, my lord.'

'I'm not your lord,' the warrior said, moving on. 'Your lords are dead. Go to your duty, and that track had best be unfrozen by the time we're ready to roll out.'

The man attempted a salute, but was hindered again by his chilled bones. 'Yes, sir.'

He went back to thawing out the tank track, using the hand flamer as instructed, but the chill never left him.

ANTARO CHRONUS LEFT the serf behind as he went to inspect the rest of the squadron, but reached out to touch the metal hull of the tank before he did so.

'*Antonius*, old friend…' he sighed. 'You'll be battle-ready for the war on this barren rock.'

Three Predators, Annihilator-patterns on account of their twin-linked lascannon turrets and heavy bolter sponsons, waited in the cold, engines growling. They had been back less than an hour and the Damnos ice had already crept back into their workings. Chronus was no Techmarine but he knew tanks and his were not at ease. Their machine-spirits were displeased.

A short reconnoitre into the wastes had revealed little. As reported, the immediate area surrounding Kellenport was free of necrons. The retreat looked to be total. It meant they would have to press further, towards Damnos Secundus, but that required a refuel and now a thorough de-icing after waiting so long in the cold.

As the serfs kept the vehicles from freezing over, his crew were performing other checks according to protocol and taking on extra ammunition before their next foray. This time they would head north into the region where Tigurius had alleged the necrons were regrouping.

Emerging from *The Vengeful's* cupola, one of the Ultramarines crewmen hailed the tank commander and disembarked to speak to Chronus.

'They work too slowly,' he said, jutting his chin at the shivering labour gangs. Fabricus was a driver as fearless as any Chronus had known, and as relentless.

Chronus cast his eye over the serfs: first the ones striving to keep their tanks functional, then the much larger workforce currently attempting to reinforce the sundered walls of Kellenport. According to Tigurius, it was the last bastion of human habitation in all of Damnos. Judging by the shattered revetments, collapsed bulwarks and broken gates, it was a poor one and not particularly defensible.

'It's the cold, Brother Fabricus,' said Chronus. 'Remember, they are merely men and cannot be expected to endure what we can. They'll do their duty. This is their city after all, their world, and we are all that stands between it and annihilation.'

They walked together in lockstep, passing first through three Predators and then between the heavier armoured forms of three siege tanks, the Vindicators *Glory of Calth*, *The Ram* and *Wrath of Invictus*. The Ultramarines who noticed Chronus as he passed saluted the tank commander before going back to their preparations.

'Have you been to see him?' asked Fabricus solemnly.

'Who?' Chronus replied as they reached a group of three immense Land Raiders, their drop-ramps down as crews within worked on thawing out the interior troop compartments.

'Captain Sicarius.'

They stopped at the edge of the improvised laager provided by the hefty Land Raiders, looking in the same direction as the tanks' hull-mounted heavy bolters towards featureless tundra and endless ice wastes. A storm had rolled in, obliterating the distant horizon line behind a wall of white.

'What purpose would that serve, brother? I know Sicarius is being tended in the apothecarion of the *Valin's Revenge*. There is precious little I can do for him when he is unconscious and at high anchor above this frozen world, is there?'

Fabricus frowned, and the ice riming his face and closely shorn scalp cracked.

'The Master of the Watch has fallen. Does that not concern you, commander?'

Chronus folded his arms, but kept his gaze on the white false horizon as Fabricus looked at him for his answer. 'Do I think his absence harms our chances of success out here? Yes, of course. He is an inspirational leader and a fierce warrior, albeit capricious. But does it concern me?' He gave a derisory laugh. 'No more than a thrown track or a malfunctioning sponson mount. We adapt, we maintain, we overcome. We are armour.' He slammed his fist against his chest with a heavy *clank*. 'We are inviolable. The necron have yet to taste our fury, and I am wholly confident it won't be to their liking when they do.'

Fabricus slammed his fist against his armour too, nodding at this declaration.

A second tank squadron idled within fifty metres of the first and comprised an identical array of vehicles, with the exception that the siege tanks were replaced by launcher-fitted patterns, excellent for long-range sustained barrage.

Alongside this fearsome alliance of armour was a void. It was waiting to be filled by a third group, one that was now almost an hour late.

'Has there been any sign of them yet?' Chronus asked.

'Sergeant Egnatius's last communication had them entering the Vogenhoff region. It's remote, plagued by ravines and ice caves. Together with the storm…' Fabricus let it hang like that, knowing there was no need to go further.

Chronus scowled, as if satisfied for now, but he was itching to be back aboard the *Rage of Antonius*, his own Predator tank, and back amidst the ice. 'Inform Sergeant Gnaeus he has temporary command of the company, and vox me the moment Egnatius returns.'

'Yes, commander.'

'Have them stand by. We move on my order. One I must delay until I speak with our captains.'

Fabricus saluted again and went to carry out his orders.

Turning on his heel, Chronus began to stride back towards Kellenport.

Labour crews swarmed over the city like ants, directed

by Techmarines and a few battle-brothers from the Tactical squads. Despite superior Space Marine engineering and fortification, the city looked far from siege-worthy. It was ragged. Only he and his armour would serve as any real protection for these people.

Despite what Tigurius believed, Chronus knew he could save this world. He had but to be afforded the opportunity.

CHAPTER TWO
FIRST MEETINGS AND OLD REUNIONS

THE ULTRAMARINES COMMAND section had made camp just within the broken gatehouse of Kellenport's north wall. Most of the officers present were Second Company, some of Sicarius's squad sergeants and honour guard. The rest were well known to Chronus, and he picked out faces he recognised as he breached the makeshift cordon of barricades and came to stand alongside the warriors surrounding a map table.

'Hololiths are out,' explained one sergeant, an officious sort given his stilted bearing, Chronus thought, but with a shadow behind his eyes. He had seen a lot of that since they had made landfall in the Thunderhawk transporters, and he wondered exactly what had happened prior to their arrival. He had not stopped to ask, just rolled out with his vehicles to secure the immediate perimeter. In the end, it had proven unnecessary, a fact that made the back of the tank commander's neck itch in irritation.

'Vintage,' Chronus replied, stepping into the circle of officers and taking stock of the parchment map they were all examining. 'I find something quite reassuring about that. Antaro,' he added, offering a hand.

'Brother-Sergeant Manorian,' said the sergeant, clasping the tank commander's wrist in the traditional Ultramarines greeting.

'I know your rank, brother. It's on your armour. Tell me your given name.' Chronus was already absorbing all the information on the map and matching it to what he knew of the landscape first-hand from his initial reconnoitre and futile harrying mission. 'If we are to bleed together, then I would know who you are.' He looked back at the sergeant, his eyes bright and alert.

The sergeant nodded. 'Praxor.'

Chronus smiled. 'Excellent.' He looked up at the rest of the gathering, who had been in the midst of determining strategy when he arrived. 'So then, who can provide me with a situation report and who else around this table have I yet to become acquainted with?'

At the head of the table loomed a massive and imposing figure, the veteran Brother Agrippen, now encased in a holy Dreadnought sarcophagus. He was roughly a third taller than any of the assembled Ultramarines and easily twice as broad. Out of the vox-emitter built into his sarcophagus churned a machine-growl that Chronus took to be laughter.

'It is good you are here, Brother Chronus. I see you did not wait to make greeting after landfall.'

'Securing the perimeter of the city was more of a priority, Ancient.' Chronus crafted a small bow to the Dreadnought, who gave a nod of sorts in return. 'I was informed you have command?'

'Yes,' answered Agrippen, 'together with our Chief Librarian.'

Chronus smiled at the hooded psyker, who kept his distance from the strategy table. His eyes glowed with power in the dusk that had settled over Kellenport.

'Varro and I are well known to one another.'

Tigurius nodded. Even in the shadows, Chronus saw the Librarian's jawbone tense at the informality.

Chronus did not linger on it. He gestured to another of the gathering, one armoured in black. 'And Chaplain Trajan, also.'

He knew all of Sicarius's Lions, too. Daceus, Vandius, Malican and Gaius Prabian. Only Venatio, the Apothecary, was absent. Doubtless, there were many injured who required his attention. Two others, besides the sergeant called Praxor, were unknown to him.

'Strabo,' said one, his markings indicating him as an Assault Marine. 'Mathias,' he corrected, before the tank commander had to request it.

'Maxima Atavian,' said the final officer, his bionic eye suggesting his position as a Devastator. 'It is an honour to fight alongside you.'

Three line sergeants from each of the three squad dispositions of Second. 'Well then,' Chronus addressed the group, nodding in turn at the warriors he had not met before. 'I don't need to be told how Kellenport fares, this city is fit to crumble, but what of the rest of Damnos?'

'From the Thanatos Hills, we saw a great force of necrons amassing to the north,' said Tigurius. 'And more phalanxes are activating in several other regions too.'

Chronus cast his eye over the map again, and the marks made in charcoal to indicate known and suspected enemy dispositions.

'We are surrounded, Commander Chronus,' uttered Tigurius. 'Kellenport is a solitary lantern amidst a sea of night.'

'I always admired your poetry, Varro,' said Chronus, rubbing his clean-shaven chin. 'I have no gift for it, myself. I am altogether a much blunter instrument.' He looked up. 'Perhaps that is what's needed now, the more direct approach.'

'I thought you a pragmatist also, Chronus,' Tigurius replied, 'and yet it sounds like you're suggesting we can still take this world.'

Chronus was impassive. 'I would see what kind of fight the necrons still have in them. Perhaps Damnos *can* still be saved. And if not, then the phasic generators present an issue for all of us, which requires an attack.'

'Withdrawal is the only strategy left to us.' A flash of power filled Tigurius's eyes in sympathetic frustration. 'Don't risk your arsenal on what would be a pyrrhic victory, commander. By destroying the phasic generators you give us precious time to evacuate. To attempt any more than that is foolhardy. Damnos is lost.'

'And yet here we all stand, stooped over a strategium,' replied Chronus.

'I find myself in agreement with Tigurius,' said Chaplain Trajan from behind the death-skull mask of his helmet. 'Even with the leadership of Sicarius, we cannot triumph here.' He bowed his head to Agrippen. 'No disrespect, Ancient.'

'None taken, Brother-Chaplain.' The Dreadnought's gaze through his vision slit fell upon Chronus, though. 'But if victory is still possible, then we must strive for it.'

'Even at the potentially futile cost of more lives?' asked Tigurius.

All present knew of the guilt he felt about Sicarius, and of the premonition he had failed to discern in time to prevent the captain's mortal wounding.

Agrippen had already decided what their course would be, however.

'What is our purpose, if it is not to lay down our lives in protecting humanity and its sovereign domains?'

Tigurius bowed to the Dreadnought.

'Wise words, Ancient.' He spared a glance at Chronus, who was studying the map and committing it to memory. 'If the commander believes there is a chance to save Damnos then we are duty-bound to pursue that unto its end. Whatever end that might be,' he added, somewhat forbiddingly.

When he was finished, Chronus looked up.

'From what I know, the majority of the necrons are on foot. They are also slow and their tactics predictable.'

'As we routed them at the gates, they were not as formidable,' Agrippen agreed. 'The loss of their leader crippled them in some gestalt fashion.'

Chronus nodded. 'The primary function of a tank is to kill infantry. It's the reason we were forged. We should look towards our defence, and fortify Kellenport. Have your warriors keep vigil on the walls, your gunships the skies,' he said. 'I can see you've drawn all defences back to the city walls and abandoned all else beyond it. Make what preparations must be made for a planet-wide evacuation. In the meantime I will seek engagement, and treat these necrons like any other enemy in my crosshairs. Piece by piece, phalanx by phalanx, I'll dismantle them. I have twenty-four engines at my disposal and several others in support. Not to mention those still in their berths aboard the *Valin's*

Revenge. We'll head north into Damnos Secundus. Soon as I get a sight of the enemy, we'll bombard them, break them apart. I understand they don't run, so if they want to engage us they'll have to advance. Slow as they are, that *will* hurt them, even these creatures. When they do, I'll bring up a second line of armour, heavy cannon and bolters. By the time they reach us they'll be a ragged mess. And if anything does remain, I'll crush it under my tracks. There's no coming back from that.'

'There could be thousands of necrons, commander,' said Trajan.

Chronus faced the dour Chaplain.

'Then I shall have to take sufficient ammunition. Rest assured, this is not arrogance or vainglory. I want to know we are beaten before we accept defeat. With all good conscience, I cannot say that I do yet. So I fight.'

Spurred on by the tank commander's rhetoric, Sergeant Manorian stepped forwards.

'I'd like to pledge my warriors to your cause, Commander Chronus.'

'Aye, and mine,' added Atavian.

Strabo's fervour was obvious in his eyes, so no offer was needed to convey his feelings.

All three sergeants looked eager for retribution, but Chronus knew he was going to deny them.

'Your courage is without question, but your place is on the wall. My armoured company can end this threat, but I need to move quickly and with what I know. I am commander of machines, not men. See to the protection of Kellenport, in case I am unsuccessful.' Chronus turned to Agrippen. 'We are in agreement, Ancient?'

'Aye, we are. Engage the necrons and assess the threat they

still pose to us, but the Chapter has lost one hero already to this enemy. I would not see it lose another.'

Chronus bowed reverently to the veteran Dreadnought. 'Understood.'

Tigurius and Trajan nodded their assent to Chronus's plan too.

A warrior appeared at the edge of the circle of officers. His armour markings described him as tank crew.

'Then if all are agreed and everything is in order,' said Chronus as he noticed the driver, 'I believe Brother Fabricus here has arrived with news of my errant sergeant's return, so I shall put actions to these words and seek engagement.'

He saluted, looking at each and every officer in turn.

'Your gunships, Ancient,' said Chronus as he was about to leave. 'I need them as my eyes, to show where my hammer should fall hardest.'

A machine-growl emanated from Agrippen's vox-emitter, expressing his eagerness to see Sicarius and all of the fallen avenged.

'They are yours to command, Antaro. Do so wisely.'

Chronus nodded curtly, saluted again and left with Fabricus.

THE SIX ENGINES idling on the snow plain expelled steam and exhaust smoke. Ice clung to the hulls of the Predator tanks, but they were, nonetheless, fully operational.

Chronus approached the lead vehicle as one of its occupants appeared out of the cupola hatch.

'Apologies, commander,' said Egnatius. 'We were caught in the storm. Our augurs malfunctioned and took us into a blind ravine. The Vogenhoff region is more treacherous than I at first believed.' He bowed his head contritely, snow cresting the ridge of his battle-helm. It bore a steel laurel, and some scars that had not been there before.

'Did you run into some trouble, brother-sergeant?' asked Chronus.

'Just the elements, sir.'

'Then let's hope you fare better against the necrons. Your squadron is second in the line after mine. We're heading north into Damnos Secundus.'

Egnatius looked askance at the serfs freighting a cache of fuel drums in the direction of his squadron, but kept most of his attention on Chronus.

'Far north, it would seem.'

'Indeed. The enemy have retreated deep and are attempting to regroup. We're not going to allow that. Take on your extra fuel and fall in as instructed.'

Egnatius saluted and Chronus left him to it. Fabricus had already returned to his vehicle, so Chronus crossed the snow plain alone to where the *Rage of Antonius* was waiting.

As he was climbing back into the open cupola hatch, he spared a last look at the white veil beyond the Kellenport perimeter.

It looked almost impenetrable.

Almost.

Ducking inside, he shut the overhead hatch with a dull *clang*.

Slowly at first, their tracks grinding and slipping on the snow until they found purchase, the tank company of Antaro Chronus rolled out.

CHAPTER THREE
ICE ON THE WIND

ICE WAS IN the air and it cleaved to the *Gladius*, riming its wings in white.

'*The storm's fouling the augurs.*'

The voice issued through the hold's vox, from the pilot in the cockpit up front.

'They're still down there, Brother Kastus,' said Scipio, standing in the hold with one hand clasping the rail above his head to keep him stable. 'How are the engines holding up?'

There was a short pause whilst Kastus checked his instruments before his disembodied voice answered.

'*One of the turbofans is a little sluggish, but nothing to threaten loft or propulsion.*'

'We need to come back down out of this cloud,' said Scipio, 'and get sight of the enemy.'

'*As you wish, brother-sergeant. I'll plot in a descent vector.*'

The roaring sound within the *Gladius*'s hold shifted in

451

pitch almost immediately, going from a dull drone to a screech as the descent thrusters eased in and slowly took them down.

'No sensors?' asked Brakkius, sitting down next to the exit hatch and his sergeant. 'We'd be coming out of this blind, and low enough for ground-to-air attack.'

Scipio unclamped the magnoculars attached to his belt and adjusted the settings one-handed.

'They've shown little interest so far, brother.' He gave a feral smile. 'Besides, I want to take a closer look at what they're doing.'

Scipio's squad, the Thunderbolts, all sat in sturdy grey grav couches, harnesses up and unlocked. They had been reduced down to combat-squad strength, just five men including the sergeant. A gunship the size of the *Gladius* had capacity for up to thirty armoured Space Marines, including their wargear. With just the five of them aboard, the troop hold felt cavernous.

Most of Second's squads had been redeployed, the warriors from the more intact squads re-tasked to those with diminished combat efficacy in order to provide solid operational efficiency overall. Weapons too had been reappropriated and redistributed according to need. All retasked squads operated under their sergeant's preferred honorific. In Scipio's case this was the Thunderbolts, Squad Vorolanus.

Most of Second's warriors were back at Kellenport on wall duty, and this included some surviving Thunderbolts. Recon patrol did not usually require a gunship's hold to be encumbered with troops but Agrippen wanted protection for the Thunderhawks he had sent out in case they were shot down. Besides, more souls aboard meant a greater chance of someone surviving and being able enough to send a message if the necrons decided to move or change tactics. The extra guns aboard did not hurt either when trying to put a dent in their vast phalanxes.

Scipio got back on the vox. 'Bring us in, pilot.'

The hull shuddered with some minor turbulence, but the engine noise began to return to its previous drone. Scipio could feel the *Gladius* levelling off. The gunship's pilot confirmed it.

'*Breaching cloud layer now…*'

Brakkius was on his feet, bolter low-slung but with the slide racked ready to fire. Garrik joined him, the heavy's missile launcher braced against his shoulder.

'Just in case,' Brakkius said to Scipio. Auris and Largo, the final two members of the squad, loitered behind him.

All five Ultramarines had mag-locked their boots to the deck. This close in, their transport might have to shift to combat speed or perform evasive manoeuvres.

Magnetically secured, Scipio let go of the rail.

'Open her up, Brakkius.'

Disengaging the locking clamps, Brakkius slid the side hatch of the gunship open, admitting the ice and buffeting wind. It hit them at once, forcefully, peppering their armour with chips of hail. The *Gladius* pitched a little as its interior integrity was altered, but Scipio and his squad stood firm.

The sergeant leaned out, hanging on to the rail again so he could extend his body a little further from the hatch without falling out. He was right – the necrons were still there, marching slowly and in phalanx formation. Despite the fact the deadly gunship screamed overhead, none of them looked skywards. Their eyes were dull, aglow, but with barely any sentience, assuming their brightness was any barometer of that. The Ultramarines did not know. They had precious little intelligence about the necrons beyond the fact that they were extremely difficult to kill.

With one hand, Scipio pressed the scopes to his eyes.

The image return was awash with grainy green resolution, but the filter cut through the cold interference and the natural obfuscation of snow flurries well. Any heat signature was weak, and judging by that the necrons appeared in some kind of semi-dormant state. They moved in lockstep, their flayer weapons held at ease across their bodies. Definitely advancing south, they still seemed without much purpose.

'Garrik,' said Scipio, still monitoring the phalanx through the magnoculars, 'put a missile in their ranks, centre of formation.'

Brakkius stepped aside to give the heavy weapons carrier some room. Garrik nodded, took a knee to adopt a more stable position and flipped up the targeter array on his launcher. The red crosshair flashed into life on the scope's small screen, overlaying a hazy rendering of the selfsame image on Garrik's eye. He closed the other to increase his focus, and gave a thumbs-up to Brakkius before getting his gauntleted finger on the trigger.

'Firing,' declared Brakkius, warning the others to brace.

A second later and Garrik's body jerked with recoil as a payload of light ordnance was spat from the mouth of the launcher with a throaty *choom* of expelled pressure. A winding contrail of white vapour snaked downwards before impacting in the midst of the phalanx and detonating.

The explosion tore through the necrons' ranks, throwing up metal bodies and plumes of displaced snow and earth.

Scipio let the incendiary flare fade from his magnoculars,

the visual briefly overloaded with light and rendering nothing but ugly green. After a few seconds, the image resolved again.

'Nothing,' he told the others, still looking through the scopes. He saw mechanised limbs and body parts strewn in all directions, and a small crater where Garrik's missile had found its mark. Already, the necrons were self-repairing. There was a single flare of light where one of the automatons had been too badly damaged and phased out. Scipio increased the range, refocused for a closer examination. Entire mechanised systems were reconstructing themselves. Metal appeared to reflow and coalesce, refashioning back into whatever shape it had previously possessed. Wires reattached themselves, fragments of shattered gears and servos reassembled with one another as if suddenly magnetised.

The necrons that were spared the blast closed ranks around the fallen, absorbing the damage, whilst those that were self-repairing found fresh positions at the end or edge of the formation as soon as they were mobile again. Barring the one necron that had phased out, the phalanx was identical to what it had been prior to the attack. Their pace had not changed, their demeanour remained the same. Despite analysing the aftermath in detail, Scipio could find no discernible reaction to what had just happened.

He lowered the scopes and leaned back inside.

'It's as if we weren't even here,' he commented to himself.

'We could try a strafing run?' suggested Brakkius. Through his helmet's vox-grille, his voice sounded tinny with a slight reverberation. It could not disguise his doubt, however.

Scipio's second-in-command was reaching. They all were. The sergeant shook his head.

'What do you think caused it?' asked Auris, his beaked

helmet giving him the same resonant cadence as Brakkius, only not as deep.

'I'm not sure,' said Scipio, still watching the necrons.

Reports from the *Thunderstorm*, also on recon patrol over the Damnos skies, gave much the same account. The remnants of the necron horde thrown back at the Kellenport gates after the heroic sacrifice of Captain Sicarius had regrouped much farther north and were advancing, but showed no other signs of aggression.

'I've seen servitors acting in a similar vein,' said a voice from the back of the hold. Brother Vantor sat apart from the rest of the group, quietly ministering to the *Gladius*'s aggrieved machine-spirits.

So circumspect was the Techmarine, Scipio had almost forgotten he was there at all.

Vantor looked up from speaking his canticles of function to address the sergeant. Both Thunderhawks in the skies at that moment each had a Techmarine in their roster. With such adverse weather conditions, together with the Second relying so heavily on the gunships' ability to track and monitor the enemy, everything was done to ensure they stayed aloft. That included taking a servant of the Martian creed, a Techmarine.

'They are following a prescribed protocol,' Vantor went on, the dull internal lighting of the hold limning the right side of his red power armour but plunging the left, where he wore his blue Ultramarines shoulder guard, into shadow. The servo-arms attached to his power generator and their various concomitant mechadendrites resembled arachnid silhouettes in the dingy hold. 'Imagine the entire phalanx slaved to a rigid doctrina wafer instruction,' he went on.

'These mechanoids are no servitors, Vantor,' said Scipio.

'Correct, and nor is their synaptic instruction methodology so crude.' His eyes widened a little and a hollow smile just curled the edge of his lips. 'It is advanced.'

'You sound almost as if you admire them.' Brakkius scowled behind his faceplate, but his distaste was obvious in the tone of his voice.

'I find them fascinating,' the Techmarine confessed.

'The more we know, the easier it will be for us to destroy them,' Scipio conceded. 'Every weakness is crucial to us, and this,' he jabbed his finger through the still-open hatch at the marching necrons, 'is definitely a weakness, one we must exploit.'

'I have a theory,' offered Vantor. All eyes were suddenly on the Techmarine. 'Based on what I've observed, I believe the necrons are an evolved cybernetic race, but not all of them have evolved to the same degree.'

Scipio found himself in agreement. The one proclaiming itself the 'Voidbringer' had spoken to them during the assault in the Thanatos Hills, displaying an awareness and intelligence beyond that of the more ubiquitous necron constructs. And they had all heard the propaganda message of the so-called 'Herald of Dismay'.

'There is a hierarchy, a command structure,' said Scipio.

'I think it's more than that, Sergeant Vorolanus. I believe it to be dynastic, and the older or the more aware the necron, the greater its influence upon the horde. A nodal structure, if you will. Remove that influence and the mass will revert to whatever basic protocols their lesser functioning brains possess.'

'These things have no brains, Vantor,' snapped Brakkius. 'They're machine, and neither flesh nor blood.'

'A figure of speech, brother,' Vantor replied, mildly

placating. 'As to them being flesh and blood, I think perhaps they were, once. No machine, however advanced, acts as the necrons do. That behaviour cannot be programmed, it can only be learned or known.'

'If what you're saying is true, Vantor, then the creature Agrippen vanquished at the gates must have been a general of some kind,' said Scipio.

'Not a general, brother-sergeant. A king.'

'So we're dealing with a kingdom of these things,' muttered Brakkius, his displeasure increasing by the second.

Vantor met his disgruntled gaze. 'That is a distinct possibility.'

'So, where is this "kingdom" then?' asked Scipio.

The Techmarine laughed, but without humour.

'An excellent question to which I have no answer. If I were to posit a theory I would say it is below us.'

Scipio's eyes narrowed. 'Beneath the ice crust?'

'I think it's deeper than that,' said Vantor. 'It has to be, or the miners would have discovered something before now.'

The crackle of static presaging the activation of the hold's vox forestalled further discussion.

'Communication from Kellenport, brother-sergeant,' came the voice of Kastus.

Scipio looked at the others, then replied, 'Put it through, pilot.'

There was a short wait and a slight vox-modulation as an external channel was fed into the hold.

'This is Commander Antaro Chronus. Respond.'

Scipio knew the veteran tank commander by reputation only. He had heard there was significant armour being deployed from the *Valin's Revenge* but had seen none during muster or transit. Chronus and his vehicle squadrons had been lodged on a different assembly deck. Until Scipio's commandos, assisted in no small part by Librarian Tigurius, had neutralised the necron ordnance on the Thanatos Hills, Chronus and his tanks had been trapped in low orbit.

'Sergeant Scipio Vorolanus, aboard the gunship *Gladius*.'

'*Good to hear your voice, Scipio.*' The signal quality was relatively poor, but the tank commander had a dauntless quality to his voice and demeanour that came across in spite of the weak vox-return. '*I have over twenty pieces of tracked armour on the ice plains. We're looking for a fight, but in need of some direction.*'

Scipio smiled and felt the faintest stirrings of hope kindle.

'We have eyes on the enemy, commander, and can guide you in along with the *Thunderstorm*.'

The others shared his sudden optimism, the fire that had been waning inside them now stoked with fresh enthusiasm at Chronus's words. Only Vantor remained pensive.

'*Glorious, brother,*' Chronus replied. '*Our coordinates are being transmitted to your augurs as we speak.*'

'Augurs are down at present, commander. Please relay hard coordinates over vox instead.'

Chronus laughed. It sounded deep and hearty, but briefly overloaded the vox-link. He came back a moment later. '*Such antiquated methodology. It gives me heart, Scipio.*'

'Commander?'

'*We of Guilliman's blood, we always find a way. Do we not, brother-sergeant?*'

Scipio nodded, and felt his smile broaden.

'Indeed, commander.'

Chronus gave Scipio everything he needed to find the armoured column. The tank company was just outside Arcona City, which they had flown over on their way north.

It was an empty shell now, devoid and abandoned of all life. Even the necrons had moved on, surrendering it to ruin and entropy.

The entire war so far on Damnos had felt attritional. Piece by piece, Scipio had seen the Second being chipped away like the ice encrusting their boots. No Ultramarine ever wanted to admit defeat. They were pre-eminent warriors and tacticians, even amongst their fellow Adeptus Astartes, but the necrons had driven them close. Perhaps closer than anyone dared to admit out loud. In his heart, Scipio had felt a deep weariness, one that afflicted the soul as well as the body. Endless winter had gripped Damnos, and there were monsters within the ice, ones that came back from the dead and were capable of killing Space Marines.

Now you know who you are, brother.

Tigurius had uttered those words to him. He had spoken of courage and self-sacrifice. Since the war had begun, there had been plenty of both. Standing in the wind-blown hold and surrounded by his brothers, Scipio had a feeling there would be more... much more, before this was done.

'He sounds like he wants to win this war,' said Garrik once the vox-link was severed.

'Perhaps he thinks he can,' said Largo, and Scipio could hear the desire to get back into the fight in his voice.

The Ultramarines had been battered in the opening salvos of the campaign. Now, they wanted to hit back. They *needed* to hit back.

'We are badly in need of reinforcement, that I do know,' said Scipio, sliding the hatch shut and returning the hold to some semblance of stillness again. 'With an armoured company as our spearhead and the necrons seemingly debilitated, perhaps there is a slim hope.'

'Hope of victory, brother-sergeant?' asked Auris.

Scipio met the gaze of the warrior through his retinal lenses. 'At the very least, revenge.'

Now you know who you are, brother.

The words of Tigurius echoed in Scipio's mind. He only prayed he would not know himself a fool for trusting to hope.

CHAPTER FOUR
WATCHERS ON THE WALL

FALKA STOOD ALONE on the wall, and tugged the collar of his storm jacket up around his neck to ward off the cold.

A bleak wind was rolling in from the north, one of the fiercest and most bitter he had ever known on Damnos. Kellenport was besieged by it, trading the necrons for the elements as its next oppressor. In the last half-hour the storm had intensified. Life had never been easy on this world. Throne knew, he had seen many men killed in the mines and known those lost to the drifts or dead of sickness. Damnos was a harsh world, but in hiding the necrons beneath its icy surface it had betrayed them more than the harsh weather ever could.

Thick drifts shawled the walls in snow but failed to hide the city's ruination. Ice clung to its stunted bulwarks and beheaded towers. Frost lay heavy over stone and metal, grey-white like a funerary shroud. It was a fitting metaphor. The city was dead, inhabited by ghosts. Falka watched them as they went about their existence. When the necrons had retreated, disappearing in a flash of actinic, lurid green, it should have been met with jubilation. Instead, a mood of sullen acceptance had descended like a pall over Kellenport. It was pregnant with mordant anticipation of an end merely delayed and not averted at all. Falka saw it in every face, every deed. Their saviours had been humbled, their greatest hero fallen, some even said killed. How could they, the simple citizens of the Imperium, trust to hope when even their champions had succumbed to doubt? Yet still the Damnosians went on, because it was all they knew how to do. It was all they *could* do.

Labour teams toiled in silence to repair the city's outer walls, shoring them up with fallen slabs of masonry or reinforcing unstable structures with metal struts salvaged from buildings inside the gates. Triage stations and makeshift infirmaries had been set up. Few actual medics had survived the initial assault, so unskilled but enthusiastic hands were put to use as orderlies in the improvised medicae teams that had evolved in the aftermath of the first siege. Soldiers not on watch huddled together around fires, muttering quietly, their faces as dark and bleak as the sky.

Falka saw Ultramarines striding through the groups of Damnosian workers and the disenfranchised Ark Guard but even sight of these cobalt Angels could not seem to stir the people's spirits. The career soldiers looked worst of all, bereft of purpose and low-spirited. At least the workers could build and repair, losing themselves in the menial routine.

Falka scowled at a sudden thought that sent a deeper chill through his marrow.

We have become no different to the necrons. We are

automatons now too, but ones of flesh and blood. Quick to die and easier killed.

What he would not give to see a gilded sunrise over the wastes and the light striking the high peaks of the mountains, casting all the way to Halaheim... But Damnos was slate-grey, the grey of tombs and unforgiving metal. Falka did not think he would see it different again during his lifetime. The old ex-miner was a hard bastard, hard as ice, but he wiped a gloved hand across his eye at that maudlin thought. In the time it took to reach his face, his solitary tear had already frozen to his cheek and broke apart as he touched it.

'Throne, Jynn...' he murmured, as more ice froze on his face. 'I pray you are at peace now, girl.'

He shook, once, with an involuntary sob and then it was over. It was difficult to grieve when your life was being measured in minutes and seconds. It seemed a waste, somehow.

Falka was a soldier now, part of the ill-fated, if brave, 'One Hundred'. It was an inaccurate name for the militia that had arisen to defend Kellenport in its darkest moments. There had never been one hundred of them... There were fewer than that now.

Despite his fear, he had caught a few hours of sleep since the siege had ended and exhaustion finally claimed him. But it had been a fitful, restive slumber in which Falka had dreamed of a cold, grey world and the metal-clad revenants who had once claimed it as their own. The passage of ages and the death of its nearest sun had veneered the world in ice while its old masters slept in their cages, dreaming of a better age when their kingdoms still thrived and they treated with the very gods themselves. Bitterness was all

NICK KYME

that was left to them now, and a remorseless desire to take back what was theirs.

They would kill everything on this world, everything on Damnos.

Feverish sweat had lathered Falka's body as he had come to in the half-ruined barrack house, some of his comrades suffering the same nightmare.

He had recently surfaced from the dream to take his appointed watch upon the wall. Even a good twenty minutes later, memories of it still lingered and made his hands shake as he tried to light up the stick of tabac pressed to his frost-touched lips.

'Here,' said a man next to him, Ark Guard judging by his ragged uniform and the shoulder patch on his coat. So deep in thought was he, Falka had not noticed him approach. The newcomer took Falka's small silver igniter and held it steady so he could light his tabac.

Falka drew deep with a shuddering, nerve-settling inhalation before expelling a plume of smoke.

'I needed that,' he said, his words ghosting in the air.

'Tanner Greishof,' said the man. 'Ark Guard, corporal rank.'

'Falka Kolpeck,' replied Falka. 'Old man freezing his arse off on this damn wall.'

He did not shake Greishof's hand, it was far too cold for that. Both kept their arms as close as they could to their bodies, hugging their chests and rubbing their arms.

Falka offered the tabac stick, but Tanner refused.

'It's all yours.'

Falka nodded. 'Your loss. But thanks, anyway.'

'You fought at the gate?' asked Greishof.

Falka grinned ruefully and his head drooped a little. *I*

should have known he was a talker. 'I was with the One Hundred.'

Falka expected surprise, perhaps even respect, but all he got was indifference. Greishof nodded, as if this was not really news.

'We fought at the gate,' he said, 'my men and I. They died, every one of them. Mechanoids got 'em. Took the flesh right off the bone, then turned what was left to ash. Didn't even have anything to bury.' Greishof started to whistle, the tune light and carefree. Fearless. What he said next made Falka realise why. 'No one's getting out of this. We're all dying here, Kolpeck. Every one of us. Dead men's boots and ghosts walkin' in 'em.' Greishof looked over. 'Another smoke?' he asked, gesturing to the tabac stick that had almost burned to the nub in Falka's hand.

'No, thank you.'

Falka left him and went to another part of the wall. Greishof did not follow, he did not move at all. He just stared into the ice, whistling. He would be dead in the morning, either having jumped or slashed his wrists. Most preferred to jump, they did not have to take off their gloves for that.

Falka wondered how long it would be until his mind gave in, until he looked down over that wall and saw something appealing at its broken footings on the other side.

A runner caught his attention. Little more than a boy, he was wearing a medicae smock under cold-weather gear.

'Kolpeck?' the boy asked, breathless. He had obviously run up the steps to the wall and kept on going until he had found the man he had been charged to seek out.

'Take a breath, lad,' said Falka. 'I'm Kolpeck, yes. What is it?'

'Infirmary Seven,' the boy said, pointing vaguely in the

direction of a unit of warehouses beyond the courtyard. Denuded of all their machinery and raw materials to make barricades and plug gaps in the wall, the warehouses had been co-opted to act as medical stations for the many hundreds of injured.

'What of it, lad? Tell me.' Falka gripped the boy's shoulders, firmly but not hard, in his frustration to hear whatever message he had come to impart.

'A woman… injured. She's asking for you.'

A thick lump swelled in Falka's throat and he almost could not speak.

'What's her name, lad?'

The boy checked on a scrap of parchment that had been thrust into his hands. Falka saw there were several names on it and guessed the runner was making the identity of survivors known to their relatives and loved ones.

'Evvers, sir. Captain Jynn Evvers.'

'Let me see that.' Falka snatched the parchment. Hurriedly reading down the list, heart beating hard in his chest, he saw the name the boy had given him. He almost did not dare believe.

'She's alive?' he whispered, tears filling his eyes and freezing on his cheek. 'Throne above…'

But he could not leave the wall, he could not leave his duty. Yet this might be the last chance, their last chance… Falka looked to Greishof, but discounted him immediately. The man was clearly imbalanced.

'I cannot leave my station, lad,' he said, 'but get a message to her for me, would you?'

The boy nodded, but was only half listening. Now he had delivered the news, he had the rest of the names on that list to work through. Falka suddenly doubted his message would reach Jynn before… He shut his eyes, desperately wishing he could leave.

And then, as by some divine hand, his prayer was answered by an Angel.

'I have your watch, Brother Kolpeck,' said a deep, gruff voice.

Both Falka and the boy looked over to where an armoured giant clad in cobalt blue was striding up to the battlements.

He looked more grizzled than when Falka had last set eyes on him, if that were even possible, the stubble on his chin like asphalt and his face set like a granite cliff. His leg greave was battered and recently repaired, but he carried the wound he had received at the gate well. If only they all had the constitution of Space Marines, perhaps then they would not all be staring down the prospect of an unpleasant death at the hands of the necrons. Despite his outwardly harsh appearance though, Brother-Sergeant Iulus Fennion was not unfeeling as stone. He had more heart than any of the Ultramarines Falka had met on Damnos.

When Iulus reached the top of the stairs, he towered over both of them and was twice as broad as Falka, who was built like a tundra-ox.

Trying not to weep in sheer awe and terror, the boy was about to take a knee when Iulus's booming voice held him fast.

'Don't bow to me, boy. Never do that. Bow when you're dead and your sword slips from your hand, but not until then, not to me. Are you dead yet, boy?'

'N-n-no, sir,' he stammered, standing again.

'Then let's try to keep it that way. Go to your duty. I'll relieve Sergeant Kolpeck on this part of the wall.'

More than a little relieved, the boy nodded and quickly scurried off.

'You're not wearing your battle-helm, Sergeant Kolpeck,' said Iulus, glaring.

'I was always just a rig-hand, Brother-Angel,' Falka answered with good nature, 'and besides, a padded hood is much warmer.'

Iulus smiled, unable to keep the pretence going any longer. 'Justly spoken.' He nodded, something like pride in his shadowy eyes. 'I am glad to see you still live.'

'And I you, Brother-Angel.'

A brief silence descended, wherein the giant Ultramarine said nothing but merely stared.

'Begone then,' he said thunderously at last, and stood aside for Falka to pass. 'You have relinquished your guard post to me, Sergeant Kolpeck.'

Falka nodded, before hurrying in the direction of Infirmary Seven.

IULUS WATCHED HIM go, and thought how desperately the humans clung to what remained of their lives here. He did not know how much longer there would be threads strong enough for them to grasp.

A dull thud that came from the opposite side of the wall made him turn. Looking across, the battlements were empty, where before there had been a solitary Ark Guard trooper standing watch. An urgent shout from one of the upper towers told Iulus another one had gone to his death. He paid it little heed, taking up his post.

'How long, indeed?' he muttered to himself.

Beyond Kellenport, the ice was still and dead. Ever-thickening snow drifts had obliterated much from view past a few hundred metres. If the necrons were out there, regrouping, readying for another assault, the watch would not see them coming until they were almost on top of them.

That was assuming they travelled over the ice at all. For the longest time since the siege, Iulus had been aware of something below the surface. It was hard to describe, more of a feeling than an explicable perception. He dearly wished to tell Scipio of it, but the brother-sergeant was abroad in the *Gladius* keeping a watchful eye on the suspiciously dormant necrons that had rematerialised in the far north.

Agrippen had yet to sanction a full-scale attack on them. With their gunships and armour planetside, it was now possible, but a lightning strike would be foolhardy against an enemy whose strength the Ultramarines could not yet gauge. And there was talk of evacuation, also.

There was much unknown, and they would not underestimate the necrons again.

If Damnos could be won, they would win it. If not, they would get every living soul off this dead world and scour it from orbit.

Unable to guess the future himself, Iulus did the only thing he could and settled in for a long watch.

CHAPTER FIVE
WE ARE LEGION

THE UNDER-CAVERNS BELOW the surface of Damnos were a lie. Unbeknownst to the parasites currently embedded on this world, they were but a shell, an outer crust formed over its true core.

Ankh knew the truth. He was the Architect, the cryptek who had borne witness to the death of the first sun and the birth of the creeping ice that came in its wake. Cold did not affect the necrontyr, not any more. Since the long sleep, such things as warmth and comfort had become but the petty concerns of lesser beings.

They no longer felt as they once had, though some still dreamed and confused that dream with waking. A great many had been damaged during their slumber, like Sahtah the Enfleshed and the Undying. The risk in reviving them, the potential damage to their memory engrams… So many curses, the Sautekh Dynasty had indeed been brought low by them.

Ankh still held to hope. Tahek, Sahtah, even the Undying – they had been but lordlings compared to the true dynasts of Sautekh. The Architect was cunning. He had no desire to make the same mistake he had with the others, lost to grief, envy and madness. A chronomancer, he knew well the importance of time. In revivifying the Undying's paltry war host, he had garnered enough of it to set the great mechanism in motion and bring about the return of the Sautekh's pre-eminent overlord.

When *he* arose, the ice would cloak their world no longer and the wretched epithet of *Damnos* would be a footnote in the empire-history of the necrontyr. As a vaunted servant and trusted vizier, Ankh would bask in the reflected glory, his status assured.

As he walked slowly through the under-caverns, every slow and measured step carrying the cryptek deeper into the subterranean realm, legions of arachnid constructs were hard at work reactivating the tomb-pyramids and revivifying the necron hosts within.

Ankh could feel their life-signatures, perceive the growing web of necron awareness as it latticed over his subconscious.

Staff in hand, he paused by the slab-sided flank of a tomb. It was partially buried in a crust of hoarfrost. Just the summit was clad in ice – the bulk of the structure went deep into the actual tomb-world's catacombs and was still locked in ageless slumber. Ankh resolved to alter that.

His skeletal fingers traced ancient sigil-runes over the surface of the tomb, manipulating an activation panel only perceivable to another cryptek. The sequence was complex and delicate. An error now could result in the dramatic and fatal deterioration of every memory engram contained within the tomb-pyramid.

Within seconds, Ankh activated it without mishap and felt the anima of hundreds start to waken.

'*Doom,*' he muttered to himself, his rictus jaw unmoving as the words emitted from vocalisers in his polished, metal skull. '*Annihilation… Let slip these chariots of retribution.*'

Through the metres-thick metal, his mind perceived the deadly war machines and their enslaved crew slowly being restored. Ankh saw their eyes alight with verdant balefire, felt the thrum of engines and power coils coming online.

In ancient days the necrontyr had waged war on the back of resplendent arks and barges. So they would again.

But more was needed, much more.

Having begun the process, Ankh could leave the scarabs and spyders to finish revivifying the war machines. At a command gesture, two canoptek wraiths, his watchdogs and guardians, materialised into being before him. Tall and serpentine, their bladed limbs clacked together in anticipation of their master's command.

'*Show me the rest,*' Ankh ordered in a sibilant voice.

His mind connected with those of the wraiths and he perceived rank upon rank of tombs, stretching ever deeper into his world's forgotten core. Some were damaged, and would have to be destroyed. This was an eventuality for which Ankh had already prepared. But the majority harboured legions. He saw foot soldiers, the gilded retainers of kings, walker constructs and the venerable overlords themselves. And at the last, something else, a malign intelligence that when unleashed would scour all life from this world and restore it to the necrontyr.

'*Good,*' hissed Ankh, myriad plans already forming as he

focused on the image of a many-limbed walker. *'We shall begin with the Triarch.'*

A BARREN ICE plain stretched before Chronus through his magnoculars. Riding in the cupola of the *Rage of Antonius*, hatch thrown back, he barely felt the bite of the ice and the scything hail hammering against the Predator's armour.

Somewhere in the storm, his enemy was lurking. From all the intelligence he had gathered, the necron force was still numerous and growing. But it also consisted solely of infantry, and slow-moving, tactically inert infantry at that. Chronus did not consider himself an arrogant man. He was logical and tried to base his assumptions only on fact, but a laborious host of foot soldiers would not last long against an Ultramarines tank company. They would be easily defeated, and he suspected there were more forces held in reserve somewhere, sterner opponents.

But he had to engage the remnants first, and goad whatever else was waiting for them out of the ice. He had seen the reports of the phasic generators, large-scale teleportation devices that had moved entire phalanxes from the battle zone to an unknown regrouping point in the northern polar wastes. If engaging the necrons was the primary mission, then finding and destroying the generator was next.

Of course, that was assuming he could even find the necron remnants left after the Kellenport siege.

Setting the scopes down on the hull, he took the auspex from his belt. The backlit screen still returned an empty scanner pulse. Since leaving Kellenport they had continued north, following the map coordinates he had given the sergeant who had contacted them earlier. Chronus led the line, a column of twenty-four battle tanks with fourteen other armoured carriers advancing along either flank. He kept them in file until engagement was imminent; it was easier to conceal their martial strength that way.

Taking up the scopes again, he first ranged left and then right, checking on formation dispersal. It was wide, just as instructed, and the column was also spread. If he was riding into a trap, if the necron reinforcements were closer at hand than gathered intelligence suggested, then the wide spread across the length and width of the formation would give those not caught directly in the ambush a chance to counter, or regroup.

He was just about to despair of ever making contact with the enemy to run such a risk when a blip came through on the auspex. A pair of markers, they flashed red against the screen and then returned a second later.

He recognised the origin of the markers. They were Ultramarines.

Chronus called down into the hold.

'Novus, I have the *Gladius* and the *Thunderstorm*.' He sent the markers to the driver's retinal display.

'*Affirmative, commander.*'

Chronus switched channels through his comm-feed to his sergeants leading the other two squadrons.

'Be advised our guides are inbound.'

'*I have them on auspex, Commander Chronus,*' replied Gnaeus.

Egnatius's comm-channel remained silent.

Chronus tried the link again. 'Sergeant Egnatius, respond.'

Still no answer. He went back to the other sergeant.

'Gnaeus, are you experiencing any comms interference?'

'*Nothing unusual, commander.*'

'What about between vehicles in Sergeant Egnatius's squadrons?'

'I've not had vox contact with Sergeant Egnatius since we left Kellenport.'

Egnatius's formation was second in column. Chronus cut the link to Gnaeus and opened up a channel to the next battle tank in the line, *The Vengeful*.

Fabricus answered his hail.

'Brother Fabricus, take front of column.'

'Commander?' asked Fabricus, nonplussed.

'That's a direct order, driver.'

Chronus shouted down for Novus to peel off the column and double back along the flanks, then voxed the nearest Razorback and Rhino outriders with the brief change in the order of march.

'Novus,' Chronus shouted down into the hold. 'I want you to bring us right alongside the *Stormwarden*,' he said, referring to Egnatius's Predator Destructor.

The *Rage of Antonius* rode down the line, running against the churning tide. Ice cracked and snow was ground to slush before the ruthless advance of the armoured column. Exhaust ports plumed grey smoke that was quickly caught on the wind and dispersed. Frost hugged the flanks of every vehicle and ice rimed their turrets where thick snow squalls had built up and then solidified.

Rolling close to combat speed, engines spitting out a throaty rumble as if grateful for the sudden run-out, the *Rage of Antonius* came up alongside the *Stormwarden* in a few minutes.

Hail and ice were slamming down hard now, chipping paintwork, and Chronus donned his helmet before the storm got bad enough to cut flesh or take an eye.

'Vutrius,' he called down to his own gunner. 'Put the searchlight onto the *Stormwarden*.'

Novus had expertly brought them around and along-side the Predator Destructor so they were rolling with the column again, directly adjacent to the *Stormwarden*. The automated lamp attached to the *Rage of Antonius*'s turret swung around and, with a heavy *chank* of activation, blazed into life. Magnesium-bright, it lit up the side of the *Stormwarden* and flooded its vision slits.

When Egnatius did not respond, Chronus unholstered his sidearm and fired off a single shot at the Destructor's front arc, leaving a dent but no permanent damage. It barely registered outside in the storm, but he knew that inside it would resonate.

A few seconds later, the turret hatch disengaged and Egnatius emerged from the cupola. Though it was difficult to tell with him wearing his helmet, Chronus could tell his sergeant was angry. When Egnatius looked over and saw the commander his ire cooled almost immediately.

Chronus tapped the side of his helmet.

Egnatius's channel came online, indicated by a single glowing Ultima rune on Chronus's retinal display.

'Why did you not respond to my hails, brother-sergeant?'

Egnatius's reply was chopped with static and bad signal return.

'Apologies, commander. We are… periencing… issue… ith… comms.'

'Find a solution. Our Thunderhawks have just made contact and will be guiding us in. We are about to rendezvous. I want you and your squadron back in vox contact before that happens.'

'Yes, comm… der. It… ill… be done.'

'See it is, Egnatius.'

Chronus went down below, sealing the hatch behind him. Disengaging the holding clamps, he removed his helmet to drink in the atmosphere. It was louder inside the Predator's hold, the engine noise exacerbated by the close confines, and every contour of the rough terrain could be felt through the shuddering hull. Though during combat there was no better place to be than riding in the cupola and seeing the destruction wrought by his war machine first-hand, Chronus had always found the interior of the battle tank calming.

It was dingy and cramped inside, the majority of the hold taken up with machinery and munitions. Novus sat up front, surrounded by instrumentation. A control panel was lit up dully next to him, providing a slew of information including fuel, speed and acceleration. The forward vision slit was open. Hands on the steering column, Novus peered intently through the gap. Internal auspex and sensorium were proving patchy on account of the adverse weather, so Novus preferred the evidence of his own eyes as opposed to the Predator's on-board systems.

The only other crewman of the *Antonius*, Vutrius, sat at the back of the hold and nodded to the commander as he descended and joined them both in the shadows.

'Are we battle-hungry yet, gunner?' Chronus asked as he took up position midway down the cramped crew compartment.

'Running final readiness procedures now, commander,' replied Vutrius without much of the hunger his commander had asked for. Chronus was unconcerned. His gunner might be cold but his aim was deadly and unforgiving.

Arrayed around Vutrius's gunnery seat were three

monitors, one for each of the Annihilator's main weapons. Ammunition counts were at maximum, though they also carried two additional drum mags for the heavy bolters and a spare power generator for the twin-linked lascannon. According to his readouts, all weapons were at acceptable temperature levels and currently running at full efficacy.

'Could it have been environmental interference?' suggested Vutrius.

'Could be.' Chronus did not sound convinced. 'I want you to send them a hail every three minutes until they're back on comms.'

Vutrius nodded, his attention still on the Predator's arsenal. He was not wearing his battle-helm, none of them did once inside the tank, and Chronus could see his gunner's lips moving in silent litanies of accuracy and function.

Satisfied, he called up to Novus.

'Get us back to the front of column. I want to meet our aerial support at the tip of the spear.'

Novus increased speed and the drone within the hold grew to a roar.

Chronus recalled his earlier words to Agrippen and the others.

'*It's the reason we were forged.*'

He smiled, knowing he was not just referring to the tanks.

CHAPTER SIX
ARMOURED FURY

THE TANK COLUMN slowed to within approximately three kilometres of the enemy and began to fan out. Its concomitant elements, formerly alloyed together in a long line of tracked steel, dispersed into their smaller squadrons.

Twenty-four battle tanks with additional armoured support faced off against six infantry cohorts. From the air, Scipio gauged each necron formation was roughly fifty warriors strong. None of them were the more advanced constructs he and his brothers had fought during the siege and the assault on the Thanatos Hills. Despite the obvious enemy threat, the necrons still appeared sluggish, but had begun to adopt some approximation of a firing line as they advanced into the teeth of Chronus's armour.

The tank commander rejoined his sergeants, forming a twelve-engine-strong phalanx of Predators. Judging from the formation Scipio could see emerging from his vantage point in the *Gladius*, he assumed Chronus would attack in two waves.

On a shallow ridge that overlooked the vast ice plain where the necrons were marching, Chronus had positioned his preliminary bombardiers. At the rear, a trio of Whirlwinds cycled their launchers and adjusted for precise trajectory. To the front of them and a little further down the ridge were the formidable Vindicators, their massive Demolisher cannons angled to maximum elevation. It was clear to Scipio that Chronus meant to soften the necrons up before he committed to closer engagement.

Six hulking Land Raiders were ranged on the opposite flank to the Predators. Pre-eminent troop transports, the tank commander had deployed them as mobile weapon platforms, a trio each of the standard and Crusader-pattern variants.

Last were the armoured outriders, the Razorbacks and Rhinos that would run interference for the larger, more destructive battle tanks.

'He's creating a killbox,' said Brakkius unnecessarily, competing with the howling gale ripping through the gunship's open side-hatch. 'The necrons will engage the obvious threat, the tanks on the ridge, and they'll be outflanked by the farther ranging engines to their right and left.'

From the air, Chronus's stratagem was obvious but, against a slow-moving infantry force, also deadly. The necrons would be destroyed, but Scipio still frowned.

'This cannot be all that is left of them,' he said, 'these rudimentary, half-functioning constructs.'

'We can only fight what's in front of us, brother-sergeant,' replied Largo, ever the philosopher.

'And that is precisely what concerns me. That this is all

there is in front of us. We fought an enemy ten times more potent than this. Not all of those necrons were destroyed in the rout at the gates. Some endured, they must have.'

Garrik pointed down to the kilometre-spanning battlefield unfolding below, his missile launcher shouldered and ready.

'Whatever their mettle, Sergeant Vorolanus, we are about to see it tested.'

The last of the battle tanks and their attendant outriders were moving into position. The order to commence bombardment was about to be given.

The *Gladius* and the *Thunderstorm* remained at the edge of the battle zone for now. Both gunships were tooled for war with dorsal-mounted battle cannons, a payload of heavy ordnance and several reserve weapons that would still be ruthlessly effective against the necrons.

Scipio was about to raise Sergeant Vandar on the vox to discuss potential attack-run vectors when something fast bolted across the skyline and shot between them. A thunderous boom shook the air and the hold, resonating down the *Gladius*'s hull.

A pair of vessels cruising at supersonic speed had just arrowed between them, making the gunships look slow and cumbersome by comparison.

'Guilliman's sacred blood!'

Brakkius tried to follow their flight path through the open side-hatch, but it was impossible.

Vandar's voice crackled over the vox.

'Did you see that, Vorolanus?'

'A pair of flyers. Sickle-shaped, I think,' said Scipio, tracking a rapidly disappearing smudge through his magnoculars. 'Extremely fast.'

'*They're headed for Kellenport. I'm going to pursue in the* Thunderstorm. *We might not catch them but we'll sure as Hera take them apart if they are bound for the city.*'

'Two birds against one, Vandar. We can guard your wing for you.'

'*Appreciated, but we'll have plenty of support when we arrive. Stay with Chronus. I don't believe this is all there is of our enemies.*'

Vandar cut the link. A few seconds later, the *Thunderstorm* streaked past on full engine burn.

There was little time for the warriors aboard the *Gladius* to watch their fellow gunship depart because, below them, a storm was about to break.

CHRONUS WATCHED THE bombardment commence from the *Rage of Antonius*'s cupola. The Whirlwinds fired in strict and regimented succession, one missile per salvo. Their rocket-fuelled payloads streaked into the air on thick contrails of white smoke, their perfect telemetry bringing the combined barrage down amidst the necrons with destructive results.

Vengeance-class missiles were solid-fuel, fragmentation ordnance. Not tank-busters by any gauge, but against densely packed infantry they were devastating. Necron bodies were blasted apart under this aggressive and sustained barrage. Three salvos went out, nine missiles in total, shattering one region of the ice plain into craters and gouging a cleft in the enemy ranks.

Through his raised scopes, Chronus saw the telltale flashes of multiple phase-outs. On a tactical screen slaved to one lens of his retinal display, the entire tank formation was arrayed and lit.

'Cease barrage,' he uttered into the vox, speaking directly to the gunnery crews of *Fury Unbound*, *Ceaseless Endeavour* and *Scion of Talassar*. 'Resupply, Castellan load-out.'

He smiled grimly, all his good humour faded as the aspect of war came upon him. 'You think that hurt,' he muttered, watching the dogged necron advance. '*That* didn't hurt.'

Returning to the vox, the icons of *Glory of Calth*, *The Ram* and *Wrath of Invictus* glowed brightest on the right lens retinal display as Chronus opened his command channel to their crews.

'Vindicators advance fifty metres and engage.'

A string of affirmation runes flashed across Chronus's display as the three battle tanks ground forwards in unison. At the fifty-metre mark, the hull-mounted Demolishers jutting belligerently through each Vindicator's siege shield spoke.

Their combined voice was terrifically loud and roared with captured thunder that shook the earth as far as the *Rage of Antonius*. Chronus laughed loud and wrathfully as his Predator shuddered with the awesome resonance of the siege tanks. Three wide and impossibly powerful explosions erupted to the front of the necron ranks. Amidst the flying limbs and other body parts, Chronus witnessed over a score of phase-outs. After the smoke cleared and the few surviving necrons had managed to crawl from the trench dug by the Vindicators' ordnance, there was almost nothing left of the first phalanx. He had done it to prove a point, to show the mechanoids that the Ultramarines yet had weapons in their arsenal that could dismantle them, just as Chronus had vowed to his comrades.

Five more fully intact phalanxes advanced after the necron vanguard, the broken remnants slowly to be absorbed into the larger formations. Their weapons were fixed forwards, intent on the artillery squadrons occupying the ridge.

Chronus watched the necrons enter the killbox and gave the order for the flanking forces to circle around and entrap them.

'All gunners on the ridge,' he voxed, as Novus got the *Rage of Antonius* moving steadily in concert with the other Predators. 'Sustained barrage until flanks reach within two hundred metres. Commence with extreme prejudice.' He leaned into the hatch to speak directly to his driver. 'Bring us in, Novus. I want to vent the guns. Vutrius?'

'We are weapons-ready, commander.'

'Good. The turret is mine, brother.'

Vutrius responded with a clipped affirmative, switching control to Chronus.

Heavy thunder was rolling down off the ridge, turning the ice plain into a wrecker's yard and the necrons into a distant memory. If he had not wanted to taste some of that righteous fury himself, Chronus would have gladly watched the faultless display of his battle tanks and revelled in its perfect destruction.

OVERHEAD IN THE *Gladius*, Scipio marvelled at the superlative tactical display being orchestrated by Chronus. A sizeable contingent of almost three hundred necrons had already been reduced to two-thirds that number, and they were but casualties of the bombardment. Chronus had yet to even engage with his flanking forces.

A stilted layer of return fire was coming from the necrons now that they had advanced far enough across the ice plain, but it was sporadic and at extreme range. Certainly, nothing to trouble the Ultramarines armour on the ridge.

Even still, the sergeant could not put his mind at ease.

'Bring us in closer, but circle the flanks,' he voxed up to their pilot, prompting an immediate shift in velocity and altitude from the Thunderhawk.

'Do you see it too, brother-sergeant?'

Scipio turned sharply at the resonant, machine-like voice. Something in his subconscious almost made him draw his pistol, but it was no necron that addressed him. It was Vantor, skulking in the shadows behind them.

'See what?' asked Scipio, though he thought he knew the Techmarine's meaning.

'A trap…'

'We all see it, Techmarine, it is Chronus's–' Brakkius began.

'Around *our* armour, brother,' Vantor corrected. 'This is but a feint.'

'How is that even possible?' snapped Brakkius. 'Look at them, they are all but defeated. There is no tactical acumen at work, just mechanised shells slaved to routine.'

'I agree,' said Vantor, 'but analyse that battlefield below us… What word comes to mind when you see the necrons?'

Brakkius snarled, still not comprehending. 'Scrap. Metal.'

'Bait,' said Scipio, believing the Techmarine but unsure what their next move should be. 'And how do you suggest I convey to the commander that he is being drawn into a trap?'

'What trap?' asked Brakkius, exasperated. He gestured to the decimated necrons. 'It's already over.'

Vantor ignored him, and looked impassive as he answered Scipio's question.

'How do you tell a hero of Ultramar his perfect strategy is part of an elaborate enemy ruse? I'm not sure you can, brother-sergeant.'

Scipio looked down onto the battlefield.

The Predators were engaging.

NOVUS PUSHED THE *Rage of Antonius* up to combat speed, leading the first squadron by the smallest of margins. Rather than envelop the necron infantry in a pincer-like movement that would amply suit a ground-based force, Chronus had the two lines attack in file obliquely so they overlapped and enfiladed the enemy prior to the point of intersection.

The *Rage of Antonius* was on its first pass, *The Vengeful* and *Hellhunter* on its tracked heels in close squadron formation, when the optimum range marker flashed on the tank commander's retinal display.

'Unleash guns!' Chronus roared, without ceremony. War sang in his heart, buoyed higher through the exhilaration of tank-mounted combat. Still rolling at combat speed, the Predator's turret swung around to forty-five degrees and released a searing lance of energy. The azure beam struck the edge of a necron formation and vaporised one of the automatons. It was followed fractionally later by a second beam. Paired phase-outs overlapped, creating a bright burst of viridian energy. Capacitors in the *Rage of Antonius* took a few seconds to build back up to power before a second volley was released.

Targets in his sights, Chronus poured on the punishment, shifting his aim and the turret as the battle tank moved. The side sponsons chattered below, spitting out shells that detonated upon impact and chewed holes in the packed necron ranks. The heavy bolters kept up a steady refrain, audible between the high-pitched whine of the pounding lascannon.

Twelve engines released their weapons on one flank, whilst on the opposite side the half-dozen Land Raiders lit up the dwindling snowstorm with ranks of explosive muzzle flare from assault cannons and hurricane bolters. Las-beams, distant on the opposite side of the battlefield but getting closer, stabbed from the shadows like spears of light and were joined by the barking report of heavy bolters. Necrons were cut apart. Those struck by the las-cannons were summarily destroyed in actinic flashes. The solid-shell weapons took a heavier toll at first, levelling a veritable deluge of fire, but several necrons were showing signs of self-repair and those felled in the earlier salvos were returning to their dauntless ranks.

Down the centre, the bombardment ceased as the other tanks came to within the two hundred metre no-fire zone. It mattered little – the necrons had been drawn into the trap and were being picked apart by Chronus's armoured squadrons.

'Dismantle you,' the tank commander said to himself, holding fire for a moment to appreciate the carnage his engines were causing, 'piece by piece.'

THROUGH THE OPEN hatch of the *Gladius*, the battlefield below looked strung out. From his vantage leaning out of the hold, Scipio saw vast gaps emerging in the necrons' previously closed ranks. Even the slow-moving automatons had reverted to defensive protocols now, recognising the danger posed by the artillery to their front and the more dynamic battle tanks to their flanks and rear.

Keeping up a steady stream of verdant gauss fire, the necrons towards the core of their now slowly collapsing formations remained still, whilst those further out and cut off began to retreat. Like the musket regiments of old Terra, they were forming square.

As part of Roboute Guilliman's teachings in the Codex Astartes, all Ultramarines were comprehensively versed in military tactics, both contemporary and archaic. Scipio recognised what the necrons were doing at once. They attempted to fight their enemy on all fronts and prevent them from breaking up their coherency. Only these were not mere cavalrymen armed with lance and flintlocks; the battle tanks of the Ultramarines Chapter assailed them. Their outmoded strategy was fated to fail. And yet, the idea persisted in the brother-sergeant that these mechanoids were just sacrificial, intended to draw Chronus and his battle tanks in.

Straying from the systematic destruction of the necrons, Scipio's gaze was drawn to the ice. The constant barrage, the heat of energy discharge from las-weapons and gauss flayers had damaged its integrity. He looked through the scopes, training them on a point just outside the shrinking square of necrons.

'Pilot, bring us in closer,' he voxed.

With the dull growl of engine deceleration, the *Gladius* descended.

'What is it? What do you see?' hissed Vantor before the others could speak.

'I'm not sure... Increasing magnification.'

The image through the scopes blurred then quickly refocused, a line of data scrolling down one side of the lens telling Scipio he was at maximum range. There were small fissures in the ice, nothing that would split it; the frozen plain was thick and densely packed. But it was not this that had caught the sergeant's attention.

'I see…' he began, 'a shadow.'

'Say that again,' said Brakkius, staring down at the point where his sergeant was looking, trying to see the same shadow but without success.

'Under the ice,' Scipio went on, his heart rate increasing with sudden, irrational urgency.

He looked up from the scopes as the shadow came so close and grew so large against the frosted lens of surface ice that even Brakkius and the others saw it.

'Fortress of Hera!' the second-in-command shouted.

Suddenly the gunship they were riding in felt perilously low.

'Kastus,' Scipio said quickly into the vox. 'Bring us up!'

The *Gladius* was rising just as a vast flash of light ignited to the west, within a half-kilometre of where Chronus had almost vanquished the necron infantry. It was massive, like a verdant sunrise only much faster and more violent. Scipio had seen its like before: it was a teleportation flare.

'Guilliman's blood…' breathed Brakkius.

The necrons had activated a phase generator and transported an entire phalanx into sudden and immediate battle.

Auris and Largo stared, disbelieving, and Garrik made the sign of the old Legion, a single clenched fist, against his breastplate.

'We've sprung the trap, brother-sergeant,' said Vantor.

Scipio snarled into the vox. 'Bring us up, damn it!'

Within the verdant light, which was slowly dying after the force of its dramatic arrival, a second necron horde had emerged.

'Not infantry,' said Garrik, sighting through his launcher's targeter.

'Something worse…' added Vantor.

The *Gladius* was rising, Kastus pushing the turbofans to achieve a faster escape velocity.

Facing down the rapidly deploying flanking force, Scipio already knew they would not be fast enough.

An entire fleet of large skimmer-tanks was surging across the ice plain, devouring the kilometres between them and the Ultramarines with alarming speed. Before Scipio could get a decent look at the force in the dying after-flare of their materialisation, a slew of crackling beams arced from several necron turrets. One struck the left wing of the *Gladius* as Kastus was attempting to turn, ripping up one of the turbofans.

Thrown back into the hold and slamming into Vantor and Brakkius, Scipio saw a spit of flame shoot up from the engine, smoke pluming a second later before being sucked up by the still-turning fan and coiling in over itself.

Alert sirens were wailing in the hold, the engine noise high-pitched, almost desperate. If the *Gladius* had a living, beating heart, some sense of anima, it had just been wounded and was crying out in pain.

'*Hold on!*' Kastus bellowed through the vox, the sound of emergency systems kicking in audible in the background as the pilot struggled to keep them airborne.

'What else does he expect us to do?' growled Brakkius, clinging to the overhead rail.

The Thunderhawk was spinning, the gaping hatch revealing ever-quickening flashes of the advancing necron host and then the harsh white of ice mountains. The former was shrinking as the latter grew inexorably closer.

Ditching fast, the *Gladius* would not clear the rugged terrain that was rapidly advancing upon them.

'Brace yourselves,' Scipio shouted above the shrieking

engine noise bleeding in from the outside. He managed to get on his battle-helm and bring up the ident-markers for his combat squad as well as one for Vantor.

The Techmarine was kneeling, his servo-arms extended and braced either side of the hold to keep him steady. Vantor had no helmet, so the Ultramarines aboard the stricken gunship could see him muttering litanies of function to soothe the *Gladius*'s injured machine-spirit.

'Maybe we should all start chanting,' sniped Brakkius.

Scipio shot him a stern look through his retinal lenses. 'Just hold on.'

With a spurt of throttle, the damaged turbofan cycled down to a full stop, leaving Kastus relying on the remaining engine to keep them up. Its protests were loud and discordant – it was not going to keep them aloft for long.

Scipio tried to catch a look out of the side hatch, but the terrain was whipping by too quickly for him to determine how far they had strayed from the battlefield. In its current predicament, directionality was not a facility the gunship had in abundance at that moment. It was taking all of Kastus's concentration and effort just to keep them going and find a safe place to land. Wherever that was, it would be far from the ice plain now.

Scipio felt a sudden shift in velocity, a brief interlude of anti-gravity followed by an acute sinking sensation, and assumed they had dipped. The *Gladius* was burning at full speed; peaks and crags jetted by in a frost-hazed blur.

Despite the disadvantage of having only one functioning turbofan, Kastus had guided them around the peaks and was racing through a narrow canyon.

The Ultramarines in the hold grimly seized the crash rails. There was no way they could reach their harnesses and strap in. The slightest upright movement could throw them out of the gaping hatch and into the white void streaking beyond it.

With the creak of sundering metal, the rail where Brakkius was clinging bent and came away from its fixings. He hung on for another second, roaring defiantly, before the railing snapped and was thrown loose.

Despite the risk to himself, Scipio reached out one-handed to grab the flailing Ultramarine. His gauntleted fingers snagged armour, then slipped as Brakkius was torn from his grasp.

'Brother!'

Horrified, Scipio thought he was about to watch his second-in-command be dragged to almost certain death when Vantor pinned him with one of his servo-arms. Brakkius cried out as his back and shoulder were pierced, but at least he was secured.

There was no time to feel relief. Kastus's voice crackled through the vox just as the engine noise rose sharply in pitch and the violent shuddering felt within the hold increased.

'We're going down,' he said. 'We're going–'

They struck earth. The engine noise ceased abruptly, overwhelmed by the sound of buckling, splitting armour. Scipio thought he saw a chunk of wing ripped off, spiralling away down their flank before the ice and rock piled through the open hatch, suffocating everyone inside the hold.

Light became dark, sound became silence. The shuddering, jolting gunship finally grew still. Scipio's head struck metal. The right side of his helm crumpled, crazing the retinal lens as he hit the interior wall or one of his brothers – he didn't know which – and felt something warm trickle down the side of his face inside his helmet before blacking out.

CHAPTER SEVEN
NOWHERE TO HIDE

FEATURELESS ICE SPED past below, so fast it blurred into a smear of seemingly endless white. Storm squalls broke against the edge of the flyer like waves striking the bow of a ship, but nothing slowed it. It was moving at hyper-velocity now, running at supersonic and cutting through the belligerent wind with sickle-edged ease.

Pilot did not notice. No chill touched his body, though he was cocooned in a cockpit open to the elements and wore no flight suit or visored helmet. He experienced no exertion of any kind, no sense of inertia as his craft knifed through the air at such a phenomenal speed. Hail whipped against the flyer's hull, against his exposed 'skin', but he paid it no heed. It was as inconsequential as the battle on the ice plain he had left behind several minutes ago. Emotion, even one as bright and blazing as hate, did not feature in his limited consciousness.

For Pilot, sentience was reduced to the data stream and what it told him.

Multitudinous stacks of operational protocols streamed across his vision, enhanced cogitation assessing each before accessing prefigured routines and responses. A shift in wind speed, a sudden airburst, and Pilot activated the secondary protocol that told him to dip his wing and change the flyer's angle of approach.

His twin craft, far too divorced from any bonds of brotherhood to be considered a wingman, performed a similar manoeuvre, reacting to the selfsame protocols. Both were acutely aware of each other's presence, but not in the conventional sense. Pilot visualised the second flyer as a line of data, only acknowledged through the inclusion of the additional protocols it afforded within his vast but prescribed decision matrix.

Proximity markers entering the data stream provided further options for Pilot to sift through. He increased speed, deaf to the atonal shriek emanating from the flyer's aggressive approach. A second concomitant data stream aligned onside the first, informing Pilot his twinned craft had mirrored the manoeuvre.

Up ahead, a large structure began to materialise through the ice fog. Pilot saw it in the data-feed first, a stream of code that unlocked a tertiary vault of responses. Then his cold machine eyes saw the city and he vectored towards the aspect which possessed the lowest threat ratio in order to increase the chances of mission success. This too was relayed and cogitated through the myriad datastacks.

Pilot felt no pity for the beings of flesh within the city's walls; only cold logic raged through his android brain. He processed, adapted and realigned with the addition of new data. He did not feel in any way. He had no desire for carnage, but that was what Pilot brought with him on scythed wings; carnage and death.

CONDITIONS IN INFIRMARY Seven were overcrowded and far from sanitary. Buckets brimming with reams of used bandages and gauze lay clustered together in the corners, waiting to be cleaned or burned. Blood slicked the floor in places, waiting to be sluiced away. The warehouse-turned-medicae centre was capacious but the injured numbered in the hundreds, just at this location alone. Herded here in their droves, the men and women inside were like cattle. Beds were stacked close together, some rigged up as bunks for the more stable or terminal patients that could not be moved. Intravenous lines were hooked up to the extant machinery too cumbersome to move out for the barricades, or looped around bed rails. Some were even held by diligent servitors slaved to that single task.

The moment he stepped past the guard detail outside and entered the makeshift infirmary, Falka had to cover his nose and mouth. The place reeked of blood and contagion, the air thick with it and ringing with the screams of those undergoing emergency surgeries. Misery touched everything, clinging like a second skin. It was a product of despair, one that had affected all of Damnos since the invasion and was slowly eroding what little resolve its people had left.

Through the dingy light of overhead phosphor tubes that did little to lift the gloom of the place, Falka saw a small army of medics, orderlies and servitors rushing to keep the Damnosian wounded alive a little longer. Most wore masks to retard the worst of the stench, a few even utilised the mouth cups from Guard rebreathers.

Pressing through the mob of walking wounded, careful not to cause any further distress, Falka found what he took to be the nearest medic and gently gripped his shoulder.

Exasperated, the medic turned. He was a young man, too gaunt for his actual years, Falka suspected, and wore a smock stained dark with blood.

'You one of the orderlies I requested?' snapped the medic, without waiting for Falka to speak.

'I– no, I–' Falka began, wrong-footed.

'Good,' said the medic, seemingly hearing what he wanted to. 'Name's Rauter.'

'Kolpeck, Falka,' said Falka, events running a little too fast for him to keep up.

'Follow me, please, Kolpeck.' He turned on his heel, wading through the waves of meandering injured men and women, shouting orders here and there. To whom, Falka had no idea. It seemed chaotic in the shadowy infirmary. With bodies pressed so close together, it felt as if he were back in the One Hundred about to face the necron assault all over again.

Somewhat dumbstruck and appalled by it all, he followed, but struggled to keep up with the medic. Thronged with bodies, beds and what little medical equipment could be scavenged, it was a labyrinth without walls; one in which Falka could see his destination, but just had no idea how best to reach it. It was only by virtue of his size and intimidating stature that he was able to catch up with the medic at all. When he finally did, Rauter had found a rare scrap of open space where several avenues of beds connected.

'There are a lot of burns, first through to fourth degree. Mostly from the weaponry those metal bastards were using, but from fires too,' he explained, gesturing in several directions whilst reading off a data-slate Falka had only just realised Rauter was carrying. 'Some amputations,' the medic went on, 'but we've got shock victims as well, burst ear drums, ocular scarring, breaks. You're not skilled, so I don't expect miracles. Make them comfortable if you can.'

Rauter turned from his data-slate to face him, wondering just how many of the able-bodied had been pressed into this service and what would happen when the injured outnumbered the fit and healthy. Perhaps they already did.

Now they had stopped and Falka was regaining his composure, he got his first proper look at the medic. A pepper-wash of stubble masked the lower half of Rauter's jaw and neck and there were blood splashes he had not noticed or had time to clean off. His hair was short, not military, but still cropped. Falka guessed he was twenty-one standard, give or take. Too young to run a facility like this, but he saw no one else answering to the description.

'Despite donations from our heavenward protectors,' his tone was cynical and Falka had to resist the urge to strike him, but realised Rauter was just exhausted and had seen and lost too much, 'we're dangerously low on any form of sedative, so most of what you do will probably be holding down patients who are in agony but can't be spared any pain relief. We're also running out of coagulant gel, synth-skin, disinfectant and bandages. You care to name it, we probably haven't got it or are almost out of it, so improvise.'

Rauter was about to hurry off when Falka put up a big hand to stop him.

'I'm not here as an orderly,' he said, stalling the young medic's anger by going on to say, 'I'm a soldier. I was told Jynn Evvers is in here somewhere and was asking for me.'

Rauter frowned, incredulous, as he opened up his arms wide to gesture at the squalid surroundings.

'Look around. Can you see any organisation here? I have no idea where your friend is. If you're not here to help please stay out of the way.' Rauter was starting to walk away again and Falka's urge to punch the medic came back with greater insistence, when he turned and said, 'There's a medical servitor with most of the patient data inloaded.' Rauter jabbed a thumb in the vague direction behind Falka. 'It's voice activated, you only have to say her name. She might not have been logged, many haven't, but it's probably your best chance at finding her.' He paused for a moment, his shoulders briefly sagging as he let Falka see the broken man he had become and was trying to keep at bay for as long as he was needed. 'Is she your wife, daughter?'

'No, nothing like that,' he said, and felt hollow. 'Just a friend.'

'I am sorry... Kolpeck, was that your name?' said Rauter. 'I don't mean to be insensitive, I don't regard myself as such, but we are at the bleeding edge here. I'm not ashamed to admit that we're ragged, but I haven't slept for twenty hours and my patience is worn a little thin. Try the servitor, maybe it can help.'

Rauter nodded curtly before hurrying off to conduct his many duties, and was quickly lost in the crowd. In his wake, his words lingered. They *were* ragged, worn thin, and when ice is like that a break is not far off. All of Damnos was cracking. If the necrons did not kill them, then the heinous conditions they were being forced to endure probably would. Life had never been easy on the colony, ice mining never was, but this crisis was fast exceeding mortal forbearance.

Following the directions he had been given, chastening

himself a second time for his lack of sympathy towards the medic, Falka eventually found the servitor.

It was a battered, half-organic model with a bare metal faceplate riveted across the nose and mouth where a vox-grille had been implanted, and all too human eyes. Given the nature of the enemy they were facing on Damnos, Falka found the spectacle of the servitor a little chilling. It was a walker, bipedal, with medical overalls and boots. It still had arms, but the organic limbs had been amputated and replaced with bionics. The servitor's back was laden with various packs and canisters now mostly denuded of the medical supplies they had once carried.

Blank-eyed, the servitor paused in its preconfigured rounds and stopped in front of Falka.

'I'm looking for Jynn Evvers. She here?' he asked, a little unsettled by the corpse-like automaton.

Its dead-eyed stare persisted for a few seconds, giving the servitor time to search its records before blurting in machine-like cadence. '*Name: Evvers, Jynn. Rank: Captain, Militia. Presence: Affirmative.*'

There the report ended.

'Where?' asked Falka, frustrated. He had got used to the smell by now, but the constant moaning and wailing from the injured was wearing at his nerves.

After a few seconds of further searching, the servitor answered, '*Insufficient data.*'

Falka scowled. 'What? She's in here, right? Where is she? Evvers. Jynn,' he repeated, and grabbed the servitor's shoulders. The metal was cold and unyielding, and Falka suppressed an involuntary shiver at the touch.

'*Insufficient data,*' it answered again, in a carbon copy of its first response.

Irrational anger gripped Falka, prompting him to try and shake the truth he needed from the automaton. The patients around him were growing agitated too, thrashing and shouting. Some had risen from their beds and were remonstrating violently with the strung-out medicae staff. The break in the ice was coming, just as he knew it would…

Falka was wiping his eyes and shaking his head to clear the sudden bout of nausea threatening to empty his stomach when he heard someone puking nearby… then another.

'*Insufficient data, insufficient data, insufficien–*' blurted the servitor, trapped in a loop.

Something was happening. Falka felt it deep in his core, but could not pinpoint exactly what. Dizzy, he let go of the servitor and backed up a step before it suddenly convulsed and a line of blood streaked out of its eye from some internal haemorrhage.

'What the hell…?'

Within a few metres of the servitor, a burn victim had kicked over his IV and collapsed on the floor. Another man, an orderly, fell to his knees and started scratching at his eyes. Farther away, he heard a woman shriek and someone else collided with a crash cart, spilling tools and equipment.

Through the crowd, which was slowly succumbing to some invisible malady, Falka noticed Rauter. The medic was slumped against the side of a bunk, his mouth slack and drooling. Then all the shouting, wailing and moaning stopped. Medical saws and machinery continued to burr and churn, but did so without human accompaniment.

Then came the keening.

It began as a low-level hum, just below the normal range of human hearing, but felt through the resonance of the hairs erect on the body or as a dull aching sensation in the gums, before growing in amplitude to an ear-wrenching shriek.

Falka did not realise what was happening until he had hit the ground, hands pressed instinctively over his ears. Somewhere close by he heard a gunshot, then the screaming began in earnest as the human voices returned. Patients were lurching up out of their beds, crawling their burn-ravaged bodies over the bloody infirmary floor. The medi-servitor Falka had been ineptly attempting to threaten was still upright but leaking a deluge of blood and oil from every one of its biological and non-biological orifices. The cyborganic was dead and no amount of augmentation would coax it back to functionality again. Never had he felt his own mortality so acutely. And as Falka looked up into the eyes of a hospitaller nurse who had fallen to her knees as he had done, he knew he was not alone. Terrified, she backed away and was lost to the darkness. Everywhere the same terror-etched faces, all experiencing the same revelation.

Death had come, and it was here amongst them.

Trembling, through tear-blurred vision, Falka saw someone he recognised emerging through the throng of slowly-maddening medics and patients. The whole infirmary was infected, the terrible shrieking an almost white-noise tinnitus that brought people to their knees or sent them into pangs of violent insanity. It was a man dressed in an Ark Guard uniform that Falka had seen. In one hand he held a simple igniter and a pack of smokes; in the other, a Damnosian ice axe already slick with blood. As he stepped into the dim light of a phosphor tube, the face of Corporal Tanner Greishof was revealed, only it was half-decayed and bloated with putrefaction.

'Need a light?' asked Greishof, the blackened tongue lolling around the cavity of his mouth slurring his voice.

Falka took out his sidearm, a simple heavy-gauge laslock, and pointed it towards the apparition. His rational mind knew what he was seeing could not be real, but his eyes were sending a different message to his brain, terrifying him.

'Stay back!' Falka warned.

Greishof frowned, flakes of skin peeling from his rotting face.

'Do you want to jump instead? Down to the ice? It's cold down there, you won't feel a thing. Not a thing…'

The ground under Falka tilted like it was seesawing to the left and a profound sense of vertigo overtook him, enhancing his nausea. He vomited, but kept his eyes on Greishof, wiping his mouth with the back of his hand.

'Keep away…'

Other shapes moved in the darkness, within Falka's peripheral vision. They were hunched and broad… skeletal.

Greishof advanced, paying the other spectres no mind, languidly swinging his ice axe.

'Sure you don't wanna smoke?'

'Go to hell.'

Falka fired and missed, struggling to remain steady with the ground pitching and yawing beneath him. A second shot flashed into the darkness beyond Greishof's shoulder. A third struck his cheek and exploded the trooper's jaw. Falka was about to unload a fourth when he caught sight of something behind Greishof.

No, not some*thing*, some*one*.

As his gaze alighted on a woman lying comatose on a nearby bunk, his heart beat a little faster, the flicker of hope rekindled in it.

'Jynn…'

She lived. After everything, after he thought she had perished, Jynn lived.

'Always knew you were a born survivor, girl,' he murmured through tears of relief.

And like smoke shadows drifting away into the cold air, the spectres at the edge of Falka's sight faded. But the crowd of half-mad Damnosians standing between them was very real. Crazed, capering figures barrelled through the darkness. Some were becoming increasingly violent, their fear turning them hostile. One slammed into Falka, but he managed to get his shoulder into the man's abdomen and haul him over his head.

Knowing he would probably be crushed to death if he stayed on his knees, Falka staggered to his feet. He was tempted to keep out his pistol but holstered it instead, afraid of what he might do if he were so armed. At least Greishof had gone. He had never been there in the first place.

Just a ghost… Falka realised. *They're all just ghosts.*

A woman wearing Guard fatigues rushed him out of the darkness. She was wailing incoherently, so Falka cuffed her across the left temple to put her down, knocking her unconscious.

'Out of my way!' he shouted, mustering what little resolve he had left, only the prospect of reaching Jynn compelling every laboured step. His concern for her was an anchor he could cling to and helped overcome his irrational fear. Even still, Falka's heart was hammering like a rock-drill and he clutched at it, scarcely able to breathe. For a moment he genuinely believed his chest might burst and imagined a host of mechanical scarabs swarming out to consume him, flesh and bone.

It's just the fear talking. Ignore it. Grit your teeth.

Falka did; he gritted his teeth and clenched his hands into fists. He had reached the makeshift avenue of beds that led him to where Jynn was lying. Clutching one of the beds' metal rails, barely noticing the catatonic figure seemingly paralysed upon it, he struggled on. It was like wading through an ice storm, only it was the phantoms in his mind and not the elements assailing him. Something lurked in the outer darkness of the infirmary, and it was slowly creeping towards him. Falka fought to maintain his tunnel vision, eyes locked on her and only her. She needed him, and he used that thought to galvanise him and reach Jynn's bed. Even comatose, she had not been spared the horrors. Whether experiencing some nightmare brought on by the coma or feeling the shared dread that had affected everyone in the infirmary, Jynn was convulsing too.

Hands trembling, Falka managed to hold her down.

'It's all right, it's all right,' he soothed, one giant hand keeping her still while he tenderly stroked her forehead with the other. No one came close. She and he were an island amidst the madness. His presence seemed to calm her but she was mewling in her coma sleep, reliving Throne-only-knew what dark moments embedded in her psyche.

Falka knew it was this deep-seeded fear that affected them, one so potent it could conjure the dead or render a grown man insensate. Without exception, the entire infirmary had capitulated before it. Perhaps all of Kellenport was lost to it? What if this were the end?

Falka rallied, forcing himself to focus on Jynn and getting her out of this alive.

'Hold on,' he whispered, clinging to his last shreds of

sanity. 'Hold on, for me,' he repeated as the far wall of the infirmary was wrenched away in a storm of tearing metal and iridescent energy.

Men and women were thrown into the air by the blast. Some were shredded, cut in half by the wreckage of the destroyed wall. Falka saw others transfixed by jade-green lightning arcs, their bodies shuddering as they were rendered down to their scorched bones.

It happened so fast, experienced through fear-dulled senses, he barely reacted. But this was no apparition brought on by the terrible din droning throughout the infirmary; it was real.

Through the gaping hole where the infirmary wall had once stood, Falka saw out into the Damnos night and glimpsed two sickle-shaped objects arcing rapidly through the sky. It was the necrons; he felt it in his marrow. They had returned at last, just as he always knew they would.

The city was under attack.

Bodies had been cast everywhere. Some lay unmoving, either dead or too scared to move. Others, farther from the blast, had noticed the burly rig-hand and the woman he was protecting. Their faces looked feral in the half-light, barely human at all. Falka saw things glinting in their hands. They looked to him like blades: scalpels, knives and medical saws. He pulled out the laslock, brandishing it in the hope they would get the message and back away. To his right, another group had seen them and was advancing. They had just finished cutting into another coma victim, his blood still on their knives.

'Cut it out,' said one, drunk with madness.

'Cut out the horrors,' echoed another, and Falka was reminded of the scarab swarm, the one he had imagined nesting in his chest. They had seen them too, only they did not possess the strength of mind to realise they were not real.

The men and women converging on him and Jynn were lost. Waving a pistol at them would do no good.

'Stay away,' Falka warned one last time as the shadows behind them came alive again with the hulking skeletal figures. He squeezed Jynn's hand, willing her to give him strength.

Falka fired, but the laslock went dead in his hand, its power cell drained. He calmly holstered the pistol, knowing the feral Damnosians would be on them in moments.

'You can't have her,' he told them, scowling. 'You'll have to go through me first.'

'Cut it out,' said the leader of the mob, a simple clerk. He seemed not to hear Falka's threat. 'Cut it all out...'

FROM HIS POSITION on the wall, Iulus swung around and tried to aim through his bolter's scope. The skimmer was moving too fast, like a bullet, and banking as it sped over Kellenport, letting out a wailing dirge from its engines.

It was not alone, either. A second craft joined the first, both small enough to be fighters and armed with under-slung weaponry. Iulus heard the wall guns answering the threat, and saw one lit up by a twin lightning arc spat from one fighter's cannons. Both the emplacement and its crew were ripped apart and splattered over Kellenport's cold stone with nothing in reply.

Down in the courtyard below, the Damnosian citizenry – runners, soldiers, militia, medics – were screaming in fear. Imagined terrors spilled from their lips as spectres of old friends or gratefully forgotten enemies came back to claim them for the afterlife. A battalion of Ark Guard sent to quell the sudden distemper had succumbed to it instead. To see them so unmanned would have disgusted Iulus once; now, he just pitied them and knew this enemy was merely beyond them. No human, as far as he could determine anyway, was immune. Only the Ultramarines seemed unaffected.

He raised his squad on the vox, following the arcing flight path of the fighters as they turned and wheeled. Hitting a flyer at that speed would be nigh-on impossible. They needed an advantage.

Iulus scowled. One had yet to present itself.

'Immortals, gain the walls if you're not already on them and try to bring these things down!'

Fortune might yet favour them. It was better than nothing, but not much better.

Staccato bolter fire echoed from the city battlements, muzzle flashes lighting the gloom and showing Iulus where his men had responded. But as the sergeant had predicted, the fighters were too fast and nimble. Hot tracer whipped through the air, but it was like chasing smoke on a gale.

Other squads joined the fusillade being levelled at the fighters and the sky ignited with explosions and spearing las-beams. The necrons ran the entire gauntlet without so much as a glancing hit. Atavian had marshalled his Devastators in the square but even the so-called 'Titan Slayers' struggled to get a bead on the rapidly moving craft.

The presence of the fighters was disconcerting. The Ultramarines had not encountered forces such as these before on Damnos. As he tried to chase one down through his targeter, Iulus wondered what else was in the necron arsenal, lurking below the ice.

Scythe-edged and menacing, one of the fighters broke off from its attack pattern and dived towards Infirmary Seven where Iulus had sent Kolpeck. With a burst from its guns, the necron tore the makeshift field hospital open and exposed its wounded to the elements and its further wrath.

Leaping from the wall, Iulus split rockcrete as he landed. Ignoring the gibbering bodies thronging the courtyard, he raced for the infirmary. Kolpeck had saved his life during the siege; he was not about to allow that debt to go unpaid by letting the man die in ignominy.

Having seen their sergeant so driven, Aristaeus and Venkelius joined him from the lower battlements.

'Brothers,' Iulus told them as they ran across the courtyard, careful to avoid the fear-gripped Damnosians, 'they will be afraid, and almost certainly not themselves. Try not to kill them.'

Both Ultramarines nodded to their sergeant.

Upon reaching the terrified guards still manning their posts at the infirmary entrance, Aristaeus stepped up and subdued the men with two swift blows from the pommel of his gladius.

'Like that?' he asked.

'There'll be more inside,' Iulus warned them both, 'and in much closer confines. Put your weapons away.'

Aristaeus had his flamer, whilst Venkelius carried a missile launcher slung across his back. Both warriors had their standard bolt pistol sidearm and Ultramarian gladius.

'And hold on to them,' added Iulus, once all three had secured their arms. 'Last thing we need in there is someone drawing your blade in the chaos.'

Iulus opened the infirmary gate with a hard kick. As they stepped inside, a hellish vista greeted them. Even the darkness could not hide what had become of the hundreds hiding within. Bloodied, wailing, clad in scraps and scuttling like beasts; the infirmary had become more of an asylum, and one in which the inmates were running amok.

Several were dead already, their bodies slumped and pooling blood. Skirmishes had broken out in places, whilst some of the victims turned their terror-fuelled anger against shadows or the inanimate. Fear-sweat drenched the air. Iulus detected heavy concentrations of epinephrine, norepinephrine and adrenaline secreted by the victims and expressed through the Damnosians' autonomic responses. The heady chemical cocktail merged with the stench of recently spilled blood, exacerbating the terror felt by those inside the infirmary.

'This is no hospital,' growled Aristaeus, unable to suppress his combat instincts. 'It's a war zone.' He slid a finger's width of gladius blade out of the sheath before Iulus's voice stopped him going any further.

'No weapons,' he stated firmly.

'Hand-to-hand then...' uttered Venkelius, nodding to a group of manic-looking Damnosians who had reacted to the Ultramarines' sudden presence.

'And no killing,' added Iulus as an orderly came at him with a surgical saw. Emitting a low grunt, he backhanded the man gently enough so as not to kill him, but still sent him sprawling.

Aristaeus deflected an IV frame swung at him by another, the metal bending around his armoured forearm before he planted the flat of his palm into his aggressor's chest, flooring him.

Venkelius broke the arm of a third, a woman, using a deft elbow strike to shatter the bone.

'Battle-brother!' Iulus warned the heavy weapon trooper.

The woman had collapsed into a heap, clutching her broken limb.

'She's not dead, sergeant,' Venkelius answered, mildly apologetic.

Iulus glanced sharply in his direction. 'Pull your punches.'

Dispatching a second round of attackers, the humans so mindless with terror that they hurled themselves at them, the three Ultramarines advanced through the masses. When faced with the giant warriors, most of the Damnosians balked and fled. Others collapsed in foetal despair, willing the nightmare to be over. Iulus did not know what these poor wretches were seeing but if it kept them at bay he was not about to question it. Only the worst affected attacked, and these fools the Ultramarines dealt with swiftly, but not lethally.

As he fought, Iulus scanned the crowd for Kolpeck. He had locked the man's image in his mind and would know it immediately.

'There!' he shouted to his comrades, who had spread out to cover more ground and subdue more of the truly insane. Iulus pointed to a nearby bunk surrounded by a clutch of blade-wielding men and women. At the heart of it was Kolpeck, an unconscious woman next to him. He was trying to protect her, roaring his defiance at the homicidal figures closing their net of sharp steel.

Ignoring his own orders, Iulus drew his bolt pistol and discharged an explosive round into the air.

The pistol report resounded in the infirmary, despite the terror-dirge. Several Damnosians in his path turned at the sound.

'Step aside!' Iulus bellowed, and the majority ran. Any

stupid enough to stay were battered by the charging Ultra-marine. He was just a few metres away. Out the corner of his eye, Iulus caught sight of Aristaeus and Venkelius converging on him. He also noticed the gaping hole in the side of the infirmary, and heard the necron fighter descending in front of it before he saw it.

Despite Kolpeck's imminent peril, Iulus stopped and crouched, aiming at the cleft in the wall.

'Venkelius,' he said over the vox.

The heavy weapon trooper was also on one knee, bracing his missile launcher on his shoulder. Knowing his flamer was of little use, Aristaeus kept his brother free of interference.

With his warriors now in position, Iulus thought back to that advantage he had sought. The sickle-edge of the necron fighter came into view. It was moving slowly, hovering to get a better shot, and believing there was no threat inside the infirmary.

Iulus smiled when he saw the pilot's glowing eyes.

'Surprise...' he murmured.

PILOT HAD BROKEN off from his twin, enacting annihilation protocols extracted from his datastacks. One would distract, whilst the other would reap the maximum damage, both biological and structural. Pilot had reviewed and theoretically tested all potential tactics and had determined that splitting the ships was the most effective.

Though he did not understand or possess the capacity to appreciate the psychological effects of terror, Pilot could determine the logic path to this form of attack and the reduction in the overall combat efficacy of an entrenched enemy because of it. Based on experiential data contained within the stacks, he knew it would increase the success ratio of further attacks and that there was a direct and statistically significant correlation between terror attacks and the eventual capitulation of an enemy force.

The punitive tesla arc he had unleashed against the structure, thus making it more vulnerable, was therefore not only logical but also the most effective course of action his android brain would allow him to take.

Decreasing propulsion, Pilot brought his flyer into a descent pattern that would place all effective weapons within lethal range of the biological matter inside the ruined structure. He calculated he had time for a single salvo before a further delay would breach acceptable threat parameters. A data stream indicated his primary weapon was the pre-eminent choice in this scenario.

Pilot engaged the death ray's capacitors, fed energy into its power coils so that by the time he had the optimum shot it would be fire-ready. But as his targeting matrices locked on the focus of his beam, new data cascaded over the old. Threat parameters dramatically increased, warning Pilot that additional, un-factored variables had suddenly intruded on the balanced equation he had just made.

Processing the appropriate responses in nanoseconds, Pilot took evasive action as explosive fire raked over the hull of his craft. It achieved no lasting damage, and it was only then, as another data stream describing an incoming incendiary washed over his visual feed, that Pilot ascertained the first attack had been a feint and this second attack was the one intended to destroy him.

Pilot had enough time to realise his miscalculation, to see his inevitable doom relayed in streams of unfeeling, undeniable logic, before the missile struck the coruscating tip of the death ray and tore him and his scythed craft apart.

IULUS CLENCHED A fist as the necron flyer exploded. Venkelius had shot well, and would be recommended for battle honour. Mercifully, no other casualties were caused by the flyer's destruction. Well acquainted by now with necron tactics, Aristaeus was already rushing over to the burning wreck but the necron inside was gone, phased out from irreparable damage.

The flamer trooper turned to the others, giving the all clear.

Through the gap in the wall, the *Thunderstorm* streaked past on screaming turbofans, engines flaring. Just before the gunship disappeared from sight again, Iulus saw it discharge a missile payload at a target beyond his limited field of vision through the ruined wall and knew it was engaging the second flyer. With the destruction of his wingman, Iulus assumed the surviving craft would disengage. That assumption was borne out as, slowly, the terror-dirge receded and with its abeyance some semblance of composure returned. The chill of fear lingered still in its wake, but the men and women of the infirmary were beginning to come around. Some blinked, as if waking from a terrible dream; others wept, appalled at what they had done or still coming to terms with the remembered nightmares of the past.

It was raw, the atmosphere choked with grief and regret, but at least it was sane.

Iulus reached Kolpeck at last. The man was slow to come down from his heightened emotional state, and he battered at the Ultramarine at first, hammering impotently at the warrior's chest with his fists.

'Stand down, Sergeant Kolpeck,' Iulus told him, holding the man to his chest, holding him steady and firmly. 'Stand down.'

Like some of his fellow Damnosians, Kolpeck blinked – there were tears in his eyes, not of fear or sorrow but defiance – and looked up at his saviour.

'Brother-Angel,' he said, voice choked with emotion. 'Is she...?' Iulus released him and Falka Kolpeck began to turn around.

'She's alive, trooper,' Iulus told him, nodding to the prone woman on the bed whom Kolpeck had been protecting.

Now the tears really began to flow, of relief, of hope, of desperation.

'Thank the Emperor...' said Kolpeck.

Iulus did not stay to watch. He summoned Venkelius and Aristaeus, and the three of them went back out into Kellenport to see what was left of the city defences and, more importantly, the resolve of its defenders.

Iulus placed little hope in the continued endurance of either.

CHAPTER EIGHT
BROKEN SWORD

With a grunt of effort, Scipio dragged himself out of the snow-choked hold of the *Gladius*. From a cursory look, the gunship appeared to be largely intact, although it had been badly raked where its hull had connected with the sides of the canyon and a large section of wing including most of the right-hand side was buried under churned ice and snow.

They had crash-landed in a rocky valley, the surrounding crags and slab-sided boulders edged with frost. In the middle distance as he rapidly surveilled the area, Scipio noticed a nest of caves. A ridge of ice-rimed stone led to the lowest mouth, which was large enough to accommodate an entire armoured column. Drifts were still descending, not as heavy as before, but swathing any tracks friendly or enemy that might recently have been formed in the snow underfoot. To the naked eye it would appear virginal, but Scipio detected heat traces and the oily remnants of fuel thronging the ice-crisp breeze. Something had passed through this way, but he could detect no further sign of it beyond these lingering spoors.

Satisfied they were not about to be attacked, he plunged a gauntleted hand into the hold and hauled out Garrik.

'We alive, brother-sergeant?' asked the heavy weapons trooper. He was still clinging to his launcher, thick clumps of hard-packed snow disintegrating off his body as the heat from his power armour melted it.

'Only in death, brother,' Scipio replied, returning to his surveilling. 'You know that.'

'Duty it is then.'

'Hold here. I want to recon our position.'

Garrik nodded, before going to dig out the rest of the squad so Scipio could scout further out.

First impressions were that the crash site was deserted. That was both good and bad. Good because it meant an attack was highly unlikely, as in their current disposition that could prove terminal. Bad because help would not be forthcoming or easy to summon.

High cliffs on either side shielded the valley basin from the worst of the elements. It was largely barren, with the caves rising up to enclose the south-facing aspect, and the jagged path that had led them to this point heading off towards the north. As Scipio scouted past the fifty-metre mark, he realised they must have travelled some distance. He could see all the way to the edge of the valley mouth, but even through the scopes there was no evidence of the battlefield they had left behind or Chronus's tanks. If they were in retreat, or worse, destroyed, there was no way of knowing.

Scipio recalled the shadow under the ice just before the flash of light signalling the massed necron phase shift. Guilliman's blood, it had been so sudden: a vast and immediate spike of teleportation that had caught the Ultramarines forces totally unaware. But that was not what had first alerted him to the danger. Chronus was caught between two enemy formations, one above the ice; one below it. Even the vaunted tank commander would struggle to overcome such odds. Just as Scipio had suspected, the necrons were far from defeated. They were not even diminished in their military efficacy – they had merely been dormant, and now they were waking up.

He tried the vox, hoping to contact one of the vehicles in the tank commander's company, but got only static in reply. According to his retinal display, all vox-frequencies were down. Scipio guessed environmental interference was the cause. They would need to gain higher ground, and try again without obstruction. With sheer cliffs on either side, that made the caves their best hope of reaching a high enough vantage to get a signal.

Largo joined him beyond the fifty-metre perimeter. This was surprising, as he had been expecting his second-in-command.

'Where is Brother Brakkius?' Scipio asked.

'Injured, brother-sergeant. During the crash, his legs were crushed. He can't walk.'

That was a blow. Scipio relied on Brakkius's counsel and experience.

'Any other injuries?'

'Brother Kastus is incapacitated. The *Gladius*'s prow bore the brunt of the impact. The glacis was shattered instantly, and it took some hits.'

Scipio met Largo's gaze. 'Is he dead?'

'Sus-anic coma, brother-sergeant.'

'At least that's something,' Scipio conceded. With both Brakkius and Kastus out of action, that limited their options. A march into the wastes was out of the question. 'What about the ship?'

'The prow is more or less intact but our Techmarine holds it must be repaired if we're to get airborne again.'

'Airborne?' Scipio asked quizzically. 'I assumed we were grounded.'

A voice a little farther away answered, the unmistakable mechanical cadence of Vantor.

'The machine-spirit of the *Gladius* yet lives,' said the Techmarine. 'I can not only repair, I can also fly it in Kastus's absence.'

'How long do you need?' asked Scipio.

'Most of the damage is superficial. There is a split in the port-side wing that must be fixed, the prow you already know about. I'll need to run a thorough diagnostic too...'

'How long?' the sergeant pressed, quickly tiring of Vantor's loquaciousness when discussing mechanics.

'I estimate an hour.'

Scipio shook his head ruefully. 'Chronus could be dead in an hour. We need to send a message to Kellenport, and raise the tank commander if we can. He might be in need of reinforcement.' He turned back to Largo. 'Gather the rest of the squad. We're going on a scouting mission.'

'What of Brakkius, brother-sergeant?'

'He stays with Vantor. Now go.'

Looking back in the direction of the crash site, Scipio could see that most of Squad Vorolanus was ready for deployment. Only Brakkius, currently laid up against the unburied side of the *Gladius*'s hull, would be absent.

'We'll be heading towards the caves,' Scipio told the

Techmarine. 'Make sure the gunship is flight-worthy by the time we return.'

Vantor nodded. 'Be wary, brother-sergeant. I have never seen such ingenuity and resilience in a foe before as I have with the necrons.'

Scipio looked askance at the Techmarine. 'I think I am starting to agree with Brakkius.'

'How so?'

'You sound like you admire these creatures.'

'As I said to him, it is merely fascination. But also respect. They are devious and possess technology about which we know almost nothing. They are deadly, Sergeant Vorolanus.'

Scipio said nothing, and returned to the downed gunship to gather his squad.

CHAPTER NINE
ARMOUR KILLS

THE HONOUR OF CALGAR was ablaze. Tongues of fire lapped eagerly across its scorched hull, its crew trapped inside and without hope of rescue. They did not try to escape. They were sons of Guilliman. They kept fighting. It burned for another eight seconds, floundering blindly, sponson guns chugging, before its fuel and ammunition cooked off and the Predator exploded. The shrapnel struck a second battle tank, *Hera's Banner*, which was mired in ice. Half its hull was sunk beneath the permafrost, tracks whirring but skidding badly and failing to find purchase. Unable to defend itself, *Hera* could only await the inevitable as an arachnid necron construct clambered over its roof and gutted it from close range with a heat ray. Metal sloughed to molten slag under the weapon's angry glow, the incumbent crew likewise. Within a few seconds, *Hera* was no more. It did not even resemble the proud war machine it had once been. 'Scrap' would have been too kind a term for it.

Glaring at Chronus on his retinal lens display, the icon for *Hera* went from amber to crimson. As the tank commander brought the *Rage of Antonius* around for another pass, he saw several other war machines were flaring terminally on the tactical feed too.

Two Razorbacks had been eviscerated by heat beams, their lascannon fusillade seemingly ineffective against the shielding of the spider-like walker that had destroyed them both. A third had been cut in half, then rendered down by a focused beam from a second arachnid construct.

Four Rhinos were blazing wrecks, still burning despite the snowfall, and pluming oily smoke. It smeared the sky, and blackened Chronus's already bitter mood.

But it was the *Vigilant* that had been the first to die.

Caught in the act of dismantling the pitiful necron infantry, the Ultramarines armour had been strung out and lacking cohesion when the phase shift manifested, bringing with it a vastly superior and more manoeuvrable war host.

How quickly triumph had turned to urgent desperation.

The *Vigilant* was a veteran war machine, a Crusader-variant Land Raider. It took three hits simultaneously, still turning as it tried to bring its guns to bear. The first tore up its steering then severed a track guard before finally wrecking the armoured tread itself. The second punched a hole into the *Vigilant*'s back, taking out any remaining motive power and damaging its secondary weapon systems. The third destroyed it, the grizzled old Raider mushrooming upwards with the force of its own internal detonation, only to crash down again seconds later in a fire-wreathed heap.

The two other engines in its squadron, *Merciless Orar* and *Lord Protector*, gave retaliatory fire but by then Chronus was ordering a full withdrawal to a more cohesive formation.

Engines fighting engines was bad. Without infantry support, especially against the anti-gravitic and hyper-manoeuvrable skimmers the necrons possessed, the tanks were at a distinct disadvantage. But even caught unawares, Chronus believed he could rally his forces back into some semblance of order and regain the upper hand.

It was only partially successful. As the tanks unleashed suppressing fire to try and stultify the swift necron assault and were forming up into a sweeping line breaker formation to scatter the enemy, a second force emerged from below.

The walkers were spider-like in aspect and came from under the ice. They broke up Chronus's hastily restored order, appearing across the battlefield seemingly at will. It was as if some overarching consciousness commanded them, one that could perceive the entire theatre of combat and predict each of its unfolding acts before they transpired. Despite their less than robust design, the arachnid constructs were hard to kill, protected as they were by some kind of energy shielding.

Faced with the almost certain destruction of his forces, Chronus had little choice but to abandon formation and give the order for all vehicles to engage the nearest target and pray to the Throne the Ultramarines could weather the storm long enough to reassert dominance later.

As his battle tanks effectively duelled with the necron skimmers over several kilometres of churned snow and ice, a close-quarters encounter despite there being at least fifty metres between most of the vehicles, it was proving frustrating for Chronus.

'All weapons!' he snarled to Vutrius below, taking personal account of their lascannon turret. 'Tear that thing apart.'

The *Rage of Antonius* shuddered, muzzle flare roaring from its side sponsons before Chronus cored out one of the arachnids with an accurate las-lance from the twin-link. They were moving at maximum combat speed, the Predator's machine-spirit and advanced systems compensating for the continuous motion over the rugged ice. A flash of verdant fire made Chronus grimace despite his battle-helm. The larger skimmers were coming in again, not content with the destruction wreaked in their previous attack run.

Chronus slewed the turret around and fired across the necrons' front arc, as Novus poured on more speed to get away from the floating, barge-like skimmers. As far as the tank commander had been able to discern during the sudden and unheralded enemy assault, there were two major necron engines involved in this armour skirmish. One was fashioned into a simulacrum of a scorpion, an ersatz tail rising from its rear aspect with its primary weapon location on its underside, encased in something approximating a metal ribcage or exoskeleton. Its single crewman was necron, of course, but appeared to be of a higher caste than the foot soldiers Chronus had been slaughtering before he had sprung the trap. The other engine was reminiscent of an anti-gravitic throne-barge, with a vast cannon array positioned above its two crewmen who were suspended in control cradles either side of the weapon's power source. Whatever drove it, the effects were terrible to behold. A single blast had shredded open *Hellhunter*, but the Predator had survived and limped on.

These necrons, the ones driving their infernal vehicles, were much more advanced and tactically adroit. That lesson had been learned now, but had cost Chronus three major engines and six support vehicles.

Amidst the chaos of chattering shell bursts, whining beam weapons and energy discharge, Chronus opened up the vox.

'Gnaeus, try to bring your flank together and put the heavier armour to your rear.'

The necrons were almost running rings around the slower Ultramarines vehicles, though the tanks could take more of a beating. As soon as it became clear they would not be able to regroup, Chronus had the company split into three separate battlegroups commanded by himself and his two sergeants.

Gnaeus's affirmation rune flashed up on Chronus's lens display, indicating he had understood and would proceed as ordered. Gnaeus had drawn together two of the Vindicators, *The Ram* and *Glory of Calth*, as well as *Fury Unbound* and *Ceaseless Endeavour* from the Whirlwind squadron. The other siege tanks had managed to disengage from the frantic melee on Gnaeus's orders, putting some distance between themselves and the enemy so they could regroup and offer stationary bombardment. With the engagement so tightly packed, the opportunity had yet to present itself.

The two Land Raiders, *Merciless Orar* and *Lord Protector*, reduced speed and dropped back behind Gnaeus's Destructor, *Secutor Maximus*, the last of his Predator squadron. At the brunt of the necron assault force when it materialised, Gnaeus's engines had been the hardest hit but were digging in now and showing their mettle.

A beam flashed overhead, hot and angry, and Chronus was forced back down into the cupola.

'Guilliman's holy blood!' he swore, checking his shoulder guard where the beam's passage had seared it. The paint was stripped down to bare armour and even the outer ceramite layer was burned off. The vox-link was still open. 'Egnatius…'

Chronus roughly held the centre, though the battlefield was ever changing and difficult to predict, leaving his sergeants to the flanks. Of the three officers, Egnatius's battlegroup was the only one unscathed, aside from minor glancing hits.

His rune flashed up on a sub-screen on Chronus's display, indicating they were in contact.

'Pull your Predators wide, brother, and send the remaining Raiders to reinforce my flank.'

There was no answer at first, and Chronus was about to curse his fellow tank commander and the malfunctioning vox-link he had evidently failed to repair when Egnatius replied.

'Manoeuvring now.'

He sounded preoccupied, but then they all were. This kind of fight, an enemy this quick and with advanced shielding and weapon technology… A human tank commander would have crumbled under the pressure. As it was, Chronus saw all. He knew the fight was still winnable. The necrons were swift and their war machines possessed phenomenal attacking power, but they lacked true grit and endurance.

'Dismantled. Piece by piece,' Chronus swore to himself beneath his breath. He would make it so.

A long-range autocannon burst from one of Egnatius's Destructors slipped through a skimmer's shielding, splitting the ark-craft in half and sending viridian energy coursing over its broken frame.

'Ha!' Chronus clenched his fist in a vicarious expression of triumph as he watched the skimmer's demise on the tactical display.

A second salvo went close to the *Antonius*, spurring alert runes in urgent warning.

'Watch your firing solutions,' Chronus snapped at Egnatius over the vox.

The sergeant did not respond, but his tanks were moving into a flanking position as ordered.

Chronus had little time to think on it, for they were headed right into the teeth of a necron formation – two of the throne-barges and a single ark. A pair of arachnid walkers scuttled either side, seen through the *Antonius*'s vision slits.

Vutrius unleashed their heavy bolters frontwards, ignoring the walkers who were stitching desultory heat beams across the *Antonius*'s battle-seared hull.

'Keep that speed up, Novus,' Chronus said to his driver, having to shout above the roaring din inside the tank. By maintaining combat speed, they were a tougher target. Thus far, three heat beams had connected but failed to penetrate their outer armour. Slow down and that would change fast.

Enthroned at his command station, Chronus pulled down the scopes that would give him a lascannon's-eye view of the battle. Verdant gauss fire rippled from the approaching enemy skimmers. Eldritch lightning arcs flashed across the visual display, but Chronus kept the crosshairs steady, adjusting each time Novus slewed the *Antonius* aside from a coruscating beam.

'Maintain heading,' Chronus ordered calmly, as the necron ark slipped into his targeting grid. The whine in his ears told him the lascannon's power coils were at maximum. Waiting another two seconds to bring the ark a few crucial metres closer, he seized the triggers.

Twin las-beams lanced from the turret, striking the ark

midway along its spine before severing the scorpion tail. Not needing to see its destruction, Chronus swung the turret around incrementally for a second shot at one of the throne-barges. It tried to jink but the beam cut it a glancing hit, ruining its aim. The second throne-barge hit the *Antonius* square.

Novus roared, his cry of pain strangely muffled by his battle-helm and the interior noise, and a series of alert klaxons began sounding.

'Can you drive, brother?' shouted Chronus across the claustrophobic hold.

He saw Novus nodding, one hand clutching his upper chest, the other firmly grasping the steering control.

With both barges slipping beyond his immediate targeting arc, Chronus slammed the scopes back into the ceiling recess and disengaged the locking clamps on his command seat.

'Pour on the power, punch us through!' he said.

Throwing open the roof hatch, Chronus took up position in the cupola, swinging around as the *Antonius* rumbled past the necrons to get a first-hand look at the battlefield and the damage they had obviously sustained.

Smoke was billowing up from the Predator's left track assembly and a section of armour plating was gouged open and bleeding fluid.

Chronus patted the hull, and muttered, 'Sorry, old friend.'

He relayed orders down to Novus to decrease overall speed and reduce the strain on the damaged track.

Across the ice plain, skimmers and battle tanks were locked in a brutal armoured engagement. The contrast in tactics was stark. Where the necrons utilised their enhanced manoeuvrability, the Ultramarines relied on their ability to absorb punishment and return it with interest. Though the tesla-lightning and heat-ray weaponry was potent, it was better suited to the annihilation of infantry. Against heavy Space Marine armour it was not enjoying the same level of dominance. The necrons did have weapons in their arsenal that could hurt them, however. The smouldering wrecks of *Hera's Banner*, *Honour of Calgar* and *The Vigilant* were testament to that.

Despite the ambush, some cohesion was returning to the Ultramarines forces. The three battlegroups, together with the pair of disparate bombardment vehicles, were beginning to work together and this was taking its toll on the necrons who could not hope to match the tactical agility of Guilliman's sons.

The wisdom of a primarch, the scion of Konor and the Immortal Emperor, flowed in their veins – Chronus saw this engagement ending only in an Ultramarines victory. All of this he processed in seconds, whilst the other half of his strategic attention was fixed on the two skimmers the *Rage of Antonius* was embattled with.

The pair of necron barges were swinging around, lightning cannons charging. One took a stray hit from *The Ram* and detonated explosively from the siege tank's heavy ordnance. The blast buffeted the second skimmer but it was intent on the stricken *Antonius*, which Novus was desperately trying to turn about, and did not deviate. An arc of tesla-lightning spat out, searing the Predator's hull but causing no significant damage. One of the side sponsons came into firing range and Vutrius gunned the heavy bolter from below. Thick shells hammered against the barge but its shielding was practically inviolable.

Both tanks had fired their secondary weapons to no avail,

and like jousting knights of old, came at one another to finish it at close quarters. Chronus had his lance, the turret lascannon turning with agonising slowness, whilst the necron barge primed its main destructor.

At the edge of his vision through his battle-helm, the intimidating forms of *Galatan* and *Strength of Konor* came into view. Lascannon sponsons on both the Terminus Ultra and standard pattern Raider were flashing deadly bolts of light across the field, cutting the legs from under the two arachnid constructs as the necrons' shields were overwhelmed. For a moment the walkers floundered on the ice, attempting to retaliate with their deadly heat weaponry. In advance of the other two Land Raiders in its formation, the *Shield of Iax* put paid to that by rolling over both walkers and crushing them beneath its merciless tracks.

Revenge for the *Vigilant*, thought Chronus, believing engines of the same template were of kindred machine-spirit.

The barges seemed to sense the demise of their walker outriders, one peeling off to escape the certain destruction of the ruthless Land Raiders, while the other was locked into its course against the *Rage of Antonius*.

A cascade of tesla-lightning flashed across the Predator's flank, tearing up a heavy bolter but otherwise leaving the tank intact.

Chronus smiled behind his battle-helm's faceplate.

'Too soon…'

Two more crucial seconds and the twin-link let out a shrieking las-bolt. Chronus drove his lance right into his enemy's heart and vanquished it. Before the kill could be confirmed, he was on the vox to the Raiders curtly expressing his gratitude. Disappearing back down below, he switched channels to his squadron brothers.

'Fabricus, Deneor, form up on the *Antonius*'s lead.'

Both *The Vengeful* and *Hellhunter* moved towards formation with Chronus's Predator. A cursory examination of the battlefield showed that Ultramarines engines outnumbered necron two to one. The enemy were also down to just their skimmers, all the walker constructs having fallen back beneath the ice. Whatever anima drove these creatures, they clearly understood the value of self-preservation.

Once the hatch was closed above, Chronus moved through the hold to the driver's location.

'Vutrius,' he said on the way, crouching down as he navigated the tight confines of the tank, 'you have all weapons.' Chronus's tactical display switched out the twin-link and transferred it to his gunner. He laid his hand on Novus's shoulder. The driver was shaking, blood seeping freely from a savage crack in his power armour.

'Switch to automatic,' Chronus told him. '*Antonius*'s machine-spirit will guide us until I can take the controls.'

Novus was a proud warrior, and Chronus knew he would not easily relinquish his station. 'I can do my duty, commander,' he said.

'Of that I have no doubt, brother. But you're wounded, and that's a direct order.'

Reluctantly, Novus reduced speed to allow the other Predators in their formation to catch up to them and form a bodyguard. He disengaged from his driver's position, and Chronus caught him as he nearly fell. 'Rest easy, brother. Bind that wound. I'd have you back at the *Antonius*'s controls before this war is done.'

'It would be my honour, commander.' Novus saluted – it lacked some of his usual vehemence – and retreated to the back of the hold where they kept the Predator's medi-kit.

Replacing him at the driver's console, Chronus slaved all systems to his retinal display and opened up the company-wide vox.

'Brothers,' he said, 'let us end this. *Ultramar victoris!*'

CHAPTER TEN
ICE CAVERNS

Standing on his vantage at the top of the ice ridge, Vantor and Brakkius looked distinctly small to Scipio. From on high, the *Gladius* appeared in worse condition than the sergeant had first believed. One of its wings had almost completely sheared off and the fuselage was battered. Brakkius was still sat up against the largely intact side, whilst the Techmarine worked at the other, sparks caused by his plasma-welder flashing in the gloom.

An hour, Vantor had said. The wing would be repaired, the glacis restored and hermetically sound, landing struts straightened and re-strengthened.

It had taken Scipio's reduced combat squad almost twenty minutes to summit the ice ridge and, looking down now, he could not see how the gunship would be ready for flight by the time they returned.

He briefly tried the vox and got more static.

Brother Auris was consulting an auspex. 'According to

the scan,' he relayed to the squad, 'we are in the Vogenhoff region.' Inputting some data, he then added, 'It's riddled with caverns and ravines. We are fortunate to have landed at all.'

'Can you tell me where this one leads?' Scipio asked, indicating the vast cave mouth yawning in front of them. Close up, it was even larger than it had appeared in the valley. Frost encrusted the rocky edge of the mouth that faced the elements, and fangs of ice protruded from the irregular arch at its apex. Superstitious men might have believed it to be the maw of some frost giant of old, entombed in the ice and asleep.

Auris stepped forwards. 'Running topographical scan now...' he reported. 'It will take a few seconds.'

Whilst Largo kept his gaze and his bolter trained on the darkness within the cave, Garrik faced north towards the battlefield they had left behind.

'When we were hit,' he said as Scipio approached, 'Chronus was not only outmanoeuvred, he was outgunned.'

Garrik had removed his helmet. It was sitting in the crook of his arm, his other hand just then lowering the scopes. He was scarred, a jagged line of pink flesh running from his chin to alongside his right eye. It was an old wound, received long ago. The hair on that side of his face was patchy too, the black fading to grey. Fortunately, his eyesight was unaffected or that would have been the end of his role as a heavy weapons specialist. Either that, or take a bionic.

He and Scipio had fought together a long time.

'You think Chronus has fallen?' asked the sergeant.

'No,' Garrik replied, 'he seems too stubborn for that. But I wonder what else waits under the ice of this world.' He turned to face Scipio. 'How many necrons are on Damnos, brother-sergeant? How many is too many?'

'We'll know that when we're back aboard the *Valin's Revenge* or lying dead on an icy battlefield, brother.'

'I don't fear death, sergeant.'

'Of course you don't, none of us do, but something has unsettled you.'

'It's Damnos,' Garrik confessed frankly. 'Ever since we arrived on this world and engaged the necrons, I've felt as if something was aware of us. I didn't understand it at first, but after the siege I spoke to Largo and some of the others. Something is buried deep, and it's not human, not remotely. I'm not referring to whatever legions are slumbering below the ice. This is a singular mind. During meditation, I have dreamed about it.'

'A beating heart at the world's core,' said Scipio. 'It's no delusion, Garrik, but we can only face what is in front of us, and not the enemies in our thoughts. Only Master Tigurius can do that.'

Garrik handed back the scopes, having said what he needed to on the matter. 'No sign of the battle tanks. I couldn't even find the *Thunderstorm*.'

'Vandar's back at Kellenport by now,' Scipio replied, locking the magnoculars back onto his armour, 'dealing with whatever flew by us before the attack.' He clapped his hand on Garrik's armoured shoulder. 'We are, all of us, being sorely tested in this campaign. But I believe we will not yield to this pressure, brother. We are sons of Ultramar and do not bend easily.'

Garrik nodded. 'Courage and honour, sergeant.'

Scipio smiled back, and felt some of the humanity he had thought lost on Damnos start to return. 'Courage and honour. It's what separates us from the necrons.'

Auris approached them, having completed the scan.

'Cave leads out to a plateau higher up the range. We should be clear of interference there.'

'Weapons ready, brothers,' Scipio told them both, facing the cave mouth. 'Be prepared for anything.'

Just before they entered the cave, Scipio opened the short-range vox to the warriors they had been forced to leave behind. The signal was patchy, but localised, so he got through almost unimpeded.

Brakkius answered.

'*All's quiet down here, sergeant,*' he said. '*Assuming you're not counting our Techmarine's labours. If there are any necrons slumbering beneath us, they'll soon be awake and upon us.*'

'Keep your eyes open, brother. Soon as we get word to Kellenport or Commander Chronus, we will return. How go the repairs?'

'*Difficult to judge. Vantor and I have yet to exchange words on the subject. I hope well, for I doubt I'll be walking back to the city.*'

Brakkius's black humour was encouraging, as was his thinly veiled annoyance at being trapped with the Techmarine.

'Guard my ship for me, brother. Keep Vantor on course, if you can.'

'*Aye, sergeant. I'll watch him too.*'

'He's one of us, Brakkius,' Scipio reminded him.

'*No he isn't, sergeant. He is not one of the Thunderbolts, and I have not fought with him before.*' He paused, then asked, '*May I speak freely?*'

'Proceed, but whatever it is be quick. We are about to embark.'

'*Something is fundamentally wrong with this world, Scipio. There is a… presence here.*'

Scipio was instantly reminded of his previous conversation with Garrik but a moment ago.

'*And I believe we have all felt it,*' Brakkius went on. '*Perhaps some of us more deeply than others, the Techmarine amongst them.*'

'The Martian creed is an esoteric and clandestine one, but Vantor still wears a white Ultima on a blue field on his shoulder, Brakkius. You'd do well to keep that in mind.'

'*I will watch his back, as you would, sergeant.*'

'Just make sure the *Gladius* is ready upon our return. Eyes open, as I said, brother.'

'*Eyes open, sergeant,*' Brakkius confirmed, '*and good hunting.*'

Scipio cut the vox-link, and waved Largo forwards. He was acting scout, and the first to snap on his helmet's luminators. A sharp magnesium glow filled the outer threshold of the cave, but revealed only further rock and ice.

Eyes open, thought Scipio and went in after Largo.

DURING HIS SERVICE as an Ultramarine, Brakkius had stood sentry many times. The fact he was technically *sitting* this duty made it no different to all those others. Scanning the immediate surroundings revealed no threats on his retinal lens display. An icon showed the position of the Techmarine relative to Brakkius, but his bio-reading was green and all was apparently well. He had no line of sight to Vantor and periodically checked in over the vox to keep apprised on the progress of repairs. Brakkius felt no regret at the loss of his legs. He would either walk again naturally or bionics would be grafted in place of his ruined limbs. As long as he was able to serve, he remained unconcerned. It did leave him feeling vulnerable, however, and the constant reports with the Techmarine helped to assuage that feeling and served to make up the shortfall in vigilance he knew was a reality of his current condition.

Both his legs had been crushed during the crash. They lay mangled in their greaves in front of him, utterly useless. Had Vantor not pinned him through the shoulder, it might be him and Kastus comatose in the hold. As it was, though, Brakkius felt of little service to the Techmarine.

'All clear on this side,' he voxed.

Vantor's few seconds' delay was infuriating, and Brakkius was about to repeat his message when the Techmarine answered.

'*Is there something you need, brother? I am currently quite preoccupied with the repairs to the* Gladius.'

'Just your status report, Techmarine.'

'*Work would proceed faster without interruption,*' Vantor replied.

Brakkius was cursing his misfortune to be stranded with this of all Ultramarines and about to give a terse reply, when he noticed the slightest seismic tremor register on his lens display.

'*Brother Brakkius?*' prompted Vantor when the expected rejoinder was not forthcoming.

'Wait…' Brakkius replied. The tremor returned, stronger than before… and again, stronger still and with greater frequency. 'Something is happening.'

'*You'll need to be more specific.*'

Brakkius raised his bolter at a spot on the ground that

had begun to shake. As he looked down the targeter, he saw small fissures beginning to form and a mound rising from the ice.

'Get around here now.'

Vantor cut the link.

'Damn it!' Brakkius swore. The mound was rising, developing into a large inverted funnel. Something burst through at its apex, the size of a gauntleted fist, insectoid and obviously metallic.

Whilst on Damnos, Brakkius had seen a swarm of necron scarabs reduce a speeder to scrap. He tried not to imagine what one would do to a prone Space Marine slumped against the side of a downed gunship.

He fired two rounds into the side of the funnel that exploded upon impact. Machine parts, insect limbs, broken mandibles and chunks of carapace fountained outwards in a plume of wreckage. In their wake came more of the creatures, scurrying over the metal carcasses of the others, pincers clacking.

To the left of Brakkius a second funnel speared up from the ice, followed by a wave of high-pitched chittering.

Switching to burst fire, he broke apart the second funnel before quickly turning his attention to the surviving scarabs of the first. Alternating from one to the other, he conserved ammunition but kept up a steady rate of fire. Slowly, the diminutive constructs were broken apart, their emergence funnels collapsed and destroyed. But, miraculously, two scarabs from the first funnel made it through the shell storm and leapt at the injured Ultramarine. Brakkius caught the first, having switched to a one-handed grip. The bolter's recoil violently jolted his shoulder and the pain came back anew, but he gritted his teeth and smashed the scarab against the gunship's flank. The second latched onto his face and immediately he could hear its tiny mandibles chewing through ceramite. He head-butted the *Gladius*, destroying the construct before it could do any real damage.

Three more funnels spiralled up from the ground.

Brakkius's ammo gauge was flashing, warning him to slot in a fresh clip. That would take precious seconds and the scarabs were already spilling out onto the ice. Firing off the last three rounds, sharing them evenly between the funnels, Brakkius cast his bolter aside and drew his combat blade. He had mag-locked it to his chest, knowing that drawing it from his thigh would be a needless hindrance in his current position.

Even so, it would not stop the twenty or so constructs scuttling towards him.

'Come on then,' he growled, determined that if he was going to fall he would do so fighting.

A sheet of flame swept over the swarm, setting them ablaze and turning the scarabs to fire-blackened metal.

Brakkius turned and saw Vantor, a flame-unit attached to his servo harness, releasing a constant plume of super-heated promethium that washed over the constructs and turned their emergence funnels into slurries of melted snow.

Only once all of the scarabs had been utterly destroyed did the Techmarine relent.

'I thought you'd abandoned me,' Brakkius told him, sheathing his combat blade so he could pick up his bolter again and rearm.

'Because I am part machine?' asked Vantor, coming over to inspect what was left of the constructs.

'Yes.'

'I will always be more son of Ultramar than of Mars, Brakkius.'

'I am beginning to appreciate that.'

Vantor turned his head, regarding the other Ultramarine through his cold retinal lenses.

'Evidently, saving your life during the crash was not proof enough.'

'Forgive me, brother.'

Vantor gestured to the fused remains of the scarabs.

'They are feeder constructs, consuming matter and turning it into energy, designed to maintain the horde. Protect it during dormancy.'

'How can you know that?' asked Brakkius, still unable to shake his disgust at Vantor's seeming admiration for the necrons.

'Since we have been here, I have watched them, studied them and the effects of their weapons on our own. Only by building a repository of knowledge can we truly fight the necrons effectively. A better question though, brother, might be: why might such creatures be needed here in this remote region?'

Realisation came quickly and starkly to Brakkius.

'There are necrons right here beneath us.'

'I would estimate in their hundreds, but that's not all the presence of the scarabs tells us.'

'What else?' asked Brakkius.

'That they are waking up.'

'VOX-COMMS ARE DOWN,' shouted Largo, scouting at the front of the squad.

Scipio called them to a halt.

545

Garrik checked Largo's findings to make sure it was not just his brother's vox that was malfunctioning.

'Mine too, brother-sergeant,' he reported, tapping the ear-bead embedded inside his helmet, but unable to provoke the unit into function.

'Brother Auris?' Scipio asked the Ultramarine consulting the auspex.

'It must be the cave walls, some mineral interference. We'll be free of it once we're on the other side.'

'What kind of scanner returns are you getting?'

'Weak, brother-sergeant,' said Auris. 'But there's a larger chamber up ahead. It's possible we could receive an improved signal in there.'

'This entire complex is large,' said Garrik. 'I have never seen anything like it, save for the old arcologies on Calth. It makes me question what it's for.'

Scipio regarded him. 'What it's for? You don't believe these caves are natural, brother?'

Garrik shone his luminators, casting the interior rock faces in pellucid white.

'Look at the walls. They're smooth, as if bored. No cave system is this vast, not all the way through. Where is the variation, the natural beauty? I see none of that here.'

Scipio saw that Garrik was right. So focused was he on getting a signal to Chronus or Agrippen back in Kellenport, he had neglected to pay attention to what was in front of his face.

The tunnels were – he hesitated, knowing the word he sought was not 'man-made' – machine-made, carved from the bedrock of Damnos. From what little he knew of the Vogenhoff region, it was extremely remote and had no mining operations. There were no cities, subterranean or otherwise, no settlements of any kind. It was far enough north of Kellenport to be uninhabited and yet these caves had seen the passage of one life form or another.

For a moment, Scipio considered what *exactly* the ice and rock of Damnos encrusted. Before the coming of the Emperor's illuminance and the Great Crusade, some ten thousand years ago, the galaxy had been a lightless place. And it was old, so Imperial scholars and the alien eldar believed. Races far more ancient than man once ruled the stars. It was only logical to assume that some of them had lived on the worlds mankind had colonised. Perhaps some, those able to withstand the entropy of time and the elements, had never left.

The chrono counting down on Scipio's retinal display was at twenty-eight minutes. They had used up over half of Vantor's time getting this far.

'Keep moving,' he ordered. 'And, scout,' he added to Largo, who was leading them out, 'stay close until we can restore vox.'

IT TOOK ANOTHER six minutes to reach the cavern Auris had specified.

It was vast. *Immense*, in fact. Ice floes trickled down ribbed walls that rose up into a vaulted ceiling prickled with distant stalactites. Swathes of frost crunched underfoot, becoming bulwarks of ice where the floor met the walls.

An entire hangar of gunships would have no difficulty fitting inside the massive chamber, Scipio realised. But like the others, it was not the cavern's sheer size that caught his attention, it was the strange vents in the floor.

There were hundreds, arranged in perfect symmetry, their wide necks tapering to a much narrower aperture at the end. Languid vapour was oozing from the mouths of these bizarre, unnatural formations. Encrusted with hoarfrost, a casual observer might have mistaken them for some genus of subterranean flora, but they were not remotely anything like that.

Scipio realised almost at once that the vents were metallic and distinctly alien in origin. The vapour spilling from their mouths was doing so downwards, carpeting the floor around them in a pale mist. He suspected this too was unnaturally produced, likely heavy in nitrogen or fluorine.

'Tell me what you see, brother,' he said to Largo, who had reached the strange crop of vents and was knelt down examining one of them.

Auris joined him, scanning with the auspex.

'Definitely inorganic...' Auris muttered.

'There are tracks here, too,' added Largo, leaving his brother to his analysis and moving further into the chamber.

With Garrik on overwatch, Scipio went after Largo to see what he had discovered.

'Two kinds,' Largo continued, throwing the light of his luminator over a deep impression of what could only be a booted imprint made by power armour. 'And here,' he added, highlighting a second example. The latter were also recognisable.

'Tank tracks,' Scipio whispered, trying to put together what he was seeing into some form of logical order. 'We are not the first Ultramarines to reconnoitre this cave system.'

'Sergeant Egnatius's tank company scouted into the Vogenhoff region,' said Largo.

'I heard of no reports of this cavern. Why would a veteran officer like Votan Egnatius not make mention of it?' Scipio looked around. They were surrounded by a veritable field of vents. He and Largo were standing near the edge, but Auris was deep in amongst them conducting further scans. There were several others, colonising the entire chamber in perfectly rectangular areas.

'Brother Auris…' Scipio began, instinctively reaching for his bolt pistol.

'Something is happening…' Auris replied, intent on his analysis.

'Brother,' said Largo.

Scipio caught Garrik's attention and signalled him to hold position.

Auris was peering down into the mouth of one of the vents. 'The gaseous vapour is abating. I can see something inside it…' He checked the auspex, before looking back. 'Retinal analysis is inconclu–'

A dark mass was suddenly expectorated from the vent. It spattered against Auris's faceplate, forcing him to drop the auspex and recoil.

Garrik was about to advance, but Scipio's raised hand stopped him.

All of the vents had stopped fuming. Something was trickling down their fluted sides. No, not trickling… *crawling*.

'It's all right,' said Auris, signalling the all clear. 'Must have been some kind of blockage, probably from–' He stopped with an abrupt jerk. A swarm of tiny insect-like creatures had penetrated his vox-grille, bored through the hairline gaps between his helmet and its retinal lenses. They had bypassed his gorget and were, even now, infiltrating his body through his mouth, ears and nose.

Hidden by the vapour cloud amassing around the base of the vents, Scipio failed to see the rest of the swarm until it crept beyond the edge of the field in an oily black mass.

'Watch your footing,' he warned Garrik, pulling Largo back a few steps and gesturing down to where the insects had begun to converge. 'Auris,' he shouted out, his voice echoing and hollow. 'Brother!' Scipio said more urgently when the Ultramarine did not immediately respond.

Auris was covered in the writhing creatures, but he made no move against them. Instead, he looked up slowly, straightening his body.

'You should not have come,' he uttered in a voice not entirely his own.

'Ghost of Hera…' hissed Largo, and carefully raised his bolter.

'This is not your world,' said Auris, *'it never was,'* and shot Largo in the chest.

Both Scipio and Garrik opened fire a half-second later, killing a warrior they had once called brother but who was now lost to some terrible affliction neither could understand.

Auris went down amongst the vapour. His ident-rune turned red on Scipio's tactical display, indicating a kill.

'What just happened?' Garrik shouted from across the chamber, sidearm still in hand. About twenty metres separated them, the width of one of the vent fields.

'Stay where you are,' Scipio told him. 'Do not cross the vents.' He went to Largo. Mercifully, the Ultramarine's armour had taken the brunt of the shot but his ribplate could be cracked. 'Can you walk?' Scipio asked, acutely aware of the oily swarm creeping ever closer.

With some difficulty, Largo nodded. Scipio got him to his feet.

'Soon as we are clear,' he called to Garrik, 'I want you to destroy this abomination.'

Garrik scowled. 'With pleasure, sergeant.'

As he helped Largo around the field of vents protruding obscenely from the ice, Scipio realised the function of this place. It was a breeding ground, both for the minute constructs oozing from the vents and the unwilling slaves they created. Here they had peeled back another layer of the necron epidermis and found yet greater aberration.

Garrik had backed up as far as the cavern entrance.

There would be no pressing ahead now. The entire cave system was enemy territory. They had to go back, and get airborne as quickly as possible.

'Bring it down, brother,' said Scipio. 'Then fall back.'

Garrik nodded, having already shouldered his launcher, and released a fragmentation missile into the ceiling. Cracking ice followed in the wake of the explosion as a rain of brittle, razor-edged stalactites cascaded down onto the vents. The entire cavern shook, but not just with the force of detonation. The Ultramarines' presence and subsequent attack had prompted a response. As the deluge of rock and ice crushed the vents, fissures were already splitting the cavern floor and walls. These were not natural clefts, but machine-engineered. Heat swept in from below, the heat of engines and subterranean power coils. Verdant light exuded through the slowly expanding cracks, melting the ice floes and liquidising the frost.

Garrik fed two more missiles into the vent field that had claimed Auris, just to be sure, stowed his launcher and then ran. He caught up to Scipio in short order, the sergeant having lagged behind to help Largo.

'Brother-sergeant, what happened to Auris?' asked the heavy weapon trooper.

'I don't know,' Scipio answered honestly. Behind them

the verdant light was growing, spilling outwards like the dawning of some viridian sun. It would herald the coming of the necrons Scipio now realised were buried below. If they had not reached the *Gladius* and got airborne by the time that happened, there would be no dawn for them.

A salutary thought penetrated his consciousness then – Damnos could not be saved. The only recourse left was to get everyone off-planet as quickly as possible, and the realisation of that fact at least provided purpose.

'He fired on Largo,' said Garrik, unnerved by what he had witnessed. 'To see him taken over so quickly, so easily…'

Largo did not meet his gaze. He was concentrating hard on staying upright and ignoring the pain in his chest.

'Something inside the vent infected him,' said Scipio.

'*Infected* him?' asked Garrik, incredulous.

'Turned his mind, I don't know how. But he might not be the only one.'

'If that's true…' Garrik let his words hang.

'We *must* reach the *Gladius*,' Scipio told them, 'and hope that when we do Vantor is ready for immediate take-off.'

CHAPTER ELEVEN
PYRRHIC VICTORY

CHRONUS COULD NOT deny a deep sense of self-satisfaction.

Despite the necron surprise attack, the battle was his. *Ultramar victoris!*

From here they could use the victory as a staging ground, bring in the gunships from the *Valin's Revenge*, bring in Rhino-mounted infantry and drive their assault deep into the heart of enemy territory. They would crush the necrons in their sleep, set charges around their tombs and purge this world in the name of the Emperor, reclaiming it for the Imperium.

He was not a man given to vainglory; what he did, he did for duty and honour, but these necrons were a singular foe he took pride in vanquishing.

The last of their resistance on the ice plain was fading. All of the arachnid constructs had withdrawn from the field, and the final few barges and arks were slowly being corralled by an unrelenting ring of Ultramarian steel. An android brain, however advanced, was no match for true will and human heart. And here was the evidence of that.

Both the Vindicators and Whirlwinds had removed themselves from the engagement and taken up bombardment positions again back on the ridge line. It was a needless contingency, but Chronus was wary of further rapid deployments courtesy of the necron phasic generators. With the withdrawal of the siege engines, that left the more manoeuvrable Predators and Raiders to chase down the more stubborn enemy elements, support vehicles acting as outriders.

Tesla-lightning and the verdant flare of gauss beams whipped across the battlefield, but it was desultory. A cohort of necron arks was bearing down on the *Antonius* and the other two tanks in its squadron. Chronus let them come on, pushing up to combat speed to draw them in. Over on the flank, he had the perfect answer to the necrons' aggression.

'Egnatius, bring in *Stormwarden*, *Titus* and *Venator*,' he voxed. 'Hammer them.'

An affirmation rune flashed up on Chronus's retinal lens. Satisfied, he kept up the pace and checked the tactical display.

The five Raiders had formed up and were taking the necrons on the left flank apart. Gnaeus had joined them in the *Secutor Maximus*, adding to their already formidable firepower with his Predator Destructor.

That left Chronus and Egnatius to destroy the rest.

'Vutrius,' Chronus called back to his gunner. 'Keep that turret on them.' Suppressing fire from the other two tanks in the commander's squadron, *The Vengeful* and *Hellhunter*, wrecked one of the arks and sent it ploughing into the ice.

That left two. No challenge for Egnatius.

Stormwarden was leading the charge with *Titus* and *Venator* close on the front Predator's heels. They had yet to discharge weapons. Three autocannons would make scrap of the necron vehicles.

Gauss fire hammered in on the *Antonius* and its fellow squadron members. An outriding Rhino was hit and went up explosively, showering *The Vengeful* with shrapnel.

'Egnatius,' Chronus barked down the vox, 'what are you waiting for? Engage!'

Still the necron arks came on, slipping into an advantageous position as the Predators' attack vector took them out of a forwards firing arc and presented their flanks and rear to the enemy.

One of the arks unleashed its main energy weapon. It struck the already wounded *Hellhunter* in the side, flipping the tank onto its roof where it convulsed explosively. Rolling hard, trying to manoeuvre back into a better firing position, the *Rage of Antonius* and *The Vengeful* left the sorry carcass of their destroyed squadron tank behind.

SCIPIO REACHED THE cave mouth with Largo and Garrik close behind him.

What he saw in the valley below turned his determination into a sense of grim finality. The *Gladius* was gone, doubtless consumed by an undulating swarm.

The crash site was obliterated from view, overrun by diminutive necron scarab constructs.

'There must be thousands,' said Largo, slumping against a rock.

Behind them, the din of machine activation still sounded and the verdant glow of necron revivification intensified.

'Can't go forwards, can't go back,' uttered Garrik. He checked his ammunition. 'I have two krak missiles and one fragmentation in my rack. How shall I spend them, brother-sergeant?'

Scipio drew his chainsword and planted it blade-first in the ice.

'This is our ridge now. I have just claimed it for our Chapter. As sovereign territory of Ultramar, it is our honour-bound duty to defend it. Let the necrons come. They'll find Ultramarines do not die easily.'

'They won't have long to learn that,' said Garrik, gesturing to the scarab swarm that swept towards them like a dark cloud.

From deep inside the cave mouth came the hollow cadence of mechanised feet marching in unison. The first warrior constructs had awoken.

Scipio wrenched his chainsword free and drew his bolt pistol.

'In my eyes, you are all heroes.'

Above them, the unmistakable burr of turbine engines could be heard as a very welcome shadow fell across the trio.

'Guilliman's blood...' breathed Garrik, looking up at the descending form of the *Gladius*. For a moment, it stayed suspended in the air, Vantor watching them through the repaired glacis. Then with a burst of the gunship's stabiliser jets, the Techmarine swung around to present the *Gladius*'s flank where Brakkius and an open side-hatch awaited.

Largo went first. Well harnessed in the flank gunner's seat, Brakkius caught his wrist and helped him aboard. Garrik went next, leaving Scipio for last. Brakkius grabbed his sergeant's shoulder guard as he came aboard and Vantor gunned the engines.

'You're late,' he said, betraying not a trace of humour.

'And you are very much alive, brother,' Scipio replied. 'A fact I find surprisingly pleasing.'

Brakkius clapped him on the shoulder in comradely fashion, but then added, 'Where is Brother Auris?'

Scipio shook his head.

'His duty has ended.'

Not lingering, Scipio went immediately to the on-board vox. Amplified by the gunship's superior communication systems and now free of environmental interference, he was able to open a channel to Commander Chronus. He only hoped he was not already too late.

CHRONUS WAS INCENSED. From a position of certain victory, Egnatius's defiance of orders had given the necrons a foothold back and endangered his engines into the bargain.

'Brother-sergeant,' he began down the vox-link, though he knew that something was seriously wrong. 'You will open fire on the enemy immed–'

The *Stormwarden* fired, but its heavy shell burst against the armour of *The Vengeful*. A second muzzle flash erupted from *Venator* a second later and crashed just wide of the *Antonius*.

'What in Hera's name does he think he's doing?' snapped Vutrius.

'Disengage at once,' ordered Chronus. 'Egnatius, you are targeting friendlies. I repeat, you are opening fire on your brothers!'

Still no response came from Egnatius. Chronus hastily tried the other two engines in his squadron but got no answer there, either.

'Have they gone mad?' asked Vutrius. 'Should I open fire?'

'No, not until I know what's going on. It could be targeting malfunction.' The tank commander did not sound convinced.

Titus was moving in, too, when one of the necron arks hovered in behind it and gutted it with a direct hit to its rear facing. The subsequent explosion pushed the tank into a violent roll, barrelling it into a Razorback that was smashed aside and disabled.

Two more engine kills flashed red on Chronus's tactical display.

Titus had just left itself open to attack. It was not a targeting malfunction.

The vox-link crackled, and Chronus answered it to find Sergeant Vorolanus on the other end.

'I thought the *Gladius* destroyed, brother-sergeant.'

Scipio did not waste words. '*Commander, one of your squadrons has been infiltrated by the enemy. I lost one of my squad to the same mind control.*'

'What?'

'*One of your squadrons is lost, commander. It is no longer loyal to Ultramar. I believe it to be one belonging to Sergeant Egnatius.*'

Chronus abruptly cut the feed, resigned to finding out further answers later. He urgently activated the vox-link to the entire company.

'All vehicles. Squadron Egnatius has been compromised. Engage as if enemy. All siege engines occupying the ridge, your orders are to neutralise the *Stormwarden* and *Venator*.'

Chronus severed the link, anger and denial warring in his heart. Whatever had happened to Egnatius, it obviously was not just comms malfunction. As Scipio had said, he was lost. Chronus only hoped he could stop him before he took anyone else with him.

'Commander, I do not wish to question–' Vutrius began.

'Then don't,' Chronus snapped. 'There is no other choice.'

Affirmation runes flashed up on the tactical display for *Scion of Talassar*, *Wrath of Invictus* and *The Ram*. All three had firing solutions on Squadron Egnatius.

Chronus tried one more time to raise his fellow tank commander, but Votan Egnatius was clearly no longer in control. He raised the three siege engines, and with steel in his heart gave the order.

'Execute.'

Thunder felt all the way from the ridge line resonated through the *Antonius*'s hull as multiple hits registered against the *Stormwarden* and *Venator*. Chronus briefly closed his eyes, asking his dead primarch for forgiveness. He knew the crew of both tanks, had fought with them on countless occasions. Egnatius he had trusted with his life. Two engine kills flared up on the tactical display. The *Stormwarden* and *Venator* were gone.

Crushing down his grief, Chronus was about to bring the *Rage of Antonius* about to engage their pursuers, when an actinic flash lit up a distant ridge. A second flash followed moments later towards the north, and then a third to the east.

Three more necron battle formations, comprising further heavy weapons and infantry cohorts, according to the ranged auspex.

The skimmers currently engaged by the Ultramarines began to withdraw. One of the barges was destroyed by a vengeful assault cannon burst from the *Merciless Orar* as it tried to fall back, but none of the other necron engines responded. Soon they were beyond optimum weapons range, and Chronus was disinclined to give chase.

During the ill-fated skirmish, he had lost no fewer than seven major pieces of armour and almost twice that number in support vehicles. Chronus called all the tanks to a halt. While they idled on the ice plain with their engines humming and exhausts fuming, he tried to ascertain the enemy strength.

Even a conservative estimate placed it at much greater than their own.

The phasic materialisation of all three battlegroups was several kilometres out. Without air support, it would be impossible to know the enemy's disposition, tactics and movements. If they possessed any gunships like the ones that had streaked towards Kellenport, that could alter the complexion of a second battle considerably.

Too many unknowns. Too few full-strength battle tanks. No Ultramarines vehicle had escaped unscathed. Necron phasic technology meant rapid redeployment was also a factor.

Steam rising off their battered hulls, a company of tanks patiently awaited their commander's decision.

'It serves no one if we die here this day,' Chronus muttered bitterly.

The direct approach had failed. The necrons were not as beaten as he had first believed. Rearm, redeploy, were his only options now.

'Full retreat,' Chronus uttered, his voice dark and full of reticence. 'Back to Kellenport.'

CHAPTER TWELVE
RESURRECTION

ANKH RELEASED THE mindshackle, returning cognisance to the tank commander as he burned inside his own vehicle.

Such arrogance and belief in their own pre-eminence; the Architect despised them. *Humans.* Even the thought of the word left a bitter trace in his memory engrams. He had proven their weakness, as all alien races were, ultimately, weak.

Discovery of one of the northern ice tombs had forced Ankh to escalate his schedule of reactivation. Hundreds of canoptek drones now scurried about the subterranean chambers, nurturing, restoring, revivifying, all for the glory of the necrontyr.

War hosts, thousands strong, were slowly awakening. Ankh perceived each and every one of their soulless flames igniting with activation. It was patient work, careful work, but then the Architect had already waited for aeons. What did a few more years matter?

According to his global analysis, one faction of resistance yet remained between the Sautekh Dynasty and dominance of this world. It was concentrated in the human city, the one the Undying had failed to sack during his abortive siege. With the recently resurrected war cells, Ankh had deterred further interference from the armoured crusaders and their crude war engines. Unmolested, the Architect could divert his complete attention to revivifying a legion of such magnitude as to engulf the surface city and wipe it from existence.

There would be no siege, only annihilation.

Then he could turn his ageless mind towards other concerns. The beating heart of this tomb world was stirring. A sliver of a *c'tan*. A pale simulacrum of what it had once been, but still potent in spite of that. Ankh could feel it through its necrodermis, the agitation of its essence. It would not be long now. The slave would awaken soon and then the stars themselves would quail.

IT TOOK TWO days to limp back to the city. The *Gladius* had shadowed the survivors of the tank company every step of the way, allowing Chronus to learn of the fate of Egnatius from Sergeant Vorolanus. Neither of them knew for certain what had befallen the Ultramarines that had entered that cavern; even Techmarine Vantor could offer little by way of explanation. Several had lost their lives to it, and betrayed their sworn brothers into the bargain. Chronus only hoped that was an end to this particular blight, and tried not to fathom what other horrors the necrons possessed that the Ultramarines had yet to see.

Muted celebration greeted the tank company as it rolled through Kellenport's western gate. Despite the improved fortifications, the city was still a ruin. Its walls carried the legacy of the previous siege, still breached in dozens of places. Many of the outer districts had been abandoned, allowing the Capitolis Administratum and the spaceport adjacent to it to be bolstered. Gun emplacements lined these walls, and Ultramarines manned strategic points along them to better support the failing Damnosian courage.

Chronus rode up in the *Antonius*'s cupola, Novus having recovered enough to drive. He did it not to appear the conquering hero, he was anything but that, but to see their faces for himself. Antaro Chronus prided himself on knowing the measure of a soldier by the strength of conviction he saw in his or her eyes. What he saw in the downtrodden Guardsmen and militia that circled the city gates or gathered in packs around what few monuments still stood, was defeat. These were a broken people. He did not know if it had happened during the terror raid Sergeant Vandar had apprised him of or if it had been growing ever since that first day when Damnos's lord governor had been slaughtered with his entire staff. It did not matter.

What he did know, what he had experienced first-hand, was that the necrons were a resourceful and insidious enemy. They could harness immense legions, far in excess of the Ultramarines' ability to defeat with their current strength.

After Chronus had entered the shell of the city, driven past the drum fires and the hollow ruins thronged by hollow men and women, and reached the end of the roadway, he learned of Agrippen's war council. Few strategies remained, but it seemed the veteran wanted to consider them all.

* * *

THEY GATHERED IN the Capitolis Administratum's debating chamber. It was a large, oval room that could better accommodate the Adeptus Astartes and their Dreadnought commander. It would also serve to keep the Ultramarines officers and the delicate nature of their council away from the prying eyes and ears of the populace.

'It is hard for me to admit this,' Tigurius began. 'Upon Commander Chronus's arrival, I dared to believe we could resist. But now we must all acknowledge that Damnos is lost.'

A few high-ranking Guardsmen, here to represent the natives, tried to stand a little straighter or show steel in the face of adversity, but Chronus could see the light had already died in their eyes. Tigurius had just given word to the fear they had all been living with ever since the invasion began, and made it real.

No Ultramarines officer present gainsaid him. Even Agrippen bowed his armoured form slightly at this admission of defeat.

A sergeant, Chronus recalled his name was Praxor, spoke up.

'So what recourses are left to us? We cannot abandon these people.'

Like all the wall guard, Praxor Manorian bore the scars of battle upon his armour. Evidently, he had been caught in the fighting during the now infamous terror strikes by the necron flyers.

Tigurius met the gaze of each and every warrior in the room, be they Adeptus Astartes or Guardsman.

'Evacuation is our only option now.'

'You want to abandon Damnos?' asked a tremulous Ark Guard captain who was trying to hold it together, his despair of the plan overriding his fear of the Chief Librarian.

Tigurius tried to be sympathetic. 'I want to save its people.'

'Doom has come to your world, captain,' Agrippen told him in his deep, mechanised voice. 'I am ashamed for my Chapter that we have been unable to turn back this tide, but we must now be pragmatic.'

'Evacuating the city will take time,' said Scipio, having joined the council whilst the *Gladius* was undergoing repairs. He had also been summoned for his report about his squad's encounter in the caverns at Vogenhoff and the necron forces amassing there. 'Yet the necrons are advancing with purpose and in numbers from every direction.'

'Can we stall them?' asked Praxor. 'Slow them down enough so we get the people out?'

'The *Valin's Revenge* and its frigates are at anchor in low orbit,' said Tigurius. 'Lighters from the surface have already begun to ferry the population to them, but we have had casualties.'

Since the re-emergence of the necron forces, some of their ground-to-air weaponry had resurfaced and was keeping a steady stream of gauss fire aimed at the skies above Kellenport.

'Our forces on the wall are depleted,' offered another, a bald, grizzled-looking sergeant with a face like a granite cliff. 'I should be back there now, keeping an eye on them.'

'They can endure without your presence for a short while, Sergeant Fennion,' said Tigurius. 'You were present during the attack on Infirmary Seven, were you not?'

Fennion nodded. 'It has left morale extremely low amongst the Guard cohorts, and we will be in need of them if we are to mount a significant defence. Many are still suffering the psychological after-effects of the attack.'

'And what would you deem as significant, Iulus?' asked Scipio. Evidently, the two knew each other fairly well.

'One that doesn't capitulate after the first assault. But my assessment, for what it's worth–'

'The same as everyone else's in this chamber, Sergeant Fennion,' Agrippen advised him.

Iulus Fennion nodded in appreciation. 'I do not think defence is even tenable at this point. If we can slow them down, if… then I'd suggest a series of fall-backs. We try to hold the walls and they will not hold. We draw the necrons into the city, behind several carefully engineered firebreaks, then we might retard their progress enough to make a difference.'

Agrippen activated a hololith of revolving blue light that described Kellenport in exact detail.

'This is from an orbital capture of the city,' he began. 'As you can all see, the outer defences are abandoned, leaving our forces concentrated on the walls around the Court-yard of Thor and the capitolis building in which we now debate. Our third strongpoint is the spaceport, which must be protected at all costs. Points of ingress for the necrons are the north and west gates. That is where their strength will likely be focused.'

'Your problem is not the overwhelming force the necrons will bring to bear on Kellenport.' Having listened to all good counsel thus far, Chronus finally spoke up. All eyes turned to him at the sound of his voice. 'It is the rapidity with which our enemy can deploy. Twice, I was outma-noeuvred on the ice plain. Vast forces simply teleported in, surrounded us and would have destroyed us had I not ordered the retreat.' This last part was hard for the tank commander to say, spoken as it was through clenched teeth.

'You refer to the necron phasic generators,' Tigurius replied.

'I do. We must destroy them first if we are to stand any chance of evacuating a significant amount of the population and wresting something from this disastrous campaign.'

For a few seconds no one spoke. Chronus had just said aloud what they had all been thinking. That did not mean it stung their pride any less.

'Ever since Sicarius fell, we have struggled,' he went on. No one denied it. Chronus meant no disrespect, he was merely stating facts at this point. 'So then, show me where the generators are and I'll try and buy us some time.'

Agrippen broadened the hololith's scope so it encompassed the much larger continental region around Kellenport and Damnos Prime.

'Thanks to your efforts out on the ice, commander, we have been able to track the position of three crucial phasic generators. The *Valin's* sensorium places them in these locations.'

Three nodes flashed up on the display in hazy red.

'We'll secure a drop-zone with low strafing attacks from *Gladius* and *Thunderstorm*,' Agrippen continued.

'Why not just destroy the generators in a series of bombing runs?' Praxor asked the obvious question.

Chronus answered. 'Because they'll be shielded just like their walkers and skimmers. We'll need to get in close, on the ground, penetrate their defences first.'

'Indeed,' said Agrippen. 'If you're looking for vengeance for Egnatius and the others, this is it. But choose your formations carefully, commander.'

Now Chronus smiled like the true lion of Macragge he was.

'I have just the warriors in mind.'

CHAPTER THIRTEEN
ACTS OF SABOTAGE

FABRICUS HAD ACCEPTED the field promotion with all the solemnity and humility Chronus had come to expect from the warrior. Someone needed to take Egnatius's place. Gnaeus had wholeheartedly supported his brother's elevation.

They had left Kellenport far behind and were bound for one of the phasic generators. A pair of Thunderhawk transporters ferried both the *Rage of Antonius* and *Triumph of Espandor*, as well as a Rhino transport bearing Squad Atavian. Two similar forces led by Fabricus in *The Vengeful* and Gnaeus in *Secutor Maximus* were headed for the other sites. The remnants of Egnatius's battle tanks, their crew having been cleared by Techmarine Vantor of any technological contagion, had been split up amongst the new command structure.

Ahead of all three forces were *Gladius* and *Thunderstorm*, who would scorch the earth heralding the armoured squadrons' arrival.

Three primary objectives: two to be hit simultaneously, the third, slightly more remote, to be attacked a few minutes later. Chronus had opted for the third and more difficult target, feeling it was his responsibility and risk as commander to do it.

A voice crackled over the vox inside the hold of the *Antonius*. Though the vision slits were sealed, the passage of air as their transporter cut through it at speed buffeted the sides of the Predator loudly and made the hull shudder. The effect was disconcerting for someone used to fighting all of his battles on *terra firma* with the grind of tracks, not the whipping of air, as his combat refrain.

So Chronus was a little agitated when he responded to the hail.

'Speak.'

'*We are two minutes out,*' came the voice of Scipio from *Gladius*. 'You sound perturbed, commander.'

'I'll be glad when we're on the ground, sergeant.'

'*Resistance is fairly thick around all three generators. You'll need to go in hard and fast once you hit the ground.*'

'Nothing would give me greater pleasure, Scipio. Burn me a path and we'll roll right up it and tear that generator apart.'

'*Affirmative, commander.*' Sergeant Vorolanus cut the link.

Chronus addressed his crew. 'Make all final preparations and adjust mission chronos. We disembark in under two minutes.'

'Any word on Gnaeus or Fabricus?' Vutrius asked from the gunner's seat.

'They should be engaging now. Focus on our part of the mission, brother. We'll know of its greater success as soon as we return to the city. Courage and honour.'

Chronus's crew echoed him.

Across the vox-link the transporter pilot issued a time warning. They were vectoring in on *Gladius*'s designated drop zone coordinates now.

Chronus opened the feed to the entire battlegroup.

'Make this for Egnatius, and the engines we lost,' he said.

THE THREE BATTLE tanks landed hard, tracks already whirring. They hit the fire-black earth running, spitting up clods of dirt and the accumulated slush that had somehow survived *Gladius*'s immolating missile strike.

Partially destroyed necron skeletons crunched and phased out under their treads. Chronus ignored them, heedless of the smoking ruins of skimmer-tanks and the hollowed-out remains of anti-gravitic weapon platforms. There was only one enemy weapon he was interested in as he drove at the front of the spear. It loomed before him on his retinal display, its crackling energy signature like a comet flare.

During the few hours they had spent in the city, the *Antonius*'s heavy bolter load-out had been replaced with a pair of lascannons. The full Annihilator-pattern was better suited to taking down a static emplacement. The *Triumph of Espandor* was equipped with identical armaments, while Atavian's Devastators, dubbed 'the Titan Slayers', earned their honorific thanks to their armour-busting heavy weapon configuration.

The phasic generator was immense. Riding up in the turret's cupola, Chronus regarded it with his own eyes. An extension of the necron form, it reminded him of a gigantic claw, albeit with three identical talons all cradling a jade crystal of energy at its centre. Alien sigils were embossed in gold upon the generator's base, and three clawed feet extending from it provided stability. And flickering at the periphery of the foul machine was its shield.

From fighting the walkers and skimmer barges on the ice plain, Chronus knew this defence could be overwhelmed with force. Riding in hard and fast as Sergeant Vorolanus had advised, he gave the order to do just that.

Lascannons bristling from the turrets and side sponsons of the Predators, a sustained salvo broke against the generator's shield. It endured this punishment for almost a full minute before collapsing under the strain. Vented power coils still charging, Chronus signalled Sergeant Atavian.

Disembarking in short order, the Titan Slayers unleashed their heavy weapons against the vulnerable necron machine and destroyed it.

It was swift, brutal and tactically exemplary.

Chronus allowed himself no satisfaction in the deed, however, as he recalled the Thunderhawk transporters. As the two massive drop-ships appeared in the sky above them and the magna-grapnels were descending, he reminded himself that they were merely delaying the inevitable.

'*A successful mission, commander,*' said one of the pilots by way of congratulation.

Chronus remained grim.

'We have bought them days, if that.'

Leaving the wreckage of the phasic generator behind them, they made course back to Kellenport.

CHAPTER FOURTEEN
BATTLEMENTS

STANDING SENTRY AT the walls surrounding the Courtyard of Thor, Iulus Fennion looked out at the legions marching implacably across the ice towards Kellenport.

It had been days, *days*, since the successful sabotage mission conducted by Commander Chronus and the Ultramarines armour. The destruction of the phasic generators should have crippled the necrons – it barely broke their stride, and now here they were again, a few hours from the gates.

'How many do you think are out there, Brother-Angel?'

At his own request, Iulus had taken up a position on the wall nearest the Ark Guard fighters, and dispersed his Immortals to do the same. Men needed courage at times like this. He resolved that they would find it in his example, and that of his warriors.

'More than we have shells and bullets for, Sergeant Kolpeck.'

Iulus knew, of all the Guardsmen and militia who fought on Damnos, he need not lie to this one. Falka Kolpeck had survived the initial assault, he had lived through the first siege, he had even endured when others lost their minds during the attack on Infirmary Seven. He was a hard man, as hard as the Damnos ice he used to cut with his rigging tools. It did not make him a better soldier, but it did make him tough and that was something Iulus found he could respect.

'You saw off her transport?' asked the Ultramarine, watching the distant skeletal hordes. Perversely perhaps, the storms had abated in the last few hours. Behind the drifts and whiteouts, a vast arctic landscape had emerged, and upon it legions of necrons.

Kolpeck nodded and checked the iron sights of the heavy stubber he was charged with manning.

In the wintry skies above, Arvus lighters and a host of other atmospheric craft comprised a steady stream of traffic coming from the spaceport. Thousands had been evacuated already, but there had been losses in the hundreds too. Verdant gauss fire from the distant necron cannons, entrenched in the northern wastes, maintained a constant barrage that gave the Damnos night the illusion of pyrotechnics on Founding Day. It was, of course, much deadlier than that and not remotely celebratory.

Every ship sent from the port, its gunwales brimming with refugees, was directed on an easterly course first. They went low to the ground, beneath the lattice of enemy fire, until rising and striking for the *Valin's Revenge* or one of its flotilla.

Iulus had heard from Vandar on the northern gate that an entire graveyard of destroyed vessels now languished out in those wastes. It was a cynical, if necessary, measure. The last thing the fragile courage of the Damnosian soldiery needed was falling skies.

'She did not wake before her medi-casket was taken aboard,' Kolpeck offered, 'but I believe she knew I was there.'

Iulus gave the facial equivalent of a shrug. He had seen how Kolpeck had been willing to give his life to protect this woman. It was a form of brotherhood, he supposed. He chose not to disabuse him of the notion that she would survive the journey to the *Valin's Revenge*, or warn him that she was most likely to be in a coma forever and the chances of them ever being reunited were remote in the extreme. That would dishonour this man, and Iulus had no desire to do that when he had earned so much more for his life.

'You could have joined her,' said the Ultramarine, turning to look at the ex-rig-hand, 'but you chose to remain.'

'How is it any different to your brothers staying behind for us?'

Iulus sniffed, incredulous. 'We are Adeptus Astartes, much hardier than mortal men. It is our duty. Our honour.'

Kolpeck met his gaze, but had to crane his neck. 'The oaths I have taken, the ones I swore to Jynn as she lay in her coma, are not so different. It is my world. I want to fight for it, even if it means my death.' He turned back to continue his weapons check.

Iulus regarded him silently for a few more seconds, before deciding he had no answer to that. But as he returned to watch the metallic horde coming down on Kellenport, he vowed to do everything in his power to save this man. To Iulus's mind, he had earned that much.

* * *

ENGINES IDLING NOISILY, Chronus stood up in the *Rage of Antonius*'s cupola and watched the necrons advancing. He suspected a great many, mortal and superhuman, were doing the same.

His battle tanks were assembled in three squadrons. The first, comprising all the siege engines, was ringed around the space port and would provide suppressing bombardment fire as soon as the outer walls were deemed no longer defensible; the second, which was made up of Predators and Land Raiders commanded by Gnaeus, assembled behind the north gate; that left the third with Chronus himself at the west gate.

There were enough breaches in the outer walls to provide adequate apertures for unleashing their long-range guns. Once that was no longer practical, their orders were to withdraw into the warren of streets and provide armoured bottlenecks to slow the necrons down and give their infantry time to effect an ordered retreat.

Of course, that was assuming the enemy could penetrate the indomitable guard of Agrippen. The Ancient had taken position at the western gate and looked in no mood to relinquish it.

Chronus knew it was partly for show. An astute strategy in terms of human psychology. By the tank commander's calculation, they were near reduced to half-strength, which meant just over fifty Ultramarines give or take pilots, crewmen and a few attached specialists. Roughly ten times that number were left in the Damnosian Ark Guard, and perhaps a further three hundred in conscripted militia. Kellenport was not a huge city by any standard, and with its outer districts abandoned, it shrank further still, but the Imperial forces were paltry in number and inhabited a virtual ghost town. The necrons were legions strong, tens of thousands, and with an abundance of esoteric heavy weaponry at their disposal.

Chronus was under no illusions about the outcome of this fight.

Fabricus pulled up alongside in *The Vengeful*, sitting up in the cupola like his commander.

'Come to wish me well for the battle ahead, Sergeant Fabricus? I do believe they may write stories about this one. No doubt our exploits in destroying those phasic generators are already being immortalised,' said Chronus, with more than a hint of irony. 'I expect we will have thrown several necron war cells into defeat and nearly single-handedly turned the fates of this war by the time the ink is dry on its parchment. Stories do seldom reflect the truth, don't you find?'

'I had come to gauge your thoughts before battle, commander, but can hear they are only bitter and lacking in the inspiration I sought.'

Chronus gave Fabricus a sideways glance. He had yet to don his helmet, and left it sitting on the Predator's roof. By the standard of most sergeants, Fabricus was youthful and bereft of scars. He also had a shock of close-cropped blond hair, which meant he must be young, but there was maturity in his eyes, born of hard experience.

'I make you sergeant and all of a sudden you are questioning my demeanour.'

Fabricus was instantly contrite. 'I meant no offence, commander–'

'Stop, please.' Chronus held up his hand. 'A poor attempt at levity. I apologise. But you're right,' he added. 'I am bitter. I don't like to lose and although we are standing defiant at Kellenport's gates, I cannot shake the feeling that we are already beaten.'

'So what would your counsel be then, commander?'

It was a fair question, one which Chronus had already asked himself and subsequently answered.

'We make them pay for their victory as painfully as we can.'

HUNKERED DOWN AMONGST the ruins by the north gate, Scipio closely observed a soulless robotic horde through his scopes.

Vast phalanxes of infantry, flanked by skimmers and walkers, descended on the city from its two gated aspects. Unlike a living foe, they did not shout war cries or even stare in that grim, determined fashion that Scipio had seen some warriors affect. It was cold, methodical, and calculated in every way. Necron strategy was a logic engine, a long and dispassionate equation that factored in nothing of courage or individual heroism. The only human facility they had ever accounted for was fear, and in that they were consummate masters.

The terrified faces of the Damnosian soldiery surrounding him attested to that fact. Scipio's Tactical squad, the Thunderbolts, had been reunited for this last defence. There were some exceptions. Auris was dead and Brakkius had become an unlikely gunner for Vantor aboard *Gladius*. The gunship had used most of its ordnance payload by now and had been pressed into service, like all atmospheric craft, ferrying citizens from the surface to the ships at low anchor above.

Eighteen runs that ship had made so far. It had survived every one without a scratch.

Say what you will about the Techmarine, thought Scipio, *but he is a determined and excellent pilot.* He suspected Brakki-us's marksmanship might have something to do with the Thunderhawk's Throne-blessed existence, too.

A flash of crackling lightning and the whip of turbulent storm winds manifested near Scipio's position, causing some of the Guardsmen to turn and aim their guns fearfully. When they saw the figure that stepped from the psychic tempest, they had to resist the urge to kneel instead.

Scipio contented himself with a shallow bow.

'My lord.'

'It does our charges good to see that we still possess power, Sergeant Vorolanus,' uttered Tigurius. He never just spoke, the Chief Librarian; he *declared*, and in this kind of mood he did so always in a resonant voice, redolent of his psychic might.

Tigurius was staring out into the icy void, but his eyes seemed far away, as if seeing far more than any mortal or Space Marine standing guard at that wall ever could. His staff, a ram-horned stave of master artifice, he clutched in one hand, sending a ripple of eldritch energy down the shaft.

'You are most welcome at the wall, my lord.'

'I am not merely on the wall, Sergeant Vorolanus. I am in all places, at once.' He gestured with his staff. 'Do you want to know what I have seen in the ether?'

'If it is our demise, then no, my lord, I do not.'

Tigurius turned slowly, the trace of a smile playing on his inscrutable face. They had fought together on the Thanatos Hills, but he was deep into the warp in that moment, all of his attention bent towards his powers and unerring prescience. He barely seemed to recognise the sergeant.

Even for a Space Marine as veteran as Scipio, it was

unnerving. To know such a being was by your side in any fight was ultimately galvanising, however, and so here Tigurius was.

'You are a curious one, Scipio Vorolanus,' he uttered. 'I see greatness in you, a potential you might yet reach, or die in agony in the attempt.'

'A sobering thought,' Scipio replied, dryly.

The Chief Librarian lowered his voice. 'Our paths here on Damnos are myriad, but none of them leads to victory. Not yet, not in this future.'

He turned away again, and Scipio was left to wonder at his meaning.

A shout ran out from one of the few watchtowers that were still standing, forcing the sergeant's attention onto the immediate present.

The distant hills rumbled and flashed, heralding the inception of the necrons' preliminary bombardment.

The final siege of Kellenport had begun.

CHAPTER FIFTEEN
DEFIANCE

GAUSS FIRE CRACKLED across the ice plain in an unending storm. It tainted the oil-black night, heating the air and turning it an ugly verdant green. It ripped apart the meagre defences, tore up the gun emplacements and rendered men to ash. It thundered from skimmer-tanks, implacable warrior-cohorts and the distant, pyramidal silhouettes of the largest terror weapons in the enemy arsenal. A green haze of atomisation hung over the ruins in the wake of rapid and collective particle fusion.

It reminded Scipio of a funeral shroud, and the corpse beneath it was Kellenport and all its desperate citizens.

Delivering valiant if mostly ineffective return fire, the defenders at the north wall had held for just under an hour. That staunch resistance had ended when the gatehouse and one of its watchtowers had collapsed into rubble, leaving a vast breach into which hordes of robotic infantry were now marching.

The skeletal faces of the necrons were pitiless as they emerged through the gloom. Their advance was slow and inexorable, preceded by a constant fusillade from their gauss rifles.

As soon as the wall came down, Scipio gave the order to fall back. He saw Vandar do the same from farther up the battlements. His helmet vox crackled with the voices of Solinus and Octavian, also sounding the retreat. He had no line of sight on his fellow sergeants, the defence being stretched and necessarily ragged, but knew they would be heading deeper into the city.

Somewhere behind him the assault squads of Ixion and Strabo were already redeploying. Across the length and breadth of the city, Devastators would be occupying their predetermined strongpoints from which they could launch support fire. As he retreated with the others – the remnants of three Ark Guard formations, a band of militia and his own Thunderbolts – Scipio heard the heavy guns give voice.

Out beyond the walls, on the crowded tundra past the city's outer defences, came a succession of missile detonations and the after-flare of a plasma ignition. Chugging heavy bolters and the hard-whine of lascannons kept up a steady chorus in the wake of these grander beats of war. And yet Scipio knew it was barely a scratch. There would be no holding here. The only way was back.

Kellenport's streets were warrens, although many of them had been flattened by clustered enemy bombardments and were little more than blackened ruins now. Guerrilla fighting favoured the smaller, native force. It would slow the necrons down and thus give more time for the civilians to evacuate.

'Fall back!' he cried, vox-amplifying his words through

his helmet. 'Retreat to the commercia-districts. Quickly and in good order.'

Hit by a stray gauss beam, an old refinery shed combusted explosively. Guardsmen and Ultramarines too close to the blast were thrown skywards. Revealed in the sudden burst of flame Scipio thought he saw Praxor, sword raised, rallying his troops as they fell back to another part of the city. The vista died as quickly as it was born. Scipio did not linger, and signalled his own forces to pull back.

Some of the Guardsmen fled, militia too. They ran blindly, and without the support of their comrades would die swiftly. Some were even cut down during the initial act of flight. But the majority did as ordered, emboldened by the presence of the Ultramarines or simply too afraid to run. Either was fine by Scipio; in these final hours, he had learned to be pragmatic.

A single round from his outstretched bolt pistol took a necron in the skull, erasing its rictus grin with satisfying lethality. A second three-round burst shredded two others. By now the combined las and bolter fire of the retreating Guardsmen and Ultramarines had joined his, impeding the necrons' efforts to overwhelm their position quickly.

From the left flank, rolling across a largely uncluttered plaza that was pockmarked with shell holes, a battle tank rumbled into view. It bucked on its tracks, its autocannon chewing a hole in the necron ranks before its heavy bolters poured on further punishment.

Those few crucial seconds gave Scipio and his men a chance to retreat. He was about to signal the driver his gratitude when the immense shadow of a monolith fell across them. The Predator's turret was still turning when the floating necron obelisk unleashed an arc of power from the energy crystal glowing feverishly at the pyramid's apex. The blast uncoiled, tearing open the Predator's frontal armour and gutting it. The fuel tanks went up momentarily, bathing the ruined walls and their fleeing defenders in more reflected fire.

One of Tirian's men, Scipio could not tell which, had crouched in the lee of a shattered gun emplacement and released a missile from his launcher. The incendiary exploded harmlessly against the monolith's shielding, a bloom of displaced energy like water flashing on oil. Before the Devastator had time to load another, a gauss salvo reduced him to a ruin of smoking armour.

Scipio muttered an oath for the warrior's passing, and urged his own troops back.

More tanks were moving in to avenge the destruction of the Predator. Three lascannon bursts lit up the dark. One even penetrated the monolith's armour, but barely slowed it. They were priming for a second shot when the vast obelisk began to move, crashing down half-ruined wall sections as it simply pushed through them.

Falling debris claimed several militiamen unwise enough to seek refuge behind the stunted remains of the walls, but their death cries barely registered in the chaos.

The tanks fired again, but still the monolith endured. It ripped the treads from one vehicle with a wicked gauss arc. It tore the turret off a second, leaving a smouldering crater in the metal and the hull. Its commander emerged from the flaming crevice, bolt pistol firing. It was more out of defiance than a belief that he could actually stop this thing.

'All weapons,' shouted Scipio, out of a desire to go down fighting when he realised they could not escape the monolith. 'Fire at will!'

Bolter shells and las-beams roared up at the vast floating edifice, mere insect stings against a hide of alien metal. There would be no stopping it, and Scipio began reciting his final litanies, until he saw the lightning storm.

A figure hung within it, suspended several metres from the ground. His body shimmered with coruscation as he sent an arc of bolts hammering into the ground. The necrons pushing for the breach jerked and spasmed in the lightning storm, each jag leaping from one to another until more than a score were smitten into ruin.

Muttering psychic canticles and arcane rites known only by the Librarius, Tigurius hurled a fork of azure power against the monolith. The bolt split against its flank, tearing back the plates of armour and exposing the circuitry within. Chained lightning followed, rippling from the psyker's brow and tearing off a side bank of gauss flayers.

Its apex crystal flaring in sympathetic anger, the monolith released an energy lash, but Tigurius threw up a kine-shield and bore the blast against it. The psyker staggered, his armour scorched in the violent throes of the particle whip's dispersion, but not yet finished.

Tracing the sigils of his order in the air before him, Tigurius fashioned a vortex in the very fabric of reality, ripping open a passage to the warp in the monolith's very midst. Howling, ethereal winds tore at the necron war engine. Potent energies of unmaking cascaded through it. The obelisk endured for a few moments before crumpling in on itself as the destructive fury of a star's death was ignited in its midst and then faded like a flare of solar wind.

Tigurius resealed the breach in reality. The vortex had left a gaping hole in its wake and an empty crater in the vast necron ranks. The reprieve would be brief. More were coming, undaunted by the fate of the others.

The surviving battle tanks pushed on into the gap in the wall, allowing Scipio and his men to continue their withdrawal.

'Do you hold here?' Tigurius asked him as he returned to the ground. He looked tired, but the fury of a psychic storm still raged in his eyes.

Scipio shook his head. 'We make for the streets. These walls are lost.'

'Then go quickly,' the Librarian replied before stepping back to summon a gateway of light. He was gone in an eye blink, manifesting in some other part of the city where his supreme prescience told him he was needed.

'Back, back,' Scipio urged his men, as the battle tanks sitting in the breach began to fire. They could not hold it for long and would soon need to retreat, too. The city streets beckoned, as well as the prospect of bitter, close-quarter fighting.

THE WALLS AROUND the western gate were barely standing, yet one warrior had not moved from his post.

Chronus had not known Agrippen as he was before being entombed, but if his flesh-and-blood predecessor was anything like the war machine that now stood sentinel in the Courtyard of Thor, the tank commander suspected he would have been a stubborn bastard.

Necrons littered the ground before the mighty Dreadnought, their wreckage unable to phase out fast enough before Agrippen added to the ruination surrounding him. Nothing could fell him, although his armour was rent and torn by dozens of minor wounds. A burst from his plasma cannon gouged a hole in the tight ranks of automatons, before the exhaust vents spiked to cool the weapon down again. There was no respite for the enemy, though, as Agrippen laid about him with his power fist. Chronus saw one necron, armed with claws and draped in a grisly hide of human flesh, seized and crushed by the Dreadnought's massive fist. Agrippen then used the broken robotic corpse to club another, before pulverising a third beneath his foot.

With a hiss of vented pressure and a low-energy hum, the plasma cannon was fire-ready again. The resulting bolt vaporised an arachnid walker shouldering through the mass to reach the gate. More followed, acting as vanguard for a squadron of arks that trailed close behind them.

Chronus opened up the vox to *Reckoner* and *Triumph of Espandor*, directing the Predators' fire at the more distant arks through gaps in the withered Kellenport defences. He then issued a string of pinpoint coordinates to the Whirlwinds and more advance-positioned Vindicators. A hail of ordnance from the vicinity of the space port and the surrounding region descended a few seconds later, engulfing the walkers and a sizeable portion of necron infantry.

The order to fall back from the walls had been given, so the tanks had moved up in accordance with that to provide much needed covering fire. According to his retinal display and the tactical feed scrolling across one of the lenses, all Ultramarines sergeants who still lived had made an effective withdrawal into the streets.

Chronus ordered the siege tanks back into their defensive positions and told his two commanders to do the same with their engines. He would follow in short order. There was but one matter to attend to first.

'Ancient,' said Chronus over the vox. 'We are falling back.'

'*Then go with Guilliman, Antaro,*' Agrippen replied, not for a moment breaking his destructive rhythm. '*I shall hold the line here.*'

'None shall pass, Ancient,' said Chronus, the guns of his battle tanks both close and distant thundering in his ears, despite his battle-helm.

'*None shall pass. Courage and honour.*'

'Yours has been an example to us all.' It was a bittersweet moment, for Chronus knew the sacrifice Agrippen was making to allow his brothers a chance at escape. Thumping the roof of the *Antonius*, Chronus signalled the retreat.

THE STREETS WERE clogged with bodies and rubble. Most of the necron skimmers had reportedly been diverted to attack the Ultramarines tank divisions, their unarmoured frames and much-reduced manoeuvrability making them too vulnerable in the close confines of Kellenport's warren of roads and avenues. Instead, the enemy deployed their ground troops in force: roving packs of flesh-cowled horrors, hulking heavy infantry and the ubiquitous raiders.

Though Falka had no vox like Sergeant Iulus Fennion, no means of keeping apprised of the greater warfront, he had discerned that the walls had taken severe punishment across the entire city and would likely not last much longer. They had abandoned their post, him and the few Guard and militia that remained, on the orders of Sergeant Fennion and his men.

They retreated in phases, hunkering down in what scraps of cover they could find before unleashing suppressing fire, rushing to the next scraps and then doing it all over again.

Fire. Run. Hide.

Then repeat.

During the last hour or so, it had become his mantra.

For the moment at least, Falka, sixteen other men and a battle-brother called Venkelius were taking cover as Iulus and another group raked the end of the alleyway with las- and bolt-shells. He saw one Ultramarine step out into the street and release a plume of fire from his flamer. It roared across the ground like some serpent of old myth, devouring the skin-wearing necrons scuttling into its path.

Several made it through, still burning, but the others brought them down with a brutal salvo.

Iulus waved them on, urging, 'Retreat in good order!'

Venkelius filtered the Guardsmen and militia in single fire, whilst Falka did what he had done for the last hour. Head down, he ran. He kept his lascarbine close to his body, just as he had been shown. It was not his original weapon. When his power pack had run dry, he had taken a fully charged replacement gun from one of the dead. He could not bring the man's face to mind and was surprised at how much that bothered him, even as he was struggling to survive the chaos of the streets.

As far as Falka could tell from the snatched pieces of vox-communication between Sergeant Fennion and his warriors, they were not the only ones. He got the impression the Ultramarines were stretched across the length of Kellenport, dispersed amongst the few Guard and militia regiments that were alive and holding their nerve. On more than one occasion, Iulus had tried and failed to reach one of his fellow sergeants. Falka took this to be a bad sign, but said nothing and kept his eyes down when confronted with the wrathful-looking Space Marines protecting them.

Death was part of duty, Falka had learned that about the Ultramarines from Iulus, but this was tantamount to slaughter.

As if to emphasise the fact, gauss fire from the necrons following up their skin-clad comrades fizzed and crackled in the tight alleyway. An Ark Guard trooper who had run ahead of the line and caught up to Falka was spun, his innards terminally flayed away. Falka did not see him fall; to look back now would mean death. Another did, though, and barrelled into the ex-rig-hand, recoiling in horror from the dead man's extremely visceral demise. He took Falka off his feet, and sent him tumbling to the ground. Falka's last sight was of Sergeant Fennion, putting up a hand and rushing towards him.

Something hot lashed his face and for a moment he thought he had been struck, but it was the fleeing trooper's blood as a gauss beam eviscerated him and pasted his remains across everything in close proximity, including Falka.

He got to his knees, dimly aware of the men screaming around him and the Space Marines urgently shouting in front and behind. He heard the necrons too, the cold metallic sound of their footfalls, the crackling burr of their gauss weapons re-powering.

Out the corner of his eye, as he broke into a shambling run, Falka saw Venkelius shoot one necron at close range, thrusting the muzzle of his borrowed bolter into the creature's midriff and pulling the trigger. It broke apart, its soulless existence ended by the Ultramarine's fury, but more were coming.

As the telltale whine of a gauss flayer discharge made the hair on the back of Falka's neck prickle, Iulus suddenly arrived out of the shadows and was putting his armoured body in harm's way. The beam seared him, raking his plastron and left shoulder guard.

Thrown into cover, Falka cried out just before he hit the ground, 'Brother-Angel!'

Iulus staggered, almost to one knee, but cracked off a three-round burst that destroyed his attacker. Venkelius hurried by a splitsecond later and hauled his sergeant from the path of further return fire. The entire alleyway was stitched with it, an unrelenting swathe of viridian gauss beams from rifles and the heavier cannons wielded by the hulking necron elite.

Venkelius and Aristaeus, the one who had stepped out with the flamer, were replying in kind, but the firestorm levelled against them was fearsome and they barely got off more than a shot each.

Gasping in pain, Iulus slumped to his haunches and they hunkered down behind an empty ore silo. It was reinforced adamantium with a ceramite over-layer, so Falka knew it could take a battering. But it would not last indefinitely.

'How far?' asked Iulus, rasping as he removed and dis-carded his battle-helm. It was wrecked to all hell, and without its functioning systems impeded his breathing. He wore a rebreather underneath it, but tore this away too as he took a gulp of air.

'Not gakking far enough,' Falka replied. He scowled, try-ing to gauge the distance from their position to the necrons and then the end of the street. 'Thirty-three metres for them to advance, twenty-six for us to run.'

Iulus sagged a little further, then checked the ammo gauge of his bolt pistol. His expression suggested what he had seen was not welcome news.

'Sorry, Sergeant Kolpeck. I said I'd save you...' he breathed, making an abortive effort to struggle to his feet with Falka's help.

'I'm not a sergeant, Brother-Angel, and you already did save my life. More than once. Our debt is paid.'

'It was never to you that I was indebted, Kolpeck.'

The necrons were closing, a firing line of raiders as a dogged vanguard with a rear echelon of heavier elites behind them.

Falka closed his eyes and thought of Jynn, glad that she had made it off-world. He hoped she would find the strength she needed to rebuild her life and begin again, just as all the refugees of Damnos would have to.

Venkelius ducked back into cover to make a quick report.

'At least thirty raiders and half as many in immortals, brother-sergeant. And I saw reinforcements en route, also.'

'We are the Immortals, brother,' Iulus told him. 'Never forget that, even if that honorific is about to be sorely tested.'

Venkelius nodded.

'What about the others?' asked Iulus, inquiring about the rest of the squad and the staggered Second Company.

'Seems long-range is down in this district. We have no way of knowing.'

Iulus snorted ruefully. 'Let's hope they're doing better than us, eh? Are you ready to die on your feet with a bolter in your hands, Venkelius?'

'I have prayed for this day to be so glorious, brother-sergeant.'

Iulus angled his head towards the other Ultramarine, who had exhausted his flamer's ammunition and was down to his sidearm. 'And you, Aristaeus?'

'Venkelius and I are of the same mind, brother-sergeant.'

They helped the injured sergeant to his feet, with Falka's aid. Intense gauss fire reflected on the stern-faced

Guardsmen and militia who remained as they contemplated their almost certain, imminent deaths.

'You are all heroes of Damnos,' said Iulus as he drew his chainsword and set it growling. 'Show me why, one last time.'

But the charge into death never happened. The left flanking wall collapsed instead, a half-dozen necrons crushed beneath it and the emergent bulk of *Merciless Orar* and *The Vengeful*. Their names were daubed on their battle-scarred hulls, but Falka scarcely had time to read them as the tanks turned and punitively hammered the mechanoid foot soldiers thronging the alleyway. It took eight seconds of sustained fire before the necron ranks had been thinned enough to earn a brief respite for the survivors.

With the smaller *The Vengeful* maintaining a sentry position in the middle of the broken alleyway, the imposing form of *Merciless Orar* turned about and lowered its embarkation ramp. An Ultramarine emerged from its roof hatch and beckoned them inside.

Iulus stepped forwards. 'What news from the wall?'

'Completely overrun, barring the western gate where last I heard the Ancient was holding firm,' said the tanker.

'And the streets?'

'According to the Thunderhawks, a fresh necron offensive is moving in. Much larger than this last one. Streets are being abandoned. We're pulling back, all the way to the space port. Final evacuation.'

Iulus nodded, and ordered all of them aboard.

Falka stalled as the shadow of the immense battle tank fell upon him.

'It's just a Land Raider, Kolpeck,' Iulus assured him. 'I am sorry for your world, but it's beyond saving now. But you are not. Now get aboard.'

THE RAGE OF ANTONIUS was close to shutdown. Warning sirens screamed inside the hull, accompanied by flashing crimson icons across every console. Despite exploiting the natural cover and giving a good account of themselves against the necrons, the data feed rolling across Chronus's retinal lens display told him that the battering they had taken was close to reaching the venerable battle tank's limit.

'Just a little more, old friend…' he muttered, having already rerouted power and jerry-rigged a half-dozen battlefield 'fixes' to keep the Predator moving and its weapon systems functional. Reports from the *Triumph of Espandor* suggested it was also on the brink of expiry, and they had lost *Reckoner* a short while back when three heat beams had finally transfixed it and resulted in the engine's catastrophic failure.

The ball of fire it had made was still etched onto the back of Chronus's eyelids; his roar of grief and defiance still echoed in his mind. *Reckoner* was gone, but others yet lived.

'Gnaeus, are you still with us?' He had opened vox and was trying to contact his other commanders.

'*Taking heavy fire, commander,*' Gnaeus replied. Chronus could hear it on the vox-link, the ugly shriek of necron weaponry. '*Everyone is falling back. The walls are gone… so too the streets. Fabricus is non-contactable. Lord Tigurius has issued orders for final evacuation.*'

'Confirmed,' said Chronus, having received the same orders.

Fabricus was likely dead, along with his squadrons. Nothing could be done about that now. Nor was there any way to substantiate that belief either.

'*I will reconnoitre with you if you ask it of me, commander.*'

'Get your men out, Gnaeus. Follow Tigurius's orders. It's over, brother. The *Antonius* and I will try and hold the west avenue as long as we can. I want to keep an eye on Agrippen before the end.'

Gnaeus paused, as if processing.

'*I'll see you on the* Valin's Revenge *then, sir.*'

'Aye, Guilliman willing, you may indeed.'

Chronus ended the conversation, then went on to order the *Triumph of Espandor* back.

Everyone was leaving, except for Agrippen.

The Dreadnought had been pegged back to the centre of the Courtyard of Thor, but fought just as fiercely.

Necrons were teeming through the gaps in the western wall now. Chronus fired sporadic bursts into the melee from a distance, but it was like shooting at a dirty, silver ocean.

'*We have power for another four salvos, five at a push,*' his gunner's voice came through the vox.

'Then push, Vutrius. I don't want Agrippen to be alone if we can help it.'

Through his magnoculars, Chronus watched as the Dreadnought continued to rip the necrons apart. They were crawling over him now as he thrashed at them and crushed their bodies as if they were ants, but he was slowly being overwhelmed. His plasma cannon was destroyed and sparks flashed angrily from his damaged servos and machinery.

Chronus knew he could not stay much longer. More enemy contacts were moving in via phasic insertion and would be upon them soon. He had to think of his crew.

The fifth lascannon burst sounded, the beams hazing through dust-choked air and spearing a clutch of the mechanoids advancing into the courtyard. They paid the *Antonius* no heed, their attack protocols slaved entirely to the destruction of the Dreadnought.

Lowering his scopes, Chronus bade a final farewell to Agrippen and then called down to his driver.

'Novus, get us out of here.'

As they began to reverse, Chronus witnessed the huge form of a necron monolith materialise in the courtyard.

'Bring those cannons back on line!' he bellowed down to Vutrius.

'*I cannot, commander. Our power coils are spent… Worse than spent, they are burned.*'

The data feed confirmed it – all main weapon systems were non-functional.

'Hera damn it!'

The monolith's anterior gauss array unleashed a concentrated salvo into the Ancient.

When it failed to bring Agrippen down, he stepped forwards and punched through the war machine's armour with his fist. The monolith shuddered, viridian lightning coursing over its ruptured shell as it suffered an unexpected but catastrophic malfunction. The resulting explosion, hot and verdant, forced Chronus to look away.

When he looked back, Agrippen was still standing but near the end of his strength.

THROUGH THE MERCILESS *Orar*'s vision slits, Falka saw Ultramarines fighting and dying in Kellenport's battle-choked streets.

Every metre, the Land Raider's guns punished the necrons with deadly shellfire. A whirring cannon mounted on its front chewed through debris and mechanoid alike, whilst its side guns kept up a steady rate of burst fire.

Falka and those aboard the *Merciless Orar's* troop hold fired out from the slits too, las and bolter adding to the tank's destruction. It felt good to fight alongside the Space Marines, to not be so afraid when riding in the belly of this metal beast. That determination and resolve had spread to the other Guard and militia too. They fought with their pride, their vengeance and it made Falka's heart soar to be a part of it.

A pair of necron walkers scuttled into view from behind the smoking remains of a battle tank they had just destroyed. Falka's sense of invulnerability wavered as he saw the walkers about to turn their heat rays on the *Merciless Orar*. They were intercepted by an arcane-looking figure, lightning cascading from his brow and eldritch words upon his lips that Falka did not understand. But he did not need to know their meaning to realise they were words of power.

The Librarian almost moved faster than sight, blurring around the clumsy attacks of the walkers as they reacted to the threat and tried to neutralise it. With phenomenal strength, he cut one walker in half before lifting the other off the ground with what seemed the merest thought, and casting it to ruin against the side of a silo.

'Who was that?' Falka heard one awe-filled Guardsman ask.

'Lord Tigurius,' Iulus replied.

The *Merciless Orar* was rumbling on as a squad of Ultramarines joined Tigurius in the street and went to engage a necron infantry force that had just phased in.

Though Falka tried to see as much as he could through the vision slit, the warriors were soon lost from view and he did not get to witness how the fight would end.

* * *

It was the first time Scipio and the Thunderbolts had been reunited with Tigurius since that first defence at the wall. During that time, he had seen the Librarian rip a monolith apart and lay waste to half a necron phalanx with the power of his mind. Potent as he was on the Thanatos Hills, this was something else entirely.

Scipio was not ashamed to admit to himself that he was intimidated as the awesome figure of the Librarian returned to their midst again.

'The battle's over,' said Tigurius, unleashing a storm of lightning at the necrons trying to force their way through the rubble-strewn streets at them. A flurry of gauss fire answered. Drained from his exertions, Tigurius's psychic shield was a little slow to manifest and he cried out, falling to one knee, as several beams struck him and went through his armour.

The Thunderbolts moved in ahead of him, raking the necron survivors with bolter fire and cleansing the street of enemies for a precious few seconds.

Scipio leaned down to help Tigurius to his feet and saw the Librarian's eyes were aglow with power. He spoke in a voice like prophecy as his unerring prescience stared out into the ether.

'We cannot stay. We will be overrun. The sun will rise again for one last time over Damnos, igniting all with its fury.'

It had been dark for weeks, some symptom of the necrons' mass awakening or simply a result of the season, Scipio had no idea. But looking up into the eternal night, he wondered how the dawn would ever rise again for Damnos.

There was no time to consider further. A second and third phalanx had moved into the street Scipio's men had just cleared. With a flash of phasic energy, a vast slab-sided monolith materialised behind them. More necrons were emerging through a portal that warped and cracked within its dark armour plating.

'If you have any power remaining, my lord, now would be the time,' said Scipio.

Tigurius smiled. 'I have a little…'

As the Thunderbolts prepared for a last stand, the Librarian threw up his arms and uttered a final incantation. In a split second, Tigurius was gone, taking Scipio and all of his men with him.

THE SKY OVER the spaceport was threaded with gauss fire.

Realising the interlopers were attempting to escape, the necrons had brought all of their siege cannons into the city itself and were now strafing the heavens.

Entire flotillas of ships, Thunderhawks and Arvus lighters, soared desperately into the deadly beams as the last defenders of Damnos finally accepted defeat and fled.

Chronus was amongst the last.

After taking more punishment than any battle tank had a right to endure, the *Rage of Antonius* had shut down a quarter of a kilometre from the space port. Its saviour appeared out of the night, screaming down towards the tank commander on its turbine engines. Two other Thunderhawks alongside it, *Gladius* and *Thunderstorm*, peeled off from their flying formation in the direction of the space port itself.

The familiar sight of magna-grapnels came down out of the darkness, took hold and began hauling the Predator into the transporter's waiting vehicle clamps. Then they were aloft, engines blazing again.

Despite his better judgement, Chronus cranked open the

side hatch and looked out in the direction of the Court-yard of Thor.

Far below him, diminishing as the Thunderhawk rose up, he saw Agrippen.

Debris was hitting the roof of the transporter, Chronus could hear and feel it resonating through the dormant shell of the *Antonius*. It was from other vessels, torn down by enemy flak fire. Soon they would be headed into that maelstrom and Hera help them.

Agrippen was far from these concerns, though. He fought gloriously, an end worthy of the great Dreadnought. Necrons swarmed the Courtyard of Thor, their broken remains lying thick around Agrippen's feet. He could no longer move, only swing with his power fist. Still he refused to fall, and for a moment Chronus dared believe he could somehow prevail.

When it came, the end was swift.

His armoured frame already split, oozing blood and oil, Agrippen staggered at last. Thick fumes were spewing from his reactor, suggesting an imminent meltdown. A cascade of beams erupted from the shadows at the edge of the courtyard, ripping through the thronging necrons to strike the Ancient.

Chronus was reminded of a beast of myth, the great *drakon* or *khimeraera*, pierced by a dozen lances as its hunters finally brought it down.

Agrippen stood transfixed for a few moments, his last breaths devoted to his Chapter and his brothers, before his reactor overloaded and took most of the courtyard and the necrons around him with it.

FALKA HAD TO turn away as the light blazed through the vision ports of the gunship they were riding in. He caught the impression of an immense and terrible fire raging through Kellenport, one much too bright and fierce for him to watch. His gaze went to the Ultramarines instead. There were just under ten of them in the hold and all were staring out at the blaze engulfing his city.

One of them even stood by the open side-hatch of the gunship, letting in the light and the distant reek of flame.

Someone had died. It was ash Falka could smell on the hot, whipping breeze. Ash, and retribution.

STANDING IN THE hold of the *Gladius*, Scipio watched as the sun rose for one last time over Damnos, banishing the perpetual night. It was a firestorm that emanated from the Courtyard of Thor, bright, beautiful and fierce. It obliterated hundreds of necrons. The resultant shock wave warmed the air with atomic heat and buffeted the ships aloft upon it, and it tore the enemy siege guns apart. Rolling outwards in a vast trembling wave, it immolated everything in its path.

Vantor's voice crackled through the hold's vox.

'Rough skies ahead, Sergeant Vorolanus.'

'Agrippen has shown us the way, brother,' Scipio replied.

Above them, the lattice of gauss beams promising certain destruction flickered and broke apart, until only a few sporadic salvos cut into the night.

As they prepared for atmospheric entry, Scipio closed the side hatch and looked around the hold.

Together with those that had escaped aboard the *Thunderstorm*, there were barely four squads of Ultramarines and half that in Damnosian Guard and militia that had escaped. Thousands of refugees had made it aboard the *Valin's Revenge* and her frigates. But it was small recompense for the millions who had lost their lives.

He met the gaze of Iulus, who was wounded and slumped against a bulkhead. A thick-set, bearded man sat next to him and the two were in conversation when the other sergeant nodded to Scipio.

Praxor had survived too, though Scipio had seen little of him during the conflict. He was aboard the other gunship, both of which now broke into the upper atmosphere, beyond range of the necron guns and bound for the *Valin's Revenge*.

EPILOGUE
OATHS

ANTARO CHRONUS STOOD in the apothecarion of the *Valin's Revenge* for the very first time since what had recently become known as 'The Damnos Incident'.

Massacre or slaughter was too incendiary a word, but all those of the Second Company and the menwho fought beside them knew the truth of that.

He was standing next to a medi-casket, regarding the warrior slumbering fitfully inside. The casket was fixed upright to the wall, its occupant held aloft by the viscous solution within. A rebreather was clamped around his face, but Chronus knew who this was.

Cato Sicarius.

The Master of the Watch would not be best pleased he had missed the final hours of the fight on Damnos.

Apart from Venatio, who was deep into his work monitoring Sicarius's vitals, Chronus was alone. Daceus, the captain's faithful retainer, stood vigil outside the chamber.

Chronus placed his gauntleted hand against the hard glass of the medi-casket.

'We of Guilliman's blood, do we not always find a way? Rise soon, brother-captain,' he whispered.

Even in suspended animation coma, Sicarius looked belligerent. He was fighting as he slept, remembering all and vowing revenge. And as he watched him, Chronus was certain of two things.

Sicarius would return. The battle was over, but not the war.

ABOUT THE AUTHOR

Nick Kyme is the author of the Horus Heresy
novels *Deathfire* and *Vulkan Lives*, the novellas
Promethean Sun and *Scorched Earth*, and the
audio drama *Censure*. His novella *Feat of Iron*
was a *New York Times* bestseller in the Horus
Heresy collection, *The Primarchs*. Nick is well
known for his popular Salamanders novels,
including *Rebirth*, the Space Marine Battles
novel *Damnos*, and numerous short stories.
He has also written fiction set in the world of
Warhammer, most notably the Time of Legends
novel *The Great Betrayal*. He lives and works in
Nottingham, and has a rabbit.

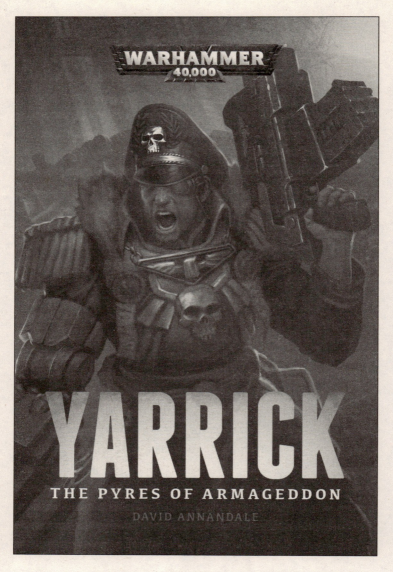

WARHAMMER 40,000

YARRICK

THE PYRES OF ARMAGEDDON

DAVID ANNANDALE

 ® READ IT FIRST

EXCLUSIVE PRODUCTS | EARLY RELEASES | FREE DELIVERY

blacklibrary.com

THE BEAST
ARISES

THRONEWORLD

GUY HALEY

WARHAMMER
40,000

 READ IT FIRST

EXCLUSIVE PRODUCTS | EARLY RELEASES | FREE DELIVERY

blacklibrary.com

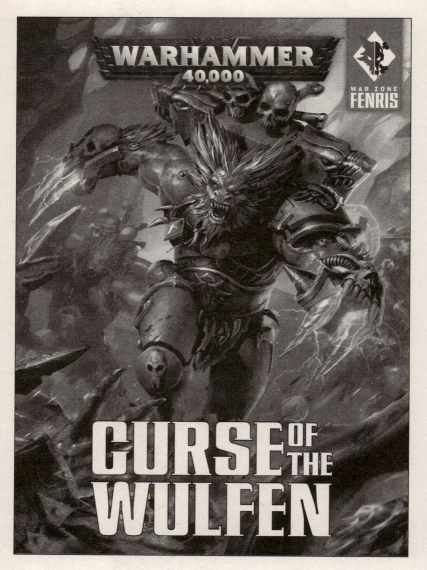

WARHAMMER
40,000

WAR ZONE
FENRIS

CURSE OF THE
WULFEN

 READ IT FIRST

EXCLUSIVE PRODUCTS | EARLY RELEASES | FREE DELIVERY

blacklibrary.com